More praise for Sharon Shinn and her novels

"The most promising and original writer of fantasy to come along since Robin McKinley."
—Peter S. Beagle, author of *The Last Unicorn*

"Taut, inventive, often mesmerizing."   —*Kirkus Reviews*

"It doesn't get much better than [this]—interesting characters, an intriguing mystery, a believable love story, and a satisfying ending."   —*Starlog*

"Smoothly written. Shinn has a talent for creating vivid, sympathetic characters. Nuanced and intelligent. A thoroughly entertaining reading experience."   —*SF Site*

"A delightful world to escape into."   —*Locus*

"A solid read."   —*Booklist*

"Rich with texture and diversity, and genuine characters."
—Anne McCaffrey, author of *Dragon's Fire*

"Romantic . . . delightful. I'm eagerly awaiting her next novel."
—*The Magazine of Fantasy & Science Fiction*

"Warm and triumphant."   —*Publishers Weekly*

"Inventive and compelling."   —*Library Journal*

☞ P9-CEC-429

THE THIRTEENTH HOUSE

SHARON SHINN

ACE BOOKS, NEW YORK

THE BERKLEY PUBLISHING GROUP
Published by the Penguin Group
Penguin Group (USA) Inc.
375 Hudson Street, New York, New York 10014, USA
Penguin Group (Canada), 90 Eglinton Avenue East, Suite 700, Toronto, Ontario M4P 2Y3, Canada
(a division of Pearson Penguin Canada Inc.)
Penguin Books Ltd., 80 Strand, London WC2R 0RL, England
Penguin Group Ireland, 25 St. Stephen's Green, Dublin 2, Ireland (a division of Penguin Books Ltd.)
Penguin Group (Australia), 250 Camberwell Road, Camberwell, Victoria 3124, Australia
(a division of Pearson Australia Group Pty. Ltd.)
Penguin Books India Pvt. Ltd., 11 Community Centre, Panchsheel Park, New Delhi—110 017, India
Penguin Group (NZ), 67 Apollo Drive, Mairangi Bay, Auckland 1311, New Zealand
(a division of Pearson New Zealand Ltd.)
Penguin Books (South Africa) (Pty.) Ltd., 24 Sturdee Avenue, Rosebank, Johannesburg 2196,
South Africa

Penguin Books Ltd., Registered Offices: 80 Strand, London WC2R 0RL, England

This is a work of fiction. Names, characters, places, and incidents either are the product of the author's imagination or are used fictitiously, and any resemblance to actual persons, living or dead, business establishments, events, or locales is entirely coincidental. The publisher does not have any control over and does not assume any responsibility for author or third-party websites or their content.

THE THIRTEENTH HOUSE

An Ace Book / published by arrangement with the author

PRINTING HISTORY
Ace hardcover edition / March 2006
Ace mass-market edition / March 2007

Copyright © 2006 by Sharon Shinn.
Map by Kathryn Tongay-Carr.
Cover art by Donato Giancola.
Cover design by Annette Fiore.
Interior text design by Kristin del Rosario.

ISBN: 978-0-441-01414-9

ACE
Ace Books are published by The Berkley Publishing Group,
a division of Penguin Group (USA) Inc.,
375 Hudson Street, New York, New York 10014.
ACE and the "A" design are trademarks belonging to Penguin Group (USA) Inc.

PRINTED IN THE UNITED STATES OF AMERICA

10 9 8 7 6 5 4 3 2 1

For Debbie,
who knows the rest of the story

↦GILLENGARIA↤

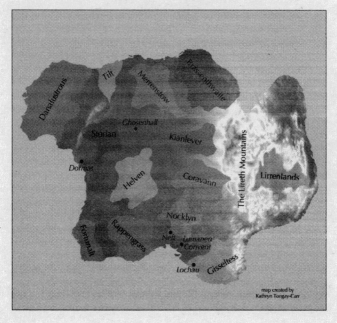

map created by
Kathryn Tongay-Carr

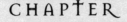

CHAPTER

I

THE three men sat in the mansion's elegantly appointed
study and discussed their options. They had drawn their chairs
close to the fire, because the room was huge and the spring
night was chilled and drearily wet. The only true circle of
comfort was within the warm glow of the leaping flames.
They were all drinking port and relishing the well-being that
came from the consumption of an excellent meal and the ac-
complishment of a difficult task.

"We could kill him outright," said the oldest of the men. He
was tall, silver-haired, and dressed in very fine clothes. It was
not his house, but his proprietary air would make an outsider
think so. "That sends a strong message to the king."

"I am not so fond of looking a man in the eyes and stabbing
him in the heart," one of the others grumbled. He was short,
dark-haired, less fashionable, and a little fretful in his manner.
He was the sort of man who would point out all the risks in
any enterprise, even the ones least likely to bring the whole
project down. "I say we hold on to him for a while."

"There are ways to kill a man that do not involve violence,"
said the elder. "Merely forgetting to feed him. Merely ne-
glecting to give him a fire on a night such as this."

"But those methods take time, which we have very little
of," objected the third one. He was balding and heavyset, even

pudgy, the kind of man who would normally appear genial. But tonight there was a calculating expression on his face. Even by friendly firelight, a certain ruthlessness molded his features. "By now, his men will be back in Ghosenhall, telling tales of outlaws on the high road. Surely even such a casual king as Baryn will guess that his regent did not fall afoul of simple highwaymen."

The elder turned his silver head to give the portly man a considering look. "Then you want him dead more immediately and with more intent?"

"If we kill him, no matter how, there will be consequences," said the fretful one. "I know you say the servants here are hand-picked, but many a servant has betrayed his lord before this."

"I vouch for the servants," said the first man coldly. "There are only four in the whole place, all loyal to me."

"Have they seen you commit murder before?" the other asked skeptically. "If not, I do not think you can be so sure of them."

The elder man looked annoyed. "We must make a decision. The man is in our hands. The king will want him back. Do we trade him in return for some concessions? And thereby bring attention to ourselves and show for certain where our alliances lie? Or do we kill him and let his body be found and therefore send a different message to the king? 'We are readying ourselves for war. We distrust you, and your royal house, and the paltry counselors you have installed to guide your daughter. You cannot mollify us by any measures.'"

The other two murmured approval at this stirring speech, and the elder man leaned back in his chair to sip from his glass. "Yes, but what if the king doesn't interpret our message just how we wish?" asked the short man after thinking it over. "What if he sees *treason*, not an honest cry for change? For we play a tricky game here. We are still very early in the game. Anything could go awry—and here we are in Tilt lands, on Tilt property. Marlord Gregory will be blamed for any cold body found lying about in Tilt fields."

"Marlord Gregory has been gracious enough to lend us his estate," said the heavy man in a purring voice. "Surely he cannot cavil at the uses to which we put his house?"

The short man was shaking his head. Someone who was looking closely might have noticed, even in the dark room, that he was wearing an aquamarine stud on the lapel of his jacket. A Tilt man, wearing the Tilt colors. "Gregory is very clever. He does not see how the wind blows, not yet, and he has not shown even his most loyal vassals what cards he holds. He dislikes the king—yes, and this ridiculous regent set up to rule over us if something happens to Baryn—but he is not so sure he wants to usher in the age of Gisseltess rule, either."

The silver-haired man gave a growl of annoyance. "Trust a Tilt to merely want to stir the pot without wanting to taste the stew," he said in a voice holding some contempt. "Gregory cannot have it both ways. Either he works for revolution, or he does not. And revolution, my friend, is dressed in the garb of Gisseltess and wears the falcon clipped to its cloak." Someone looking closely at *him* would have noticed that very same falcon embroidered on his vest. A man of Gisseltess.

The portly man gave a light laugh. "Revolution wears more motley colors than that," he said. "The maroon of Rappengrass, the scarlet of Danalustrous—you can find them all, if you look hard enough." Though he himself wore no such identifying marks; it would have been hard to guess which House he represented—or plotted against. He continued. "All of us want the same things—the recognition and prestige that are due to us, which have not come our way under this king."

"And who's to say it will come under Halchon Gisseltess?" demanded the Tilt man. "Eh? If he steals the throne from under Baryn's nose? Who's to say he will turn over any land or power to the lords of the Thirteenth House?"

"So he will call together the nobles of the Thirteenth House," the portly man said in a mocking voice. "He will say, 'Too long you have been regarded as the "lesser lords." Too long have you been vassals to the marlords of the Twelve Houses who consider themselves your superiors in every way! Let us redistribute the property and give you a higher place in society.'"

"He swears he will reward us all with lands and titles of our own," said the Gisseltess man. "If we help him win the throne."

"I have been promised many things by marlords in the past," said the Tilt man in a bitter voice. "Many of those promises have been forgotten."

"And many have been remembered," the older man said sharply. "Halchon has honor."

"As do all men who depose their king," replied the heavy fellow in a sardonic tone.

The older man spread his hands. "Late to be having doubts now that Romar Brendyn is locked in the attic of this house!" he exclaimed. "Whether we kill him now or we trade him back to his king, we have committed ourselves to civil dissent. And I tell you plainly, if we do *not* kill him, we have less room to maneuver, for we will have shown our hands. We will have stated in the clearest possible fashion that we are in opposition to our king. Whereas if he is dead . . . well, who knows whose hand may have done him in? We might be entirely guiltless. No one will be able to point at us and say, 'You did this thing.' We might change our minds altogether about which side we choose in this war, and no one will be the wiser."

"You want to kill him then," said the Tilt man. "You see no choice."

"I see many choices," said the Gisseltess man, "but I admit that I would like to see him dead."

They both looked at the heavyset man, the one who had been so very cagey up till now, careful what he committed himself to either in writing or in words. Yet he had been the one to supply the funds and the manpower; he was in it up to his neck, no matter what the outcome. He was silent a long moment, as if debating, as if considering for the very first time which of the possible outcomes he preferred and what consequences they might set in motion. At last, his shoulders seeming both bulky and weightless in the shadows thrown by the firelight, he gave a shrug.

"Well, I don't suppose—" he began, but his voice was interrupted by a furious pounding that seemed to come from the front of the house.

The three of them looked at each other with wide-eyed dismay. "Was that the door?" said the Gisseltess man in disbelief. "Has someone come calling—at this place, at this time, on such a night?" They had chosen the mansion to conduct their business for a variety of reasons, one of them being its remote inaccessibility. Only someone familiar with the rocky northern stretches of Tilt would have any idea where the house lay, or know which of marlord Gregory's many vassals was its landlord.

"Perhaps it was only thunder, rattling the casements," offered the heavyset man.

The Gisseltess man stalked to the window and threw back the heavy curtain. Nothing could be seen but a liquid black-

continued . . .

ness, midnight washed clean by heavy rain. "I can tell nothing from here."

"Perhaps—"

But there it was again, a hailstorm of blows on wood, and now the sound of upraised voices crying out for admittance. "Will the servants answer?" the Tilt man asked in a voice barely above a whisper, as if those standing outside below could hear him if he spoke aloud.

There was more rough knocking on the door. "They will have to," the Gisseltess man said with some grimness. "Or I fear our callers will bring the house down."

The three of them were on their feet by now, and they moved silently to their own door, closed firmly on the rest of the house, and held themselves still to listen. Voices in the hall, some calm, some excited—no doubt the admirable butler greeting these most unwelcome visitors. The three men waited, unmoving, barely breathing, attempting to catch a word or a sentence that would explain how these travelers had so disastrously come calling. Within minutes, the voices died down to a murmur and then were gone entirely.

"He's escorted them to some parlor or another," the Gisseltess man said. "He's admitting them to the house."

"But why—"

"He must have his reasons."

Indeed, a few moments later, they could hear the measured sounds of the butler's footsteps ascending the stairs. Before he could knock on the door, the older man jerked it open.

"Well?" he demanded. "Who has arrived? Surely you realize this is not a house that can afford to take in chance-met travelers."

The butler nodded with complete tranquillity. He looked to be quite ancient, his face lined and wrinkled, his gray hair so thin around his face it was almost only a memory of hair. But his eyes were imperturbable and hinted at so many secrets known that he could not begin to recount them all. "These were not the sorts of people who could be turned out into the weather," he said—adding, after a pause so long it might almost be considered insolent, "my lord."

The fretful Tilt man hissed out a long-held breath. "Who, then? Who are they?"

The butler addressed the older man as if the other had not

spoken. "One is a servant girl, two are guards. But the head of their party is a woman who is clearly highborn. Twelfth House. Serramarra, I believe. She has fallen ill on the road and looks to be in a high fever, which is why they have sought shelter here."

The Gisseltess man regarded the butler steadily. "Did you recognize her or are you just guessing?"

The butler chose not to answer directly. "She has long golden hair and exceptionally fine features," he said. "Her clothes were quite expensive. I saw the crest of Danalustrous on her cloak and on her servant's luggage."

Another hiss from the short, anxious man. "Kirra Danalustrous," he said bitterly. "Malcolm's shiftling daughter."

The butler nodded. "So I believe. My lord."

There was a moment's silence while the Gisseltess man clearly tried to decide what to do next. "What have you done with her? And her retinue?"

"At the moment they are in the small parlor. My lord. I have asked the housekeeper to make up a room for them on the second floor. In the other wing. Her servant girl is quite affected and refuses to leave her side for even a moment. Her guards are—"

"We cannot have fighting men in this house," the Gisseltess man interrupted. "They must be placed elsewhere. In the stables, perhaps."

"We cannot put them in the stables," the Tilt man countered. "Romar's horse is there. It bears the Merrenstow brand. Anyone familiar with the aristocracy—"

"The kitchens, then! Bed them somewhere else!"

"As to that," the butler interrupted, his voice still calm, "they seemed most interested in staying at their mistress's side. I think they would—quarrel—if asked to leave her. I doubt they have plans to roam the hallways, looking for trouble. No doubt they want to do what they can to help the maidservant nurse the serramarra."

The Tilt man looked up at that. "What's wrong with her? High fever, you say? Will she be bringing infection into the house? There's a complication we didn't think of!"

"It might solve one of our problems, though, don't you think?" asked the heavyset man. "Depending on who came down with the illness."

The Tilt man grunted. The older man turned back to the servant. "Did they ask for food?"

"They requested merely a bed for the night and shelter from the rain. It is a most wet and miserable evening," the butler added, as if he did not trust the lords to glance out the window and draw this conclusion on their own. "I must presume they have travel rations with them."

The Gisseltess man turned away, pacing toward the hearth. "Very well, then! A bed for the night. Two nights, if she is really as ill as they think. And a fire. Water. But tell them there is almost no one in the house. Tell them the lord has shut the place up for the season and there is only a skeleton staff on hand. We will stay out of sight until they're gone."

"Very well, my lord."

The man turned to give the servant a hard stare. "And make sure they don't go wandering through the corridors once we're all abed. Post someone at the stairwell to the upper story. At all times. If one of them goes investigating—well. We will have some time later to think up a reason for why we overreacted to their presence."

"Indeed, my lord. Very good. I will give you a report tomorrow. We will hope that the fever lifts and the weather breaks and they are gone by morning."

He bowed and went out. The three men clustered before their fire, two of them gulping their port and the third one holding his hand out to the flames. "Kirra Danalustrous!" the heavyset one said as he bent over the fire. It was as if the very sound of her name made him cold. "Why couldn't it have been anyone else?"

CHAPTER 2

Kirra lay on the bed, motionless, listening to the sounds of people bustling around her. The housekeeper's voice was soft, sympathetic, as she apologized for the dustiness of the room and promised the butler would bring up water soon. She herself seemed to be kneeling before the grate, building a fire, a chore a chambermaid would ordinarily do. "But there's only the few of us here, what with the house shut up just now," she said in a contrite voice. "This is the best we can offer."

"It is most adequate," Justin answered in a clipped voice. If Kirra hadn't known better, she would have thought he was genuinely worried about her, taken ill so unexpectedly on the road. "We appreciate everything you have done for us—for the serramarra."

Small hands brushed across Kirra's forehead, pushing the golden hair out of her eyes, checking again for fever. Donnal sitting by her side, having shape-shifted himself into the very picture of womanly servitude. "Cammon. Do you think you could make some broth?" Donnal asked, pitching his voice in a feminine key. "I think she might swallow some of that. She hasn't eaten for more than a day."

A rustle of skirts, no doubt the sound of the housekeeper rising to her feet and brushing cinders from her dress. "We've got a few apples in the kitchen if you'd like me to bring them to you," she said. "You could mash them up and see if she'd eat something like that. Brandy, too, if you think it would help."

"We have our own supplies," Justin answered curtly. "Thank you. Again. But I think it might be best if you—if none of you—returned to this room more than you can help. Whatever this fever is—" Kirra guessed he paused to shake his head. "I pray to the Silver Lady that we don't bring illness down upon this house."

The woman's voice sounded a little fainter, as if she had opened the door and spoken from the hallway. "It won't be the worst thing to come to this house in recent days," she said, her voice oddly sad. "I'll have the butler bring up more firewood and leave it at the door. We won't trouble you again."

Cammon, Justin, and Donnal murmured their thanks, and Kirra heard the door shut behind the housekeeper. They all held still, listening with some tension, until Cammon said, "She's gone. Back downstairs."

Kirra sat straight up in bed and began to laugh. "Well, that was easier than I expected," she said. "I thought we might be barred out of the house altogether."

Cammon smiled over at her. Even three months of study in the royal city hadn't been long enough to make him look halfway respectable. Though recently cut, his light brown hair was shaggy; his clothes, newly purchased, still managed to look like something he'd sorted from the beggar's bag. "It was the Danalustrous crest on your cloak," he said. "That old butler couldn't turn away someone from the Twelve Houses."

Justin was stalking around the room, investigating what hazards it might hold, though Kirra thought its plain walls and spare furniture were unlikely to conceal any menace. Justin was dressed in red-and-gold Danalustrous livery and carried himself like the most elite member of a marlord's escort. She thought his scowling presence might have been another reason the butler admitted them so readily.

"If he respects the Twelve Houses so much, why is he here helping to plot against them?" Justin said with a snort. He peered behind the threadbare velvet curtain hanging over the room's single window. No one leapt out at him ready to do battle. Kirra thought he might be disappointed.

"They're plotting against the king, not the aristocracy," Kirra pointed out. "And, anyway, the servants might not know exactly what's being planned here. I don't imagine their masters confide everything to them."

Justin made that sound again. "Well, they must suspect that *something* is a bit irregular. Look at this place! As far from civilization as you could possibly hope! It was practically built for intrigue. It must have been the cradle of conspiracy since the day the walls first went up."

Donnal smiled. In this female shape, with a shy, beardless face that held a conciliatory expression, he was completely unfamiliar to Kirra. She had seen him countless times in wolf or bear form and not found him as strange to her as she did right now. Until he smiled; that was a look she recognized. "Justin's right, you know," he said, his soft voice even softer in the feminine register. "A good servant knows whatever's going on in his master's house—even if he hasn't been told. Those few working here are aware that something devious is afoot."

"Well, I can only hope they don't get in our way," Kirra said. "Cammon, can you tell how many we have to contend with?"

"Give me a minute," he said, and settled onto the floor right before the fire. He frowned in concentration.

"And while you're at it, can you tell us if Romar Brendyn is actually in the house?" Justin asked. "And where he might be? Didn't look like there were dungeons, not when we rode up, but these old places can hide all sorts of secret stairwells."

"Dungeons at Danalustrous, though you wouldn't think it," said the woman sitting in Donnal's place.

"There are not!" Kirra exclaimed. "There are—well—rooms that are not so pleasant that are under the main part of the house, but they haven't been used for centuries, and they're not *dungeons*. They're just—rooms."

"I wouldn't want to pass much time there," Donnal said.

"Could you be quiet?" Cammon asked. "I can't get a read on the people here with all of you arguing."

Immediately, the rest of them grew entirely still. Donnal, of course, had a predator's instinct for absolute motionlessness; he could go hours without drawing attention to himself at all. But Justin became just as quiet, just as watchful. He was so annoying and could be so loud that Kirra always forgot how good he was at stealth, at the sinister skills that defined the career warrior. At everything, really. He stood with his hands resting lightly on his blade hilts, his sandy hair undisturbed by the slightest motion of his head. Like the others, he watched Cammon.

"I count six people in the house, in addition to us, and two in the stables," Cammon said finally, his face still furrowed in concentration. "Three of them are together, in a room in the other wing."

"Those would be our rebels," Justin said.

"Two are downstairs. I think we've met them—the house-keeper and the butler," Cammon continued.

"And one of the men in the stables must be the groom who took our horses," Donnal said.

"I doubt he's a groom," Justin drawled. "He wasn't wearing a sword, but I'd bet he's a soldier. No doubt the other one is, too."

Kirra nodded. "That was my guess as well. And the eighth person? What can you tell about him?"

"He's upstairs, I think. Not in this wing of the house."

"But he's alive? Conscious?"

Cammon gave her an uncertain smile. "Alive, certainly. And I am picking up a strong sense of rage. So I'd guess he's conscious. But that might be pain he's sending. Sometimes the two are hard to distinguish."

"Where is he exactly? Can you tell me?"

Cammon shook his head. "I'm not good with things—with places. I can tell you body count and general direction, but I have no idea how the house is laid out. I can't—" He waved a hand. "Brick and stone don't talk to me the same way."

"Well, you've come up with more information than any of the rest of us, so you don't need to apologize," Justin said, squatting down beside him on the hearth. "Anything else? Anything at all? Reinforcements riding in from Tilton City? Knives being sharpened down in the kitchen? The guards from the stables getting ready to come in and murder us in our beds?" He glanced around the room. "Bed," he corrected.

Cammon shrugged. "A great deal of uneasiness from the three men gathered together. They probably don't like that we're here. But they don't seem to have formulated any plan of action. At least, their thoughts aren't very focused at the moment."

"I wouldn't say *my* thoughts are all that focused at the moment," Kirra murmured. "I can hardly blame them."

Cammon grinned at her. "Oh, you're fairly bristling with purpose. Not hard to read at all."

Justin came to his feet and swung around. "So?" he challenged. "What next? Do you actually have a plan?"

Kirra slipped off the bed and started pacing. Indeed, as Cammon said, she was alive with energy and speculation; she thought adrenaline might burst through her skin in a bright, excited flare of light. "I suppose we should wait till the household is more or less asleep," she said. "Then I'll take some other shape and creep up to the attics or wherever Romar is being held. Hoping he doesn't scream to wake the whole mansion when he finds me knocking at his cell door," she added.

"I'll come with you," Donnal said.

She shook her head. "No. I want you to take my shape and lie on the bed. In case anyone comes calling in the middle of the night and wonders where I am."

"They'll wonder where your servant girl is if they don't see *her*," Justin said.

"Oh, I doubt it. They probably only registered her, if they noticed her at all, to note that I had a chaperone. She could disappear from the room and never be missed."

"Another charming instance of the insufferable arrogance of the aristocracy," Justin commented.

"But then, you've got so much charm of your own," she said sweetly. "Or is it insufferability?"

He laughed and dropped back down to the fire to sit next to Cammon, not bothering to reply. Donnal watched her continue to pace through the room, making plans in her head.

"I'm serious," Donnal said. "I don't like the idea of you sneaking through this house alone—no matter what disguise you're in."

"I don't think I'll be in any danger," she said. "And if there are only two soldiers on the premises—" She shrugged. "I think I can handle them."

"Two soldiers, three desperate aristocrats, and two loyal servants," Donnal reminded her. "Seven might be a lot, even for you."

She laughed. "Well, Cammon will know if I'm in trouble, and then you can all race to my rescue. But I don't think it will come to that."

"You'd better eat something before you go off exploring," Cammon said. Apparently he had been putting together a meal while he sat before the fire. "We've got some time to kill before the household settles down for the night."

There weren't enough chairs for all of them, so they made themselves comfortable on the floor, facing each other in a small circle. They talked idly and easily while eating Cammon's simple dinner. Despite the fact that Donnal looked so unfamiliar and she couldn't stand Justin, Kirra thought the whole mood was very companionable. Almost as companionable as the journey that had ended three months ago after these four and two others had crossed the country of Gillengaria on a mission for the king. When Baryn had asked her if she would go after Romar Brendyn, scandalously kidnapped in broad daylight on the king's road, she had immediately told him yes. She had immediately told him who she wanted as her confederates, too. It would have been good to have Tayse and Senneth beside them as well—but perhaps not; perhaps it was better this way. A larger party would definitely have aroused suspicions— and Tayse was too big and too intimidating to willingly entertain if you were bent on any malicious activity. No one plotting treason would have permitted him into the house.

It was as if Cammon had read her mind—which, in fact, he probably had. "Any word from Senneth?" he asked her. "When's she getting back from Brassenthwaite?"

"Soon, I think, but I haven't heard from her in weeks," Kirra said. "She did send me a note that said the reunion with her brothers had gone more smoothly than she'd expected, though neither had improved as much as everyone kept assuring her." She glanced at Justin. "Have you heard from Tayse?"

Justin's eyes glittered in the firelight, so she knew he was about to make some boastful statement about the pride and brotherhood of the King's Riders. "Riders don't send *notes* to each other," he said. "They send dispatches to their king—or their bodies come back strapped to their horses."

"Yes, well, fine. Sorry I asked," she said. Cammon muffled a laugh and even Donnal's girlish face looked amused. "Wouldn't want Tayse to do anything unbecoming to a *Rider.*"

"He would not," Justin said in a lofty voice.

She rolled her eyes and turned away from him. "Anyone bring a pack of cards? We're going to be sitting here awhile."

Donnal pulled out a deck and shuffled, then let Justin deal.

Much as it went against his grain, Justin trusted the other three—all mystics, all possessed of some form of magic—but not when it came to playing a fair card game. Then he suspected them all of using sorcery to cheat him out of a few pennies and often wouldn't play unless he was the one who handled the cards.

"Fours and sevens wild," he said, skimming the cards neatly to each of them. Kirra had to repress a smile. The four of them; their seven adversaries on the property. You never knew when Justin was going to make a poetic gesture.

They had been playing for about twenty minutes when Cammon tilted his head and frowned at the door. Justin's hand automatically went to the knife on his belt; his eyes checked the placement of the sword he had laid aside during dinner. "Someone in the hall?" the Rider asked softly.

Cammon shook his head and appeared to be listening. "One of the men from the stables just came into the house," he answered. "And is moving—upstairs. Toward the prisoner."

Kirra felt alarm flash through her. "Is he going to kill him? Do we need to move *now*?"

Cammon shook his head again. "No, I don't think—I don't sense violence on him. I think he's just—he's stopped moving. I think he's just there to guard the stairwell. To keep any of us from wandering through the hall and coming upon Lord Romar by accident."

Kirra smiled, that wide, mischievous smile that could dazzle most men, though usually not these three. "Oh, I don't think it'll be an accident if we find Romar Brendyn," she said. "I think we'll find him because we know exactly where to look."

I⊤ was another three hours before Kirra went looking. She napped for a while, half from boredom and half because she didn't know when she'd next get a chance to sleep, and she'd rolled out of bed when the hour seemed advanced enough. Donnal lay beside her and woke as soon as she stirred. Justin and Cammon, sitting before the fire, apparently hadn't bothered to try to sleep at all.

"Anyone else awake?" she asked Cammon.

He shook his head. "Only the guard on the stairwell."

"Then it's time."

She curled her fingers into claws and thought through her transformation. She would be a cat, a blotched calico, something likely to blend with the moon-spattered walls of the hallways. She felt her bones shrink and her muscles tighten; the contours of her face shifted as her whole body compacted. She had watched other shiftlings—Donnal, for one—transmogrify so swiftly, so fluidly, that she was a little jealous of their ease and fleetness. For her, it had never been an unthinking act.

But it had always been successful. "Mraurer," she greeted Donnal, coming close enough to rub her head against his plain gown. For a moment, he seemed so big, and Justin terrifyingly huge, but then she adjusted; she was used to her body and her perspective. "Mrau."

Donnal bent and scratched her under the chin, a gentle and incredibly gratifying sensation. "I can still come with you if you want," he said. But she turned daintily on her soundless paws and took three bounds toward the door.

Justin opened it and she slipped out into the hall. It was most pleasant to be able to see so well in darkness, to glance into shadows and instantly classify them. There were other advantages: the sure sense of balance, the keen sense of smell, the heightened hearing. Kirra trotted through the halls, at first just enjoying the mechanics of a body built for running. She heard a mouse whimper against the baseboard and all her instincts urged her to lunge for it, chase it down the corridor for the sheer delight of motion. It took an effort of will to force herself to continue on her course.

This was an accusation often leveled at serramarra Kirra Danalustrous: She never knew when she should be deadly serious and when it was permitted to play.

The truth was, she knew the difference, but it was hard for her not to take every opportunity for spontaneous joy.

She had resigned herself to the notion that this would get her into real trouble some day.

It was ridiculously easy to navigate the halls of this darkened mansion on the rocky edge of Tilt territory. The rain had finally stopped, and a distempered moon made fitful appearances from behind bunched and massive clouds. Kirra could catch glimpses of the sky from the narrow, arched windows that lined the outer corridors she was following, hoping to come across a main stairwell. Pray to the Silver Lady that the weather held and that they could ride out of here tomorrow in something more charitable than a relentless rainstorm.

No, she would not pray to the Silver Lady, the Pale Mother. It was a comfortable habit born from years of casual swearing, but during the past six months, Kirra had come to greatly mistrust the moon goddess and her fanatical followers. She would pray to Senneth's sun goddess instead, the Bright Mother, the Red Lady. She seemed more likely to chase away the thunderstorms, anyway.

Kirra had gone up two levels and turned into an interior corridor before she found the stairwell blocked by the guard. She kept to the shadows as she surveyed him, trying to assess his level of skill. He was seated halfway up the crooked stairway that led to what had to be the top story of the house. He had rested his head on one fist and looked quite bored, though he was wide-awake. It would be hard to slip by him completely unnoticed, at least in this present form. She could change into a spider or a butterfly and cross him at a higher altitude, but that would take time and energy, and she was already impatient. What were the chances this soldier knew the identities of the visitors to the house? What were the chances he knew that a shiftling was among them?

Low, Kirra decided. Though not completely nonexistent. She would have to be prepared for the possibility that he would suspect her identity and sound the alarm. Or try to. She would have to be prepared for the possibility that she would have to stop him.

So she stepped with a queen's haughtiness out of the shadows, making a choked meowing sound in her throat. The guard's head instantly swung her way, and his hand went to his weapons, but then he relaxed. Kirra paused in a convenient patch of moonlight so he could get a good look at her, then minced closer as he laughed.

"Up chasing mice, are you?" he asked in a friendly voice, holding his hand out to be sniffed. Her lucky night; he was an animal lover. She could smell horse and dog and even cow on his clothes. "Now's the time to find them. They're all awake down in the stables from sunset to sunrise, rustling through the hay. I don't mind them walking up to pat my face so much as I mind the fact that they're so noisy they keep me from sleeping."

She came close enough to scent his fingers, cleaner than

one might expect from a man bedded down with horses, then butted her head against his palm. He laughed again and stroked her head. "You're a pretty one," he said. "Indoor cat. Not all scarred up like the toms down in the stables. The cook must feed you all her scraps. Maybe you're not a mouser after all."

She was in a hurry to be through this checkpoint and on to her main destination, but she didn't want to make him suspicious. She settled onto her haunches and let him continue to pet her, to talk nonsense to her, while she offered up a satisfied purr. Something else she loved about taking feline shape—that ability to express happiness in such a distinct and pleasurable fashion. She loved the way the vibrations ran across her ribs, the way her throat carried the muted music. She loved her own sense of simple well-being.

"Well, I've got a few scraps you might like," the guard said, lifting his hand so he could go digging in his pockets. "Meant to eat this later if I got hungry, but—"

This was a fine chance for her to make her exit. Kirra allowed her whole body to grow tense while she lost all interest in the man. Her eyes focused on something invisible down the hall. She was on her feet, but low to the ground in a feral crouch, inching away from the soldier's side.

He caught the significance of her pose and glanced over his shoulder. "See something? Smell something? I bet there's all sorts of creepies and crawlies slithering through this place. You aren't going to want my jerky after all, are you?"

She ignored him, moving forward at an extremely slow pace, almost on her belly, attention never wavering from that spot just ahead of her. Suddenly, she flung herself forward in a pounce, then bounded into the shadows after an imagined prey. Behind her, she heard the guard laugh again.

Well, that had been simple.

She hoped they were able to spirit Romar out of here without resorting to violence. She hoped she was not going to have to watch Justin cut this man down. How could you help but like a man who talked to stray cats in the dark? But Justin would not be moved by any such considerations. Indeed, Donnal wouldn't be either if the skirmish went that way, if Donnal was the one taking on this particular soldier. He'd be in some savagely threatening shape: a wolf, a lion, a creature that men instinctively feared and usually fell to. He would show no quarter, if it was a choice between this man's life or his own. Or Kirra's.

Kirra would show no mercy, either, if it came down to the lives of herself and her friends. But if it was possible to get through the mission without bloodshed, she would like that better.

She was on the top floor of the mansion now, proceeding down a low and not particularly clean corridor. It was easy to follow the tracks in the dust, made by the housekeeper or perhaps the guards as they brought food and water to the prisoner. It was easy to catch the human scent wafting toward her despite the stillness of the air. A few quick turns, a detour down a cramped hallway, and she was there.

Romar Brendyn had been locked behind a very efficient door, a grille of metal that completely filled the roughly made opening. Kirra approved its construction, which would allow guards to keep a close watch on some recalcitrant prisoner. A tricky thing to carry a tray of food into a room when you had to open an opaque wooden door. Hard to know if your captive had positioned himself there on the threshold and was ready to strike you down. A barred door was much safer—for the jailor, anyway. It left no room for surprises, for errors.

Kirra crept up to the grille and stuck her head through, looking around the room with interest.

It was even more bare than the one she was sharing with her companions. There was a mat on the floor, where a man lay sleeping. There was a fireplace grate, currently without a fire. There was a bucket that must be substituting for a chamber pot. A bowl and spoon placed near the door. A good-sized window cut into the wall, but set with thick rods in vertical stripes.

Not much else.

Kirra concentrated for a moment on the sleeper. In this shape, and under these conditions, she couldn't tell much about coloring, but she remembered him as a man with shoulder-length hair just a few shades darker than her own gold. He was somewhere in his mid-thirties, she thought, and generously built—not as big as Tayse, but solid, a natural athlete who probably spent much of his time training with swords and horses. At the moment, he lay on his side, under a thin blanket. There was clearly no weapon he could lay his hand on anywhere in the room, but he faced the door, as if ready at any moment to respond to danger, and this was the direction from which he expected it to come. Even asleep, he did not look helpless, Kirra thought. She wondered suddenly if the guard had been posted more to keep Romar in than to keep Kirra and her friends out.

She pulled her head out from between the bars. Slowly, silently, still keeping her eyes on the prisoner, she shifted to her natural shape. Certain details fell away from her; others became clearer. Absurdly, it was the color of his hair that she noticed most right now. Dark blond, even by moonlight. She thought his face looked proud and passionate, sculpted into a frown by whatever he was dreaming. He looked very much like the sort of man a king would trust to be regent.

"Romar Brendyn," she called in a low voice. "Romar Brendyn, wake up."

CHAPTER
3

ROMAR Brendyn was awake and on his feet, the blanket bunched around his ankles, before Kirra had even finished speaking his name the second time. As far as she could tell, he felt not a moment's disorientation; he seemed to know exactly where he was and where the voice was coming from. Still, it was clear he had no idea who was confronting him here in the middle of the night—his body was ready, but his face was puzzled.

They stared at each other for a moment. The moon gathered her strength enough to push the clouds aside, just for a few minutes, and came curiously peering through the square window to see if there was anything interesting inside. By its light, Kirra could see Romar Brendyn try to guess what fresh danger had presented itself and if there was any way to turn it to his advantage.

She knew she should speak up right away, identify herself, reassure him, but she allowed herself the luxury of admiring him just a moment longer. Despite being woken from sound sleep and confronted by a mystery, he did not look to be worried or at a loss. She thought he might be wondering if he could get close enough to the grille to reach through it and strangle her, and then steal any keys she might have hanging from her belt.

The thought made her laugh out loud.

His expression changed from one of calculation to one of complete bafflement. "Who *are* you?" he demanded.

She thrust her hand through the bars and hurried to introduce herself. "Kirra Danalustrous. I've come to rescue you."

He had taken a step forward, but at that he came to a halt, astonished. "Kirra Danalustrous! What? Why would—" He shook his head.

"The king got word of your abduction," she said, trying to explain quickly because it really did seem improbable, a serramarra of Danalustrous riding about the countryside with the aim of delivering noblemen from danger. "He sent me after you with a team of friends. I think we'll be able to free you tomorrow night."

He came close enough to grip the bars. She had dropped her hand by this time, since he didn't seem eager to take it. "Why not tonight?" he said. "Why not now?"

She felt a rush of admiration again. He probably didn't remember he'd met her before and certainly couldn't figure out why she'd been sent on this mission, but he didn't feel like lingering here any longer than he had to. *You've come for me? Good. Get me out.*

She laughed. "We need to put a plan in place, and we don't have time to do it tonight. You don't seem to be in any immediate danger—and I certainly don't think your captors will kill you while they've got guests in the house. But I think we can free you tomorrow and be halfway to Merrenstow by the following morning."

His fingers closed even more tightly around the bars and he glowered down at her. He was radiating irritation and impatience but seemed as if he was trying to retain some scraps of courtesy. "If we're not going to try to file down the window bars tonight," he said at last, "then let's start from the beginning. Why did the king send a Danalustrous serramarra after me? Did he at least send anyone with you who might be able to help?"

She couldn't help grinning at that. "Yes, indeed. I've got a King's Rider with me and two other mystics. Between us—"

"Mystics," he interrupted. "*That's* why he sent you. You've got some—magical ability. You can do something special."

"Change shapes," she said calmly. "And heal people. Have you been wounded? I can fix you right up."

He shook his head. "No, no. Except for abducting me in the first place—and conveniently forgetting to give me a fire—my captors haven't done much to abuse me. But you—even if you can change shapes. What good does that do me? How will you get me out of here?"

"Well, among other things, my shape-shifting ability allowed me to slip past the guard and find you tonight," she said. She was still amused. "And tomorrow—"

"That's it! You can shift me, too," he said. His voice was brisk, unalarmed. He hadn't paused to consider the wonders or the horrors of being turned into some other creature; he just assumed such a transformation would serve his ends, and he accepted the necessity. "So why can't you do that *now*?"

"Lord Romar. Please. You go too fast," Kirra said, using her most winsome voice. "I cannot shift you. I can only change myself. We will have to use other methods to free you."

"Why can't you change me?" he argued. "You mean, you've never tried it? I'm willing to risk being turned into a rather ugly rat if it means getting out of this cell a day earlier."

How was it possible that in this situation, with so much else to cover, she was being drawn into this particular discussion? "I cannot change you because it is forbidden for shiftlings to transform any living creature except themselves. I can change objects. I can change plants. I can change myself. I cannot change other people."

"But—"

"Can't, because I do not have the ability. Won't, because the prohibition is something I hold sacred," she continued, cutting him off. "We will find another way. Trust me. I have come this far."

He stared down at her another moment, still mutinous but clearly deciding he should channel his energy into more fruitful discussions. "You said you had a Rider and two mystics with you," he said. "There are at least five people in this house. Can you kill all of them with your small group?"

"I would prefer it didn't come to killing," she said. "And, in fact, there are seven people arrayed against us—two guards, two servants, and three men who appear to have arranged your abduction. And, yes, I think my companions and I can outwit them."

He finally decided he had no choice but to submit to her will. "How, then? What's your plan?"

Before answering, she glanced at the barred window set in the wall. "What do you overlook? What part of the grounds?"

"The back of the house. Kitchen gardens. The stable's off to the left some distance."

It would have been too much to hope that his window gave out over some deserted flower garden on a track that none of the occupants ever followed. "How often does someone come to the door? To bring you food or ask you questions?"

"So far, twice a day. Breakfast in the morning, dinner in the evening. My captors have not been to see me at all."

That caught her attention, changed her train of thought. "Your captors. Do you know who they are?"

He shook his head. "We were surprised on the road. I had four men with me and I saw three of them die in the attempt to save me. I don't know if Stellan escaped—"

"He did," Kirra interrupted. "That's how we learned you'd been taken."

Romar nodded. "One small piece of good news, then. At any rate, there were possibly twenty of them arrayed against us. At first I thought they were bandits, but it quickly became clear their plan was to take me alive, whatever the fate of my men. And if I was being kidnapped—well, there had to be a political motive. So I looked for crests and insignia, but I didn't spot any. We traveled two days to get here—" He glanced around his cell. "Wherever here is. I have no idea who took me or even where I am. I assumed the king would know more than I would, if some kind of ransom has been demanded."

"There may have been. We left before any demand arrived, within hours of Stellan's appearance. So I know very little more than you do—not even who owns this house. I can tell you that we are on the northern edge of Tilt territory, very close to the sea."

He was staring at her, the expression easy to read even by moonlight. "If you don't even know who took me—how were you able to find me?"

Kirra grinned. "Magic," she said. "We have a reader with us."

"What?"

Oh, he was going to be worse than Justin, wholly skeptical

of a mystic's skills. "A young man named Cammon," she explained. "He's a reader—a sensitive. He has a tremendous capacity for picking up on the auras and emotions of the people near him. Actually, he's getting better at picking up those emotions from a distance, too. He was able to lead us to you."

Romar was still stupefied. "All the way from Ghosenhall?"

Kirra felt her laughter bubble up. "No, don't be ridiculous. Stellan told us where the attack had occurred, and Donnal tracked you most of the way north—"

"Who?"

"Donnal. Another mystic who accompanies us. He's a shiftling, like I am, and he took wolf shape to follow your scent. Till we lost it in the rain, but by then Cammon had located you, and he brought us straight to the house earlier tonight. He says you're full of rage," she added inconsequently.

"Yes, well, who wouldn't be enraged to be attacked in bright daylight by traitors to the throne?" Romar demanded. "And then to be left in a cell for close to a week, not told why, not told what's going to happen next—I want to pull the house down with my bare hands. I'm not surprised this magical boy of yours picked up some anger."

"We haven't seen our hosts, either," Kirra said. "The servants say the house has been mostly shut up, but Cammon says there are three men here who exude the air of authority. We feel they must be the ones who have arranged your capture. He doesn't know the members of the nobility well enough to recognize personalities at this distance. If I get a chance, I'll go looking tomorrow, but—"

"But that's a lower priority than getting me out of here," Romar interrupted. "Yes. How are we going to do that?"

"We need to get you a rope," she said, "so you can climb out the window after dark."

Once again he was staring at her as if she was a complete lunatic. "I can't climb down the wall, even if I have a rope," he said in a tight voice. "There are bars across the window. Perhaps you didn't notice."

Kirra bit her lip to keep from laughing again. People unaccustomed to magic never consciously thought about how to incorporate it into every situation. "The bars are not a problem," she said. "I will change them to something brittle. I am more concerned with finding you a rope. And perhaps a knife—some kind of weapon."

"Yes, indeed," he said. "I would most like to have a weapon."

She grinned. "I'll see what I can do. It would be much easier if we had a fire to see by, or at least a candle, but I can't call flames with my fingertips as Senneth can."

She could see the word "who?" hovering on his lips again, and then he remembered. "Senneth. The missing Brassenthwaite serramarra. I met her at the palace a couple of months ago."

"So you remember Senneth, but you don't remember me," Kirra said lightly. "And yet, I've met you more than once. I even attended your wedding."

"I remember you," he said, sounding surprised that she would think otherwise. "You wore red the day I was married."

"I often do. Danalustrous crimson," she said, more lightly still. What an odd thing for a man to remember. But she had much more important matters to focus on. "Let me come in there and look around and see what I can turn to my purpose."

"Come in here," he repeated. "How will you—oh. You'll change shapes, I suppose, and crawl under the door. Perhaps I shouldn't watch."

"Watch or not, makes no difference to me," she said cheerfully.

But he turned away. "They left me with a candle and some flint," he said over his shoulder. "I'll get us some more light while you—do your magic."

Romar stepped back toward his sleeping mat while Kirra shrank herself into mouse shape, scurried under the grille, and resumed her human form. She thought he must have been watching, at least surreptitiously, because he was at her side with a lighted candle in his hand just as she was throwing back her heavy hair.

"What are we looking for?" he asked, sounding as if he was trying hard to keep any sense of marvel out of his voice. "What basic materials do you need to change something into something else?"

She paced gracefully across the cold stone floor of the cell, using the gliding step that her stepmother had taught her was proper for a lady. Absurd to even be thinking of such a thing at such a time, but she had been so eccentric already; she didn't want Romar to think she was wholly without social graces. "Oh, ideally, the objects should have some relation to each other. We could tear your blanket into long strips and tie them together, and that would alter quite nicely into a rope, but then you wouldn't have a blanket."

"I can sleep cold," he said instantly.

"Yes, but whoever brings your breakfast in the morning would notice you had a rope on your bed instead of a cover, and that wouldn't do you much good," she pointed out. "The next best thing might be—what were you wearing when you were taken? Does your coat have any braid?"

It turned out that Romar Brendyn wasn't much for elaborate dress, so neither his shirt nor his overcoat sported any fancy trim that Kirra could rip free. But she was able to tear the silk lining out of his topcoat and shred that into ragged strips, and she knotted these together into a respectable length. She passed the thin, frayed cord through her fingers, touching silk but thinking about hemp, and she felt its weight and texture change against her palm.

"Rope," she said, coiling it before her on the floor.

"That's not even remotely credible," Romar said flatly. "That someone can do such a thing. I watched you, and I can't believe it."

She smiled. "Very handy, don't you agree?"

"Can you change anything you please to anything else?"

"No. For instance, I can't change a bird into a rosebush. I can turn *things* into other *things*. And I have to be touching the object in order to effect the transformation. And if I try to change too many things—or myself too many times—I can exhaust all my power and have to rest for a while."

"For how long?"

"An hour, a day. It depends on how much of my magic has been used up." She handed him the rope. "Let's hide this under your mattress. I'm afraid you won't have a very comfortable sleep tonight."

She was not even surprised when his immediate response was, "I don't need to be comfortable." He was as prickly as Justin, in his way, impatient of delay and scornful of comforts.

Less irritating than Justin, of course, though she supposed that could change if she spent much time with him.

"Now then," she said, glancing around by wavering candle-light. "What might we turn into a knife?"

The obvious choice was the spoon that lay by the bowl at the door, but Kirra didn't want anyone to notice that something crucial was missing. She pulled a hairpin from the tangle of her hair and used that instead, shifting its form, its material, and its purpose.

"A wicked little dagger," she said, handing it over to Romar, who slipped it inside a pocket of his trousers. "I wouldn't use it if you didn't have to, at least until the trap is sprung. If you kill off the servants before we free you, you might not get out of here alive."

"I may not anyway," he said. "I still don't understand what you have in mind."

Kirra took those ladylike steps across the room to the window and wrapped her hands around the bars. Before working any magic, she gazed out to see what she could determine by capricious moonlight. That open space right before her must be the gardens, soggy and unappealing after the rain. The dark silhouette to the left was probably the stables. There wasn't much cover for a good hundred yards, till a line of scrubby trees hunched themselves into a windbreak along the western edge of the property.

Romar had come to join her by the window, and Kirra pointed. "There. We'll have a horse and another rider waiting for you right past that line of trees tomorrow night. Wait till it's full dark—wait till your last meal has been brought to you. Break the bars, climb out, run for us. We should be able to cover a lot of ground before anyone knows you're gone."

"If they come after us—"

"The important thing is to get you out of here and back on the road," Kirra interrupted. "If there's a pursuit, you and Cammon will ride for safety while Justin and Donnal and I attack the others."

"You! And two men!" he exclaimed. "If there is a fight on my behalf, I will lead the charge."

"You are the valuable individual here," she said, her voice a little sharp. "Yours is the life to be protected. And, believe me, between us, Donnal and Justin and I can account for more than two soldiers and three noblemen. We've done it before."

Now he turned to look down at her. He had left the candle over by his mat, so she could only see what portion of his face the moonlight chose to illuminate. He was an amazingly handsome man, she thought, though this was not the time and place to be noticing such things. He had an aristocrat's fine features, stamped with intelligence, and his face was quick to show his emotions. Just now he seemed to be struggling with respect, protest, and curiosity.

"I hate the thought of running like a coward while others defend me," he said in a quieter voice than she was expecting. "But I find myself wondering what in the silver hell has brought a serramarra of the Twelve Houses to the place where she thinks she can take on professional blades and kill them on the road."

"Yes, it's a most interesting story," Kirra agreed. "We'll tell it around the fire on our journey tomorrow night."

"Something to live for," he said.

Kirra smiled. "I imagine you have many other items on that list."

He laughed but did not reply. "What else is left to be done here?"

Kirra ran her hands up and down the two center bars of the window. "I must turn these into something you can break easily with your hand. There—these two are old wood. You should be able to snap them without much trouble. Give me a moment to convert them all."

"Not all of them," he said. "I must have something to anchor the rope."

She laughed. "Naturally. I shall leave this one on the left pure iron."

Romar watched her more closely this time, seeming fascinated and a little fearful. "How long will the sorcery last?" he asked. "When will these items revert to their proper materials?"

Kirra shook her head. "This is what they are now. They will not revert." She could not help but give him a look of limpid mischief. "Oh, they do say that sometimes magic dies with the mystic. So I suppose if I am accidentally killed in a brawl tomorrow while you're in the process of climbing down the wall—well, you could find yourself in desperate straits, clinging to the end of a slip of silk as you try to find purchase on the side of the house. But I plan to live out the day, so you should be quite safe. Don't give it another thought."

He looked as if he wanted to be irked with her but found himself, against his will, amused. "In fact, I am happy to learn you will be alive at day's end," he said instead. "You have that story to tell, after all."

Kirra ran her hands once more down the changed bars, just checking, but all of them seemed splintery and ready to break. She glanced around the room, wondering what else she could do to improve Romar's comfort or his odds for survival, but nothing occurred to her. "My best advice now would be to sleep as well as possible and eat what you can," she told him. "Keep yourself strong. If you hear a commotion tomorrow afternoon, that will be us leaving. But we won't go far. We'll be waiting for you behind the trees tomorrow night."

"I'll be there," he said.

Kirra glided back toward the door, and he followed her. "Wait till it's safe," she cautioned him. He seemed like the kind of man who needed such a warning, and probably wouldn't heed it even then.

He laughed. "No part of this enterprise seems safe, but I will try to proceed with some care," he promised. "Thank you, Kirra Danalustrous. It is very possible you have saved my life."

"Don't thank me too soon," she said. "You're not free yet."

He surprised her by taking her hand and bowing over it very low, though he did not kiss her fingers as a courtlier man might have. "Then I shall thank you merely for the intention," he said, straightening up. By the dim light, his face looked very serious. "It is what we should all be judged on, anyway."

Ridiculous; she really didn't want to leave. She didn't want to shrivel down to mouse size and scamper down the halls, away from him. But she would see him tomorrow, unless everything went unthinkably awry. No need to linger now.

"Till tomorrow," she said. "Try to be patient."

She let herself collapse, like a dress cut from the laundry line, turning a thing that was full and round and vivid into something small and uninteresting. She could feel Romar's eyes on her, or she thought she could, as she ducked under the low iron of the grille and skittered with her tiny claws down the uneven stone floor.

"Be careful, Kirra," Romar called after her, but she did not look back. She did not change herself into a woman again to make a more dignified good-bye from this side of the door; she did not even don her calico colors and slink along as a cat. Her small heart was beating hard enough as it was. She would not give it something else to contend with.

DONNAL was furious when he flung the door open, probably three hours after she'd left. "Where have you *been*?" he demanded, addressing his scold to the brown rat who scurried in after scratching timidly at the door. "I've been thinking you were dead this past hour or more."

Kirra pushed herself up on her hind legs and stretched her curled hands toward the ceiling, feeling her body bulk up and lengthen. She took in what details she could while a slight opalescence hazed her eyes during transformation. Cammon and Justin had been slumbering on the hearth, wrapped in their blankets, but they had stirred when Donnal greeted her and now they were yawning and trying to wake up. Donnal, who had looked like Kirra when he opened the door, was now himself—a slim, dark-haired man with a neat beard and watchful, sober eyes. The fact that he still wore a maid's simple gown meant he was ready at any second to resume his disguise.

"It must have been harder to find Romar than you thought," Justin said. He didn't sound as if he had been too worried.

Nor did Cammon, who yawned again though he fought to keep his mouth closed. "I told you she wasn't in any trouble," Cammon said, addressing Donnal for what was probably the hundredth time.

"It shouldn't have taken that long," Donnal said grimly. "What else were you doing?"

She grinned at him, at all of them, and perched on the edge of the bed. Donnal stood beside her, very still in his gray gown; the other two sat relaxed before the fire.

"First, I talked to Lord Romar," she said. "Explained who I was, why we're here, and came up with a sort of plan for getting him out. His window overlooks the western view of the mansion—"

"Stables to that side," Justin said. He had, of course, memorized every detail of the grounds as they rode up. It was the sort of thing a Rider did automatically. "Line of trees, too. That could be a place for us to hide and wait for him."

Kirra nodded. It was a sad day when she and Justin followed a similar thought process. "Exactly. His window is too visible for him to attempt to escape before dark, but we can be in place long before then. I made him a rope, changed the bars on his window, and fashioned a knife for him out of a hairpin. He should be ready to leave."

"So that took maybe an hour—" Donnal began.

"And when I left him, I went exploring," Kirra continued. She ignored Donnal's soft exclamation. "Lord Romar had no idea who his attackers were, and we haven't seen any clues since we've been here. So I thought I'd go look."

"You crept into their bedrooms?" Cammon asked, clearly impressed. "As a cat? No, you couldn't fit under the doors."

"Mouse, spider, bat, I took a few different shapes to navigate the corridors," Kirra said, while Donnal's frown grew blacker. "And I visited a few empty bedrooms before I found our kidnappers."

"Did you recognize them?" Justin asked.

"There were two that I'm sure I've seen before, though I honestly couldn't tell you their names. One's a Gisseltess man—no surprise there—but not Twelfth House. A third or fourth cousin of Halchon Gisseltess. Very unpleasant man. The other was a Tilt vassal who's got a place on the southern edge of Tilt lands, so I don't think this is his property. The third one—" She spread her hands. "I don't think I've ever seen him before. Heavyset and balding. I couldn't tell much else while he was sleeping."

"Not much to go on," Justin said.

"No. But worth knowing all the same."

Donnal shook his head. "Too much of a risk. If you were going to do something like that, you should have come back to get me."

"I'm fine. I survived. But I admit I'm exhausted now."

"So what's the plan for tomorrow?" Justin asked. He was always the one who wanted to know what would happen next, what strategy would be in play. Cammon was just happy to be included in any adventure, and Donnal was content merely to follow Kirra's headlong lead. Usually. Until he became worried and overprotective. Her father had charged Donnal with the task of guarding her, but still. His close attention could sometimes be a nuisance.

"I have to sleep," Kirra said. "I expect the servants will be by in the morning to check on me. Tell them I had a restless night, but that my fever broke sometime near dawn. You expect that I will feel well enough to travel by early afternoon."

"That's not entirely believable," Cammon said. "Most people would lie in bed another day or two."

Kirra grinned. "Ah, but I'm a difficult and intractable woman, and you've long ago given up trying to talk any sense into me," she said. "They'll be so relieved to see us go, they won't argue."

Justin was frowning. "Still. I wonder if our leaving will put Lord Romar in danger. Let's assume they were considering killing him, and our arrival put that plan on hold. Our departure might be their signal to go ahead with the execution."

"Why capture him just to kill him?" Kirra objected. "Why not simply murder him on the road?"

"Many an outlaw before this has found a dead body more convenient than a live hostage," Justin countered. "They might not have thought this whole thing through to the end. Or they might have been spooked by our sudden arrival here and wonder who else might show up at their door before they've determined what to do with their prisoner. I hate to leave Lord Romar here—if our presence is all that's keeping him alive."

"But we can't very well wait to leave till nightfall," Donnal said. "That would seem very odd. Especially with a sick woman in our midst."

"All right, then, we'll leave in the afternoon as planned," Kirra said, thinking rapidly. "But Donnal will tell the housekeeper and the butler and whoever appears to see us off that he thinks I am weaker than I will admit. Tell them that we might not get very far on the road before we have to turn around and come back. If they're expecting us to reappear, they won't have the nerve to kill Romar."

Justin nodded. "That should do it. And if you can manage to look both ill and ill-*tempered* as we leave tomorrow, they won't know what to expect from us next."

Donnal scowled, but Kirra was grinning. "I think my acting skills can encompass such a role," she said. She yawned and stretched. "Silver hell, but I'm tired. Try not to wake me up tomorrow till noon or later—unless something important happens."

Justin snorted. "What makes you think *we'll* be awake by noon?"

She ignored him. It took only a few short pulls to undress as far as she was going to in a room full of men on a night when she might have to flee at a moment's notice. Within minutes, she was under the covers, drowsing against the pillow.

Donnal waited until she was settled, then curled himself around her, fitting his front to her back, adding his welcome warmth to the rather thinly furnished bed. They had slept so most nights of the hundreds, the thousands, they had traveled together, though Donnal frequently was in animal shape and thus even warmer. Now, formed like a woman again, he generated less heat than she was accustomed to, and she felt herself shiver a little in the chill of the room.

"You take too many chances, serra," Donnal whispered, his voice so low that not even Cammon would be able to hear it, and Cammon heard everything. "You are too valuable to lose."

"You won't lose me," she whispered back.

He didn't answer; he didn't have to. She knew what he was thinking. *Someday I will.* She was a serramarra of the Twelve Houses. He was the illegitimate son of a tenant farmer. Even if she didn't die in some ill-conceived pass through dangerous territory, there were so many ways he could lose her. Till then, she knew, Donnal was hers, heart and soul, to do with as she chose. Since she could neither rebuff him nor reassure him, she merely closed her eyes. Sleep claimed her while she was still wriggling on the bed trying to get entirely comfortable.

CHAPTER
4

THE housekeeper actually seemed concerned that Kirra was not well enough to travel, but the butler was happy to see them go. He didn't say so, of course, but he offered them fresh canteens of water and warned them that the northern road was generally impassable after this much rain. "But you've got a nice clear day for travel," he told the travelers as he waited with them on the front walkway while the soldiers-cum-ostlers brought their horses around. "You should make excellent time."

"Thank you for your hospitality," Kirra told him, handing him a coin.

"But, serra . . . you were so sick yesterday—" Donnal began.

"If we stayed another night," Cammon added.

"I'm fine," Kirra snapped.

"What if you fall ill upon the road?" Donnal demanded. "We may have to return here."

"I am *most certain* that will not be the case," she said. She smiled at the butler and scowled at her servants. "I'm *fine*," she repeated.

"Of course, serra," Donnal said. But the look he gave to the butler said something else entirely.

She mounted her horse somewhat shakily but managed to ride out at a pretty good clip. Her strength returned amazingly fast as soon as they were out of sight of the mansion, and they covered another five miles before reining in.

"Long wait till dark," Justin said, slipping from the saddle to look around and make sure they were safe during this particular rest stop. "I'll take the watch if anyone else wants to sleep."

At first, no one slept. Donnal hunted and returned with fresh meat, so they had a better dinner than they'd had the past two nights. Justin and Cammon practiced swordplay, and Kirra was interested to see that they both used metal blades. On the road last winter, Tayse had insisted they use wooden practice swords. Either Justin was getting careless—an impossibility— or Cammon was getting better.

"I thought you were studying with the mystics in Ghosenhall," she said to Cammon when they took a break. "How'd you get better at fighting?"

Cammon wiped his mouth with his sleeve and grinned down at her. Bright Lady, he looked as much like an urchin today as he had when they found him almost six months ago, serving out a sentence of indenture at a lowlife tavern in Dormas. "I train with the Riders once a week," he said. "Well, not all the Riders. Justin and his friends. I'm not good enough to train with them, but Justin makes them practice with me."

Justin took the water bottle from Cammon and downed half of it with a swallow. "Mystic with a sword," he commented. "Makes your blood run cold, doesn't it?"

"But then, all mystics give you a chill, don't they, Justin?" Kirra replied in a dulcet voice.

Justin laughed. Cammon grinned. "He's become a lot more tolerant," Cammon said. "Not just of us. The other day in Ghosenhall there was a girl doing magic tricks in a city park. Justin went up and watched and even said she was pretty good."

"Was it real magic or trickery?" Kirra asked.

"Real magic. Changing small objects to other objects— rocks to coins, that sort of thing. She wasn't very powerful. She couldn't do much. But the crowd liked her." Cammon glanced at the Rider. "Justin even gave her a copper."

Kirra put her hand to her heart. "My hero."

Justin rested his sword point-down and shook back his

sandy hair, damp with exertion. "Anyway, I've been giving Cammon lessons. He's always been good at defense, so we're working on attack. But he doesn't really have the heart for it."

Kirra let her gaze wander over Cammon. How old was he now, nineteen? Beefing up a little since he'd come under their care, but still thin, shabby, all sharp angles and flyaway hair and wide, wise eyes. He had nothing in the world except his friendships with this oddly assorted group and a strange mental power that none of them quite understood. Senneth had set him up with teachers who could hone his skills, but Kirra could imagine no situation in which he would turn those abilities toward hurting anyone else. No, Cammon was not a killer.

"Well, as long as he's good enough to keep himself alive, that's all we really care about," Kirra said. "And as long as you're around, he doesn't even have to worry about that."

Justin laughed again and swung his sword up. Cammon dropped back into a defensive crouch, and the battle went on. Kirra stretched out before the small fire, deciding she had enough time to take a short nap before the evening festivities began. "Wake me when it's dark," she said, and closed her eyes.

A FEW hours later, the moon was up and they were all in place. Donnal had taken wolf shape and was prowling the grounds of the mansion. He would raise the alarm if anything went amiss during Romar's escape—and he would be the first line of attack if one of the soldiers tried to stop the regent. Justin was positioned just behind the windbreak of trees, holding Donnal's horse for Romar to ride. Cammon and Kirra were almost at the main road, watching to make sure no other untimely arrivals came cantering up at this crucial hour. All of them were poised to gallop out.

"He's climbing down," Cammon whispered suddenly. "No one else in the house is moving."

"Both soldiers in the stables?"

"I think so. Wouldn't swear to it, but I think they're sleeping. He's the only one in motion."

A long, tense silence, and then Cammon said, "I think he's on the ground. He's moving faster, at any rate, probably running. He's—" A short pause. "You probably should have told him about Donnal."

"Damn. Well, I did—I mean, I said he was a shiftling, but I didn't mention that he might be roaming around—is Lord Romar afraid?"

A very faint laugh for that. "Well, he's certainly aware of all the potential hazards, and a wolf pacing alongside him seems to have added to his tension, but he's still running. He's—ah. He's with Justin." Cammon looked over at her and grinned by moonlight. Kirra had no doubt at all that he could see her face perfectly plainly, or as well as he needed to in order to read every thought in her head. "Justin on one side of him, Donnal on the other," he said. "I'd call him safe."

Kirra nodded briefly and swung her horse around, ready to fall in with the others as soon as they charged into view. Cammon brought his mount alongside hers, but kept his head half turned as if to listen to the conversation of those behind him. The night was so still that Kirra could catch the thrum of hoofbeats before she could glimpse the riders. Donnal loped up beside her a moment or two before the horses appeared, his mouth half open in a lupine grin, and she nodded at him but said nothing. He trotted up to the road, nose down as if to scent for trouble.

The hoofbeats grew louder and there they were, both men bent forward in their saddles, traveling fast. Justin swept his arm up in an arc and then pointed forward, but Kirra and Cammon were already in motion. In a tight, fast-moving group, they all raced for the road and kept riding.

IT was dawn before Justin felt they were safe enough to call a halt. They had not traveled at that breakneck pace the whole time; indeed, they had not even stuck to the main road for more than an hour or two. Kirra had been content to let Justin plan this part of the trip because he was the campaigner, after all, but she essentially agreed with his strategy. Speed and distance for the first part of the escape, then stealth and misdirection. Hard to know how long they might be pursued, but it would be more difficult to find them if they took cross-country ways with no discernible track.

"I think we can rest now," Justin said, and they all immediately pulled up their horses. Kirra was weary to the bone and imagined the others must be as well—though neither Justin nor

Romar showed it, of course. In fact, Romar immediately announced, "I can go farther if necessary." Kirra had to smother a laugh.

"We have to rest sometime," Justin said practically. "Just for a few hours. We'll split a watch."

"I can take a watch," Romar said.

Justin glanced at Kirra as he slid from the saddle but did not answer. Justin didn't admire aristocrats any more than he admired mystics and wasn't about to set himself up to argue with one. Kirra swung down with the ease of much practice and waited till Romar was on his feet before she gave him a somewhat calculated smile.

"*You* will not stand watch," she said, her voice almost flirtatious. "*You* are the one we have come to save. You will have something to eat, refresh yourself with a nap, and be ready to ride on when Justin says it's time."

Romar frowned. Even after a week of captivity, a daring escape, and a long night of forced riding, he did not look worn or beaten. They must breed men of incredible stamina down there in Merrenstow. "I hate to feel helpless. I hate to feel like I am relying on the efforts of others while I do nothing," he said.

Justin was unstrapping a spare sword from his saddle. "Here," he said, handing it over to Romar rather casually, considering he cared about his weaponry more than he cared about his friends. "If we're attacked, you can join the fight. I'd guess you've some skill with a blade."

Romar looked deeply pleased and pulled the sword from the scabbard to inspect it. "Thank you. This is a fine piece. Yes, I am a fairly good man in a fight. Thank you again—" And he hesitated as if searching for a name to complete the sentence.

Kirra stifled a sigh. There had been no time for introductions as they pounded out of Tilt. "That's Justin. King's Rider. I mentioned him to you the other night. The fact that he will entrust you with a sword he owns is either a mark of high favor or a sign of deep desperation."

Romar immediately reached out and shook Justin's hand as if they were men of equal rank. Kirra could see Justin appreciated the gesture, but she had a better idea of what it meant. Twelfth House aristocrats rarely even noticed the existence of lesser folk, unless to issue orders or reprimands; they certainly didn't fraternize. But she had had a few chances to observe Romar when they were both in residence at the royal palace in Ghosenhall. She had noticed then that he was impatient of pomp and careless of class distinctions. Here might be a man who knew all of his servants by name and who could win love, not just respect, from any men under his command.

"I will hope our need is not so desperate that I need to bloody the blade," Romar said to Justin. "But if it is, I promise you won't be sorry you lent it to me."

Justin grinned. "Now I'll almost hope for an engagement just to see you in action."

Kirra was motioning Cammon forward. "And this is Cammon. He's the mystic who can read people's minds, so think only courteous thoughts when he's nearby."

"I can't," Cammon said, giving Romar a little bow. This time there was no handshake, but Romar gave Cammon a long and interested inspection. "Can't read minds. I can sense emotions pretty clearly, though. And—and—just general existence. It's hard to explain."

"I'm sure those are very useful skills," Romar said.

Kirra couldn't help laughing. "You can't even begin to guess," she assured him. She was looking around. "Donnal's here somewhere, or he was."

Romar also glanced over both shoulders, as if searching for someone. "Yes, I thought you'd said there were four of you, but there were only three of you riding with me last night."

"The wolf," Justin said. "Running alongside you as you escaped the house. That's Donnal."

Comprehension played across Romar's face. "The—ah. I admit to a moment of panic when I saw him there, but then I decided I'd rather be eaten by a wild animal than killed by a faceless guard, so I ran for the trees anyway. And after that, I seemed to forget him."

Justin made a little grunting sound, as if about to make a reluctant admission. "Always a mistake to forget Donnal," he said.

"Well, I don't know where he went," Kirra said, giving up. "Hunting, maybe. He'll probably stay in animal shape for most of the trip. His senses are keener when he's a wolf, and that's pretty handy when you think someone might be pursuing you. Anyway, we don't have enough horses."

Romar glanced around again. "So it's Donnal's horse I'm riding? I hate to dispossess him."

"We couldn't take yours from the stables without raising five kinds of alarm," Justin said. "This was the most practical solution."

Kirra could see protest forming on Romar's face again. Really, his sense of pride could be most inconvenient. "Don't apologize," she warned before he could utter a word. "Don't tell us you'll keep up by jogging along beside us. Don't try to give the horse back to Donnal and tell him you'll walk back to Merrenstow. If Donnal takes human shape to ride, I swear to you I'll take animal shape, and it's *my* horse you'll be riding to complete the journey."

For a moment there was deep silence as Romar looked both offended and astonished. Justin and Cammon had prudently turned away and pretended to be engaged in conversation. Kirra held Romar's gaze, her own unwavering. She couldn't help but notice that his eyes were a dark brown, thickly lashed, meltingly beautiful even as they brightened with anger.

A moment longer he held the stare, and then he gave a small laugh and shrugged his shoulders. "You think me some kind of thoughtless autocrat," he said. "And I know I appear ungrateful. It's just that—"

"It's just that you're not used to being rescued by strangers and ordered about by frivolous young women who ought to be entertaining callers on their fathers' estates," Kirra said, giving him her widest smile again. She could tell it was starting to dazzle him, just a little, as it should; he was not as susceptible as most men. "You're used to being in charge. And you don't like being beholden to anyone. You don't know how to act."

He laughed again, a little more freely. "All that. Except I have a feeling you are very rarely frivolous."

Kirra was fairly certain she heard a muffled "Ha!" from Justin, but she was able to ignore him. "We are in unusual circumstances," she said, her voice most friendly. "But it will be easiest on all of us if you will just surrender the burden of responsibility till we get you to safety. Justin is wholly despicable, as far as personality goes, but he is really a splendid fighter and I would trust him to save all our lives if we were pitched into battle. Cammon and Donnal are amazing guards, with the ability to sense danger when it is miles away. And I have an assortment of skills not to be found among most of your serramarra. I have seen my share of adventures these past six months, and I will never again be content to sit in a drawing room discussing fashion and bloodlines. Though I can do that, too, if it will make you more comfortable," she added. "But I just want you to—relax. Let us handle the details of this journey. We are very sure of what we're doing."

Romar nodded and then, as if that were not acknowledgment enough, gave her a deep bow. "You want me to be gracious," he said, straightening up. "I can do that. I swear. I can also thank you—and your companions—for rescuing me. I appreciate it more than I believe I will be able to find words to say."

"We acted on our king's request," Kirra said, because she knew Justin was itching to say the words, and she thought they might sound better coming from her. "But we were happy to do it."

Justin glanced over from where he and Cammon had been laying out provisions. "Breakfast is ready," he said, "if anyone's hungry."

They were all starving, and they devoured bread and dried meat as if they hadn't eaten for a week. Donnal padded up while they were taking second helpings, but since he showed no interest in the meal, Kirra assumed he had fed elsewhere. He sat beside her on the damp ground and gave Romar an unnervingly direct stare. He was still in wolf form, and his yellow eyes peered with a totally inhuman intensity at the king's regent.

"This is Donnal. Perhaps you remember him." Kirra made the awkward introduction as coolly as possible. "I'd have thought he might take a man's shape for a few moments to greet you—but I guess not. He can take any form he wants, but when he's not human, he's most often a wolf. Some affinity there, I suppose."

"Indeed, he looks most—convincing," Romar said. Kirra suspected the lord wasn't entirely comfortable with the wolf sitting so close—but then, few men were. She supposed that was why Donnal had chosen to retain this shape. As a man, he was lean and supple but not particularly imposing. As a predator, he inspired a quick and instinctive reaction of fear, even in those who knew what he truly was. Unlike Justin, Donnal didn't have a deep-seated hatred of the aristocracy—but he wasn't above taking the opportunity to flaunt his superiority when he had the chance. She supposed that was only natural. Or perhaps it was completely male. By the grin on Justin's face, she would wager it was the latter.

Romar regarded the wolf a moment longer, then he pulled his gaze away with some effort. "So. What's our plan?"

Justin picked up a stick and made a rough sketch in the dirt. "We're approximately here," he said, indicating a point about dead center in the triangular domain of Tilt. "We've been heading southward because the traveling's easier, but we probably need to turn straight east. Get to Merrenstow as quickly as possible. We won't leave you until you're with a garrison somewhere inside Merrenstow lines."

Romar nodded. "How long do you think that will take?"

"Three or four days, maybe," Justin said, "if we continue cross-country like this. Faster on the roads, but—" He shook his head. "I'm thinking you shouldn't be on the main roads without a battalion at your back anytime soon."

"Yes, I think I've learned that lesson," Romar replied.

"So what did they think to accomplish?" Kirra asked. "By taking you? Even if they'd killed you—what would that have achieved?"

"Depends on who was in charge of the enterprise," Romar said.

"I did a little reconnoitering," Kirra said. "Looked to me like they were Thirteenth House men. From Gisseltess and Tilt. But that doesn't mean they weren't acting at the behest of a higher lord."

Romar shrugged and looked tired. "Or they could have been acting on their own. There's been an upsurge of—discontent, I suppose you'd call it—from some of the Thirteenth House lords in recent months. Everyone senses change in the air, and no one wants to be excluded from the spoils."

"But would lesser lords band together outside of traditional fiefdoms?" Kirra asked. "I've never heard of such a thing."

"No, and you have to ask what kind of power they could really muster even if they did so," Romar admitted. "Most of them live on lands held in trust to the marlords—they run the estates, but they don't *own* them. Are they organized enough to plan war strategies? Are they truly a threat worth worrying about, or merely an annoyance at a time of great general disturbance?"

Kirra ground the heels of her hands into her eyes. Bright Lady, she was so tired. If she didn't sleep soon, she would disintegrate into a pile of weary dust. "There are so many threats on so many fronts," she said. "There is Halchon Gisseltess whispering that the king needs to be overthrown because he is old and his daughter is incompetent. There is Coralinda Gisseltess spreading the gospel of the Pale Mother and claiming that all mystics are evil and must die. Don't we have enough to contend with? Now we must make war on the Thirteenth House as well? It is too much."

"It is all of a piece," Romar said. "The realm is in discord. Change is at hand and everyone wants to influence what the new kingdom will look like. We may yet see more factions emerge before Amalie is on the throne."

Kirra dropped her hands to stare at him. "Change is at hand," she repeated. "But why is everyone so certain that Baryn is ready to die? He's only sixty-five."

"His father died before he was sixty," Romar said gently. "As did his uncles and his grandfather. Trust Halchon Gisseltess to know that. He would be an unusual man of his line to live even another five years."

Kirra bit her lip. She hadn't had that particular statistic; she wondered if Senneth knew it. She turned her head to look at Romar more closely. He was sitting next to her on the ground, so he sat in profile to her, the shape of his head illuminated by sunlight now for the first time since this journey had begun. He had pulled his matted hair back to tie it in a ponytail, so the angles of his cheeks were exposed; the stubbled line of his jaw seemed to set even as she watched. Not only a handsome face, but a strong one. No soft, indulged, pretty-boy lordling was Romar Brendyn of Merrenstow.

"You have been given a hard task," she commented in a low voice. "If Baryn dies, you will be the one to usher in a new era. With all these foes arrayed against you."

He smiled a little. "I will stand at Princess Amalie's side as she ushers in that new era," he corrected.

"She's a child."

"Eighteen now."

Kirra shook her head. "Eighteen is only seven years behind me, and I know that I would not even have been ready to rule Danalustrous at that time. I doubt I would be ready now. This burden will fall on you."

Romar stared before him a while longer, completely motionless, while Kirra watched him. Then he gave a small shrug. "If the king dies. If war comes. If diplomacy fails. We are not yet at a dire crossroads, though darkness looms in many directions. None of these terrible things may come to pass."

"Still," she said. "You are a brave man to answer the king's call for a regent."

He smiled. "Amalie is my sister's daughter. I would protect her with my life even if the king had not given me such a charge. The rest of it, all the political maneuvering, that makes the job more challenging, I admit—but I would have had some part of the job regardless. I am just as happy that he has given me ultimate authority."

"He may have written your death warrant," Kirra said.

Romar laughed and shook his head. "No," he said. "I will be more careful from now on. I will not be taken a second time."

Kirra fought back a yawn. "Well, if we want to make sure you are not taken again today, we must be on the move again soon," she said. "Which means, first we must sleep." She glanced around the camp, suddenly aware that she and Romar had been the only two conversing for quite some time. Cammon and Justin were asleep already, stretched out side by side on the ground. Donnal sat a few yards away, ears up, nose twitching, scenting the wind that blew in fitfully from the north. Guarding their back trail.

"Donnal must have taken first watch," Kirra said, a little unnerved that all this had been decided around her while she had been oblivious, deep in conversation with Romar. "I assume he knows when to wake Cammon or Justin. You and I should merely sleep."

Romar nodded. "I am too tired even to protest. Wake me when it is time to move on."

Kirra tried to smother a yawn and let herself fall back, right there on the ground, with nothing but a light cloak between her and the grass. "Someone will," she said drowsily. "Sooner than you'd like."

CHAPTER
5

WHEN she woke, the warmth of Donnal's body was at her back, but everyone else in camp was astir. The sun was high and remote; the cool spring air was sticky with humidity. She sat up and pushed her hair back over her shoulders, feeling irritable, dirty, and far from rested.

"My clothes are damp," she said with a touch of petulance. "The ground was a lot wetter than it looked."

Justin gave her a quick, unsympathetic look. "Better get yourself something to eat. We ride out in ten minutes," he said.

She shoved herself to her feet. "Thanks for the generous warning," she grumbled, as she took off for a little privacy.

Her usual sunny temperament had reasserted itself by the time they were on the move again. She had always been able to make do with minimum amounts of water to freshen up her hair and face, and she had always been able to manufacture clean clothes out of soiled ones. Justin must have lent Romar a razor, because the regent was clean shaven for the first time since they had found him, and he, too, managed to improve his appearance before they took off. Justin always looked presentable, in a rough and dangerous sort of way, and Cammon never did, so nothing had changed there. And naturally, the wolf had not bothered with a toilette at all.

They were heading southeast at a deliberate pace through

countryside that was rocky, uneven and sparsely covered with low brush and spindly trees. Justin was in the lead; Cammon was in the back to pick up any intimation of pursuit. Donnal was roaming, though he came back periodically to pace alongside Justin as if waiting for the Rider to issue him orders. Not much love lost between those two, either, though Justin had a grudging respect for Donnal's fighting and scouting abilities. They worked together like jealous brothers, understanding each other even when their dislike was at its strongest.

Kirra rode alongside Romar and had a grand time of it. They had been successful in their mission; they were out of danger; and she was the lone woman in a crew of men, the most handsome of the four riding at her side. She could not help but enjoy herself hugely.

"So, you promised to tell me the tale of your adventures," Romar said shortly after they set out. "The story of what turned the silly and superficial serramarra into a cold killer in service to the king."

"I don't think the transformation was quite that dramatic," she said with a laugh. "But it certainly was an adventure."

She spent the next hour or so giving him the colorful details of her trek across Gillengaria last winter with Cammon, Justin, Donnal, Tayse, and Senneth. He was familiar with the general outline, of course, because the king had shared the story with him. He knew that Halchon Gisseltess had told Senneth to her face that he wanted to be named heir to the throne. He knew that Halchon's sister, Coralinda, had styled herself the head of a devout order known as Daughters of the Pale Mother, and that she was sending her novices out to proselytize for that revived religion. He knew that mystics had been prosecuted and murdered throughout lands held by many of the southern Houses. But he hadn't heard the tales of their exploits in Dormas, Neft, and Lochau—or the story of Tayse's capture and rescue from the Lumanen Convent—or confirmation of the rumor that Halchon Gisseltess wanted to wed Senneth Brassenthwaite before he took over the throne of Gillengaria.

"But he's married," Romar exclaimed.

"He seems to not consider that an obstacle," Kirra said.

"It would be a good match. For him, I mean—for a man bent on taking over the throne. Brassenthwaite and Gisseltess—at least six of the other Houses would follow their combined lead. I applaud him for his strategy even as I hate him for his treason."

"No need to worry," Kirra said. "Senneth will never marry him."

"Her brother Kiernan had better be looking for another match for her," Romar said. They had effortlessly slipped into one of the favorite pastimes of the aristocracy: plotting bloodlines and alliances. "What about Rappengrass? Ariane seems most loyal to the king. That strengthens the crown in the southern region and gives Rayson Fortunalt a reason to think twice before joining a rebellion."

"I think only one of Ariane's sons is unmarried, and he's almost ten years younger than Senneth."

Romar made a dismissive sound. "What does that matter when there's a kingdom to secure? But if not Rappengrass, then Nocklyn, perhaps. I know that Els has only got the one child, a girl, but I think his brother was widowed a year or so ago. Senneth could marry there."

Kirra laughed. "Actually, I fear there is little chance Senneth will marry to oblige her king," she said. "Regrettable but true. She's found love in a less—conventional—place, and I doubt either Kiernan or Baryn will persuade her to give it up."

Romar looked instantly intrigued. "Really? A mésalliance? With whom? Kiernan must be beside himself."

"Kiernan lost all hope of influencing Senneth when he allowed their father to turn her out the door when she was seventeen," Kirra said. "He's lucky she's willing to attempt reconciliation now."

"Yes, no doubt," Romar said. "Who's she lost her heart to?"

Kirra bubbled with laughter. "A King's Rider. Tayse. He rode with her to Brassenthwaite a couple of months ago and I'm dying to hear how the journey went."

Romar appeared to be completely dumbfounded. "Senneth Brassenthwaite in love with a *King's Rider*? Surely not. Never. I won't believe it. There's—there are standards to uphold, even among the most wayward of the serramarra. She can't be considering marrying him, can she?"

Kirra pulled her horse to a halt, and Romar, after continuing on for a few paces, reined back around to face her. She was suffused with fury. "You know, I hate the smug, suspicious, *stupid* aristocrats who believe an accident of birth makes them better than all of the *ordinary* people in the realm. I hate that sense of privilege and entitlement and outright *arrogance* that makes people like you believe someone else isn't as good as you are, not fit to touch your hand, or—Bright Lady forbid it!—the hand of your wife or daughter or sister—"

Romar, incredibly, was laughing. He flung up a hand to stem her tirade. "I was only joking," he said. "I think it's marvelous."

She was so angry that it took a moment for his words to register. "You're so— What did you say? And it's not funny. I don't know why you're laughing—"

Ahead of her, she could see Justin had turned around to see what the holdup was, while Cammon was no doubt just a few yards behind and greatly entertained by what he could pick up of the argument. Kirra kneed her horse forward and battled back her rage.

"I was joking," Romar repeated. "I don't feel that way at all. Frankly, I think the bloodlines could stand a little mixing up. Though, it's true, it's rare that a serramarra would mate with a soldier, even a high-ranking one, or someone else of a lower class—say, a household servant. In fact, the only instance I can recall is when Kallie Fortunalt ran off with her husband's steward, and you know that affair didn't end up so well."

Kirra took a couple of deep breaths to dispel the lingering effects of anger. In the calmest voice she could muster, she asked, "What happened to them? I was only seventeen when the story came down, and my stepmother wouldn't tell us the details. And my father never bothered with gossip of that sort."

"Rayson won't talk about it—she was his mother, you know. The story at the time was that Reynold hunted them down and had them killed. For the dishonor to the name. But I've always wondered about that. It's just the story Reynold would have put out, even if he'd never been able to track them down. I like to think they escaped on one of the small ships you can always find in Forten City and took off for foreign lands, where they built themselves a small house and settled down to live happily for the rest of their lives. Certainly anyone who'd been married to Reynold Fortunalt deserved such an ending."

That made Kirra laugh, and her good humor was almost completely restored. "Right about now you're thinking I need to apologize for my outburst," she said.

"No. Now I'm thinking I should apologize for seeming to be the kind of person you despise."

He said it so seriously that she was caught completely off guard. "I despise the type," she said. "I don't know you well enough to know exactly where you don't fit the mold. From the outside," she added with a small laugh, "you seem to embody it."

"What, privileged, pompous, and stupid?" he said, grinning. "Thanks for the compliment."

"Privileged, intelligent, pure-blood, related to the royal house, blessed with royal favor, most likely to benefit greatly from maintenance of all current conditions."

He gave her a quick sideways look from those deep brown eyes. "And in what way does this description not also fit you?"

"Oh, no, I'm a complete mongrel. Not only was my mother Thirteenth House, but she—or someone in her family—was a mystic. I can play serramarra well enough, but I'm only in the higher echelons on sufferance. If my father ever lost his standing among the marlords—or ever lost his patience with me—I'd be ostracized so quickly it would be hard for you to remember my face."

Another sideways glance, this one accompanied by a quick little bow, neatly accomplished even from the saddle. "Serra Kirra, I do not believe I will ever forget your face."

A giggle for that. "Well, no, you're bound to remember me since I saved your life," she said. "And now you're bound to answer my questions, too, since you owe me for the favor! What makes you so different from the marlords and their kin? How have you rebelled against the strictures of the Twelve Houses?"

He gazed before him, his face meditative. "I don't know that the rebellion has been by action so much as by attitude. The man I trust most in the world is the captain of my guard—a man not much different from a King's Rider, in fact, all duty and honor and loyalty. He has run of my house and can interrupt me at any point, night or day. I dine with him and several of his officers at least once a week." He shrugged. "But many an aristocrat will tell you he values his servants and his soldiers. I try to see every man as my equal—perhaps not in intelligence, perhaps not in wealth, but having some knowledge or some skill that I do not possess, as well as the intrinsic appreciable qualities that make him a good soul. I look everyone in the eye. I deal honestly with any man or woman. I admit, I haven't looked ahead to marrying my children off to farmers' daughters and merchants' sons, but I wouldn't disinherit them if that's what they wanted to do." He laughed a little. "Or so I say *now*, before I have a precious daughter who wants to go off to be the blacksmith's bride. I may find myself a whole pile of class arrogance then."

"I hope not," Kirra said, speaking with assumed lightness. She had been stirred more than she liked to admit by his thoughtful avowal. Her father was something of an egalitarian, too, though she'd never heard him put the philosophy into words; merely, Malcolm considered any man good enough to use, and then reward, for service to Danalustrous. "I would like to see a blacksmith's son running estates in Merrenstow someday!"

"Well, once I have a daughter and she grows up to fall in love with a smithy," Romar replied, "I shall most certainly invite you to the wedding."

"I shall most certainly come."

Their conversation continued much this way for the next couple of hours, interrupted only by their infrequent stops for food or privacy. True to his self-description, Romar always spoke directly and with unforced respect to the other men of the party, asking them if they'd noted anything of interest on the road or how long they thought they might be riding this day. Justin seemed to take his fellowship as a necessary consequence of their proximity, a camaraderie that would last only for the journey, but he also seemed to find that completely understandable. Cammon, of course, blithely accepted Romar as a kindred spirit, a delightful new friend, and over lunch pelted him with questions about his capture and his escape.

"Did you kill any of the men who tried to abduct you? Did you know where they were taking you? Were you afraid? What did you think when Kirra appeared at your cell door?"

Romar answered everything patiently or playfully, laughing at the final question. "I thought, 'They must have drugged my food. I'm having hallucinations. I better not eat tomorrow's breakfast.'"

"Did you see her changing shapes, then?" Cammon said. "Everyone says it's very unnerving, but I can't follow it myself when Kirra and Donnal shift. They always just look like themselves to me. I mean, I *know* Donnal's a wolf. I can see the wolf shape, but he still looks like Donnal. It's hard to explain. But everyone else says it can be a little eerie to watch a transformation."

Romar glanced at Kirra. "No, she didn't wake me till she was standing before me in human shape. They say that sometimes a goddess will come visit you the night before you die. I didn't want to die, but she looked like a goddess to me. That's why I was hoping for hallucinations instead."

After the quick meal, Romar volunteered to help Cammon refill the water containers in a sinkhole Donnal had found. Justin and Kirra worked in silence to erase evidence of their passage. But after a moment the Rider looked over at her with something of a smirk.

"There's a lord who's found something he likes," he said. "You might tell your father you can find a husband on your own."

Kirra felt a little chill pass over her. If Justin, the least sensitive of the lot, could see the little coil of attraction that was tightening around her and Romar, how terribly obvious must it be? "He's just flirting, the way all nobles do," she said in a neutral tone. "He's married."

Justin dropped a tin plate, his hand no doubt made nerveless by surprise. Not until he had picked it up and dusted it off against his trousers did he speak again. "He certainly doesn't act like he's married. And you don't act like he is, either."

She gave him a frosty look, wishing she had Senneth's power but in reverse, so her glare could chill him into a statue of ice. "Since when did my behavior become a concern of yours?"

He shrugged. "Well, you're always telling *me* when I do something you don't like."

"Again—"

"He seems like a decent fellow, though," the Rider went on. "I can see why the king picked him for regent." He shoved the plate and a few sundry items into his saddlebag and worked the buckle closed. "If he lives long enough to do the part."

She tried to let go of her irritation and her little nugget of fear and turn her mind to other worries. "You think those men will come after him, then?"

Justin patted his horse on its nose and let the animal lip at his face for a moment. "If not them, others. He's a target. He's going to have to get himself an awfully good personal guard."

"He says he has one back on his estates."

"Well, then, let's get him there as quick as we can."

Hearing voices behind her, Kirra turned to see Cammon and Romar approaching, the younger man laughing at something the older one had said. She also saw Donnal sitting a couple of yards away, having arrived silently at some point during her conversation with Justin. His amber wolf's eyes were fixed on her face; his own face, shuttered at the best of times, was absolutely unreadable now. She had no idea how long he had been there, what he had heard, what he had gleaned from his own observations.

"Any trouble on the road ahead?" she asked him. She always talked to him, no matter what form he was in, because she knew he understood her. He would understand her even if she spoke some language he'd never heard before, some tongue she had fabricated on the spot. The connection between them had always gone that deep.

He didn't answer, of course, just came fluidly to his feet and padded over. She put her hand down and he nuzzled at her fingers, then sent his tongue in one quick, sticky lick across her palm. That made her laugh, and she bent down to ruffle both his ears, putting her nose against his cold black one, daring him to lick her chin, her mouth. But he didn't. He waited for her to release him, then turned his head away to give an appraising glance to the two men who had just arrived. Cammon had instantly gone to Justin's side and was telling him some story in a lively voice, but Romar was standing on the edge of the camp, watching her. Watching Donnal. Kirra knew he must be wondering just why she had been so eager to champion the friendships between serfs and serramarra and just what her relationship was to the shiftling at her feet.

IT was nearly sunset when the attack came. They were riding through a little gully, and Justin had just said, "This would be a nice place for an ambush," when Cammon cried out a sharp warning. They had bunched together against the oncoming dark, so Cammon and Donnal were both with the main party, and Donnal immediately loosed a low growl of menace.

Instantly, the men raised their swords and formed a neat circle with Kirra in the middle. Cammon quietly called out numbers and details. "Two over the hill, both on foot. Two before us and one behind, mounted. Another one some distance ahead—I guess in case one of us tries to run."

"Fair odds," Romar said, not sounding at all discomposed. Kirra could not help but notice that he seemed perfectly at ease with Justin's borrowed blade in his hand. "Do you think they've come across us by chance, or that they've been hunting for *me*?"

"This place, probably bandits," Justin said, his gaze fixed on the top of the hill where Cammon had indicated two of the attackers lay. "We're in open territory between Tilt and Merrenstow—not that well patrolled. And the force isn't big enough to have been sent after you specifically."

"The ones ahead of us are coming closer," Cammon reported.

Justin glanced down at Donnal, who was standing stiff-legged and snarling a little ahead of Cammon's horse. "Guessing this lot will be more impressed by a man with a sword than a wolf at our feet," the Rider said, his voice carefully holding no hint of command. "Extra blade on Cammon's saddle if you want to fight that way."

Kirra's attention was caught by Cammon's yell and the sound of pounding hoofbeats, so she missed the moment when Donnal transformed. Suddenly, she was in a thicket of upraised swords and descending arms and struggling bodies. Donnal was at a disadvantage on foot. "Donnal!" she cried, kicking her feet from the stirrups and scrambling up so she was almost standing in the saddle. "Take my horse!"

She sensed Romar turn wildly her way, a bloodied blade in his hand, but she was already changing shapes. "Kirra!" he cried. She thought he grabbed for her, but the world was first hazy, and then very, very clear. She flung herself from the horse's back just as Donnal leapt up to take her place. She shot herself in a straight line for the top of the gully, the ambush site where one man still waited. She was not high enough, she did not have the altitude for a truly dizzying, spectacular plunge, but she could frighten him well enough. She was a spring hawk, small and light-bodied but bred for hunting. She aimed herself directly at the man who was just now cresting the hill and starting to clamber down.

The horse shied before the man reacted, and then he flung up his sword arm as if to stab the hawk from the sky. She loosed a shrill, furious cry and dove for him, a short quick plunge, catching one eye with the point of a talon. He shrieked and dropped his sword, clutching at his face, snatching at empty air as if to catch and strangle her. She dove again, raked her claws across his scalp, coming away with hair and skin and blood. Now his screams were truly unnerving, and he had both hands up to his head as he writhed in the saddle. His horse whickered and backed up, dancing away from the battle scene below and acting as if it wanted to throw the rider from the saddle.

Kirra didn't figure this assailant would be much of a factor in the remainder of the brawl.

She beat her wings to attain some altitude and circled once over the gully where the main skirmish was going on. The men of her party had the clear advantage, all of them still mounted and in fighting mode, while one opponent lay lifeless on the ground. Three men to four, even if one of those men was Cammon. Kirra cawed out a guttural greeting and Donnal looked up quickly to spot her overhead. He pulled his horse around and followed where she led, straight to the covert where the final bandit lay, awaiting any who tried to flee. The man was ragged and almost as thin as his blade, but he willingly crossed swords with Donnal for a brief, spirited encounter.

Red and silver hell, the man looked like he hadn't eaten for a week; the whole lot was probably just as shabby. Kirra felt a sudden reluctance to mete out the ultimate punishment, and by the careful feint of Donnal's weapon, she could tell he felt the same. She waited for an opening, then swooped down in a swift, threatening dive to claw for the outlaw's face and shoulders. Like his compatriot, he flung his hands up to protect his head and cried out in deep disquiet. Donnal lunged for him again, pricking the man's rib cage and opening up a red gash. Donnal pulled back; Kirra dove down and raked her claws across the man's forearm.

It was enough. The man jerked his horse around and pounded off, abandoning the fight itself and any assistance he might render his friends. Donnal stood up in his saddle to watch him go, then settled back and glanced up at Kirra. Sunset was painting a vivid scarlet across the western horizon, and his dark face looked ruddy and smiling.

"That's taken care of the whole crew, I think," he said. He crooked his arm as if to offer her a perch, but she wanted to be sure there were no more enemies lurking just outside Cammon's circle of perception. She drove her wings down hard, then skated along the higher air currents, making a wide, slow loop around the gully where they'd been attacked. Nothing to be seen, so she widened her search, perhaps a mile in each direction from the central point. Twice her circuit intersected with the path of Donnal's last opponent, still racing away as fast as his horse would take him. She followed him for a while, curious to see if he would hook up with others, but he seemed most interested in fleeing far enough to save his own life.

She didn't spot any other signs of an outlaw camp in her spiral around the countryside.

Full dark had fallen by the time she circled back to the gully. There was a body lying facedown in the dirt; not one of her men. Her own party was gone, no doubt deciding to put a certain amount of ground between them and the site of the ambush. Romar might have protested at moving on before Kirra returned, but all three of the others would have convincingly insisted that she could find them anywhere they traveled.

In fact, it was only a few more minutes before she caught up with them in a small camp on open land where a watcher could see in all directions. They'd built a fire, so Justin must have decided their risks were equal at this point: Either every outlaw in the area had already spotted them, or they'd already vanquished the only band likely to attack. And anyway, he'd no doubt already assigned watches for the night. It was cool enough now to make the thought of a fire welcome.

Kirra drifted down in a lazy loop, wishing she'd thought to catch a rabbit or a squirrel for the night's dinner. It was strange, for a moment, to see four male shapes grouped against the firelight, instead of the three she had traveled with thus far. Donnal had chosen to remain human, which she thought was a hopeful sign. She wondered if he'd exchanged any words with Romar—and guessed that Romar would certainly have made a point of thanking him directly for the help he'd provided during this enterprise.

She was a little sorry she'd missed the conversation. A little glad.

Hard to say who spotted her first, Cammon or Donnal, but Cammon was the one who said, "There's Kirra," while she was still aloft. Romar spun around, peering through the darkness behind him. Justin dropped to his knees beside the fire, not much interested. Donnal stood unmoving, hands laced behind his back.

Cammon was laughing. "Not on the ground. Up there. Put your arm out. You'll see."

Romar, clearly confused, held his hand over his head as if signaling to a friend across a room. Cammon extended his own before him, bent and braced, to demonstrate. "She's a spring hawk," Cammon explained.

Uncertainly, Romar angled his elbow and clenched his fist. Kirra promptly landed on his forearm. She caught his slight hiss as her talons closed over his sleeve, and then he slowly drew his wrist closer to his face. Somberly, his expression disbelieving, he studied her by the flickering firelight.

"Are you sure it's Kirra?" he asked. "She looks— completely wild."

A muffled "Ha!" from the direction of the fire. "Then it's Kirra," came Justin's voice. "Because she's certainly wild."

"No, she's not," Cammon said. "She's just not entirely civilized."

That made Justin laugh out loud. Romar was still studying the bird. Kirra rustled her feathers and redistributed her weight. "How can you be sure it's her?" he asked. "Just because she can change shapes—how do you know *this* is the shape she's taken?"

"Well, how often have wild birds just come up and settled on your shoulder?" Justin said with a certain sarcasm. "It's her."

"Yes, but—"

Cammon shrugged. "I don't know how anyone else can be sure. But *I* can tell. She looks like Kirra to me."

Kirra cocked her head to one side and tried to lay a melting expression over the hawk's deadly features. Not much good. She winked her eyes a couple of times, but had a feeling the signal didn't come across as sultry in her current disguise.

Romar smiled. "You'd almost think she was flirting with me."

There was elaborate silence from Justin. Cammon said, "She likes to be stroked under her chin."

Romar's left hand came up, slowly, as if he didn't want to frighten her, and he ran his index finger slowly along her throat. Bright Lady, *that* felt better than it had a right to. Kirra stretched her head a little, to give him more acreage. He repeated the motion.

"Well, I don't think a wild bird would stand contact like this for very long," Romar said. "Maybe it is Kirra, as you say."

Justin stood, dusting dirt off his knees, and sauntered over. "Strange, isn't it, though," he remarked, "that we haven't seen Donnal and Kirra both together in human shape since we started out on this trek?"

Romar's arm straightened out before him, as if to put some distance between himself and the creature on his arm. "You mean—you think this might be Donnal?"

"Donnal's right over there," Cammon said.

Justin sounded like he was enjoying himself. "Is he?"

The fourth man stepped over to join the others—but revealed himself to be not a man at all. He was Kirra, all splashing golden hair and perfect, haughty features. "I wondered how long it would take you," he said in Kirra's voice.

Now Romar held his hand as far away from his body as it would go. "But you—how did you—I saw the wolf change into Donnal, but I didn't see Donnal change into a hawk—"

"They're teasing you," Cammon said patiently. He pointed. "That's Donnal. That's Kirra."

Romar looked almost fearfully between the woman's beautiful face and the hawk's fierce one. "But how can you ever be certain?" he asked.

"Well, that's the thing about shiftlings," Justin said blithely. "You really can't be. They'd just as soon trick you as talk to you."

"Watch your mouth, gutter boy," Donnal said in Kirra's voice.

Justin was having the best time. He put his hands in his back pockets and grinned. "Well, you can't tell by *that*," he said. "Donnal doesn't like me any more than Kirra does." That was so true that Kirra spared a moment to wonder why Donnal was playing along with Justin's charade. Her only conclusion was a gloomy one: He was relishing a chance to discompose Romar, to put him at a disadvantage. To make him look foolish while she was watching.

Justin was still talking. "But why don't you investigate? See who's wearing a housemark? That'll tell you which creature is who."

Donnal immediately pulled down the high neckline of his traveling gown to reveal a small brand burned into the flesh. A tiny D, red in the raised skin, acquired when Kirra was too young to remember the pain. All high-ranking heirs bore such marks, customized for their Houses.

"You have to admire the detail," Cammon admitted. "But it's still Donnal. And, no, don't bother looking at the bird. She won't have a housemark in this shape. She changes *everything* about herself, physically, when she becomes something else. There are no clues left behind."

"I'm completely confused," Romar admitted. "I no longer know whom to believe."

Kirra tightened her clutch on Romar's arm merely to aid her balance and set all her veins and muscles into motion. After one quick spasm, Romar held firm, his eyes wide with wonder as he watched her undergo transformation. In a moment or two, she was herself again, feet on the ground, both hands clinging to Romar, holding on till she had regained her sense of body and her sense of balance.

"In situations like this," she said, "it's always best to trust Cammon. Justin rarely lies, and never when it matters, but he's so good at it that you really can't tell when he's doing it. But not only does Cammon *always* tell the truth, he really can tell when someone else is lying, and he's never confused by magic."

Romar was staring at her, fascinated. He didn't seem to mind that she was still grasping his arm. "And Donnal?" he asked. "Is he better at truth or lies?"

She glanced at Donnal—who was no longer Donnal, but a wolf again. It had been too much to hope that he would sit around the fire with them tonight like a civilized man. "He never lies to *me*," she said. "But I think he can be flexible with the truth when he's talking to others."

"Well, I'm not lying when I say I'm hungry," Justin said, still in that disgustingly cheerful voice. "Let's get something to eat."

The meal was a couple of unwary rabbits and yesterday's water, spiced with talk about the ambush. "I saw one body left behind at the campsite," Kirra said. "Did the others flee?"

Justin nodded, swallowing a mouthful of meat. "Didn't even mean to kill the one, but he came at me and wouldn't stop, so I—" He shrugged. "But they were a sorry bunch. I wish they had all just run."

"Hard to know how they ended up outcasts," Romar said in a quiet voice. "Did they commit a crime? Or were they just poor and unlucky, too many bad crops in a row, not enough skills to get a job in one of the small towns? I can't condone outlawry, of course, but I wonder sometimes if we should go after the causes of it, and not the outlaws themselves."

Justin raised his eyebrows at that. He'd been something of a brigand himself in the days before Tayse found him, and he had some sympathy with a lawless way of life. "Go after it how?" he asked.

"Offer some kind of monetary aid in the bad years—lower taxes, maybe, or loans that can be paid back over ten years. Make work available in the towns where they've lost some industry, where the mines have gone bad or the trade routes don't go through anymore." Romar took a sip from his water container, then added, "In Merrenstow, we've been trying to recruit some of the men like this. We're building up the civil guard, and we need more bodies. But a lot of them don't trust the offer of amnesty. They think it's a ploy to get them to turn themselves in. So not many have joined."

"Say it's the king's summons," Justin suggested. "I think even the most desperate men would believe the king's word, even when they don't trust the marlords. Get Baryn to write a proclamation. They'll sign up then."

"That's a good idea," Romar said. "And it's even true. If we go to war, we'll be warring for Baryn."

"At least, Merrenstow will be," Kirra said. "Let's not let them use such proclamations in Fortunalt and Gisseltess."

"Or Tilt," Justin said darkly.

Kirra shook her head. "We can't be sure Gregory Tilton was involved in our own little escapade. I admit, I don't trust him myself, but we have no proof."

Romar closed his eyes for a moment and rubbed his hand across his forehead. "Lady's tears," he said in a weary voice, "I hope it doesn't come to war. I have no idea who would fight with us and who against. I'm far from certain we would have the numbers to win."

"Well, you'll have the Riders and the mystics on your side," Justin said. "That will make you harder to defeat."

Kirra could not help glancing at him across the fire. It was the first time she could remember Justin ever naming the mystics as potential and welcome allies. But perhaps he only had Senneth in mind when he spoke that way. He had managed to overcome his dislike of magic when it came to Senneth.

"I don't think fifty Riders and—what?—a couple hundred mystics will be able to turn aside armies raised from more than half the Houses," Romar said. "But at least it's good to know we'll go down only after a hard-fought battle."

"Maybe there won't be a war," Kirra said softly. "That's what we'll work toward, at any rate. Peace in the realm."

CHAPTER
6

THEY had traveled about three hours the following day when Cammon called for a halt. "Men ahead of us—a lot of them," he said.

Justin pulled them all together for a conference. "Men cutting cross-country like we are?" he demanded.

Cammon shrugged. "I can't tell. They're—this way. Traveling—that way." He pointed. He was hopeless at compass directions.

Justin was never lost. "They're northeast of us heading straight west," he translated. "Probably on the main road. A large party."

"Merrenstow men looking for me," Romar said.

Justin nodded. "Probably. But I'd hate to be wrong." He glanced around. "Donnal." The wolf was already on his feet and poised for travel, one paw lifted from the ground, eyes trained on the Rider. Justin told him, "We'll just wait right here for you to come back."

The rest of them slipped from the saddle and ate some dried rations. Too early for lunch, but riding always made everyone hungry. Justin and Romar cleared debris from the scrubby grass and laid out maps with rocks and pebbles. Kirra and Cammon made little pallets on the ground and sat there, bored. Well, Kirra was bored. Cammon continually looked around him with interest, as if listening to the conversation of the wind or the thoughts of the passing jays. Kirra had never seen anyone else who could always be counted on to be delighted. At times—like now—she found it the most maddening trait of Cammon's entire personality.

Donnal was back within the hour, too stubborn to change out of wolf shape, which made for an interesting exchange of information. "Men in Merrenstow colors?" Justin asked. Donnal bobbed his head, his mouth wide in a silent pant. "How many? Twenty?" Donnal made no sign. "Fifty?" Donnal nodded again. "About fifty Merrenstow men," Justin repeated to Romar, who looked just about as annoyed as Kirra felt about that ridiculous pantomime. "Still doesn't guarantee that they're looking for you, but—"

Romar shouldered up next to Justin. "Did you notice the man in charge? Was he big-boned and black-haired, riding a gray stallion?" Another sharp nod for that. "Colton, most likely," Romar said. "My captain."

Justin nodded. "It's probably safe to intercept them. Let's go."

They all swung back into their saddles and changed course. Even so, Kirra could tell Justin was just a little nervous about it, not wanting to be wrong, wanting Romar to hang back long enough for the rest of them to create a desperate diversion if this platoon turned out to be hostile. But, as Romar so reasonably pointed out, "I'm the only one who will recognize my men. I can't ride in the back." Nonetheless, Donnal stalked in the lead and Justin and Kirra rode on either side of Romar as if to defend him with their own particular skills.

The precautions turned out to be unnecessary, which they could tell as soon as they trotted in sight of the oncoming party. The soldiers rode in strict formation, their chests proudly sporting the black-and-white checkerboard of Merrenstow, the lead rider carrying a Merrenstow flag. Just behind the herald rode a big man with hard features, his eyes restlessly scanning the way ahead for any sign of trouble. He was first to spot the small group stopped in the road before him.

"That's Colton," Romar said, but prudently didn't push past Justin and dash straight up to the guard. This was a group, Kirra thought, that might react a little too quickly to the sight of a headlong stranger.

Colton had flung up a hand, and the whole cavalcade came

to a disciplined halt. "Who rides there?" the captain called out in a booming voice. He didn't put his hand threateningly on his sword, but he didn't have to; every other man in his party did.

"Someone you'll be glad to see," Justin called back. "Romar Brendyn of Merrenstow."

A collective gasp for that and an impressive change of expression for Captain Colton. Kirra wondered if even her father's loyal guards would look so pleased at the notion that Malcolm was not dead after some risky enterprise. "Lord Romar!" the man exclaimed.

Romar nudged his way forward, both hands extended and empty in case his men couldn't recognize him from a distance and thought he might be playing the impostor. "Captain," Romar said in a warm voice. "I have been looking for you on the road these past two days. I knew you would come for me."

Now there were cheers from the amassed men, and a few of them tossed caps and gloves into the air to create a little black-and-white snowstorm over their heads. Colton leapt from the saddle and knelt in the road, his right hand crossed to his left shoulder in a quiet gesture of respect. "Lord," he said, his deep voice much softer now, "we feared you were dead."

Romar was also off his horse, and, taking quick strides forward, bent to put his hands on Colton's shoulders. "I feared death might come for me, too, but instead, friends arrived," he said. "Sent by the king."

That pushed Colton back to his feet, for it wasn't good to be prostrating yourself before anyone but royalty when the king's men were around to see. "We came as soon as we had word," Colton said.

Romar nodded. "I knew you would." He half turned to motion the others forward, and Kirra was amused. Was he really going to introduce all of them to his captain? "They had information sooner, and were on the road almost immediately. This is Justin. A King's Rider."

Colton nodded curtly and Justin nodded back. Kirra supposed that was some high mark of recognition from fighting men; no one offered a hand. Romar continued, "Cammon. Kirra Danalustrous." He glanced around, and Kirra wondered if he would actually introduce the man in animal form. "The wolf is one of our party as well," was all he said.

Colton's eyes snagged on Kirra's face, and he bowed again,

not quite as deeply as he had to his lord. Truly, this was most entertaining. She couldn't remember the last time her name had been offered to an attendant or a guard.

"Lord Romar was speaking of you just yesterday with a great deal of admiration," Kirra said. "I am glad to have a chance to meet you."

"I would have been less worried had I known who was in the party sent by the king to fetch him," Colton said in a gallant voice.

Kirra laughed. "But now that you are here, we will happily let you do all the worrying about him from here on out! You can escort him back to Merrenstow while the rest of us go on our way."

She caught Justin's quick look and Romar's troubled one. "We will discuss that by and by," Romar said. "First, let me confer with my captain and my guards, and then we'll decide where to travel next."

Justin showed a grin at that, which was the first time Kirra realized what was afoot. Romar had never quite believed he was the helpless one who needed to be protected by a soldier, mystics, and a *woman*. He certainly wasn't going to be happy about the idea of Kirra setting off by herself on any return journey.

She wondered if it was only the aristocracy that felt such inconvenient impulses to chivalry, or if all men behaved the same way. If she'd thought Justin was a typical male, she would have asked him. Sighing, she reined her horse to one side and said, "We'll wait over here while you and your men talk."

So she and Cammon and Donnal had another round of rations while they sat at the side of the road. Justin had joined the conference between Romar and Colton and appeared to be doing at least half of the talking. Tayse would have been proud of him, this trip out, she thought. She would have to remember to tell the senior Rider how cool Justin had been, how prepared, how cautious.

Her attention turned quickly away from him, though, as she studied Romar Brendyn. The late morning sun struck his matted hair and turned it a burnished gold, shaped his tired face into a model of strength and endurance. Mostly he was listening, to Justin's comments, to Colton's; once or twice he asked a question in what Kirra imagined was a clear, incisive voice. He looked the very picture of a commander on a battlefield, sifting through the reports of his men, making swift and well-informed decisions, ready to act, ready to defend, certain to win.

Sweet and silver hell, she hoped he never *was* on a true battlefield. She hoped there wouldn't really be a war.

She wondered what it would feel like to wave good-bye, here on this empty road at the north edge of the kingdom, and turn back to Danalustrous, while Romar headed on toward Merrenstow. She'd only been with the man three days, and yet she found him more appealing than almost anyone she'd ever met—certainly the best of the Twelfth House lords. A solid man, a thoughtful one, quick-tempered and quick-witted, impatient and humorous and fair. She hadn't come across anyone quite like him, inside the aristocracy or out.

"Don't be sad," Cammon said unexpectedly in her ear. "You'll see him again."

She automatically looked for Donnal and found him on the other side of the road, snuffling at something. Probably out of earshot. "So now you're predicting the future in addition to reading minds?" she asked with a smile, hoping her bright tone covered her brief moment of shock.

"Well, it only makes sense," he said practically. "You spend so much time in Ghosenhall, and he'll be there more and more often in the next few months. Learning to be regent."

"Maybe," she said. "But I might have other traveling to do. I might not see Romar Brendyn again for a long time."

Cammon gave her one long look out of his strange, flecked eyes and decided not to answer that directly. "I'll be glad to get home," he said. "Senneth should be back by now."

They talked idly another twenty minutes or so, while the soldiers discussed topics that Kirra doubted were all that interesting. Eventually, Colton turned back to issue orders to his men, and Justin and Romar strode over. Kirra came to her feet, her best smile on her face. She had an inkling of what was coming.

"We're going to take the main road back to Merrenstow. Neither Justin nor Colton expects us to run into any trouble," Romar said. "You can either travel with us back to my house, where my wife will most happily make you welcome, and then

continue on with me to Ghosenhall later. Or, if you are in a
hurry, I will pick a company of my men to escort you to Ghosenhall now."

Justin's face was perfectly expressionless, but, just her
luck, she knew exactly what he was thinking. She wished it
was possible to kill him and still retain use of his formidable
fighting skills. "I choose—neither option," she said, her voice
easy. "I will be perfectly safe traveling with my small party
back to the royal city."

Instant dissent pulled Romar's face into a frown. "That's
not acceptable," he said stiffly. "A serramarra on the road with
only three men to guard her—it's not safe. My own experience
testifies to that."

"Well, no one has any reason to abduct me, so I don't think
our situations are comparable," she said. "And, lest you forget,
it was with this very same small group that I traveled *from*
Ghosenhall to find you. And we are halfway home already! So
much less ground to cover! You do not have to fear for us."

"I cannot agree to this," he said, shaking his head.

She appealed to the Rider, since she had no other allies.
"Justin. Tell him. I'm safe with you."

Justin nodded. "The serramarra is safe with me and our
other companions," he said. "I do not expect we will have any
trouble on the road."

"We will discuss this further," Romar said. "Let's eat something and hash this out."

"I already ate. Twice," Kirra said, but the suggestion seemed
to find favor with everyone else. In a few moments, the whole
company had dismounted and broken into orderly groups for a
noon meal. Kirra found herself in a small circle with Justin,
Colton, and Romar. Cammon had instantly made friends
among the Merrenstow soldiers—it was a knack he seemed to
have, no matter where he went—and the Bright Lady alone
knew where Donnal had disappeared to.

In the end, she got her way, but only because she was absolutely unyielding—in the most pleasant, friendliest, sweetest
fashion. And because she had, after all, the ultimate trump
card. "Romar, if you try to send a squadron with me, I shall turn
into a bird and fly away from them all," she said with a laugh.
"I swear to you I will. Now take your men and go home. Cap-

tain Colton is practically shaking with his desire to get you to safety. Do not keep him fretting much longer."

"My lady, I am not fretting," Colton said in his deep voice.

"I wish you would not be so foolhardy and thoughtless!" Romar exclaimed. "What if something happens to you on the road? How would I ever forgive myself?"

"Nothing will happen to me," she said. "I will be well defended. Now mount your horse and go."

It was not that simple, of course, and Kirra found it harder and harder to maintain her smile and her carefree attitude as the final moments of the parting dragged out. All the Merrenstow men had to mount their horses and turn them in the road; her own small group had to be rounded up; good-byes had to be spoken all around.

The last one was the most difficult, of course. She stood there, with fifty-two men and one wolf watching her, letting Romar grip her hand a little too tightly and hold it a little too long.

"I will never forget what you did for me," he said in a quiet voice. Still, it was a windless day and probably everyone could hear. "You and your friends. I will never forget your courage or your resourcefulness or your great heart. You are unique among serramarra, I believe, Kirra Danalustrous—unique among women. I have never met anyone like you."

She spoke in a light voice that was very far from mirroring her actual emotions. "We shall be friends forever then," she said. "What do they say about people bonding together over tumultuous experiences? Your abduction and your rescue have given us a lifelong connection."

"Something has," he said, bending to kiss her hand. The silence all around them was absolutely undisturbed. They might have been statues of soldiers—and wolves—witnessing this little farewell. Romar straightened and gave her a somber look from those dark eyes. "I will see you soon in Ghosenhall, I hope."

"Or somewhere," she said gaily. "Good-bye, Lord Romar."

"Good-bye, serra Kirra. Travel safely. And thank you again—for my life."

• • •

KIRRA and her party kept to the back roads as they traveled westward for the rest of the afternoon, angling south in the direction of Ghosenhall. They did not bother with much conversation. Donnal, still in wolf shape though Romar Brendyn was miles away, was clearly not in a position to talk. Justin, in the lead, and Cammon, at the rear, were watching closely for any sight of bandits or other kinds of trouble. Kirra was lost in her own thoughts, which tended to self-absorption.

Ridiculous, really, to feel so low. Anyone would have been attracted to Romar under the fabulously romantic circumstances of their escapade. He probably wouldn't seem nearly as appealing next time she saw him, at an interminable royal dinner or some Kianlever ball. Or discussing strategy with the king, going on and on about the hopelessly boring topics of manpower and deployment. Then he would seem quite ordinary, even dull.

She probably should have accompanied him to Merrenstow. Met his wife. That would have cured her of this slight infatuation.

She would have to start flirting madly the minute she returned to Ghosenhall. Maybe Darryn Rappengrass would be in the royal city with a missive from his mother. Maybe a Storian lord would come by, resplendent with self-importance and glamour. There was always someone suitable for dalliance at the royal court.

Except she wasn't going to Ghosenhall. Not just yet.

She didn't break this news to her traveling companions till the following morning, when she judged they were so far from the Merrenstow men that there was no possibility Romar would change his mind and come after them.

"Well, this has been enjoyable, almost like last winter," she said, shaking out her riding skirts and preparing to mount. "But here's where the group breaks up. Donnal and I are going on to Danalustrous. I don't know when we'll be back in Ghosenhall."

She saw by his expression that she had managed to surprise even Cammon, and Justin's eyes narrowed with suspicion. "When did you decide this?" the Rider asked.

"I should have been back in Danalustrous two weeks ago. I had a letter from my father telling me he wanted me home. But then the news came about Romar and the king asked me to join the expedition to rescue him, so I—" She shrugged. "So I let my father wait. But he never waits patiently for long."

Justin glanced at Cammon with his eyebrows raised, and the mystic shook his head. Justin turned back to Kirra. "We're in no hurry to get home," he said. "We'll accompany you to Danalustrous."

Funny. *That* she hadn't foreseen at all. "Oh, Justin, don't be silly," she said. "I'm perfectly safe traveling a few hundred miles with Donnal."

"You'll be safer traveling with us."

"Justin. I have crisscrossed Gillengaria by myself, or with only Donnal beside me, more times than I can count. I'm always on the move. It's one of the reasons my father has summoned me home—I haven't been inside Danalustrous for six months or more. I am perfectly able to take care of myself, and I won't be alone. You don't have to have any fears for my safety."

The Rider looked unconvinced. "And if someone attacks you on the road? Bandits, like those we came across just the other day? You and Donnal alone aren't strong enough to fight them off."

"We don't have to be," she said patiently. "We can run faster than they can chase. We can fly. We'll be fine."

"But if something happened to you," he argued, "what would I tell Senneth? What would I tell Tayse?"

"What would we tell Romar Brendyn?" Cammon asked, earning a sharp look from Kirra. But his face remained innocent. "He left you to our care, you know. He never would have ridden back to Merrenstow without you if he'd thought you'd be going on to Danalustrous alone."

"I know," she said, giving him a smile of some mischief. "That's why I didn't mention it to him."

"I don't think Tayse would let you ride on alone," Justin said.

"I don't think Tayse would be able to stop me if I decided to change shapes and slip off in the night," she said. "I don't think you'll be able to, either. And I don't want you coming after me to Danalustrous to make sure I've made it safely," she added because his speculative expression made her guess his intent. "Justin! You know what I'm capable of! You know you don't have to be afraid for me!"

"She's right," Cammon said to Justin. To Kirra he added, "I wouldn't mind riding to Danalustrous and meeting your father, but I don't think we have to go. I don't think you need us."

"Thank you," Kirra said, and kissed him on the cheek.

Justin was still thinking it over, his face creased, his eyes troubled. Kirra knew that it was Tayse's opinion, more than anyone else's, that Justin valued, that he was trying to determine what decision Tayse would make in a similar situation. Last winter, they had all seen evidence that Tayse would lay down his sword, sacrifice his life, to save Senneth's; Tayse would refuse to abandon Senneth no matter how little she might appear to need him, and Senneth was the most powerful mystic in the kingdom. By that code of conduct, Kirra knew, Justin would consider himself honor bound to protect Kirra, no matter how she swore she could protect herself.

Still, Tayse was in love with Senneth. That changed every equation.

"Anyone else who asked this of me, man or woman, I would refuse," Justin said finally, slowly. "I would insist on following to the end destination, if my charge was to keep that person secure. But I do believe you are as safe solitary as you are under my protection. And may the Bright Lady forgive me if that turns out not to be true."

Kirra was actually surprised. She was all poised to tumble into anger when he stubbornly refused to abandon her on the road. "Thank you," she said, her voice a little faint. "I think this is the nicest compliment you've ever paid me."

He grinned. He still seemed uneasy, but she thought he would abide by his decision. "The only compliment, I think," he said.

"*I* can't recall any others," Cammon said.

Still, the moment was slightly awkward; all partings were, Kirra thought. "Good, then," she said, making her voice brisk. "Let's divide the rations and be on our way."

That was quickly done. From horseback, they all waved and called out farewells. "Send word from Danalustrous that you're safe," Justin shouted back at her a few moments after he and Cammon had set off. "Or I really will come after you, and you don't want that."

"*You* in Danan Hall?" she called back in mock horror. "I'll do anything to prevent it! Ride safely."

"You, too."

It was a relief to be on her way finally. She clucked to the horse and felt it move smoothly underneath her, straight west. Automatically, she looked around for Donnal, to find him a few yards ahead of her, investigating some scent on the rocky ground. As if feeling her gaze, he glanced back, his amber eyes very dark in his white wolf's face. It was so odd to look at such a foreign creature and know exactly what he was thinking, to feel such kinship with him that it was almost like talking to a familiar ghost or a manifestation of herself.

"Lead the way," she said. "Danalustrous."

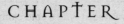

CHAPTER
7

KIRRA and Donnal were on the road four days before they made Danan Hall. The trip would have gone much faster if she indeed had changed to hawk or falcon or even songbird shape and navigated the miles by air. But there was the horse to consider—a fine black mare from her father's stables who deserved a better fate than to be set loose in the countryside. If danger threatened and Kirra had to assume animal shape, of course Kirra would leave the mare behind. But no such crisis occurred. They traveled steadily through unaligned territory, just below the southern tip of Tilt and above the northern boundary of Storian. They easily navigated the open land that smoothed from Tilt's rocky gullies to the green undulating hills of eastern Danalustrous. They met no trouble at all along the way.

Kirra had always loved these solitary journeys, no one but Donnal to share the time with. Even in human shape, he was a taciturn and undemanding companion, able to go days without speaking if she did not appear in the mood for conversation. On the other hand, if she was feeling low, he could entertain her for hours with stories picked up from disreputable relatives and his handful of friends. He had a charming, easy way of telling tales and a subtle sense of humor. Though he showed it to almost no one but her.

At night, she sometimes built a fire and sometimes did not. It was late spring, so the nights never grew too cold. And anyway, Donnal slept always with his body to Kirra's back, the heat pouring through his thick fur to warm her skin. A couple of times she changed shape before she slept, making herself into a fox or a lion or a wolf, just because it was more comfortable that way when she was faced with a cold camp and a hard bed. She felt safer in animal shape, too, as likely as Donnal to catch any hint of danger that might creep up on them in the night.

But nothing threatened them. Nothing slowed their progress. They crossed into Danalustrous property on the morning of the fourth day.

Almost instantly, Kirra was aware of passing some invisible boundary. The holdings of the twelve marlords were a mix of land owned outright and land held by vassals who paid a complex series of taxes in return for protection and some recognition of status. These were the lesser aristocrats who made up the Thirteenth House, who were far enough down the hierarchy of power to never expect to inherit the great lands surrounding the Twelve Houses, but who nevertheless had connections of blood and history binding them to the highest lords. There had always been some jealousy between ranks, Kirra knew, but also a great deal of pride. A Danalustrous vassal wore Danalustrous red and gold, quoted Malcolm Danalustrous's every pronouncement and considered himself a faithful, integral part of House Danalustrous.

In turn, Malcolm considered them all in some sense an extension of himself, his land, his holdings. All the marlords did, of course, but with Malcolm—as in so many instances—the intensity of the possessiveness was several degrees higher. He could tell you—often, to the dismay of his daughters, *insisted* on telling you—who owned every square inch of property in the entire domain, who had owned it before that tenant, and when the land had changed hands. He seemed to know when rain fell along the coastline, when drought hit the southern croplands, even before a rider arrived with the news. It was as if the land itself communicated with him, sent its heartbeat of buried river and seasonal blooming like a slow, steady pulse into Malcolm's body. So often that it had long ago ceased to surprise her, Kirra had come across her father standing motionless and alone, his head cocked to one side, his eyes fixed on nothing, simply listening. She had asked him several times what he was doing, and he had only shaken his head. "Noticing things," he had answered once or twice. Or, "Concentrating." Her only conclusion had been that he had been giving his whole attention to Danalustrous itself.

It was Senneth's theory that all mystics drew their power from one of the old, forgotten gods. These days, most of Gillengaria worshipped the Pale Mother, the moon goddess, but Senneth believed her ability to call fire came directly from the goddess of the sun. The Wild Mother, who extended her protection to all the animals of the realm, perhaps watched over shiftlings like Donnal and Kirra. Who knew what strange deity might give Cammon his uncommon gifts? Kirra had never heard of a land god, a divinity with power over the soil and rocks themselves, but if there was one, she was sure it had laid its hand across Malcolm Danalustrous.

It was clear to Kirra from the minute they crossed into Danalustrous territory that her father was preparing for war.

Danalustrous was a rich, fertile property on the northwestern corner of Gillengaria. Considered second only to Brassenthwaite in terms of power, prestige, and prosperity, it drew half its wealth from the foreign trade and fishing industry available off the coast, and half its wealth from the arable farmlands that spread over most of its flat and even plains. As she and Donnal traveled at a steady pace toward the heart of the domain, Kirra saw all those lush fields heavy with crops. Even the fields that were usually fallow had been planted and were green with promise.

Most of the workers she saw laboring in the fields were women or young boys. When she spotted any men, they were in uniform and in training, gathered in some warlike formation on the back lot of a lesser lord's property. Every smithy she passed was clamorous with the sounds of hammers hitting iron. Every seamstress sat in a welter of red fabric, or gold, sewing sashes and vests in the Danalustrous colors.

If Malcolm Danalustrous expected war, war would very likely come.

It was late afternoon on that fourth day before Kirra and Donnal came in sight of Danan Hall itself. She had disguised herself somewhat as they rode through the industrious little town that was situated just outside her father's estates. If she had not, everyone in the streets would have recognized her, and she would have been stopped every few yards by someone calling out a friendly greeting, wishing to hear the tales of her recent travels. Some other day, perhaps; right now she just wanted to get home. Donnal had modified his appearance as well, and now he ran alongside her horse as an unalarming mixed-breed dog in rough black fur. No one noticed them at all except the vendor from whom she bought an apple, and he was too busy hawking his fruit to other potential customers to pay much attention to her face.

At the wide gates that led to Danan Hall, of course, it was a different story. She presented her true self to the six guards who stood at full attention, scrutinizing anyone who would pass through. Normally there were only two guards at this check-point, another sign that Malcolm was preparing for trouble.

"Good evening, friends," she hailed them, because her father had taught her to greet any man in your employ, by name if you knew it. In this instance, she did not; they were new to Danalustrous service. Malcolm would know their names, though. That she would bet on. "I have come home to Danalustrous at my father's bidding."

"Serra Kirra!"

"Serramarra Kirra!"

Each guard called out her name and gave her that low bow signifying greatest respect. No doubt they were familiar with her face from portraits and descriptions; no doubt every guard knew who should be admitted without delay.

"Would you like an escort to the doors, serra?" one of them was asking. The door to the estate lay a half mile away, winding through sublimely green grass and well-tended hedges.

She laughed. "No, I think not. We should be safe going that far alone."

The "we" caught their attention. Three of them sought for a companion and settled on the dog that was looking around with bright interest. Two of them exchanged glances and nodded, so she supposed they'd been briefed about Donnal as well. "Then go on to the door, serra," the guard said. "Welcome home."

She nodded and kicked the horse forward.

Oh, Danan Hall was the most beautiful estate in the entire

kingdom. Kirra always felt a small clutch at her heart when she rode up to the doors, especially after a long absence. The house had been exquisitely designed more than five hundred years ago and not marred with clumsy additions built on by misguided heirs. Its perfect proportions encompassed three stories of honey-beige stone supported with white marble columns and graced by white shutters at each of the many windows. Wild roses had completely taken over the western edge of the house, climbing almost to the roof, and they lay their explosions of green and red with unabated fervor along every gutter, around every open window. The lawn seemed to spill behind the house like the train of a bride's dress, embroidered at the hem with flowers and beckoning statues. Farther, beyond the open expanse of green, were woods filled with thin birch and slender aspen, and laced with two delightful streams.

A person could live forever at Danan Hall and never tire of its beauty or its peace.

Servants were pouring from the door before she had gone halfway down the lane, so either someone had been watching from the windows or the guards had signaled from the gate. A groom ran up to help her from the saddle and take charge of her horse; a footman unstrapped her insignificant bundles of luggage and carried them inside. Another footman whistled for Donnal, but he veered off, heading for the kitchens, where he was likely to be fed. The head cook was familiar with Donnal in most of his forms; she always made sure he was taken care of.

The butler and the steward were both standing on the wide front porch, smiling more broadly than their positions usually allowed, and Kirra thought she glimpsed a gauntlet of maids and footmen gathered just inside the door.

"Serra," the steward said, stepping forward to take her in an embrace. Carlo had been with her father since before she was born; she couldn't remember a day she hadn't been familiar with his slim shape and carefully curled dark hair. "Your father will be so pleased to see you."

"Not as pleased as I am to see you!" she said, returning the hug and kissing him on the cheek. "And Menten!" she added, greeting the butler. He was a handsome but generally impassive man of about fifty years, but today he was smiling benignly.

"Serra Kirra," he said, bowing again. "How good to see you."

She gave him her hands, since she knew he wouldn't suffer the indignity of an embrace. "How is everyone? My father? My stepmother? Casserah?"

"Well and happy, serra. Happier now that you're here, I'm sure."

"Are they home?"

"Your father is. Serra Casserah is out riding. She should be back shortly."

"Your father is in his study," Carlo said. "I know he wants to see you as soon as you arrive."

She laughed at him. "Shouldn't I pause to change my clothes?"

"Such a trivial thing as a little travel dust will not matter to your father," Carlo replied.

Kirra felt the smile die on her lips. Perhaps her father had been deadly serious when he wrote her a few weeks ago. *It has been too long since we have seen you. Come home*, had been the terse message. But that meant nothing—Malcolm Danalustrous was always terse. Stranger would be the day when he wrote a long, effusive missive, ending with how much he missed her.

"Then I'll go right up to see him," she said. She nodded at them both, and stepped inside.

The interior of Danan Hall was even more beautiful, more thick with serenity, than the grounds. Every arch, every niche, every piece of furniture in every room was designed to be pleasing to the eye, welcoming to the spirit. Kirra slowly climbed the wide, curving stairs, trailing her hand with a sense of physical pleasure along the polished wood of the banister. On ground level and on the first two landings, servants were gathered to greet her, calling out her name if they knew her well enough or merely bobbing their heads if they didn't. She smiled, waved, occasionally reached out a hand to touch someone on the arm, but her attention was not focused on the tableaux of loyal domestics and prodigal child. She was thinking about her father.

He was waiting for her in his study on the third floor. She entered the room without knocking and barely took in the familiar furnishings of dark leather and deep crimson. Malcolm Danalustrous was standing at the far window, looking out over his back lawns toward the woods beyond. The failing rays of the sun came in at an almost horizontal angle to illuminate his strongly modeled features, wide mouth, prominent cheekbones, and startlingly blue eyes. His hair, black and thick, was marked with only a few gray strands. A tall man, he had broad shoulders and the athletic legs of someone used to riding. He was still now, but when he was in motion, he gave the impression of being completely unstoppable, whether he was riding on the hunting field, arguing with a vassal, or striding across the room to refill his plate with meat. In the twenty-five years of Kirra's life, she had never seen him fail to attain whatever it was he most wanted.

She stood just inside the door, waiting for him to notice her. No, that wasn't right—he had known she was there the minute she stepped inside the room, possibly the minute she stepped inside the house. In fact, she was far from sure he hadn't realized she was in Danalustrous the instant she crossed onto his lands. He might have been expecting her since she first put foot on Danalustrous soil.

His silent communion ended; he seemed to stir and wake. With one abrupt motion, he turned from the window and plunged through the room in her direction. "Kirra," he said, putting his arms around her. "It's good to have you home."

He smelled like tilled earth and summer leaves and sunshine and horse; he smelled like woodsmoke from a parlor fire, clean cotton, home-brewed beer. He smelled like Danalustrous. She closed her eyes and tightened her hold and felt, for a moment, completely at rest.

Then she pulled away and prepared to do battle. It might not come to that, but it might. With Malcolm Danalustrous, you never knew.

"You've been gone too long," he said.

"I meant to return sooner," she said. "But this most recent delay was not my fault."

"Yes, Baryn sent me word that he had asked you to do a favor for him. He wasn't specific."

"I'll wager you know it anyway."

Her father looked a little amused. His blue eyes and his frequent smiles were almost the only things Kirra had inherited from him, but Casserah was a gentler, prettier copy of their father. "I am glad to learn you have such a high opinion of me. But in this case I am in the dark."

"Someone—still unclear who—abducted the newly named regent of the realm, holding him hostage, though we don't know why. He was unharmed by the time some companions and I found him and helped free him from the house where he was being held, an empty holding in Tilt. My party accompanied him toward Merrenstow, until we encountered a troop of his men. We left him with them, and I returned home."

Malcolm's eyebrows had shot up at the first sentence of her story, and surprise continued to shape his face. "The regent abducted," he said now. "That's about as bad as news can get." He didn't make any observation on her ability to free a man from a guarded cell. "And you have no idea who put such a plan in motion? Or what their motives were?"

"The three I saw were lesser lords. I don't know if they were acting alone or at the behest of someone more powerful. Romar Brendyn says the members of the Thirteenth House are growing restless."

"As change comes, violence hovers over our borders," Malcolm said in a musing voice. "Yes, very likely. But will it really come to armed conflict?"

"*You* would seem to think so," Kirra said, striking first. "Everything I saw as I rode through your holdings showed me a man girding up for war."

He smiled again. "You know I am cautious," he said. "I would rather be too ready than caught unprepared."

Kirra strolled through the study toward the two wing-backed chairs positioned close to the window. She wanted to sit in the fading sunshine. "And whom do you prepare to war against?" she asked in a conversational voice, plopping down in one of the chairs.

Malcolm sat across from her, seeming as relaxed as Kirra. "Who do you like for my enemies?"

"That's the thing," she admitted. "I really don't know. I would like to think you would support the king against Halchon Gisseltess and whatever insurgents he manages to persuade to his cause. But no one can ever predict you. I certainly can't."

"Well, this much I can tell you for certain," he said. "I would never take sides with Halchon Gisseltess in any bid for the throne. In fact, I can't think of too many instances in which I *would* take sides with Halchon Gisseltess."

She leaned her head against the back of the chair. "You don't care much for Kiernan Brassenthwaite, either."

"At least he's honest. You can trust his word."

"But I don't hear you saying you've entered into any compact with him."

He appeared to think a moment. "At this time, I would not commit myself to any side in a war," he said at last.

That made her sit straight up. "What? But if war comes, you cannot possibly remain neutral!"

He shrugged. "Can I not? Can I not simply patrol the borders and coastline of Danalustrous? Why should I take up arms against my fellow marlords? Why should I see Danalustrous men cut down in a stupid battle for power? Let kings fall and kings change. Why should it matter to me as long as Danalustrous is left alone?"

She gripped the arms of the chair. "You can't mean that."

"Possibly I do. Convince me otherwise."

"I'm not the sort of melodramatic person who uses words like 'evil,'" she said. "But there is something about Halchon Gisseltess that fits that word. He is blind with ambition, and he will sacrifice as many lives as it takes for him to achieve his goal of sitting on the throne of Gillengaria. He has already started killing mystics throughout the southern provinces—did you know that?—he and his sister both. They are on their way to constructing a whole new regime, based on his notions of rulership and her notions of religion. They have ignited enough passion among the southern marlords that half the Houses have united behind them. We are looking at the possibility of a coup, and a bloodbath. And you would sit inside Danalustrous and do nothing?"

"I have never been interested in bloodbaths," he said, his voice indifferent. "The word itself makes me want to bolt the doors and close the borders."

"But you can't close the borders," she said softly. "This war will run right over you."

A slight smile for that. "You think I cannot?" he said. "I think, if I wanted to, I could hold off Halchon Gisseltess and his benighted armies for as long as it took. I could seal Danalustrous off and keep everyone inside safe while war tore the entire rest of Gillengaria to pieces. I think I could—and I think I will, unless I see a stronger incentive than has so far presented itself to me."

"You have to fight for your king!" she cried. "You have to fight for your country!"

"Danalustrous *is* my country. Don't you understand? *That* was the trust I was given more than thirty years ago, when the property passed into my hands. *Protect Danalustrous.* And I will do it, too, no matter what storm rages outside my boundaries. I don't know—perhaps my land can only be saved by protecting Gillengaria as it stands today, and then I will fight side by side with Brassenthwaite and the king. But perhaps Danalustrous can best be served if I stand aside from war. I will see. I will do what I think is best when the time comes."

Kirra was suddenly tired. Once more she leaned her head back against the cushions of the chair. "Nothing else matters to you," she said in a flat voice. "Nothing. Not your wife, not your friends—"

"My daughters matter to me," he interrupted. "You are among the things I would defend with my life."

She opened her eyes to give him a bitter glare. "Because we are Danalustrous! Because you see our flesh as so many pounds of Danalustrous soil and our blood as Danalustrous river water."

His mouth quirked; he was amused. "Quaint," he said.

"And true."

He regarded her a moment. "Do you know why I married your mother?" he asked suddenly.

Wide-eyed, she shook her head. He simply never spoke of her mother, the fey, restless woman from a minor Danalustrous house who had lived at the hall only long enough to bear a single child. "I can't even guess."

"Because she promised me you. My first wife was barren, as you know. Your mother—oh, I knew she was a mystic. She made no attempt to hide it. But I didn't care. She told me she could make my baby in her womb. She described you to me, down to the color of your eyes and the curl of your hair. She told me you would be a girl. She told me you would be a shiftling. I fell in love with the picture she drew, the picture of that child who turned out to be you in every detail she predicted. I didn't want you merely because you would be a daughter of

Danalustrous. I wanted you because you would be *mine*. My child. My daughter. You. And that has never changed."

It was then Kirra knew, with sudden cold certainty, why her father had called her home. For a moment she couldn't speak, merely sat there, clutching the arms of her chair, staring at him with eyes so much like his own that, if their portraits were laid side by side, the eyes would be identical. "Casserah just turned twenty-one," she whispered at last.

He nodded. "Old enough to own property."

"You've made her your heir."

He nodded again. "I have. But I waited to make the announcement until you were home. We are having a party a few days from now and every landholder in Danalustrous will be here. We will make the announcement then."

Kirra felt dizzy, bereft, suddenly and completely adrift. She was the oldest daughter; by right and tradition, Danalustrous should come to her when her father died. It had never occurred to her the estate might be left differently. "Does Casserah know?"

"Yes. And her mother. No one else."

"Give me a moment to absorb this."

He nodded and was silent. Anyone else would have attempted to argue his point, present his reasons, but Malcolm Danalustrous liked to think things through for himself, so he always allowed others the same privilege. He stayed unmoving in his chair, watching her face or watching the fire, it was hard to tell. Kirra sat with her hands now lax on the armrests, looking out over the subtle beauty of Danalustrous, and felt her life reshape around her.

Well. She had been gone for most of the last six months. In the past eight years, she had probably spent at least one-quarter of her life somewhere else. She was as restless as her mother; it was hard for her to sit still. She was happiest when she was traveling, looking forward to another stop upon the journey. The long trip with Senneth and Tayse earlier in the year had been hazardous and full of painful surprises, but in some ways she had enjoyed it more than any other stretch in her life, because their small group had been so constantly in motion.

She was not suited for staying in one place, watching over a single plot of ground, no matter how beautiful. She had always thought Danalustrous would come to her, but the thought had been vague and distant. It had never really occurred to her that her father would die, that any power on earth could quell Malcolm Danalustrous's contentious spirit. She had made no attempt to learn the intricacies of governing the realm. She had never taken up the responsibilities of an heir.

But Casserah? Oh, Casserah loved Danalustrous with all of Malcolm's single-mindedness. She had left Danan Hall only rarely, under protest, to attend a few of the more important social events at other Houses. She was possibly as unknown to the Gillengaria gentry as the sheltered Princess Amalie and content to have it that way. Like Malcolm, she cared about nothing but the land and the people who belonged to it. Like Malcolm, she had some preternatural connection to Danalustrous.

He must have realized that years ago—almost from the day Casserah was born. He must have known for nearly twenty years which daughter he would name heir. Why had he waited so long to make his announcement?

So that Kirra would not feel like a stepchild, unwanted and unimportant. So that the lords of the Twelve Houses would be forced to treat her with honor, to acknowledge her as serramarra. So that Kirra could define her own life, driven by curiosity and excitement, not by fear and insecurity.

So that she would realize he loved her.

"It's not because I'm a mystic," she said at last.

"No. Though there are some lords who will think that's why."

"It's because I'm so restless."

He smiled a little. "It's because you think Danalustrous should go to war."

She nodded. "Yes. Because I don't put Danalustrous above every other person, place, or consideration."

"And Casserah does, you know."

She turned her head a little so she could inspect him, still leaning her back against the chair but entirely focused on him. "I would have picked her, too," she said. "I am no marlady."

"Danalustrous will always be your home," he said.

She nodded. "Casserah feels about me the way you do," she said. "I am part of Danalustrous, and so I belong to her. I am not afraid that she would ever lock me out. Unless I bring war to the borders, of course."

Another small smile for that. "Even then. She would find a way to let you in and keep your soldiers out."

"So now we must think," she said, "of the generation to follow. Have you picked out her husband yet? For suddenly it becomes important for Casserah to marry."

He was even more amused. "This from the girl who would never tolerate talk of matchmaking on her own behalf."

"Casserah is different."

"Yes," he said. "She always has been."

IT was another hour before Kirra had a chance to congratulate Casserah on her new position. She was in her own suite by then, moving slowly and carefully through the familiar rooms and furniture. She felt as if she had just risen from a sickbed, still shaky with a remembered fever. The proportions of the world looked blurry and strange; nothing was as it should be. And yet, everything was the same. The flowered bed curtains, the brightly polished armoire, the thick carpet that could choke back the severest winter chill—all exactly as they were the last time she had been in Danalustrous. She was the one who had changed.

She washed up and then dressed in a gown of dusty blue, one of the items of clothing always kept waiting for her. Often there were new pieces in the armoire, items picked out for her by Casserah or her stepmother, dresses and shawls and slippers that she instantly loved. This one was an old favorite, though, made of washed cotton that felt soft and comforting against her traumatized skin. Its color picked up the color of her eyes, provided a foil to her golden curls.

It was the right dress to be wearing when Casserah came to the door a little before dinner, knocking expectantly. "Kirra? Are you in there? Carlo told me you were home."

"Yes—come in—oh, it is so *good* to see you!"

The sisters met in the middle of the room, flinging themselves into a long embrace. "You should not be gone so long," Casserah said in her ear. "I miss you! And you have been doing dangerous things. I know, because Carlo tells me. Father won't say a word."

Kirra laughed and pulled back, keeping her hands on Casserah's shoulders and inspecting her face. Her sister looked so much like their father that there was no mistaking her parentage. The blue eyes, of course. The dark hair. The far-away expression, focused on something no one else could see or hear. In fact, on Casserah's face, that expression was most pronounced, accentuated by the exceedingly wide placement of her eyes. No matter how intense or personal the conversation Casserah might be holding, she always appeared a little abstracted. Like Malcolm, Kirra thought, Casserah was always listening to the land. Like Malcolm, she cared about little else.

Kirra smiled at her sister, feeling a surge of affection so fierce it would be impossible to articulate. "Not so dangerous, really," she said. "I had powerful friends with me."

A quick smile from Casserah. "Senneth, yes?"

"Among others."

"I haven't seen her for years. She's well?"

"She's wonderful. She's taken a commission from the king, so she's respectably employed—oh, and she's fallen in love. Most unsuitably, with a King's Rider."

The smile widened. "Kiernan must be beside himself."

"I expect so, but I haven't heard from her. She's visiting Brassenthwaite now. After seventeen years of not speaking to her brothers at all."

Casserah nodded. "Good. No one should ever be estranged from their siblings. I would never let you go seventeen years without speaking to me. No matter what."

Kirra took a deep breath. "Nothing would ever turn me against you. No matter what. There would be no rift."

"Father's told you," Casserah said.

"He was right to choose you," Kirra said. "In fact, he had no choice."

"No," Casserah said.

And that was all they said on the topic. Then, or ever.

Kirra drew Casserah over to the bed and they sat together under the flowered canopy, as they had so many times in the past twenty years. "So tell me," Kirra said, "everything that has been happening with you."

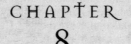

KIRRA was in Danalustrous for three weeks and was wishing she was gone within two. She couldn't help it; she could not find the calm within herself to sit quiet in any one place very long.

Not that her time in Danalustrous was quiet. Far from it.

Her very first night back she had to participate in a formal dinner with perhaps a dozen guests attending, so she had to dress like a serramarra and play the grand lady. Easy enough to do; it was how she'd been trained, after all. Her stepmother, Jannis, made sure to praise her lavishly once the meal was over.

"No one would know how much you hate such affairs," was Jannis's comment as the guests slipped into an informal parlor to play cards and conduct more relaxed conversations. "You carry it off so beautifully. I think I even saw you flirting with Simon Grelback, and he's really quite an unpleasant human being."

Kirra laughed. She had always liked Jannis, a tall, lean, dark-haired woman who was unfailingly practical and almost never caught by surprise. "Whatever grace I own I can thank you for," she said. "Though I *don't* thank you for seating me by Simon."

In the parlor, she made her way around the room, talking with totally feigned gaiety to all of the guests. She made a special point of singling out Erin Sohta, a shallow, sharp-eyed woman who owned a great deal of property and considered herself to have a special relationship with the House Danalustrous.

"Oh, Erin, I don't know if you'll think I'm wonderful or terrible once I tell you a little story about a recent escapade of mine," Kirra said, putting a hand to her cheek with mock concern. "But I think it's best you hear the story from me. So promise you'll take it in good part."

"Why, Kirra, you make me nervous. But surely nothing you did could ever be so bad," Erin said, glancing around the room to make sure everyone noted that serra Kirra had special news for her alone. Indeed, quite a number of people were listening, including Malcolm and Casserah.

Kirra took a deep breath. "Well, I *hope* you'll be flattered," she said. "I was in Forten City some months back—gathering information for the king, you know." That would impress Erin; that would impress everyone, except her father and sister. "I needed to join a group of nobles who were celebrating a wedding, because I wanted to eavesdrop on certain conversations. I couldn't go as myself, but I wanted to go as someone both respectable and welcome—"

"And you disguised yourself as me!" Erin guessed, looking quite delighted. "Oh, Kirra, what fun!"

"Actually, it was fun," Kirra said, allowing a look of mischief to cross her face. "I flirted with all the most handsome men—I'll be surprised if you haven't heard from Emory Clayton by now—and I danced the whole night through. Everyone told me how much they enjoyed my company. I would think you'd be quite popular in Forten City if you ever went back."

"And whose wedding did I attend? Can you tell me that?"

"Katlin Dormer and Edwin Seiles. Do you know them?"

"Yes, but only slightly."

"Well, you bought them a clock as a wedding gift. One of them should send you a thank-you note eventually."

Erin dissolved with merriment, and Kirra's father and sister were both smiling. But Kirra noticed that a few of the people listening were not amused in the slightest. *A mystic, taking whatever shape she pleases, imitating honest men and women and—who knows?—maybe disgracing them with her hoydenish behavior.* Not everyone would find such tricks acceptable—not even in service to the king.

But no one said anything to her face, that night or in the

hectic days that followed. Casserah and Jannis were deep in preparations for a huge banquet that would be held in two weeks, to which close to a hundred people had been invited. It was at this event that Malcolm planned to make the announcement that Casserah was his heir, and Kirra could hardly say she was looking forward to it. But she did what she could to help with preparations, docilely allowed Jannis and her seamstress to fit her for a ballgown in the color and style they chose, and even submitted to having her long hair trimmed and tamed a few days before the big event.

But she didn't enjoy any of it.

She also missed Donnal, who had disappeared the day they arrived. He was off visiting his own family, she knew—poor farmers whose close association with House Danalustrous had netted them some monetary advantages and outright ownership of their small plot of land. His father had been gone a long time, but his mother, uncle, brothers, and various other family members were always thrilled to see him on his infrequent visits home, and demanded to hear all the details of his most recent adventures. He would grow restless even sooner than she would, Kirra knew, but while he was gone, she missed his quiet, undemanding presence and the warmth of his body beside her at night.

But he would be back soon. He always returned to her.

After she had been home about a week, her father sought her out, a letter in his hand and a sour expression on his face. "If you've nothing better to do, you might ride down to see your aunt and uncle in the next few days," he said.

She had been letting Jannis's dresser work on her fingernails, absolutely disgraceful after six months of neglect, but she had been happy enough to forgo that occupation and talk with her father. "Certainly I will, but I thought they were coming to the banquet?"

Malcolm waved the letter. "Apparently not. Berric has injured himself in some riding accident and cannot leave the house, and, of course, Beatrice won't go anywhere without him."

Kirra grinned. "She probably didn't want to come anyway. She hates big social gatherings. I'll bet she's relieved."

"No doubt she slipped a burr under the horse's saddle to cause Berric to be thrown," Malcolm agreed. "Nonetheless,

they seem grieved at the thought of missing a chance to see •
you, and I'm sure they would welcome a visit."

"I am equally grieved at the thought of tearing myself
away from manicures and hair stylings, even for a day, but I
believe I can make the sacrifice," Kirra said. "Should we write
to tell them I'm coming?"

"I'll send a note. You are very kind."

She laughed. "I like them. You don't."

Malcolm spread his hands. "There are so many people I
don't like."

"I'll leave in the morning."

And she did, accompanied by two of her father's house
guards, though she protested she could care for herself well
enough. Malcolm didn't bother to argue with her, so she sighed
and accepted the escort. She thought the men had been assigned to her more to give her consequence than to protect her,
but she couldn't be sure.

Berric and Beatrice lived close enough to Danan Hall that
the trip could be made in one rather long day. Their holdings
were small but pretty, consisting of a two-story stone house set
on smartly tilled farmland. When she was younger, and just
beginning to exhibit signs of the restlessness that would haunt
her for the rest of her life, Kirra had spent many of her summers here. There was much more freedom at her uncle's house,
more to explore, fewer rules.

And Berric and Beatrice loved her, though they had never
quite forgiven Malcolm. It was their sister he had taken as his
second bride, relocating her from their modest property to
Danan Hall and then losing her altogether. Beatrice claimed
that Bayla would have been content to roam Danalustrous her
whole life, periodically returning to the home she shared with
her brother and sister, but that Malcolm showed her a different
world. Ships from foreign countries, caravans of trading goods
from other regions of Gillengaria. She hadn't realized how big
the world was outside of Danalustrous borders, and she had
wanted to see it all.

As far as Kirra knew, Bayla had never come back. Malcolm
had had her declared dead three years after Kirra was born, two
years after Bayla had disappeared. Kirra had always figured that
was a convenient fiction on his part, freeing him to marry Jannis.

She had not felt much grief for the mother she could not re-member at all—but she had, as she'd grown older, felt a certain sympathy. She knew what it was like to be unable to sit still, to find the calm serenity of Danalustrous closing in on her like an iron-bound cell. She was certain Bayla would have discovered the rest of the world on her own one day, even if Malcolm Danalustrous had never come calling.

Beatrice was waiting for her at the door when she and her guard rode up, and Kirra tumbled from her horse to fling her-self into her aunt's arms. Beatrice was short and plump, with hair as gold and curly as Kirra's, though not nearly as long. She had very comforting hugs.

"Look at you! What a fine lady you are!" Beatrice said, stepping back to admire Kirra's clothes and coiffure. "I hope we didn't steal you away from anything too important, but you're home so rarely and I didn't want to miss you completely."

"Oh, I was so *glad* when your message came!" Kirra ex-claimed. "All that sitting around being—serramarra-y. It's about to drive me to lunacy. I can't imagine how Casserah can stand it."

Beatrice put a hand on Kirra's arm and drew her inside. The front hall, like the whole house, had been designed with pleasing proportions and would have been very lovely if it hadn't been overflowing with shelves and statuary and knick-knacks. Beatrice loved *things*, from books to chairs to vases, and the whole house was crowded with examples of her prof-ligate taste.

"And how is Casserah? And your father and the marlady?"

Neither Beatrice nor Berric ever referred to Jannis by name. She was always "the marlady" to them, a constant re-minder that she had stolen Bayla's title. "Everyone is well. They're planning Casserah's birthday dinner, you know. It's a shame you can't come."

"Yes, isn't it?" Beatrice said in a dry voice.

Kirra laughed. "So is Berric *really* injured? Or did you just find you couldn't face a party at Danan Hall?"

"Injured, indeed, and quite petulant about it, too," Beatrice answered. "But here, talk to him yourself! We've waited dinner for you. It'll just be the three of us, so we can talk all night."

"That's just the way I like it," Kirra said, and followed her aunt into the small family dining room.

Berric was already sitting at the head of the table, one foot extended before him and propped on an overstuffed stool. Like Beatrice, he was stout and fair, though his hair was mostly missing and hadn't been curly when he had it. He was shifting uncomfortably in his chair, and his face looked red and displeased, as if he'd just been shouting at someone as a palliative to his own wretchedness.

But his expression cleared instantly when his niece walked in the room. "Kirra! I thought I heard voices in the hall. We weren't sure if you would make it tonight or tomorrow, but we were hoping. Come give me a kiss—it's too much trouble for me to stand up."

She crossed to his side and bent to kiss him on the cheek. His skin was hot, a little damp, and she pulled back to put a hand across his forehead. "Do you have a fever? How bad is the pain, really?"

"Bad enough," he admitted. "I don't know if I've caught an infection, but I feel like red and silver hell. Beatrice has been feeding me some vile herbal drink, but it hasn't helped much."

Kirra pulled up a chair to sit beside him. "Is it just your leg? Or does your hip hurt, too? Where's the break? And how did this happen?"

Berric sighed. "I was riding back from Storian. I'd been gone almost two weeks, didn't have a single day of trouble! I must have ridden two hundred miles without so much as a thrown shoe. Then three days ago, as I'm coming up the lane to my *very own house*, the horse shies and I fall off. Caught my foot in the stirrup, twisted my leg—*heard* it snap before I felt it. Beatrice and the groom set it for me, and between them they've seen every injury a man might get from a horse, but I'm wondering if I might need to call a physician in."

"I think I might be able to help you," Kirra said, and hitched her chair over so her knees almost touched Berric's outstretched leg. "Hold still."

She was gazing down at the leg but she didn't miss the quick, significant glance that passed between brother and sister. Bayla had been a shiftling, but she had not had the power of healing. No one could figure out where that talent had come from, what quirk in the bloodline had given Kirra two magical abilities, when most mystics could only claim one.

"Let me know if I hurt you," she murmured and laid her hand gently over the bandage visible under Berric's trousers.

He winced but didn't cry out, and she spread her fingers as wide as they would go. She could feel the layered textures beneath her hand—the silk and cotton of the clothing, the skin and hair that defined the flesh, the liquid of the blood, the porous marble of the bone. Blood and bone were bunched up in a painful lump, veins in knots, bone in a ragged break. Kirra smoothed her hand over the cotton of the outer layer, sent her energy sinking down to the interior levels. She stroked her hand again over the misaligned edges, then tightened her fingers for a moment along the top of Berric's leg. She heard him take a deep breath, but he didn't say anything. The palm of her hand felt strange, as if it danced with tiny pinpricks. The sensation continued clear up to her elbow before it dissipated.

"Does that feel any better?" she asked.

Berric let his breath out in an explosive sigh. "Yes! Pale Lady's silver tears, I knew you were a healer, but—I've never witnessed anything like that. The pain is all gone! My leg feels almost normal!"

"What a gift," Beatrice said. She had stood tense and silent this whole time and only now began to stir uncertainly through the room.

"The leg's still healing, though," Kirra warned. "It will be a while before you can really expect to be at full strength, so don't push yourself. Walk with a cane for a while—and don't go horseback riding any time soon. And *certainly* don't go jaunting off to balls and banquets and other taxing affairs," she added with a smile.

"Are you sure? I shouldn't go riding up to Danan Hall to attend your sister's dinner?"

"Quite sure," she said, pushing away from him and coming to her feet. "But I do believe you'll be feeling quite restored in no time."

"Let's have wine with dinner," Beatrice said, disappearing through a connecting door toward the kitchen. "I feel like a little celebration."

The meal was convivial, though it would have been even without the wine, Kirra thought. Beatrice had no use for pretension and could be quite sharp-tongued when she relayed gossip about the lesser gentry of Danalustrous, and Kirra found herself laughing helplessly more than once at her sarcastic comments. Berric, now out of pain, was mellow and urbane, though quick with his own less-than-flattering remarks about the lords he had recently visited in Storian.

"The man's hardly smart enough to remember his own name, let alone run a household, but he thinks he should have Rafe Storian's title and property," Berric said. "People talk about the decline of the marlords! They should talk about the utter madness in the Thirteenth House."

Kirra toyed with her wineglass a moment. "Yes. I have heard some—interesting—tales lately about the ambition of the lesser lords," she said. "I found them hard to credit, but then I have never been ambitious. At least not for wealth and property."

Berric made a sound that sounded like "faugh" and waved an impatient hand. "The lesser lords don't understand how good their lives are," he said. "What could be better than the way Beatrice and I live? We have a beautiful house. We have a prosperous property. We have social standing—good friends—a charming niece. Life is good. Life is *easy*—and I'll wager the life of a marlord, though glamorous and coveted, is not an easy one. The lesser lords don't know what they're jealous of."

"But there is jealousy?" Kirra pressed. "There is discontent? Is there—Uncle, do you hear tales of the gentry planning to rise up against the king?"

Berric looked at her very soberly. Beatrice, sitting across the table from them, was openmouthed with surprise. "Tales. Yes," said Berric. "Of how Martin Helven is weak and should be brought down, how Els Nocklyn is sick and his daughter not ready to run the House when he dies. And who better to take over such rich properties than the loyal vassals who know and love the land so well? They grumble that they don't have enough, but none of them sees that if they were ever to don the title of marlord, all of their friends would turn against *them*, wanting what they had now. They talk revolution, but will they act? I don't know. I don't believe they have the organization to act in concert."

"But they talk about it. That is bad enough," Kirra said.

Berric shrugged. "Will they rise up to depose Baryn? I doubt it. But from what I hear, the marlords are poised to do just that. Is this a time of crisis in the realm? Why, yes, I think so. Gisseltess appears to be amassing an army. So does Rappengrass. So does Danalustrous, if it comes to that. Where are all the Houses drawing their funds to support their legions of soldiers? From the lesser lords, of course. They are taxing their vassals and conscripting the workmen to toil in their armies. You can see why the lower gentry might be saying, 'If I must finance this war, I want some recompense in return. I do not want to beggar myself for the honor of my marlord, or even my king.'"

Kirra took a deep breath. "There is so much unrest," she said. "Everywhere. I don't know that Baryn can look in all directions at once to see the potential dangers facing him."

"No, and what if he dies?" Berric agreed. "For that's what everyone's afraid of, you know. That little princess can't hold off an army if the marlords choose to raise one. No, and neither can that man, that regent Baryn's picked out. What's his name? The Merrenstow fellow."

"Romar Brendyn."

Berric nodded. "That's it. I don't see him uniting the marlords to any cause, even if it is in protection of the throne. The whole realm is uneasy, Kirra, as you say."

"Then what's to come next?" she asked.

He shook his head. "Pale Lady alone can guess."

Beatrice stood up. "Dessert's to come next," she said in a firm voice. "And you can stop all this frightening talk. I don't like to hear it. I can't think anything will happen—not to Baryn, not to the princess. Let's just have some pie now and think about happier things."

"Yes, you can tell us what you've been doing lately that's kept you from Danalustrous so long," Berric said as his sister left the room. "Just back from Tilt now, aren't you?"

Kirra widened her eyes. "How did you hear that story? My own father didn't know it."

He grinned. "I didn't hear all of it. Just that you were wandering through northern parts at a time when no one was expecting you."

"Was that news all over Storian while you were there?"

He shook his head. "One of Gregory Tilton's vassals was present, and he drew me aside to ask why you'd been in Tilt. Apparently someone had been surprised to see you there, doing something you weren't expected to do. And he wondered what your interest there had been. I told him I'd ask—but that I guessed you wouldn't tell me."

She laughed at that. "No, I don't think I'm supposed to repeat the story. But I'm impressed that you know enough to ask!"

Beatrice reappeared, bearing a large fruit pie and smiling broadly. She would not want to hear any speculation about dangerous activities Kirra had engaged in. Berric said, "We'll talk about this later. Bea, it looks like you've outdone yourself."

Over dessert, Kirra related some of the more humorous tales of her recent travels, the ones she could repeat, which left out most of her trip last winter with Senneth and the others. Instead, she described bits and pieces of other events, the wedding in Forten City, a dinner in Ghosenhall, an evening she had spent in Kianlever.

"Oh, you'll appreciate this story, Uncle! There was a little girl in Kianlever—had broken her leg and *both* her arms falling down a stairwell. She said her brother pushed her, and I wouldn't have been surprised—he was a nasty little boy. Anyway, I was there two days after she fell and I put all the bones back together. I felt very good about it, too. I've never been as good at injuries as I am at sickness."

Again, Beatrice and Berric exchanged glances. "What?" Kirra demanded. "What did I just say?"

Beatrice answered. "There's a boy. The son of one of our farmers. He's fallen sick and no one can help him. Your father sent out a physician, but he didn't have an antidote. And there was a healer who passed through not a week ago—a mystic, like you. She couldn't fix him. She said nobody could."

Kirra felt her heart grow smaller. "What does he have? Did she name it?"

"Red-horse fever," Berric answered.

Kirra nodded and felt all her pleasure in the evening drain away. "I've heard of that," she said. "Even come across it once or twice. I haven't met a mystic who's been able to cure it."

Beatrice's voice sounded frightened. "None of you? Why would that be?"

Kirra shook her head. "I heard someone in Ghosenhall guess that it comes from somewhere else—Arberharst or Sovenfeld—that it's a kind of fever brought in by one of the trading ships. Our magic only seems to work inside Gillengaria. The farther a mystic gets from these shores, the weaker his power gets. So if this is an infection brought from somewhere else—" She shrugged. "Our magic won't help."

"It's a terrible disease," Beatrice said. "The physician said it sometimes takes people as much as a year to die from it. Everyone he's seen has died. And most of them have been children."

"I've heard the same things," Kirra replied.

"Well, then. We won't ask you to see him. We thought—but if you can't do any good—"

"I'm willing to go," Kirra said. "To try. I just don't want to get anybody's hopes up."

"You're so strong," Berric said hopefully. "Maybe you'll be able to do something the others can't."

"I'll try," she said again. "When should we see him?"

They decided that Beatrice and Kirra would set out the next day, as it didn't seem advisable for Berric to travel even a short distance from the house. Their moods had all been depressed by the topic of illness, but they revived a little upon eating more pie. The hour was late by the time Kirra started yawning.

"I'm sorry—goodness, that's rude—but I think I'm getting tired."

Beatrice was laughing. "Of course. You've been up since dawn, I imagine. I've put you in your old room, of course, and feel free to sleep in as late as you like."

Within the half hour, Kirra found herself comfortably ensconced in the familiar room of heavily flowered wallpaper, multiple layers of patterned rugs, and an ornate bed piled high with pillows. She was undressed and under the covers in record time. The long day had made her truly exhausted; she was instantly asleep.

KIRRA and Beatrice rode out shortly after breakfast the following day, both of them enjoying the bright sunshine that was pleasant now but promised heavy heat before the month was out. Kirra laughed and talked easily, but she felt herself getting more tense as the thirty-minute ride progressed. During her roving days, she had spent some time studying traditional medicine at institutions in Ghosenhall and Rappengrass, and what she couldn't repair with magic she often could cure with science. But red-horse fever was beyond her capabilities; she was pretty sure of that. Worse, it culminated in a grue-some, lingering death that was agony for everyone—patient as well as family.

She had heard horrifying tales of children and ancients being left to die, put out on a winter night or left behind on some in-frequently traveled road. She supposed that poorer families, in particular, didn't have the resources to lose a pair of healthy hands in the care of someone who would not recover; there were too many chores to do, too many other uses for that per-son's energy. But there might have been another side to it—a man who knew he might linger in pain for another six months might ask to be put outside on an icy night, preferring the quick, hard death to the slow, impossible one. She didn't know what she would choose if her own options were so grim.

They eventually arrived at a small, well-tended cottage, bright with flower gardens. It was owned by a couple who had rented the property for years from Beatrice and Berric. Kirra thought she might even have met them before.

However, she did not recognize the woman who came out to greet them, her face still with long-held grief, her hair pulled back into a knot clearly designed to keep it out of her way. She said a quiet hello and asked them to tie up their own horses, as both the boys were out helping their father in the field. With a word of thanks, she accepted the basket Beatrice offered and led them both inside.

The sick child lay in a narrow bed in a small room at the back of the house. Kirra was glad to see the window was open to let in the fresh air and brisk sunshine. The boy, who looked to be about ten, was propped up in bed, playing with some string game that changed patterns as he moved his fingers. His face was pale and all his bones looked sharp. He was concen-trating very hard on the string.

"Davie, here's a mystic come to see if she can help you any," his mother said, putting a hand on his shoulder. "It's serra Kirra, Lady Beatrice's niece. Isn't that something, a fine serramarra coming all the way here to see you?"

Davie glanced up without much interest. His eyes were rimmed with red, and a little pus had gathered in the corners. "Hullo," he said. "I don't think you can help me."

Kirra pulled up a chair and sat next to him. "Maybe not,"

she said. "But maybe I can make you feel a little better while I'm here. Do you mind if I touch you? Sometimes that tells me what's wrong inside someone's body."

He shrugged and kept folding and refolding his string. Kirra leaned a little closer and ran her hands lightly over his shoulders, his head, his chest, his legs. She could feel the fever running through his body, just under the skin; she could sense it like a skein of venom threading its way through the red weave of blood. There should be a way to change it, she thought, alter its composition from poisonous to pure. But she could not locate its source, could not tell what infected organ pumped out a continuous deadly stream. She pressed harder on Davie's stomach, poked a finger between his ribs, but the disease remained elusive. She could not identify or dissolve it.

"How long have you been sick?" she asked him, but he didn't answer.

"Three months," his mother said at last.

"Anyone else in the house come down with symptoms?"

"No. But a young girl over near the village . . . She died last week. She'd been sick a little longer than Davie. They didn't know each other, though. Davie said he didn't even know what she looked like."

Kirra nodded. "It doesn't appear to be contagious. I've heard of cases where several people in a family all got sick, or in a town, but it doesn't seem like it passes from person to person the way some fevers do."

"Some people think so, though," the mother said darkly.

Keeping her hands on the boy, Kirra glanced over her shoulder at the mother. "What do you mean?"

The woman gestured toward the window. "Some of our neighbors. When they heard Davie was sick, they wanted us to take him to the island."

"The island?" Kirra wondered if that might be some countryman's euphemism for death. "Where's that?"

Beatrice answered. "Off the lower coast of Danalustrous, there's a little place called Dorrin Isle. Mostly fishermen live on it. About six months ago, some folks set up a community there for people sick with red-horse fever. I think a couple dozen patients are there by now, some with their families, some by themselves. The physician told me he and some of his students were going to go out there and spend a week or two."

"Even though they can't cure the disease?"

Beatrice was quiet a moment. "Not to cure," she said. "To study the bodies afterward. For the students to learn—about cadavers."

Kirra was filled with a welling of distaste that felt as toxic as the fever in this boy's body. "That's horrible."

"Maybe they'll learn something," Davie's mother said. "I wouldn't mind so much if something good came out of it."

She was right, but even so, Kirra found the very idea opportunistic and coldhearted. She turned back to concentrate on Davie. Well. She could not reverse the fever, she couldn't even find its source, but she might be able to mitigate its effects, at least for a short time. She concentrated again on the silver current of corruption running through the boy's veins and imagined it turning pale, turning pink, evaporating. She put her hand over his eyes, forcing him to close them and abandon his string game, and she pushed the fever down, chased it out of his skull. She laid a fist on his chest and squeezed her fingers tight, and the cramped bundle of his heart imitated her, shaking off its sluggish rhythm. The lungs she cleared with a sweep of her fingers. The accumulated pain she eradicated with a touch of her palm upon his throat.

When she lifted her hands, Davie was staring up at her, his busy fingers lax in his lap. "What did you do to me?" he demanded.

"What? What did you do?" his mother repeated fearfully.

Davie sat up straight in bed, twisted his head from side to side. "I feel funny—I feel *good.* What did you do to me?"

"By the Pale Lady's silver tears," the woman whispered. She was crying. "You've cured him."

Kirra stood up, her sober face enough to make the woman reassess. "I haven't. I don't even know if I've bought him much time. I've taken away the pain, slowed down the infection, maybe. But it's still in there. It'll go to work on him again. But he'll feel better for a few days, at least. It's all I could do."

Davie was actually on his feet, laughing at the way his wasted legs buckled under him. "Mama, look, I haven't been able to walk for three weeks! And I'm hungry. What's in the kitchen?"

His mother gazed at Kirra and then at her son, halfway across the room now, his hand out to the wall for support. "No one else was able to do even this much for him. No one could even take away the pain. How can I thank you?"

Kirra shook her head. "Don't thank me. He'll be sick again soon. But maybe—for a few days—"

"He'll be my boy again," she said. "My boy."

And without another word to her visitors, she followed her son out of the room, catching up to him in the hall and laughing. Kirra saw her put her arm around him and guide him toward another room. The kitchen, no doubt. Where she would make his favorite meal for him one more time and watch him while he bolted down every bite. And maybe tonight, when his brothers came home, he'd wrestle with them before the fire, or race them across the field. And maybe, so happy that her son was out of pain for a day, the woman would turn to her husband for the first time in months, offer him the affection she had been too tense to summon up since the child fell sick. Maybe the respite, though brief, was bountiful. Maybe it would ease the whole family through one week, or two, give them back a measure of peace, remind them that love could be free of pain.

Maybe not. Maybe the gift would be unbearably bitter as it broke in their very hands, as the illness returned with redoubled force, choked the child's lungs, twisted his limbs. Maybe magic was a bright sparkling lure that drew the unwary deep into haunted and inescapable woods, where monsters and demons lay in wait. Maybe it would have been better for Kirra not to have come here, better for her not to possess magic at all.

Dark thoughts. Kirra shook her head and tried to clear the gloom from her mind. "I guess we're not needed here any longer," she said, trying to make her voice light. "I suppose we'll show ourselves out."

SHE stayed another day with Berric and Beatrice. Nothing else so dramatic occurred, though she and Beatrice rode out that afternoon and met a few of the other tenants. Berric had improved rapidly overnight and was even able to navigate the stairs without much trouble, marveling aloud at the impressive magic Kirra had in her hands.

"I can't cure everyone," she said when the topic came up again at breakfast as she prepared to leave. "I didn't cure Davie."

"Still, I envy you," Berric said. "I wish I had your kind of magic."

"You do, a little," she said. "When I was a girl, you were something of a shiftling."

Berric grimaced. "I could alter my appearance a bit— change my hair color. Make myself look thinner. Not much else. And I can't even do that anymore." He held out his hand as if to prove something, so Kirra obediently looked down at his fingers. "See? Nothing. I can't even make my age spots disappear."

Beatrice sighed. "I never even had enough magic to alter the expression on my face," she said. "That would be a useful skill, I always thought! Change your grumpy look to a happy one. You could still be grumpy, but no one would know it."

Kirra smiled. "I'll have to try that. Perhaps at the banquet next week. I'll show everyone a smiling face, but I'll only be able to fashion it by magic."

They parted with many expressions of affection, and Kirra promised to visit next time she was in Danalustrous. "You're leaving again soon, then?" Berric asked, waving to her from the porch as Kirra sat astride her horse.

Kirra laughed. "I imagine so. I planned to stay a few months, but already I can tell—" She shrugged. "But I'll try not to be gone so long this time."

"We'll look for you when we see you again," Beatrice said.

"I'm sure it will be sooner than you think." Another wave, a nod to her escorts, and she was on the road back to Danan Hall. Not as glad to be returning to her father's house as she was glad simply to be in motion again.

CHAPTER
9

As far as Kirra was concerned, nothing of much interest had
transpired while she was gone. The house was still in a state of
constant turmoil as servants and tradesmen worked toward
readying the house for the grand event. Donnal was still gone.
Casserah was still too busy being fitted for gowns and writing
thank-you notes for her many birthday gifts to have much time
for her wayward older sister. Kirra thought she very well could
have stayed with Berric and Beatrice another few days and no
one would have noticed she was gone.

But she was glad enough to be at Danan Hall a few days
later when a package arrived from Ghosenhall, accompanied
by a letter from Cammon. She had never seen his handwriting
before and couldn't guess who had written to her until she
flipped the page over to see the signature on the bottom. Even
more mystified, she turned the letter back over to read it.

The letter began without any formal salutation.

*Justin would not rest easy until I assured him you had
made it safely to Danalustrous. But I told him when you
arrived—yes, I can tell such things, even from this far
away!—and he finally relaxed. A few days later, a package arrived from Merrenstow, addressed to Justin and*

filled with presents from Romar Brendyn. Wasn't that kind? He sent Justin the most beautiful dagger—I don't think any of the other Riders has a blade so fine, and Justin will not step out of the barracks without it. He sent me a shirt such as the great lords wear—the finest material I've ever had against my skin. I'm torn between never wanting to take it off and never wanting to put it on, because I don't want to ruin it! I suppose he thought I was very ragged while we traveled. Little does he know that I always look so disreputable, but I wrote him right off to thank him anyway.

The last package was addressed to Donnal. Justin and I couldn't figure out how to open it without leaving behind any traces, so I have no idea what's in it. I wish I were better at things, but it seems I can only read people. Anyway, we've sent it on for you to give to Donnal.

There was nothing for you in the packet, but maybe he sent you a gift directly. Or maybe he thought such a thing would not be appropriate—I never know what sort of behavior is considered proper among the aristocracy. But we thought Donnal should have this right away. We have no idea when you'll be in Ghosenhall again—though I, at least, wish you were back right now! Justin doesn't seem to care one way or the other.

Kirra could imagine Cammon laughing as he wrote that last line, and the thought made her own face brighten with a smile. Though nothing else about the letter amused her so far. Gifts from Romar Brendyn! Kind, indeed, especially since the two that had been described were thoughtful presents chosen with a real eye toward pleasing the recipients. She was dying to know what was in Donnal's package and hoped a respect for privacy would prevent her from opening it before he returned.

She didn't expect any gifts for herself, oh no. Didn't want any. Inappropriate, indeed, on every level. One might reasonably give tokens to servants or vassals who had performed a heroic service—that reflected well on both the giver and the receiver—but one didn't pass out trinkets to unattached women with whom one had spent a certain amount of time under highly unusual circumstances. No one would think well of that.

It was with some difficulty that she forced herself to concentrate on the final paragraphs of the letter.

> *Before I forget, I want to tell you that Senneth is back. And Tayse, of course. When she heard that I was writing you a letter, she said, "Be sure and tell her that everything with me is going quite well, and underline those last two words." So I am. She has been very busy because she has been accompanying Princess Amalie on all sorts of outings. The king and queen had a grand ball here a few nights ago, and Senneth came down to the Riders' barracks to show us her dress. I happened to be there having dinner. She said the king is making her go out in public with the princess to protect her from anyone who would harm her—which I think is a very good idea, don't you? Because no one gets hurt when Senneth is nearby. Well, usually not, anyway.*
>
> *That's all I have to tell you, I think. I can't remember the last time I wrote anyone a letter, so I'm not sure I've done it right. Do come back to Ghosenhall soon. Unless you'd rather stay in Danalustrous, of course, but somehow I don't think so.*
>
> *Cammon*

Those last two paragraphs were almost as interesting as the first few, and had the added benefit of changing the direction of Kirra's thoughts. Senneth's message could only be a guarded reference to the relationship with Tayse, which had been promising but unconsummated the last time Kirra had had any news. She wanted to grab a pen and write Senneth a teasing note that very instant, but fear of who might see the contents made her pause. Well, she would be back in Ghosenhall soon enough. She could not linger much longer here. She had already missed the king's ball, the traditional opening of the summer social season. The other Houses would be holding similar entertainments in the next few weeks, and perhaps Kirra would attend them. One or two, at least. If nothing else, as an excuse to continue gathering information for the king.

Or to see old friends. You never knew who might go to a

ball or a summer banquet. Anyone at all might show up. She really hated the thought of missing the entire season.

THE banquet she attended in Danan Hall the following night was not calculated to make her eager to join the rest of the social whirl throughout Gillengaria. She performed her own part flawlessly, dressed in an exquisite gown embroidered all over with red flowers, her hair cascading down her back like raw gold. Her father had placed her at his right hand, the seat of highest honor, and circulated through the room afterward with Kirra on his arm. All marks of great favor, all reiterated proof that he valued this daughter, the oldest, the mystic, above all others.

Except one.

"Guests—lords and ladies—most loyal friends," Malcolm called when the meal was over and the mingling had gone on long enough to allow everyone to get a little inebriated. "I am so happy you have all been able to join me on this most important occasion. As many of you know, my daughter Casserah turned twenty-one this spring, and this dinner is in some way a celebration of that great event." He turned to smile down at Casserah, who stood beside him looking utterly serene. Kirra stood on the other side of Casserah, trying to imitate that calm, assured demeanor. Her whole life, whenever she had been in doubt about what expression to hold on her face, she had painted on the one she thought Casserah would choose. "Happy birthday, my dear," Malcolm said.

"Happy birthday, serra! Happy birthday, Casserah!" a few voices from the crowd called out. A handful of people lifted their wineglasses and drank to the serra's health.

Malcolm turned back to face the well-wishers. "Now that she is twenty-one, she takes up great responsibilities and prepares for a hard future. For I have decided to name her heir to Danalustrous. She will hold Danan Hall after me."

The silence in the room was profound. Kirra felt a hundred pairs of eyes trained on her face, with expressions that ranged from shock to satisfaction to outright malice. She imagined the thoughts the audience must be having. Everything from *What a disgrace! How can he treat her so?* to *Thank the Silver Lady! Danalustrous is saved from a mystic's hands.* Still, she kept that tranquil look on her face. She waited for Malcolm to bend a little and kiss Casserah on the forehead, and then she leaned in and kissed her sister's cool cheek. That particular move had been choreographed.

The next one had not. Casserah took Kirra's hand in hers and lifted it so their entwined fingers hovered over their heads. "I could not take on such a heavy task without the full aid and support of my sister," Casserah said in that smooth, perfectly pitched voice that everyone fell silent to hear. "It is to her that I will look for strength and guidance, for she is the one I trust above all others."

A halfhearted cheer from the crowd for that. Kirra let Casserah's hand sweep down and pull them both into a bow. Traditionally a sign of subservience, the bow meant something special now, Kirra knew: *I am subordinating myself to the land. I will sacrifice myself to its service.* The words a vassal might utter to his marlord, that a marlord might speak to his king. No one had to say the words aloud now for everyone in the room to know what Casserah Danalustrous meant by the gesture.

Once they straightened, it was Kirra's turn to talk. "It is a time of great hope and promise for Danalustrous," she said, her voice quieter than Casserah's and a little less assured. "The land cannot fail to prosper with such a one as you to guide it."

So that was it; there ended the few most agonizing public moments of Kirra's life. But the rest of the evening was not much fun, either. Casserah attempted to hold on to her hand, but the press of the crowd was too great, and soon they were separated. The well-wishers clustered around Casserah; the backbiters made a wall around Kirra.

"Well! I bet you're feeling terrible right about now," said one of Erin Sohta's cousins, a green-eyed woman with high-piled hair. "I know how it is! My own sister always got all the attention at our house, and *I* was the oldest, *and* the prettiest, but it was always my sister whom my mother thought would marry well. I didn't just sit back and whine about it, though—I found a good man, with an excellent property, and I married better than anyone thought I would. So don't let them push you aside."

"Really—it's not quite like that—"

"You can't hang around here, though, and be treated that way, can you?" asked an older man who looked half sympathetic and half greedy for dark details. "You'll have to leave. Show them how you feel."

"In fact, I have been so much on the road lately that my father feels Casserah is far more connected to the land than I am. I have to say I agree with him. I love Danalustrous, but I love Gillengaria even more."

"I'd be hurt, though, if I were you," said another voice.

"I'm sure it's not because he doesn't trust you." Still another voice. "I mean, Malcolm's never been afraid of mystics like *some* people are. Has always treated them with absolute decency."

"Still—a mystic in House Danalustrous—well, serra, you can't really blame him, can you?"

"There are no other mystics heading the other eleven Houses, that I know. Don't think Malcolm had a choice."

The voices went on around her, pushing against her, making her want to scream out in protest or cover her face with her hands. For a few moments, she wished her father or Casserah would come over and rescue her, but she knew they were too deep in their own conversations to save her; she had to take care of herself. She had a brief, crazy idea of turning herself into some kind of startling creature—the legendary lion from the king's crest, perhaps, or even a red raelynx, terrifying to behold. *That* would make anyone think twice about taunting her while pretending sympathy. But that, she knew, would just make the situation worse. *Did you see serramarra Kirra at her sister's birthday ball? Turned herself into a wild animal, she did. Can't control herself in society—oughtn't to be let out to mingle with regular folk. Mystics—you can't trust any of them. . . .*

So she didn't change. She didn't scream. She didn't look desperately around for succor. She merely smiled mechanically and answered comments when she could and prayed to the Bright Lady to end her torture by bringing daylight back a few hours sooner than scheduled. But the red goddess did not answer her pleas. It was the Pale Mother who peered in through the leaded windows, her mouth round and soundless, but her whole silver presence one of suppressed delight. The Pale Mother was always happiest when a mystic was in distress, and so this was, for her, a night of uncommon enchantment.

• • •

Kirra was still asleep the next morning when Casserah came in without knocking.

"You have to attend the breakfast," Casserah said, going to Kirra's armoire as soon as she had shaken her sister awake. "Otherwise everyone will think you're sulking."

Kirra sat up in bed, yawning. "I didn't know there *was* a breakfast."

"Informal. Mostly my friends. Maybe twenty people there, the sons and daughters of the vassals."

Kirra forced herself to kick off the covers and stand up, but she was grinning. "And those are the people you consider your friends?"

Casserah had chosen a pretty, simple dress of spidery cotton lace over antique linen. "Here, this makes you look docile and devoted," she said. "No, in fact, there are a few I truly can't abide. But it's important for *them* to feel a connection with me. So I'm having this breakfast. I thought I told you."

"I don't know, maybe you did. Wait a minute. I have to wash my face and—horrors, look at my hair."

"I can fix your hair," Casserah said.

Kirra, bending over her nightstand, grinned at her sister in the mirror. "We haven't done each other's hair in years. I can't imagine you even have to brush your own at night. Don't you have servants for all that?"

Casserah's face showed its customary faint amusement. "So would you, if you lived here. Who styles your hair for you when you're traveling? Not Donnal, I would think. The mystic Senneth? She never struck me as a woman who cared much about fashion."

Kirra had to laugh. She had cleaned herself as well as she could with the contents of the pitcher and basin, and now she was running a brush through the knotted tangle of curls. "No, indeed. Senneth much prefers dressing in a man's leathers and cutting her hair so short she doesn't have to bother with it at all. Maybe Kiernan has convinced her to invest a little more energy in her appearance, but I doubt it."

Casserah was behind her, pushing Kirra into a backless vanity chair. "Sit. I'll do this very quickly."

Quickly and well, as Casserah did everything. Fifteen minutes later, Kirra had to admire her own appearance. Casserah had devised braids of hair and gold ribbon and lace, and wound the whole heavy mass around Kirra's head, so that she seemed to wear a halo of her own hair. The linen dress did indeed make her look demure and eager to please. Casserah had heightened the effect with a choker of lace and pearls tied around Kirra's neck. The largest pearl fell just over Kirra's housemark, right above her breasts.

"Now if you can only contrive to keep your high spirits in check, I think you'll do very well," Casserah said, stepping back to take one last look.

"Anyone would think you were ashamed of me."

Casserah leaned in to give her a quick hug. "You know that's not true. I'm trying for an effect here. It's as much for your sake as mine. We want everyone else to love you as much as we do."

Kirra put a hand to her heart. "Is such a thing even possible?"

Casserah smiled again and pushed her to the door. "We will work to achieve it."

At first, the breakfast went smoothly enough. As Casserah had said, there were only about twenty people gathered with a semblance of intimacy around the table in the mansion's smaller dining room. Strong sunlight made the room seem quite cheerful, the food was tasty, and all the guests were so pleased to be included that everyone was in an excellent mood. Casserah sat at the head of the table, Kirra at the foot, and they handed around plates of eggs and pastries with an easy informality. Kirra even enjoyed her conversation with the two young men sitting on either side of her, vassals' sons who didn't take themselves too seriously and didn't think the breakfast hour was too early to start flirting.

"Why are you gone so much?" one of them asked after Kirra had made them both laugh with some story about traveling. "You're a great deal of fun. Sometimes Danan Hall isn't always—fun."

"Oh, I'm much less entertaining the longer you know me," Kirra assured him. "You only appreciate my wit and sparkle because you see it so rarely."

"How long are you staying?" the other asked. "We're leaving the day after tomorrow, but we could go riding later today. Even hunting. Your father has superb hounds."

Kirra would hunt if she knew the game would be eaten, but

she didn't really enjoy hunting as a sport. Too much fellow feeling for the animal being chased down. "Oh, let's just go riding," she said. "Why spoil a lazy outing with the necessity for making any kind of effort?"

That caused them to laugh again. The men were instantly diverted into talk about dogs and horses, and Kirra listened as intently as if she was really interested. The fact that she wasn't made it easier for her to monitor the conversation going on a few places away from her in the middle of the table. There, another young man was leaning forward to express a passionate opinion to two ladies sitting across from him. They nodded wordlessly, as though mesmerized by his commentary.

". . . hardly accidental," he was saying. He was good-looking in a bluff and stupid way. Kirra recognized him as Chalfrey Mallon, the son of her father's richest vassal. "The point was to humiliate her so publicly that she won't make any attempt to wrest back the inheritance. He's sent her away from Danalustrous over and over, but she keeps crawling back, trying to work her way into his good graces."

Oh, red and silver hell. He was talking about *her*. It took all of Kirra's energy to keep her gaze trained on the young man next to her, going on at some length about a purebred bitch who could be trusted to fetch back *any* game, even if it was bigger than she was and weighed more. Casserah would not like it if Kirra created a scene. Casserah would not like it if she metamorphosed into a lion and ripped Chalfrey's throat out.

"Now, purebreds—I know some people swear by them, but I like a mongrel any day," the other young lord was saying. "Something about them. They're smarter. And more loyal."

One of the women sitting across from Chalfrey Mallon glanced in Kirra's direction and lowered her voice, but Kirra could still hear her. "Do you think it's because she's a mystic?"

Chalfrey wasn't speaking very loudly, but he didn't put any effort into moderating his voice, either. Kirra was beginning to suspect that she was not the only one at the table who was eavesdropping on this conversation, though they were all pretending not to listen. "Of course it's because she's a mystic! He doesn't trust her, and he's just sent a message to the rest of Danalustrous not to trust her. Mark my words, this is just the first step. In a year—maybe six months—he'll bar her from the

Hall. He'll cast her out. He knows Danalustrous is too important to risk in the hands of a sorceress."

Kirra couldn't help herself; she flicked a glance up toward Casserah's end of the table, to see if her sister had heard any of this. But Casserah had motioned one of the footmen over and was speaking quietly in his ear. He bowed and left, and Casserah turned back to give the whole table her usual sleepy smile.

"I've had a special treat ordered," she said. "It's a fruit and cream concoction, and you won't believe how delicious it is. I had it last winter at Erin Sohta's and I made her give me the recipe. So next time you see her, you'll have to tell her how much you loved it."

"I had a cake at Erin's last spring," someone said. "She must have the best cook in Danalustrous."

"Better steal him for the Hall," someone else called out.

Casserah smiled. "No, I shall keep my own cook and steal all her recipes. Much better."

Similar banter followed as they awaited the arrival of dessert. There was a step outside the door and the steward came through, bowing very low to Casserah. Kirra saw two footmen and two guards in the hall, and she sat up hastily, alarm tingling up her spine.

"Carlo," Casserah said, her voice not raised at all from its usual calm cadence, "Chalfrey Mallon is leaving. Help him pack his clothing and see that he's escorted to his parents' house. He won't be back to Danan Hall."

Shock held the occupants of the room absolutely silent. Carlo bowed in the young man's direction. "My lord," he said, his voice hushed with respect. "When you're ready."

The young lord was gaping at Casserah. "Serra! What did—I—no, I'm not leaving! What have I *done*?"

Casserah's face showed its usual smooth serenity, but her voice was icy. "You spoke slightingly of my sister. That will never be tolerated in Danan Hall."

Chalfrey Mallon shot a look of pure venom in Kirra's direction, then scrambled to his feet. "Serra! It is true I fear the influence of a mystic on the House Danalustrous, but I will not apologize for that! No, and I am not the only lord to feel that way. But I would never speak out against *you*, against marlord

Malcolm—my heart is dedicated to the House Danalustrous. From now till I die."

"I am glad to hear it," Casserah said coolly. "You will show that dedication from your parents' estate, for you will not be welcome back here. Carlo?"

The steward came close enough to lay a hand on the young lord's arm, though he bowed again as he did so. "If you'll come with me—"

Chalfrey shook off Carlo's hand and strode to the door, his cheeks red with anger or humiliation. *Or both,* thought Kirra, *and that's a bad combination.* He stopped at the doorway.

"I will never honor a mystic, serra," he said in a low voice. "But you use me cruelly if you think I will ever have anything except love and admiration for you." He bowed to her, so low his hair swept the floor, and marched out of the room. His footsteps were swallowed by the tramp of the guards' feet as they accompanied him down the hall.

No one at the table could think of a thing to say. Kirra felt as if everyone in the room was straining to recall anything they had uttered that was even remotely uncomplimentary to Kirra in particular or mystics in general. She wondered if she should make a remark—to thank Casserah, to exonerate Chalfrey Mallon—but her mind was empty. No one else seemed willing to break the silence.

Fortunately, within a minute one of the servants returned, bearing a platter of berries and cream. He set it down in front of Casserah to the accompaniment of rather too enthusiastic oohs and aahs.

"Excellent," Casserah said, and her smile was mischievous. "Now there will be more for the rest of us."

CHAP†ER
10

KIRRA had thought her father might be displeased by
Casserah's show of family loyalty, but, in fact, he seemed
to think she had done exactly the right thing. "The Mallons are
always testing me, hunting for a weakness," he said to his
daughters as they gathered in his study once the breakfast
was over. "It is wearisome. They can be powerful allies, but
they expect too much indulgence. It is good that you made it
clear from the outset that you will not tolerate their disobedience."

"But she's made an enemy!" Kirra exclaimed. She had flung
herself into one of the wing-backed chairs before the window
and let all her muscles finally release their accumulated tension. "He will not forgive the public insult."

"I won't forgive the insult to my sister," Casserah said. Her
voice was as serene as ever. She might have been discussing
whether to serve milk or tea with the noon meal.

"But if his parents turn against you—"

"They can lose their property," Malcolm reminded her. He
was leaning against a heavy table, facing his daughters. He
looked just as relaxed as Casserah, though a little more serious. "They hold it in trust for me. It is not theirs by right."

"They've held it for two hundred years! I think they *do* think it is theirs by right! Is this really the time to be antagonizing the Thirteenth House?"

"Is this really the time to give in to the fears of weak and superstitious men?" Malcolm countered gently. "You would know we were right if you were not the source of contention."

"You don't have to prove to me that you will not cast me aside," Kirra said in a low voice. "I know that. I am not afraid."

"You're not the one we were proving it to," Malcolm said.

There was a little silence after that. Malcolm appeared to be thinking something over. Kirra waited to hear what it might be. Casserah, leaning back in her own chair, seemed equally content to sit in silence or engage in conversation. She was not merely pretending to be unruffled by the morning's events; she was genuinely unmoved.

At last Malcolm stirred and stood away from the desk. "I have been looking through the many invitations we have received for receptions to be held over the next few months," he said. "Kianlever, Coravann, Nocklyn, and Rappengrass are all gearing up to be very social. I think perhaps it is wise if we attend a few of these events."

"No," Casserah said. "I don't want to go."

His eyes were on his youngest daughter. "It is you they will want to see," he said, "now that you have been named my heir. They will want to know which way Danalustrous leans if there is a rebellion."

"We lean against rebellion altogether," Casserah said. "Write and tell them that when you tell them I won't be coming."

"Kirra thinks we cannot stand aside from war, if war comes."

Casserah gave her sister a quick sideways look. "That's because Kirra has a temper herself."

"I don't know," Malcolm said. "She might be right. In any case, the other Houses need to see that Danalustrous can be gracious and visible. They need to have a chance to make themselves friendly with the new heir."

"I'm not going to all these stupid balls," Casserah said.

"No," Malcolm said. "But I was thinking perhaps Kirra might go. Styling herself as you."

Kirra sat up in her chair. "What?"

Casserah clapped her hands together, laughing. "Oh yes! I like that idea very much."

Kirra felt doubtful. "I don't know if I could pull that off. To pretend to be Casserah for days at a time? I don't know."

"You mean, physically you can't do it?" Malcolm asked. "You can't retain the shape so long?"

"Oh, no, that's not the problem. It's playing the part. It's acting like Casserah and saying what Casserah would say."

Her sister gave her an abstracted look from those indifferent, wide-set eyes. "You know me better than anybody does," Casserah said. "I trust you to portray me accurately."

"You'd trust Donnal to portray you if it meant you didn't have to go to the balls," Kirra retorted. Casserah merely smiled.

"She's right," Malcolm said to Kirra. "It's unlikely you will make a slip."

"I don't know who you know and who you don't!" Kirra exclaimed. "I could come across fifty people in Kianlever alone that you've met casually at some function or another, and they'll think you know them and I'll think you don't! Or—just as likely!—I'll come across someone that *I* know, but you've never met, and I'll start talking to her as if we're old friends."

Casserah was unimpressed. "I never talk to anyone as if we're old friends," she said. "I don't like most people. And I never remember anyone I've met before. People constantly expect to be reintroduced to me."

"That must have won you many friends among the Twelve Houses."

Malcolm wore a faint smile. "She's too much like me. She cares about only one of those Twelve."

"I'll make you a list," Casserah promised. "The people who might actually expect me to remember their names—maybe I'll even write down a conversation we've had in the past, so you know a few details. Everyone else you can be rude to. And if they say, 'Don't you remember? We sat next to each other in Ghosenhall last year,' you can just say, 'I'm so sorry. People rarely make an impression on me. What was your name again?' It's what anyone would expect of me."

"I think it would be easier if you would go yourself," Kirra said.

"Well, I won't."

"You don't have to do it," Malcolm said. "But I do think it would be interesting for Danalustrous to be represented at these events—and if you go as yourself—"

Kirra nodded. "Too many people distrust me. And they'll be far more interested in courting Casserah than Kirra. I agree. I just—"

"It'll be fun," Casserah said. "Remember how many times we used to fool my mother when we were little?"

"Never more than five minutes at a time!"

"I think Jannis is one of the few people who knows Casserah as well as you do," Malcolm said. "One would expect her to recognize her daughter."

Kirra sighed and thought of more objections. Pointless to voice them, though. She actually agreed with her father that Danalustrous should have an emissary at the summer social events and that Casserah was the perfect person to send. And the charade appealed to her adventurous spirit, no question about it, but there were just so many ways to fail. She didn't want to embarrass her sister, herself, or Danalustrous.

"If I do this," she said to Casserah in a warning voice, "you better be prepared for the damage I might cause."

"Accidentally or on purpose?" Casserah inquired.

Kirra laughed. "Either! Though I have to say, it will be hard for me to resist—oh, shall we say, playing a few games when I'm dressed up as you."

"I don't care what you do," Casserah said.

"Even if I go flirting with some of the handsome lords? Even if I kiss a few young men at midnight on some ballroom balcony? You might be surprised to find how many younger sons come calling in Danalustrous once the season is over."

Casserah looked amused. "Just let me know what promises you've made to them so I know what debts to pay."

"Father and I were saying, just the other day," Kirra said, "now that you're heir, it's time to find you a husband. Maybe I'll pick out someone who seems suitable and encourage him to come back here to make you an offer. You wouldn't mind that, would you?"

Casserah shook her dark head and leaned back in her chair, perfectly relaxed. "No," she said, "I wouldn't mind at all."

IT was not as easy to be Casserah as it was to be Kirra, at least in terms of physical baggage. Once she'd agreed to the impersonation, Kirra found herself bogged down in details.

Casserah rarely traveled outside the borders of Danalustrous, and when she did, she never traveled alone. "I always bring a maid and two or three guards," she said. "Most people do, you know. Everyone will expect it."

"Donnal can be my maid."

Casserah looked at her for a moment. "I don't think so," she said. "Now, you'll need at least five ballgowns as well as a dozen or so dresses for other events, and the jewelry that I always wear with each outfit."

"Donnal's posed as my maid before," Kirra argued.

"Donnal, I think, cannot guarantee my appearance is exactly as I would want," Casserah said. "I will send Melly with you. She will know how to make you look exactly right."

"And will Melly know I'm me and not you?"

"I think she'd better," Casserah said with a laugh.

"You can trust her not to tell anyone?"

"You can trust Donnal?"

Ah—well—if that was to be the standard, then Melly could be counted on to give her life for her mistress. "This is getting complicated," Kirra said. "I'm used to traveling light."

"Well, I require a retinue," Casserah said. "You will find they come in most handy."

Kirra escaped the plotting and the planning as often as she could. While the young Danalustrous lords were still on hand, she went riding with them—and the day after they left, Donnal returned. He was in her room waiting for her as she went up after dinner, a black hound curled up on the foot of her bed.

"Hey, you're back," she said, giving him a rough pat on the head and tugging on his silky ears. "I assume everyone in your family was well? Happy to see you?" He made no answer, just tilted his head up a little so she could scratch under his chin. "It has been *quite* the interesting few days here."

He brought one ear forward as if to ask for more information, and she dropped to the bed next to him, burying her fingers in his fur. "Oh, let's see. I spent some time with Berric and Beatrice, then I came back here for the banquet. Where my father announced to all his vassals that he was naming Casserah heir."

Donnal scrambled up to all fours, somewhat unsteady on the soft mattress, and gave a little bark. "Yes, it *was* a little unsettling, though he'd told me already, so it wasn't a complete shock." She hesitated, then sighed. "Actually, it wasn't a shock even when he told me. I had been thinking for some time that I didn't know what I would do with Danalustrous when it fell to my hands. I just didn't follow my thoughts to the obvious conclusion. But trust my father to refuse to flinch away from a hard task."

Donnal whined and came closer, his paws scrabbling on her thigh, his wet nose against her face. He whined again and licked her cheek. She laughed and put her arms around his neck, laying her face against the brushy fur for a moment.

"Thank you, but I don't think I need any sympathy," she said. "Just time to get used to the idea. I'm almost used to it already."

He licked her again and sat back on his haunches, watching her closely. He could tell there was more to the story and was clearly interested in the rest.

"The next day, my father revealed his great plan," she said. "He thinks Casserah should go to the Twelve Houses for the summer season—see how people react to her now that she's heir. But she says she won't go."

Donnal uttered a short, sharp bark, his tail beating twice against the coverlet.

Kirra laughed. "Aren't you a smart doggie! You're exactly right. They want me to go in her place. And, Bright Mother burn me, I think it will be fun. Though it requires much more—" She waved her hands in the air. "More *preparation* than I would have thought. We'll probably leave at the end of the week."

Again, the single ear brought forward to create a quizzical look on the furred black face. Kirra nodded.

"Yes. A maid, two or three guards—a whole entourage. I said you could be my maid but Casserah said no. You can be a guard if you like."

Donnal sank back down on the bed, resting his nose between his paws. "Or you can go as you are," Kirra said. She patted the top of his head and drew one of the satiny ears between her fingers. "And who knows? It might be fun. Perhaps we'll run into someone we know at one of the parties. Darryn Rappengrass, maybe, or Mayva Nocklyn—though Mayva's not my favorite person—or, I don't know, anyone." *Romar Brendyn.* Best not to hope for that. The thought of his name triggered a memory and she jumped to her feet. "Oh! I forgot. A package came for you a few days ago."

Donnal lifted his head and looked unconvinced. "Really, for you. Apparently Romar Brendyn purchased gifts for you and Cammon and Justin to thank you for your part in rescuing him. The package went to Ghosenhall, and Cammon sent yours here." She rummaged through the clutter on top of her armoire before she found the gift, bulky and soft, still wrapped in plain brown paper. "I didn't open it," she said.

Donnal pushed himself up to his forelegs when she approached the bed and sniffed at the paper but didn't seem curious enough about the contents to change himself to human shape and rip it off. "Would you like me to open it for you?" Kirra asked, because really she was dying to know what was inside.

Donnal yawned, his pink tongue making a perfect curl between his pointed white teeth.

"Well, if you won't tell me no, I'll assume you mean yes," Kirra said, slightly annoyed. She climbed back on the bed beside Donnal and slipped the string off the four corners and then tore at the paper. What she could instantly see was a pile of fine-spun wool in a midnight color, and she loosed an exclamation of pleasure as she buried her hands in the soft folds. Then she stood up and shook it out to discover Romar had sent Donnal a cloak, long enough to fall from shoulder to booted heel, that closed at the throat with a silver clasp cast in the shape of a wolf's head.

"*Oh,*" Kirra said, holding it up for Donnal to see, then slinging it around her own shoulders because she could not resist. "This is beautiful. Look, it fits me perfectly, so you know it will fit you, because we're exactly the same height. And did you see the clasp? What a thoughtful gift."

She twirled around once and then went to stand before her mirror, turning this way and that to admire the way the fabric flirted around her ankles. The cut and the color were both too severe for her but she admired the craftsmanship anyway. She was astonished at the thoughtfulness that had enabled Romar to choose three such perfect remembrances for three such different men. Not one noble in fifty would even have thought to thank servants or soldiers for any special efforts expended on his behalf; those few who did present a reward were most likely to offer money. But Romar had noted the personalities and preferences of the individual men and had given each one a customized and perfectly gauged gift. Kirra wasn't sure even her father could have succeeded so well.

She spun away from the mirror to make some other comment to Donnal, but he had lost interest in the gift, in Romar Brendyn, in her. He had settled back on the bed and closed his eyes and gave every appearance of having fallen immediately asleep.

TWO days before they left for Ghosenhall, their first stop on the summer circuit, Kirra and Donnal took a much shorter excursion to a site in the interior of Danalustrous. Kirra was very tired of pomp already—before her trip had even begun!—so she changed herself into a brush lion and loped alongside Donnal through the flat green countryside. They were careful to skirt the farms and small towns that fell along their route, but now and then they spotted riders from a distance, or farmers working in the fields. Twice they startled hunters stalking through the occasional stand of trees. A sight to dumbfound anyone privileged to see it—a sleek golden lion pacing side by side with a white-faced wolf—but no one in Danalustrous would be amazed. No hunter in Danalustrous would lift his bow, no farmer would run back to his house crying of abominations. *That's the marlord's shiftling daughter and one of her mystic friends,* they would say to themselves or their companions. Even those who distrusted mystics, even those who feared them, recognized Kirra in this guise. No one would lift a hand to hurt her.

At least in Danalustrous.

It took most of a day of hard running to make it to their destination, a place that only Donnal had been before. It was a small, broken building deep in a stretch of untouched forest situated very near the center of Danalustrous. Kirra could not imagine there had ever been any kind of trail to lead people to the site. She slipped slowly from animal shape to human as they came to a halt outside it.

"You, too," she said, her hand on the back of Donnal's neck. "Just for the afternoon."

Moments later, he stood beside her dressed in drab country

garb, his beard as neat as if he had trimmed it the night before. Arm in arm, they slowly stepped through the rubble and into the building's remaining foundation.

They were deep enough in the woods that not much sunlight broke through the tree cover to illuminate the small space. There was even less light because it was early evening and the sun was already close to the horizon. Not that there was much to see, for the whole place was essentially a ruin. Kirra could tell that it had once been roughly square, maybe twelve feet by twelve. What walls remained stopped shortly above her head, so she guessed the ceiling had been low; if there had ever been a floor, it had all rotted away. Three sides of the building were open to the elements, leaving behind only partial walls and tumbled stones.

The fourth wall was completely whole—and marvelous. The entire surface was an intricate mosaic of dozens of colors and hundreds of images. Birds of all descriptions crowded each other through the opal sky; the emerald hills and onyx woods were inhabited by a fantastical menagerie of beasts. Kirra saw deer, rabbits, foxes, lions, snakes, squirrels—even an animal or two she did not believe ever existed—worked into the stone tapestry. The detail was astonishing, the workmanship exquisite. She stood before the wall, utterly silent, her hand upraised but suspended in midair. She wanted to touch those smooth, flat stones, but she could feel the power emanating from them, as tangible as heat. More respectful—less dangerous—to merely look.

"It's beautiful," she said at last. "It makes me want to pray."

Donnal nodded. He was standing beside her, but now he pivoted to survey the rest of the space. "I'd suppose that was the altar," he said, pointing to what could have been the front of the building. "Probably used to be a window right behind it. I'd guess it was positioned to catch the morning sun—light up the whole mosaic. That would be a sight."

Kirra turned beside him and slowly they began strolling the whole broken perimeter. "Why does no one ever speak of her?" she wondered. "The Wild Mother. Senneth's one of the only people who ever talks of the old gods."

"And there's more of them whose names we've forgotten," Donnal said. "How many, I wonder? And what were their powers? And will we be sorry we've neglected them?"

Kirra smiled a little. "How many? Twelve, I'm guessing. Why else choose twelve for the number of Houses to be established in Gillengaria? But I can only name a few. The Wild Mother. The Pale Mother. The Bright Mother. The Dark Watcher. And the only one we know much about is the Pale Mother. I don't even know what symbol the wild goddess might take as her own. We know the Silver Lady resides in moonstones. Senneth wears that gold charm, so I'm guessing the Bright Mother loves gold. But what about the goddess who watches over shiftlings like you and me? What emblem does she choose? What could I carry to ensure me her protection and to let her know that I consider myself her own?"

"Maybe you should learn more about this feral goddess before you start giving her your blind worship," Donnal said, a note of laughter in his voice. "She might require blood sacrifices on a regular basis. Violence and death."

She stopped to look at him, or what she could see of his face in the fading light. "I don't think so," she said softly. "You must be able to feel it, too. This is a place of peace, where all the animals of the earth can come together in harmony. She loves them all, protects them all, as far as they can be protected."

"She gives them claws and teeth and the ability to kill," Donnal reminded her. "She is not a mild goddess."

Kirra gave him a glittering smile. "I have not been so mild myself these last months. I think I am glad for the fierceness the Wild Mother puts into the hearts of her creatures."

"Maybe she has been watching over you all this time without you even knowing."

They found a section of half-formed wall at right angles to the mosaic and settled themselves on the ground, leaning against it. The peace of the shrine was so deep that Kirra did not want to leave. She sat with her back against the rough stone, her right shoulder leaning against Donnal's, her left hand idly sifting through the loose soil of the ground, and she merely listened. From the forest, crowding so close, she could catch intermittent sounds—the patter of squirrels' feet as they leapt from branch to branch, the munch of mice as they tried the taste of their gathered seeds, the brush of wing feathers as birds darted through the air. There must be water somewhere not too far away; she could hear the sleek splash of fish and the hoarse conversation of bullfrogs. Something large and stealthy prowled nearby—a wolf, she thought—she could sense its intentness, its absolute focus. She caught the rapid rhythm of white paws tapping against the ground and smiled a little. A hare escaping the attention of the hunter. From every direction, the scents of early summer pressed down on her, full of green promise and floral abandon.

"This is odd," Donnal said in a low voice. "I can't—Usually I have to be in animal form before my senses are so sharp."

Only then did Kirra realize how distinctly she had been hearing sounds and catching odors that were too subtle for most humans. She felt a slight shiver pass over her. "It's this place," she said. "It's the gift of the Wild Mother."

Donnal nodded and didn't answer. Kirra listened a few more moments to the questioning call of birds and the industrious work of the squirrels before she turned to Donnal. "Do you think anyone would have the same experience, coming here?" she asked. "Would hear what we're hearing—smell what we can smell?"

"No," he said at once. "Only shiftlings. Only those under the wild goddess's protection."

"That's what I think, too."

"She has put her hand on you."

"On you as well."

He shook his head, a small smile almost hidden in his beard. "I am one of the gifts she presented to you."

She held up her left hand and he met it with his right hand, and they sat there a moment with their fingers interlaced.

"You could choose to make your life something other than the shadow of mine," she said at last. "You could go study with other mystics in Ghosenhall, as Cammon has. You could offer your service to some lord who would value your abilities for espionage. You could travel across Gillengaria in any shape you choose, man or beast, lead any life you wanted. I wouldn't stop you. You are free to go."

His fingers tightened slightly; he smiled at her. "Ah, but marlord Malcolm might have a few words to say about that," he said, a teasing note in his voice. "He bound me to your service when I was ten years old. He has never released me. A Danalustrous man always serves the House of Danalustrous."

"I would release you," she said. "If you wished to go."

"I will only leave you if you want me to."

"I cannot imagine that day ever coming."

"Well, then," he said.

They were silent a few moments longer, Kirra both comforted and saddened by that last exchange. She had been twelve when Malcolm Danalustrous found Donnal, the only other shiftling he knew of in the region, and brought him to Danan Hall to train with his daughter. She could remember only a handful of days since then that Donnal had not been at her side, in some form or another. He was her second self, he was her guard against darkness, he was her safety and her memory and her tether to the world. She knew that nothing could harm her if Donnal was nearby—and still alive. Yet it was a burden sometimes, that absolute devotion; she had inherited from her father a formidable sense of justice. Donnal had given himself to Danalustrous, so Danalustrous owed him something in return, and she knew these scales were out of balance. Donnal gave more to her than she did to him. He seemed content, but in his place, she would not have been. In his place, she would have moved on long ago.

The thought of life without Donnal by her side was terrifying.

Feelings too complex to try to sort them out. She closed her eyes and leaned her head back against the rough rock. Donnal had released her hand, and now she toyed with the dirt again, breaking up small hard clumps of soil with her fingers. Tiny rocks she tossed aside, then she dug again, deeper, making a small hole in the floor of the shrine. The dirt was cold against her fingers, as if even high summer sun would not penetrate long enough to warm it. She wondered how far down she would have to go to find water.

She encountered another small rock, this one encrusted with mud but smooth against her fingers when she idly scraped away the layers. Not a rock, then; maybe one of the tiles from the mosaic, fallen out over time.

She brought it up to examine it in what was by now gray twilight. "Look at this," she said in a soft voice, sitting up straighter and working with more energy and both hands to clear away the grime. "I think it's—look at this."

Donnal lit a taper, using a small dried branch for fuel, and held the light closer for them both to see. The firelight revealed both the shape and material of the tiny object in her hands. It was a young lioness, no bigger than the first joint of Kirra's thumb, caught in the act of a flat-out run. She had been carved out of some kind of dense, chatoyant stone of striated golds and browns, and her fur seemed to ripple and move in the flickering flame. On either side of her perfectly shaped head, tiny sapphires had been set to indicate her eyes. A minuscule ruby marked her mouth.

"Look at that," Donnal echoed, his voice admiring. "The blue-eyed lion on the hunt. That's you."

Kirra touched the jewel at the mouth. "Wearing Danalustrous red, no less."

"I think the Wild Mother heard you ask for a token."

Another chill up the back for that, but still Kirra couldn't bring herself to lay aside the small charm. It was so beautiful. The stone felt so silky on her palm. And there was something—a tickle of power, a frisson of magic. When she held it, she could almost feel it glitter against her skin. "So you think I should take it with me?" she asked in a low voice. "I don't want to desecrate a shrine."

"I think you would insult the goddess if you left it behind."

She closed her fingers over the striped stone. "I really want it. Maybe if I left an offering behind?"

"A lock of your hair," he suggested.

Kirra paused a moment to consider that; the mood of the temple seemed benign. "Do you have a knife?" she asked.

In a few moments, Donnal had cut an inch of curl from her head and she had buried it in the loose dirt before the mosaic. The gesture seemed small but welcome. All the stone animals on the frieze seemed to exude goodwill.

"Do you want to find something for yourself?" Kirra asked. "If we look, something else is bound to turn up."

He shook his head. "Not today. Maybe I'll come back sometime."

She sighed. She didn't really want to leave, but if they spent the night here, it would be late on the following day before they were back at Danan Hall, and they were scheduled to ride out the day after that. It was dark already, at least inside the forest; they needed to cover some miles before they curled up to sleep.

"We'd better get started, then," she said.

"Where do we go when we leave Danalustrous?"

"Ghosenhall first. Then Kianlever." She searched his face, what she could see of it now that he had blown out the taper. "You'll come with me?"

He made a small bow. "Serra," he said solemnly. "Where else would I go?"

CHAPTER
II

A DAY and a half later, a small party rode out of Danan Hall: Kirra, Melly, two guards, and Donnal, who had chosen to keep the form of a black dog. Kirra had been gloomy when she learned that Casserah expected her to sit in a coach the whole way, since she was more used to riding horseback or following the track on her own four feet. However, she cheered up considerably when the morning brought with it a chilly, determined drizzle. Even Donnal chose to ride in the coach.

The roads between Danalustrous and Ghosenhall were excellent and well traveled, passing over fairly flat land or easily navigated hills. All along the way were inns used to serving the nobility. A far cry from her last few journeys, Kirra thought, when she had slept in the open most nights, and in barns and stables much of the rest of the time.

Melly was a practical and efficient young woman, seeing to Kirra's comfort without much fuss, though she pitched a fit at one of the inns when there wasn't enough hot water for Kirra to take a bath.

"I can wash up well enough with a couple of pitchers of cold water," Kirra said, amused. "Does my sister usually throw a tantrum when the innkeepers don't meet her every demand?"

"Serra Casserah is always most gracious," Melly replied in a stiff voice. Kirra interpreted that as meaning the casual

Casserah really didn't care that much if everything was exactly in place. "But Danalustrous must be treated with respect. Honor is due to the House."

Despite her notions of what kind of respect should be shown to a serramarra, Melly was a pretty good traveling companion, Kirra found. She would make ready responses if Kirra had idle observations to offer about the countryside or the weather, and was willing to talk about her sisters and her little brothers when Kirra asked questions about her family. But most of the time she was quiet, wrapped in her own thoughts or thinking ahead to what clothes must be washed out at the next stop, Kirra supposed. She treated Donnal like a favored pet, which either meant she knew how much Malcolm Danalustrous valued his dogs or she knew who Donnal really was.

She never once called her mistress Casserah in private or Kirra in public, and Kirra had a healthy respect for both her intelligence and her devotion by the time they finally arrived at Ghosenhall. A short ride through the bright, crowded streets of the royal city, and they arrived at the palace compound. The warm granite and tall turrets of the palace were guarded by high walls and a visible ring of guards.

Casserah Danalustrous, of course, quickly made it through the various checkpoints and was welcomed at the door by the king's steward himself. Milo bowed very low while servants began unloading luggage from the coach.

"Serra," said the portly man as he straightened up. "It is good to have you here. We so rarely see you at the palace."

"I know," Kirra said in Casserah's voice. She had dozed through the last stage of the journey, but she was wide-awake now, energized with the anticipation of playacting. It had all been very easy up to this point; she had to be extremely alert from here on out. One of the things to remember was that Casserah never made unnecessary conversation. Short answers, just complete enough to avoid being rude, characterized her sister's speech. Still, Kirra thought even Casserah might add a phrase or two to that bald statement. So she said, "It is good to be here."

Milo motioned her escort to the care of palace guards, then led the rest of them through the gorgeous hallways of the palace. "We have reserved a suite for you in the eastern wing," he told her. "A handful of other guests are staying with us as well. There is a dinner tonight—not very fancy—and then in two days, a much larger banquet. We hope you will attend both of these."

"Of course."

Her suite, when they finally arrived, was restfully appointed in soft blues and golds. Melly would have not just her own bed, but a small room all to herself.

"It is acceptable for my dog to stay with me?" Kirra asked, gesturing at Donnal, who had soundlessly accompanied them through the corridors.

Milo didn't even glance down. "Of course, serra."

"If he causes any disturbance, in the kitchen or elsewhere, let me know and I'll confine him to my room," she added. That was for Donnal's benefit. She kept her face serious, though it was an effort not to laugh.

"I'm sure he'll be no trouble, serra."

He showed Melly the various features of the room, then bowed to Kirra again at the door. "The king asked me to tell you he would be happy for a private conference with you, once you were settled in," he said. "Sometime before dinner."

"Of course," she said. "May I have an hour to refresh myself?"

"I will send someone to you then."

He was almost out the door when Kirra called out a question. "Senneth Brassenthwaite—is she still staying at the palace?"

"Yes. She will be here until she leaves to accompany the princess to Kianlever."

Kirra could not hide her pleasure. "Senneth is attending the ball at Kianlever Court! That should be entertaining." Milo put an expression of polite interest on his face. Kirra said somewhat hastily, "She has a reputation for not enjoying opulence. It has been years since I have seen her, of course. But I am hoping to renew our acquaintance."

"We have put her in the green suite down the hall," Milo said, pointing. "You may visit with her when you like."

But Senneth was not in her room when Kirra hurried down to knock. Unlike Kirra, she wasn't burdened with servants, either, so there was no one to predict when Senneth might return.

Not that Kirra had much time to waste, anyway. She had to submit to Melly's ministrations and make herself fit to meet with her king.

Baryn was a tall, thin, wispy-haired man who looked more like someone's eccentric uncle than king of the realm. "Serra Casserah," he said, greeting her with a handshake instead of the hug he would have given Kirra. "I was so pleased when we got your father's note that you were coming. It has been too long since I've seen you."

She swept him a curtsey as perfect as any Casserah would have managed. "My father tells me I must learn to be more sociable," she said solemnly. "I confess, I am not always at ease with other people."

"No, they can be most trying," the king agreed. "And yet friendship between Houses is good for the realm. So any effort you make would be likely to pay you back twelvefold."

Kirra allowed a small smile to come to her face; he might interpret it as skeptical if he liked. "Yes, majesty."

"Come! Sit down! Tell me what you have been doing with yourself. Malcolm's note contains other interesting news."

Kirra took a seat in a straight-backed chair that faced the king's settee. "Is it possible he wrote you about the next heir of Danalustrous?" she wondered.

Baryn laughed. "Indeed, he did! I was surprised—and not surprised. My instinct tells me he made an excellent choice, but I worry about the reaction of your sister. I would not want her to be unhappy. Kirra is one of those rare people whose very presence brings me joy."

That was certainly nice to hear. But how to answer this question as Casserah would? "I appreciate your concern for my sister, majesty," she said in a cool voice. "But I assure you, you need not fear for her. She may not own Danalustrous, but Danalustrous owns her, and Danalustrous never gives up what belongs to it. She is ours still. She just has more freedom now to roam as far as she likes before she returns home."

He smiled. "Elegantly said. You reassure me."

"I am glad to hear that with so much else to occupy you, you still have time to think about my sister and her heart."

At that, he sighed. "I'm certain she told you of her latest adventure on my behalf?"

Kirra nodded. "I assume the regent made it safely home once they parted on the road?"

"Yes, although—"

His sudden pause made Kirra want to sit up straighter in alarm. But Casserah would never do that. "Did something else happen to him?" she asked in Casserah's incurious voice.

"Perhaps. Perhaps not. There was an incident one day when he was riding, but it could have been accidental. I have urged him to double his personal guards, but Romar is not a man who likes to be confined and overprotected. He has many, many strengths, but excessive caution is not one of them."

"It still is not entirely clear to me," Kirra said, her voice calm though her heart was pounding, "why anyone would want to harm him. Would you not just install another regent?"

"Would I not find it difficult to find someone willing to accept such a post if his predecessor had been murdered?" Baryn countered. "Unless the man I chose had been selected for me by, say, a consortium of marlords with some interest in the succession. Then I believe my regent would have a reasonable chance of survival."

"Who is behind the attacks on Romar Brendyn?" she asked. "Do you know? My sister came back with strange and brutal tales of Halchon Gisseltess, but—"

"But it seems a little obvious for him, doesn't it? Besides, he has been confined to Gissel Plain for several months, with a troop of my own guards stationed on his estates to watch him. In theory, one of my men reads every letter that passes into or out of his house. In practice, I am sure he has ways of communicating with friends who are not entirely friendly to me. And yet Halchon does not seem like the kind of man to waste his time with a subordinate. If he were going to assassinate someone, I would expect him to come directly after me."

Kirra felt her eyes widen. "Do you think he will?"

"Eventually."

"Then, sire! Take steps now to rid yourself of the threat!"

Baryn looked rueful. "Yes, Romar says the same thing. But I cannot find it in me to execute a man merely on the suspicion that he might want to do me harm. I am not ruthless enough."

"My father would," she said. "If he thought someone was trying to harm me. Or Danalustrous. He would take action."

"Yes, one of the many things I admire about Malcolm. Such a single-minded man."

"It would seem to make sense to be single-minded about preserving your own life."

Baryn spread his hands in a gentle gesture. "If I try to confine Halchon, what kind of turmoil do I loose in the realm? If he is blocked, who else might rise up to confront me? I am trying not to precipitate events that I cannot control. Instead, I am trying to prepare for eventualities and put safeguards in place. Much less spectacular. Perhaps less effective. Who knows? It is the way I have chosen."

Kirra had no answer for that, though she imagined Casserah might have argued the point. In any case, she had no time to reply because the door opened and two women stepped inside. Kirra was instantly on her feet, making another curtsey, because although Casserah had never met either of them, everyone in the kingdom would recognize both: the king's wife, Valri, and his daughter, Amalie.

Valri stopped on the threshold, her hand still on the doorknob, and looked displeased for a moment. She was a small and exquisitely beautiful woman, black-haired and white-skinned, with eyes of such an amazing green they were impossible to look away from. The king's second wife, Valri was about Kirra's age and highly mysterious; nobody knew a thing about her background. "Oh. I'm sorry. I didn't realize you had a visitor," she said. She sounded, Kirra thought in some amusement, even more ungracious than Casserah could. "I was coming to see if you were ready for dinner."

Baryn motioned both women into the room. "Indeed, yes, I was just about to suggest that we go down to the dining hall. My dear, do you know Casserah Danalustrous? Malcolm's youngest daughter."

"Oh. No, I don't believe we've met." Valri hesitated, then came close enough to hold out her hand. "I like your sister very much."

Surprising, if true, but perhaps it was just her attempt to be civil. "Majesty," Kirra said, curtseying again. "How good to meet you."

"And this is Amalie, whom you may not have ever met,"

Baryn said. His voice was filled with pride and affection. "She's a little shy, because she has never gone out much in public, but she's been joining us at our balls and dinners lately. Amalie, this is Casserah."

"Serra," Amalie said in a soft voice.

Kirra repeated the curtsey, and then bestowed a genuine smile on the girl. Kirra herself had not seen the princess since Amalie was a little girl. It would not be rude to take a moment to assess her now, she thought, and so she did. The first thing anyone would notice about Amalie was her hair, a thick red-blond that was arranged in a very simple style, loose on her shoulders. Her face was thin, not entirely filled out, dominated by large brown eyes and marked with an expression of great sweetness. She looked nervous and eager to please, but she did not look stupid, Kirra thought. Her big eyes were watchful and her generous mouth looked as if it could be pressed tightly shut if she did not want to speak a secret. She was dressed in a plain gown that didn't do much to hide the gawkiness of her eighteen-year-old body, but Kirra thought Amalie would grow into a beautiful young woman.

But a good queen? Impossible to tell.

"Princess," Kirra replied. "What a great pleasure. My sister will be so jealous that I had a chance to visit with you."

"Tell Kirra to come back to us, and she shall have breakfast with the princess every day," Baryn said. "That should be incentive enough, don't you think?"

Kirra smiled. "It's hard to ever guess what will appeal to Kirra."

"I don't think you're very like her," Valri observed in her abrupt way.

Kirra shot her a quick glance. "No? And yet I am very close to her." Ah, great gods, she could hardly say that without laughing.

No one was required to answer that, for there was another knock at the door. This time it was Milo with the news that dinner was ready to be served. "The other guests are gathered, liege," Milo said. "Shall I tell them to wait the meal?"

"No, no, we're all done here," Baryn said briskly, rising to his feet. "Come, my love, my dear—and serra—let us hurry down before all our guests expire of hunger."

Indeed, there were perhaps two dozen people awaiting

them in a small salon attached to one of the more informal of the palace's many dining rooms. Kirra quickly identified the ones she knew and then subtracted the ones that Casserah did *not* know and concluded she would have to be introduced to almost everyone in attendance. She spotted Senneth on the far side of the room, talking quietly to an older woman in a dark green gown, and she felt a sudden unreasonable pang that she could not rush up to the other mystic and give her an excited hug. *Senneth, Senneth, I want to hear everything about your trip to Brassenthwaite! And wait till I tell you about my journey to Tilt!* But Senneth and Casserah were hardly more than acquaintances—and anyway, Casserah didn't run up and hug anybody. And Senneth would have no idea who she really was. The confidences would have to wait.

Kirra looked again for the one face that she had hoped to see here, even though she knew it was unlikely, it was stupid even to hope, stupid even to think about it. Of course Romar Brendyn was still in Merrenstow, recuperating from his wild journey and apparently inviting new assassins in to try to kill him. Of course he was not in Ghosenhall. Surely the king would have mentioned it if he were here.

Surely Kirra had no business feeling such deep disappointment at his absence.

Baryn had caught everyone's attention merely by stepping into the room, and now all the gathered nobles were offering quick bows and curtseys. "I'm not sure all of you know our newest arrival," the king said, holding out his arm. Kirra came forward and made yet another little curtsey. Really, she was already getting tired of the tedious formality. "Casserah Danalustrous, here for a few days. I'm sure you'll all welcome her."

There were a few murmurs of "serra," and everyone nodded or smiled or offered some other sign of recognition. Kirra glanced at Senneth again and found the other mystic's eyes on her, a speculative expression on her face. *Why has Malcolm Danalustrous sent Casserah here, when Kirra was so recently at court?* When she could figure out how to phrase it, Senneth would no doubt ask.

But the chance wouldn't come at dinner, since they were widely separated by other members of the party. As a new arrival and high-ranking serramarra, Kirra was seated next to the king at the head of the table; Senneth, serramarra of the First House of Gillengaria, sat closer to Valri at the foot of the table. The others were scattered in between them.

The food was excellent, the conversation witty enough but very light. No one talked politics or other disastrous topics. Kirra tried to pay attention to how well Amalie was doing, seated between her father and an avuncular man from Cora-vann. The princess wasn't exceptionally animated, but she did seem to hold her own when speaking and appeared to be listening to talk going on in several conversations around her. There was something about her eyes, Kirra thought. Expressive. Curious. Intelligent. This was a girl who didn't miss much, no matter how little exposure she had had to the world.

"And how is it I have not ever encountered you before?" the man on Kirra's left asked before the first hour of the meal had elapsed. He was a Storian man, Rafe's cousin or some such—Twelfth House, at any rate, and damn proud of it. "Serramarra Casserah Danalustrous! Shouldn't we have met at any of a thousand balls or banquets in the past three years?"

Kirra gave him a small, cool smile. He was maybe in his early fifties, still good-looking but no longer the stunningly handsome man he must once have been, though he didn't seem to realize it. He was pleasant enough, but a touch too arrogant to appeal to Casserah. "I rarely attend such affairs," she said. "Almost no one has met me."

"A loss for all of us."

"You could be useful to me," she said. Casserah would have said it, and just that bluntly.

He laughed. "Tell me how!"

"Who are these people? Should I know them? What are their Houses?"

"Do you recognize *any* of them?"

"I've met Senneth Brassenthwaite. She's done work for my father."

His eyebrows rose at that but he made no comment. "Well, the man to her right is from Merrenstow—"

Most of the rest of the meal passed with her companion giving her detailed gossip about everyone else gathered around the table, leading Kirra to feel that she knew them all a little more intimately than she'd wanted. She also devoutly hoped he never heard of any of her own escapades that he could then describe with malicious amusement to another stranger at some distant date. She almost wished she hadn't told him she knew Senneth; she would have loved to hear his comments about *her*, which were sure to be unflattering. He seemed to have a preference for the conventional and a slight aversion to mystics. Senneth would hardly have suited his notions of aristocracy.

When the meal finally ended, the group moved to another salon for a more relaxed evening of wine and conversation. Kirra had hoped to get a chance to whisper her secret to Senneth, but it turned out that Casserah Danalustrous was in high demand that evening. She soon had a press of people three deep all around her. Others at the table had been gossiping, she surmised. They all knew she was her father's heir, and they all wanted a chance to show her how much they valued Danalustrous. By the time she had finished having a small, personal conversation with each of them, it was close to midnight. Most of the room had already emptied, and Senneth was gone.

Red and silver hell. If Senneth was spending the night in the barracks with Tayse, Kirra would never have a chance to talk to her.

But maybe she wasn't.

Making her way back upstairs, Kirra headed directly to Senneth's door and knocked. There was a moment of silence inside the room, then footfalls crossed the floor, and the door was pulled open. Senneth was here, after all.

CHAPTER
12

SENNETH was still wearing her dinner dress, a severe and formal blue that turned her gray eyes cobalt and added highlights to her white-blond hair. She was looking a little mussed—the short hair, always untidy, looked as if Senneth had run her hands through it about fourteen times. Her feet were bare. Kirra could only guess Senneth had answered the door after yanking back on a dress that had already been discarded.

"Senneth." Kirra spoke in Casserah's voice. "I hope I haven't caught you at a bad time."

Senneth's face was absolutely blank. "Casserah. I didn't get a chance to speak to you at the dinner. I had no idea you were coming to Ghosenhall."

"Entirely my father's idea."

Senneth hesitated a moment, then stepped back in a tacit invitation. Kirra strolled in and glanced quickly around, but didn't see any sign that Tayse was hiding behind curtains or under the bed. "It is very good to see you, of course," Senneth added belatedly.

Kirra turned to face her, her expression cool, a little supercilious. "We've heard strange tales of you. The lost heiress of Brassenthwaite! And all this time my father knew."

"And your sister," Senneth said with a little grin.

"Oh, yes, my sister," Kirra drawled. "She told me, if I saw

you, to give you an urgent message." She glanced around the room, a little more deliberately this time. "But before I spoke, I was to make sure that you were *entirely alone.*" She looked around again. "I don't see any Riders under the covers, though. I suppose it's safe to speak."

There was a moment of dead silence while Senneth's face was completely unreadable. And then, "You brat," Senneth breathed. "I can't believe you tried to trick me."

Kirra couldn't hold back the laughter. "I *did* trick you."

"Kirra!" Senneth was upon her in two strides, throwing her arms around her neck. The heat of her body was so high it was like being embraced by summer. "Oh, it is so good to see you!"

But Kirra was pulling back, yelping in pain. "Ow! Ow! What are you wearing—silver hell, you've got another moonstone bracelet on. I thought you'd learned your lesson by now."

"Sorry. Forgot," Senneth said, stripping the opalescent stones from her wrist and tossing the bracelet to the bed. Then she hugged Kirra again, hard. "What are you *doing* here? And styled like your sister?"

They arranged themselves on the bed to talk. Kirra sat at ease, cross-legged under her dress. Senneth had her legs stretched out before her, the folds of the blue gown bunching around her knees. Kirra pointed at the bracelet without touching it. "I can't believe you got another one of those. It almost killed you last time."

"It didn't almost kill me. I was hurt. It doesn't bother me at all when I'm healthy."

"*No* mystic should be able to wear a moonstone. It's unnatural that you can tolerate it."

"I like it. It makes me aware of things, like how much energy I have to expend to keep it in check. Anyway, it makes people trust me when they see I can wear a moonstone. They forget I'm a mystic."

"I can't believe Tayse thinks this is a good idea."

"You're right about that," Senneth admitted.

"And is Tayse in a position these days," Kirra said with exaggerated delicacy, "to—approve or disapprove of your conduct? To make any comments on your behavior or your accessories or your—self?"

Senneth threw a pillow at her. "I can't believe you would actually ask me that."

Kirra leaned forward. "Oh, I can be more direct. Are you sleeping with him? What kind of a lover is Tayse, the King's Rider?"

Senneth hesitated, blushed, and then laughed. "I can't even talk to you when you look like Casserah. I can't. If you want this conversation, you'll have to change to Kirra."

"I want this conversation." Kirra concentrated a moment, felt the contour and structure of her face shift, felt her hair lift and curl against her shoulders. "There. It's me. Tell me everything."

Senneth had drawn her knees up to her chin and linked her hands around her ankles. "Oh, Kirra. This is unlike anything that's ever happened to me before. I mean, there have been men from time to time—"

"You never told me about any of those!"

"But Tayse is—I feel so—nothing has ever been like this," Senneth ended helplessly. "It's almost as if the world has changed, or the sun has started moving in a different direction. I'm *pulled* to him. He's become my point of reference. That's where I start every day, by knowing where Tayse is. I can't explain it. I wouldn't have expected it. I would be afraid that this would end, that somehow something like this couldn't last, except I know he feels the same way about me. Only it doesn't frighten him, because Tayse doesn't know what it means to be afraid."

The words struck Kirra to the heart. She felt a sudden deep desire to experience something so all-encompassing, encounter some outside agent that would transmogrify her completely. But she spoke lightly, waving a dismissive hand. "Yes, very pretty. But how is he in bed?"

Senneth giggled and dropped her head to her knees. "If people had any idea how crude you are," she mumbled into the fabric of her dress. "So beautiful, and so depraved."

"Well, you *have* taken him as your lover, haven't you? Because otherwise I can't stand it."

Senneth lifted her face, suffused with mirth. "Yes. He's my lover. It's perfectly marvelous. I enjoy it very much. I sleep beside him every chance I get. In fact, I walked into my brother's house in Brassenthwaite and told him I was bringing a Rider into my bedroom."

Kirra's mouth fell open. "You didn't!"

"I did."

"You haven't seen your brother in seventeen years, and when you do, you stroll into his house as the most powerful mystic in the realm, the confidante of the king—and you say you're having an affair with a *guard*? Kiernan must have been ready to die."

"Actually, Kiernan was too focused on essentials to really care, which I have to say raised him a little in my estimation. He just said, 'Fine, do what you please. You always did.' Nate acted all offended, talking about propriety and the distinction between the classes, but I just said, 'Nate. I have consorted with thieves and killers and beggars and slaves. I have taken food from their hands, fought at their backs, called them my friends, and trusted them more than I will ever trust you. Don't try to lecture me about where my loyalties should lie.'"

Kirra had pressed her hands over her mouth to choke back the laughter and now she spoke through her fingers. "And what did Kiernan say *then*?"

"He said, 'Are we done talking about this now? Can we move on to more important matters?' So Nate shut up, but he never did get used to Tayse being in the house."

"And how did Tayse act? Was he ill at ease? Or not?"

Senneth laughed softly. "Oh, he was in full Rider mode. Very stone-faced, very serious. Always watching everybody as if waiting for someone to pull a knife and go on the attack. He was having a grand time. At first I thought he was doing it just to annoy Nate and Kiernan, but then I realized he was trying to make a point."

But the point was obvious to Kirra. "He was telling them they had done a lousy job of protecting you when they had the chance, and now that it was his job, he wouldn't fail."

Senneth nodded. "Yes. And Kiernan at least got the message."

"So, how did it go? With you and Kiernan?"

Senneth leaned back against the headboard and stretched her legs out again. "We were not easy with each other. I have much to forgive, and I haven't really forgiven. And he's a hard man to like in general. If I met him in Baryn's dining room, knowing nothing about him, I would not be drawn to him for his wit and charm. He is very stern. He is practically humorless. But—there *is* something about him. An honesty. A sense of honor. I believe he will always do what he perceives to be the right thing, even if it is bitter. Seventeen years ago, he thought my father was right to cast me out of Brassenthwaite. But he said he came to regret that decision even before my father died—and, Kirra, I believed him. I think he would have searched for me and welcomed me back—with as much emotion as Kiernan is able to muster—even if I was not a powerful woman who could offer him alliances. Just because it was the right thing to do. So I found myself respecting him. And I found myself not hating him. That was more than I had expected."

"And Nate?"

Senneth waved a hand. "Oh, Nate is the most infuriating man! So righteous and *not* very smart. But I was able to find a few good points in him, too, while I was there. He believes in Kiernan, that's one thing. And his passion for hierarchy and order leads him to try very hard to live up to his part of the bargain. He's a good landlord, a good master, very fair. And he is absolutely loyal to his king. He has *no* idea what to do with me, but he thinks it's right that they take me back in. He'd like to see me married off to someone in Rappengrass or Helven—build an alliance, you know—but he accepted it when I flat out told him no. I'm sure we'll have other battles, though."

"And what about the others? Aren't there two younger boys?"

Senneth grinned. "Hardly boys anymore. Harris is thirty and Will is twenty-seven. I didn't see much of Harris—he's married, can you believe it, and lives on property of his own. But Will was there. It was wonderful to see him again. He was always my favorite when I was growing up. He told me he cried every night for a year after I was turned out of the house."

Kirra was frowning, trying to do bloodlines in her head. "Kiernan's married, isn't he?"

"Yes. To a Brassenthwaite girl. The most patient woman you could possibly imagine. They've got two boys and a girl now—who found Aunt Senneth a *very* peculiar individual. Nate's not married, though. No one said why, though I had some idea there was a disappointment in love. Hard to picture, but I suppose even Nate has a heart."

"Well! I think it sounds like a most successful trip! The prodigal child returns to a warm reunion with her family and they talk—what? Politics? Strategies? Or family reminiscences?"

"Only Will and I talked over old times. With Kiernan and

Nate, it was mostly strategy. They were very interested in my tales from our trip last winter. We sat there—sometimes for whole, uninterrupted days—in front of a map of Gillengaria, arguing over which Houses are loyal and which ones are likely to betray the crown. And, of course, we could never be sure."

"I guess that's something we can try to find out," Kirra said, "when we go off on our giddy social whirl."

"So, tell me about you!" Senneth exclaimed. "Why did your father send you here? And *what* happened on the road to Tilt?"

"Oh, the trip to Tilt was a lot of fun," Kirra said, and launched into the tale. "I was glad to turn the regent over to his own men, though," she said as she finished up.

"What did you think of him? Once you'd spent a few days with him?"

I thought he was the most fascinating man I've ever met. "Will he be a good regent?" she said instead. "I give him high marks for loyalty, passion, leadership, and intelligence. He was a little too eager to risk himself, which probably plays well in Merrenstow but won't be so smart in Ghosenhall. But all in all I thought the king could hardly have made a better choice."

"Cammon liked him," Senneth said.

Kirra spread her hands. "There you have it, then. Cammon is never wrong about people."

"Justin liked him, too."

"Another ringing endorsement! Since Justin hates every-body."

"I've only had about three brief conversations with Lord Romar, but I confess he appealed to me as well," Senneth said. "So, we are all agreed that he is an excellent choice—except that people want to kill him."

"Maybe that will be the next charge the king gives you," Kirra said, trying to make her voice flippant though Senneth's words had bruised her heart. "Protecting the regent."

Senneth sighed. "No, I still appear to be carrying out my most recent commission—protecting the princess."

"And how is *that* going? I met her today, for what must have been the first time since she was a child."

"What did you think of her?"

Kirra considered. "I thought she was a very mature eighteen.

But still eighteen. You're the one who's been spending time with her. What do you think?"

"Well, now, that's the interesting thing," Senneth said. "I haven't spent that much time with her at all. I've been beside her half a dozen times in the past month—at the king's summer ball, a few dinners in Ghosenhall, things like that—but I'm never *alone* with her. Valri is always standing right next to me. Usually right between me and the princess. Even when I have a few moments alone with the girl, I have trouble guessing what she's thinking. She's something of a cipher. Her face is very alert—her eyes are always watching. But she never comments. I can't tell if she's a wise child or a silly girl. It makes me a little nervous."

"Maybe you'll get more of a chance to talk with her when you travel. Milo said you'd be going to Kianlever."

Senneth nodded. "Doing the entire summer circuit. And so will Valri."

Kirra's eyebrows shot up. "I thought the queen never traveled."

"She's making an exception this year."

"I foresee an entertaining summer season," Kirra said. "At least we won't have to attend any balls in Gisseltess!"

Senneth laughed. "No, for Halchon is under interdiction, though I'm sure he's still plotting against the king. And Coralinda is still sending her Daughters out into the southern provinces, stirring up ill will against the mystics. But at least, as you say, she won't be arranging any grand masques in Gisseltess, so that's something to be thankful for."

"So—nothing has changed, really, since this past winter," Kirra said slowly. "We're still dancing around with all the marlords, trying to determine loyalties. Halchon Gisseltess is still scheming, and Coralinda is still spreading poison. And the princess is still mysterious, and no one knows anything about Queen Valri."

"Yes," Senneth said. "We're exactly where we were three months ago."

"Except that you're in love with a King's Rider."

"Ah. Well. *That's* different."

"So what happens next? With you and Tayse?"

Senneth shook her head. "I don't know. I think what happens

next is whatever unfolds in Gillengaria. Most of our attention will go to that."

Kirra yawned and shook back her hair. She concentrated a moment on calling up the colors and proportions of Casserah's body. "Gods and goddesses, but I'm tired. We'll have to talk more tomorrow. Don't make the mistake of forgetting who I'm supposed to be."

Senneth watched her until the transformation was complete. "Don't make the mistake of forgetting who you really are."

THE morning was taken up with a formal breakfast and an exceedingly dull conversation with a woman from Merrenstow who had decided she wanted to form a close friendship with Casserah. When Kirra was able to escape, she looked around for Senneth but couldn't find her. So she collected Donnal from where he lay behind the kitchen, sleeping in the sun with about fifteen other dogs, and headed down to the training yard.

The palace complex was so huge that it was practically a small city, divided into districts and graced with dozens of parks and gardens. One whole neighborhood belonged to the King's Riders, the fifty elite fighters personally chosen by the king, who devoted their lives to serving their liege. Many of them clustered in a large, well-appointed barracks, though a handful lived in their own cottages situated nearby. These were the few who were married and had children. Most Riders preferred not to allow such distractions in their lives.

Kirra wondered if Senneth and Tayse might take possession of one of those homes. It was hard to picture. Senneth was such a wanderer it was difficult to believe she would ever settle in one place, and Tayse did not project the image of a man it would be possible to domesticate. She decided she would go shopping for housewarming presents, some embroidered pillows, perhaps, or monogrammed bedsheets, and present these gifts with a totally innocent air. *I thought—I just assumed—won't you be setting up house together?* The thought made her grin.

Not far from the barracks were the extensive fields where the fifty Riders and their assorted trainers could take part in daily fighting practice. Kirra could not remember any time she had passed by these enclosed areas and seen them empty. Often there were spectators leaning against the fences—young girls who thought the Riders were handsome, teenage boys dreaming of being Riders themselves one day, merchants who had come with their families to tour the royal city for a week and who did not want to miss one of the most impressive sights Ghosenhall had to offer.

Kirra had thought Senneth might be among the gawkers, but she was out of luck again. However, eight or nine other people were already stationed along the main fence, standing on the lowest rail or resting an elbow on the top one, watching the Riders trade blows. Kirra was not even remotely interested in the finer points of combat, but she paused anyway just out of curiosity. Yes, there were twenty or twenty-five men swinging swords at each other's heads and looking as if they were determined to achieve a decapitation before the morning was over. Another group had stripped down to their trousers and were going at each other with bare hands, while their muscled bodies gleamed most interestingly from a combination of sweat and sunlight. Still others were on horseback, charging forward and rearing back. The yard rang with triumphant shouts and the clang of metal on metal.

Donnal settled on his haunches and peered through the lower bars of the fence, watching the maneuvers with more attention than the average hound would muster. To please him, Kirra lingered. She wondered if he might be tempted to turn human for a day or two if it meant he'd have a chance to work out against the Riders.

It was only after she had been watching the combatants for a few minutes that Kirra realized she actually knew some of them. Not twenty yards away, battling it out on foot, were Tayse and Cammon. Tayse was the one she spotted first. He was big, both tall and brawny, and if he wanted to he could dominate a room with his physical presence. His black hair and dark eyes added menace to a face that was intense even during his lighthearted moments, which were few. And even Kirra, who knew nothing about swordplay, could tell that he handled a blade with exquisite ruthlessness.

But Cammon did not appear to be dead, even mock-dead, since Tayse was seeming to find it difficult to land a blow. More of Cammon's uncanny sensitivity; it was impossible to take the boy by surprise. Kirra watched as Tayse dropped his sword and said something to Cammon. From the expression on the dark face, it looked like the Rider was offering high praise to the mystic. Kirra could not help but smile.

And then Cammon looked over at her and gave a shout.

In the ten seconds it took him to reach her, she had a chance to make sure she *did* actually look like her sister, she *had* actually remembered to hold her disguise as she left her room this morning. But, of course, subterfuge was completely lost on Cammon.

"Kirra! What are you doing here? When did you arrive? Hey, Donnal. See, I told Justin you were both safe."

Kirra made a hushing sound and looked around, but none of the other spectators were likely to know who Kirra was. "No, no, don't call me that!" she hissed. "I'm Casserah—I'm Kirra's sister. And this is a dog."

"I can tell he's supposed to be a dog, but you—I'm sorry, I haven't given anything away, have I? It's just that—"

"I know. I look like Kirra to you. But call me 'serra' if you can't bring yourself to call me by the wrong name."

"Yes, serra. Sorry, serra." He was grinning. "When did you get here? Have you seen Senneth?"

"Yesterday. Yes. I saw her last night. *She* had no idea who I was, so I had fun for a few minutes."

He shook his head. "You can't be trusted."

During this quick exchange, Tayse had made his way over at a more leisurely pace. He gave Kirra the small bow of acknowledgment any Rider would give to any high-ranking noble and said to Cammon, "Are we done for the day? Are you ready to quit?"

Cammon gave Kirra an imploring look. "No, I just wanted to talk to—I saw someone I knew and—"

Tayse gave Kirra a sharper look this time. She assumed a haughty expression, but she had a feeling Senneth had already betrayed her. "I'm Casserah Danalustrous," she said in her coldest voice. "I believe you're acquainted with my sister."

Now Tayse was smiling broadly, showing a rare and deep amusement. "I believe I am. Quite the hellion. Glad to see the last of her when she rode out of Ghosenhall."

Kirra shook her head. "Senneth told you."

"She didn't like the idea of you playing tricks on me."

Cammon was clearly relieved. "And that's Donnal."

Tayse glanced down and gave Donnal a friendly nod. "I was sure it would be."

"How was your visit to Brassenthwaite?" Kirra asked him in a honeyed voice. "Did you get acquainted with Senneth's charming brothers? I hope you took every opportunity to enjoy yourself."

Tayse still looked amused, but Cammon didn't pick up the undertones. "Senneth's brothers don't seem like the kind of people you really enjoy being around," the boy said.

She smiled at him. "Perhaps Tayse found other ways to entertain himself, then."

"I see you're as much of a hellion as your sister," Tayse said.

"No, she *is* her sister," Cammon said helpfully.

Kirra was giggling helplessly. "Don't confuse him."

"Oh, I assure you," Tayse said, "I am not at all bewildered."

Someone drifted over and Kirra looked up to see that Justin had joined them, as always gravitating to whatever group included Tayse. He gave the serramarra an indifferent bow and clouted Cammon on the shoulder. "You done with him? Want to fence with me a little?"

Cammon looked between Justin's face and Kirra's, obviously desperate to tell the truth but bound by the fear of Kirra's disapproval. No such restraints worked with Tayse. "Say hello to an old friend," Tayse said. "She's masquerading as Casserah Danalustrous, but it's someone you know."

Justin stepped forward and peered into her face. "Really? Is that Kirra? And is this what your sister looks like? She's pretty."

"Happy to see you, too, Justin," Kirra replied. "Good to finally learn what kind of woman you admire."

He was grinning. "I don't have much time for women. But I prefer dark to fair." He glanced down at the dog at Kirra's feet. "That Donnal? Hey, if you want to work out with us, just come on by some afternoon."

Donnal offered a sharp bark that Kirra figured no one could interpret. Possibly Cammon, who did not translate. "So are any of you going with Senneth when she leaves for Kianlever in a few days?" she asked.

Tayse just looked at her; of course he was. Justin glanced at him. "You're leaving? How long will you be gone?"

"I was going to ask if you wanted to go along," Tayse replied. "We'll need a handful of Riders because we'll be accompanying the queen and the princess. We'll need to make our presence felt."

"I'll come," Justin said.

Cammon looked wistful. "Would there be room for me?"

Senneth's voice answered from behind Kirra. "Ah, here's where you've all gone off to. Kirra, where have you been?"

"Looking for you, mostly."

Senneth bent down to ruffle the fur on Donnal's head. He had scrambled up to greet her and managed to run his tongue across both her fingers and her cheek. She laughed and held still so he could lick her again, then she straightened to survey the others. "I was trapped in the most boring conversation imaginable with some woman from—who knows? Tilt, maybe. Maybe Storian. I couldn't tell. I just cannot endure the thought that I'm about to set off on a social round that will bring me nothing *but* such conversations for the rest of my life."

"Six weeks, maybe," Kirra said. "It won't be so bad."

"We were just discussing our travel plans," Tayse said. "Justin's coming with us. Cammon has expressed an interest in joining us, too."

"Excellent! I hoped you both would," Senneth replied. "I'm assuming Kirra and Donnal will also travel with us, since they're heading to all the same functions."

Kirra was surprised to see the look of satisfaction that crossed Justin's face. Surprised, because it was exactly how she felt, but she hadn't expected Justin to be the one to experience the same emotion. "Just like last winter," he said. "The six of us."

"Well, and probably twenty more guards, and Valri and Amalie and who knows how many servants," Senneth said. "But yes. The six of us."

Cammon was smiling and that *didn't* surprise Kirra because Cammon was the one who valued connections more than any of them. *We should be together.* No one spoke the words, but Kirra could feel a net of friendship and affection tightening over their whole small group, binding them in invisible ways. She had been eager to meet up with Senneth again and pleased to see the others, but she hadn't expected this, the sense of camaraderie or something even stronger. Fellowship. Trust. Belonging.

"Good," Justin said. "When do we leave?"

CHAPTER
13

A WEEK later, a caravan left Ghosenhall for Kianlever, bearing half the royal house with it. In addition to Tayse and Justin, their party included two more Riders, a troop of twenty soldiers, and three carriages. One held Valri and Amalie, one held Kirra and Melly, and one held the three servants imported to care for the princess and the queen. Kirra had been unable to shake Melly, but she *had* taken the opportunity to send her own guards back to Danalustrous. Doing away with just the tiniest bit of her retinue made her feel appreciably lighter in spirit.

They spent four days on the road, the travel tedious but tolerable. Kirra hated being cooped up in the carriage, so she was always the first to alight when they stopped for informal breaks along the way. She would take a brisk walk with Donnal or stroll up to the lead carriage to see if Senneth had anything interesting to say. During one of these breaks, she spotted Cammon and Donnal sitting together, Cammon earnestly and unself-consciously carrying on a conversation with the black hound.

"That young man you brought along is a lunatic," Kirra joked to Senneth. "He keeps talking to that *dog*."

"Something of a simpleton," Senneth agreed. "He claims the dog can understand him. He even thinks the dog can talk back. I've told the queen and the princess not to be alarmed, but I think they wish I'd left him behind."

"I'm sure at some point he'll earn his keep."

"Cammon always does."

So there were entertaining moments during the day, but the nights spent at roadside inns were exceedingly dull. They dined according to caste, which meant spending too much time with Valri, who had no inclination for small talk, and Amalie, who was not a chatterer. Kirra could usually charm anyone, but in character as Casserah, she merely let the dinner hours pass in near silence. After each meal, they all scattered to their assigned rooms, which had mistress paired up with maid—not much chance for stimulating conversation there. As part of her mission to guard the princess, Senneth always slept solitarily in the room next to Amalie's—though Kirra suspected many of those nights she did not lie alone. She never caught Tayse coming in or out of Senneth's room but she had to believe he spent some nights there. And who better to help a serramarra guard a princess than a Rider? No one would complain.

Finally, after four days of this monotony, they arrived in Kianlever Court.

The lands owned by the Kianlever family formed a roughly rectangular shape, much longer from east to west than from north to south. The terrain shaded from fairly flat arable land on the west end to rougher, rockier, more picturesque foothills as the eastern edge climbed toward the Lireth Mountains. The principal city was situated almost exactly dead center from all boundaries. It was a pretty, rather muddled sort of place, built from a profusion of often dissonant styles and serving as home to a widely disparate group of people. Kirra, practically hanging out the window in her excitement to finally have something interesting to look at, could spot enclaves of nobles, farmers, merchants, servants, soldiers, and hunters traversing the city streets. On one corner, she noted a half dozen Daughters of the Pale Mother, dressed in novice white and sprinkled with moonstones, offering their benedictions to the passing crowds. On another corner she saw a close, watchful, edgy group of men who gave off the indefinable essence of wildness, even though they were dressed much like everyone else. Kirra wished Senneth was in the coach with her. She thought they might be from the Lirrens, that strange, half-hostile land that lay just a mountain range away from Kianlever. Senneth would know. She had lived in the Lirrens during her long years of exile and could even call some of those tight-knit clansmen her friends.

The coaches moved on and the Lirren folk—if they were—fell behind. Now they were rolling through the wealthy district, featuring large, expensive private homes and discreet inns. If Kirra craned her head out the window, she could see the ancestral home of Eloise Kianlever, as appealing and disorganized as the city itself. It featured a crazy-quilt lawn of gardens and hedges surrounding a sprawling building constructed of a hodgepodge of architectural styles. No walls or gates separated the estate from the rest of the city, though Kirra did note the presence of guards at the front entrance and the upper battlements. Still. She was sure Tayse and Justin would be appalled at the haphazard security measures Eloise had put in place. Tayse must already be wondering how he would protect the princess during their stay.

It was soon clear that that was something Tayse and Senneth had discussed in advance.

The coaches pulled up before the wide, welcoming entrance. Kirra disembarked with alacrity, Melly following more slowly. Servants were already pouring out the front door, a steward calling orders to underlings. Senneth and the royal servants were also out of their coaches.

Valri and Amalie were nowhere to be seen.

Tayse and Justin and the other Riders crowded up on horseback to follow Senneth almost to the door itself. Kirra, hopeful of a good show, hurried behind them.

The steward was bowing very low in Senneth's direction. "Welcome, serra. You have been expected. Rooms are ready."

"I am concerned about the safety of the people in my party," Senneth said in a stern voice very unlike her. "The princess and the queen are used to the most stringent security measures, with many levels of protection between them and the outside world. Kianlever Court is too undefended. We must take additional steps."

"The marlady Eloise has always felt adequately protected, serra."

"Perhaps. But a princess of the royal house, forgive me, is

even more precious than the marlady and consequently is often in much graver danger. Therefore, one of the King's Riders will be within call of the princess at all times, whether she is asleep in her room or dining in your great hall. These Riders will not be questioned or detained for any reason whatsoever—in fact, any attempt to remove them from the vicinity of the princess will be considered an act of aggression. They will be allowed free range of the house and the grounds. They will be authorized to question anyone who appears to be suspicious. They will remain unobtrusive if they can—but they will not hesitate to act if they must."

The steward looked appalled. "Serra! I assure you! Such measures are not necessary! See, we have soldiers at the entrance and down every hall—"

"If the princess is not guarded by Riders, she does not stay in this house. We will spend the night at some more accommodating establishment and return to Ghosenhall in the morning."

Now the steward was nervous, not sure where his greatest offense might lie. He could not afford to be the one who turned the princess away from the door—when the princess had not been seen outside the gates of Ghosenhall for years—but he could not recklessly commit his lady to such a course of action. "Serra," he said, as calmly as he could, "be pleased to wait. I must consult with the marlady."

Senneth nodded. "I understand. Please be swift."

The steward disappeared. The Kianlever servants had stopped their feverish unpacking and now stood uncertainly near the coaches, bags in their hands and trunks at their feet. Melly and the other royal servants climbed back into the coaches to wait.

Kirra crept close enough to Senneth to whisper in her ear, "What a fuss! Whose idea was this?"

"Tayse's," Senneth breathed in response. "War strategy. Establish your position early. Make a show of strength. Your enemy will think twice before attacking."

"Will she allow it?"

"I don't think she has a choice."

Indeed, fifteen minutes later, Eloise Kianlever herself came flowing out the door. At least that was how it looked, for she was wearing a filmy dress of aqueous colors and many layers that seemed to swirl about her like the currents of a river. Her hands were flung before her in a gesture that was half welcoming, half conciliatory. She was a middle-aged woman with regular features and unremarkable brown hair, but she always dressed in such vivid colors and outrageous styles that she had a certain flamboyant presence nonetheless. Kirra had never thought she was exceptionally intelligent, though infinitely likable.

"But, Senneth! What is this?" Eloise demanded, taking both of Senneth's hands in hers. Surprised at the warm greeting, Kirra belatedly remembered that Senneth had relatives in Kianlever; her grandmother had been born here. Though Senneth had never seemed too eager to call on those Kianlever connections once she severed her ties with the nobility. "Not even across my threshold and you are already ruffling the whole household!"

Senneth permitted Eloise to lean forward and kiss her on the cheek. "I am sorry to seem so demanding," she said, though she did not sound sorry. "I am charged with making sure Princess Amalie is secure. To me, in a place as open as Kianlever Court—charming as it is!—she does not seem safe. I want assurance that the king's men can be deployed around her at all times."

"You mean, standing beside her chair at dinnertime?"

"I mean, within call of her voice. They will stay out of the way. They will cause no trouble—unless trouble comes hunting the princess."

"Yes—yes—of course, they shall follow her wherever she goes, if that is your condition," Eloise said. "I am certain she will be entirely safe—but the king's only daughter! I understand he cannot be too careful."

Senneth nodded. "Thank you. You are most gracious."

She turned to signal to the occupants of the final coach. Eloise more enthusiastically waved everyone back in motion. "Come! Carry those trunks inside! Let us not keep our guests waiting any longer!"

Then followed the usual flurry of arrival, with shouts and curses and questions accompanying the great migration indoors. Eloise curtseyed very low to both Valri and Amalie, and looked absolutely delighted at the thought that her house was the first one these exalted guests had deigned to visit. "You'll want to go to your rooms, of course," Eloise said, leading the way, "but then I want you to come right down and visit with me! All of you—Senneth, and both your majesties."

Senneth flicked Kirra a quick look and Kirra gave an infinitesimal shake of her head. "I think it is possible you do not know my traveling companion," Senneth said, "for she has been almost as reclusive as the princess herself. She hates to leave her own home but has been persuaded it is time to visit more of Gillengaria."

Eloise stopped right there in the hallway, causing a corollary confusion in the long line of people following her. "Is that Casserah?" she demanded. "I haven't seen you since you were a baby! Forgive me for my terrible manners—it has been *such* a distracting morning."

Eloise kissed Casserah on the cheek as well; she seemed ready to bestow warmth on anyone. Kirra gave her back Casserah's guarded smile. "Serra Senneth has a way of creating distractions wherever she goes," Kirra said. "It is rarely quiet in her vicinity."

Senneth flashed her an indignant look, though she couldn't put any real force behind it and still maintain her righteous attitude. Eloise continued, unheeding, "I have met your sister dozens of times and liked her very much! I'm so happy you're here! Do come down with the others and we'll have a nice little visit without too many other people around."

Finally the whole lot of them had navigated the many corridors to find a wing that seemed to have been set aside for the royal party. They sorted themselves out into rooms, Kirra marking the rooms assigned to Senneth, Valri, and Amalie. She briefly followed Melly into her own room and found it very agreeable, all white lacy curtains and canopies, airy and serene.

"Try not to shed on the rug," she said to Donnal, who merely opened his mouth in a canine laugh.

"What would you like to wear to dinner tonight, serra?" Melly asked.

"Mmmm. Something with Danalustrous colors, I suppose, but not the red dress. I'll wear that to the ball in a couple of days. Something a little less forceful."

"The pale gold dress and your ruby pendant?"

"Yes, thank you. That would strike just the right note."

Donnal followed her back out to the hall a few minutes

later. A Rider she did not know stood outside the room that must be Amalie's, but everyone else had disappeared. Probably all in Senneth's room. She knocked and then entered without waiting, Donnal at her heels.

Tayse and Justin and Senneth stood together in the center of the room, talking quietly. Cammon sat in the window seat, watching a new arrival. "Storian, by the crest on the coach," he said. There had been a day not so long ago when Cammon couldn't even name the Twelve Houses, but now he could recognize colors and heraldry. "Some old guy. He doesn't look very interesting."

"He'd probably say the same about you," Justin remarked.

Cammon glanced at him. "I'm not *old*."

Kirra joined the others. "Making plans? Anything incendiary?"

"No, Senneth's going to try not to set the place on fire," Justin said. "Want to place any bets on the outcome?"

Kirra grinned. "My bet would be—fire, sometime on our trip. Maybe not at Kianlever Court, but before we get back to Ghosenhall."

"I'm trying to decide," Senneth said, "if I need to sleep in the same room as the princess. Valri has her own room, so it's just Amalie and her maid."

"And a Rider outside the door," Tayse pointed out.

"Sometimes things come in through the windows," Senneth said.

"Sometimes things come in through the walls," Kirra added. The men looked at her, and she shrugged. "When I was wandering the halls in Tilt, I was a bird and a spider and a cat. I don't know that a Rider would have stopped me."

Justin was grinning. "If I see any spiders, I'll step on them."

Kirra glanced down at the dog. "Let's try it. See if Donnal can get inside the room with a Rider watching. I am positive he can."

A wolfish grin from Donnal. He was sure he could, too.

"But are there any mystics who have the kind of power Kirra and Donnal have?" Tayse asked. "Who can transform themselves so completely to another shape and size?"

"I'm sure there are," Senneth said. "Bright Mother knows I haven't met every mystic in Gillengaria."

"Mystics willing to ally themselves with Halchon Gisseltess?" Tayse pursued. "A man who hates and persecutes mystics?"

Senneth shrugged. "They might have their own agenda. Or they might have been promised—who knows?—anything. People have betrayed their own natural allies long before this."

"It seems obvious," Kirra said. "You're here to protect the princess. You have to sleep in the room with her." She glanced at Tayse, whose face was expressionless. "No matter what your preferences might be."

Senneth ignored the comment. "So then we have this room empty. I think Justin and Tayse should use it when they're not on guard. I feel certain Eloise Kianlever would prefer not to house soldiers in one of her finest bedrooms, but as no one will be able to keep track of the Riders anyway, she won't know who's here when and why. And if the two of you are sleeping nearby, and there's a Rider outside the room and I'm inside it, surely the princess will be safe."

For the first time, Kirra took this whole exercise seriously. "You really expect an attack on her?" she asked. "That wasn't all for show?"

Senneth spread her hands. "The king is very, very nervous about this trip outside Ghosenhall. Is he overprotective of his only daughter and his only heir? Or is he right to have kept her so close all these years? I don't know. I do know that there's unrest in the kingdom and she could be a target. And I'm here to make sure she survives."

"As are we all," Tayse said.

"I'm here to find a husband for Casserah," said Kirra. "But I'll do what I can to help you, too, of course."

Cammon looked over from the window. "What about me? Is there anything in particular you want me to do?"

Senneth turned his way. "I want you to sleep in this room at night with Justin and Tayse. And—pay attention. The way you do. Wake us all up if something odd seems to be happening. Even if it turns out to be nothing. Wake us up anyway."

He nodded and turned back to the window to watch another new arrival pull up at the front entrance. Suddenly he was up on his knees, wriggling on the window seat, waving out the window as if trying to catch someone's eyes. "Hey, look! It's Romar Brendyn!" he cried. "He's come to Kianlever for the ball!"

CHAPTER
14

THE first dinner at Kianlever Court was the most intriguing and most excruciating period of time Kirra had passed since she'd escaped from Tilt. So much was going on that it was difficult to note and analyze everything.

And she was distracted. All she really wanted to do was make a curtsey to Romar Brendyn, ask urgently after his health and safety, and then spend the rest of the night talking to him, uninterrupted by lesser and less-interesting mortals. Conversely, she hoped she never had to speak to him at all, that she managed to get through the pre- and post-dinner socializing without being introduced to him, that he was seated on the opposite side of the room from her when they went in to dinner.

But she was always aware of him. She always knew where he was standing, to whom he was speaking. Like the sun, he cast a bright circle of illumination around himself, and anywhere he moved, the world grew brighter.

This was going to be problematic, Kirra thought. This was going to make it awfully difficult to get through the next few days.

She didn't do so badly during the hour all the guests gathered in the salon outside the dining hall. Melly had worked hard on her toilette, and she knew she looked beautiful—or rather, that Casserah looked beautiful. The filmy gold dress was cut with a square neckline that showed off the large, smoldering ruby she wore just over her housemark. Melly had twisted her dark hair into some kind of complex weave of braids and curls, using gold ribbons to tie the whole confection in place. Everyone had been most responsive, both strangers and acquaintances murmuring words of praise or admiration.

Eloise Kianlever had made a point of showing Casserah around, almost as if she was as big a prize as Amalie. It was clear to Kirra almost immediately that all the people in the room, all thirty-five or forty of them, were Twelfth House; not a single Kianlever vassal was in attendance, no one whose blood wasn't absolutely pure.

She took the first chance she had to make this observation, and Eloise laughed. "Oh, they'll all be here in two days for the big event! But today's their Shadow Ball, so, of course, none of them could attend."

Kirra felt her eyebrows rise in one of Casserah's haughty expressions. "'Shadow Ball'?" she repeated.

"What? Don't you have such a thing in Danalustrous? Perhaps you don't. Malcolm was never much of one for entertaining. At most of the Houses, whenever they've organized some grand event at the hall, the primary vassals plan their own big dance or dinner. There's a reflected prestige, you know, and I think lesser lords from all over the realm often come. I know that there will be visitors from Coravann and Storian and Nocklyn—even Gisseltess, I believe—at Kell Sersees's ball tonight. Kell and his family will be here in a couple of days, of course."

It was not too hard to guess what Casserah would have thought of such a tradition of codified segregation, and Kirra allowed some of Casserah's contempt to show. "I cannot imagine something like that ever occurring in Danalustrous," she said.

"Can't you, dear? Well, perhaps your vassals would enjoy it more than you believe. It's all very well to think you know what's best for everybody, but sometimes it's easy to guess wrong."

That made Casserah open her eyes even wider—how unlike Eloise!—but her hostess had flitted off to a small group of women who had just entered the room. Kirra followed in time to hear Eloise say, "Majesty! Princess! Serra! How pleased I am that you are here tonight! I hope you will enjoy yourselves."

"I am certain we will," Valri answered in a cool voice. The young queen was wearing a dress of emerald-green silk that perfectly matched her eyes; if she had a housemark, it was hidden under the high neckline.

"Thank you for inviting us," Amalie added in a soft voice. Her own dress was much more subdued, a rose-tinted ivory that brought out the warmth of her strawberry-blond hair and made her brown eyes seem even darker and richer. More modestly cut than Kirra's, her dress still dipped low enough in front to show a slight swell of adolescent bosom. The pendant she wore to cover her housemark was most cunningly designed, an oval-shaped weave of flat gold bands studded with the twelve gems of the Houses of Gillengaria.

"I like your necklace," Kirra said.

Amalie gave her a sideways smile. "Do you? I had it made after my own design."

Which was the most surprising thing she could have said. What eighteen-year-old would be thinking of politics when she was dreaming of finery? And yet, what gems appeared around the throat of the queen and her daughters was always an issue of some concern among the ladies of the Twelve Houses. No one wanted to see the colors of Brassenthwaite favored, for instance, or the ties to Merrenstow flaunted. Queen Pella had always worn a gold charm in the shape of a stylized lion, forgoing jewels altogether. Amalie, it appeared, would be a bit bolder than her mother.

"The princess has a most subtle elegance of mind," Valri said. Kirra found it impossible to tell if the queen's voice was sincere or sneering.

"The princess is the most welcome guest I've ever had," Eloise replied.

A slight smile on Valri's perfect face. "She was pleased to be invited," the queen said. "It is time for her to become better acquainted with the realm that will be hers someday."

"Not for some time, I hope," Senneth said, speaking for the first time. Although she was taller than both the princess and the queen, Senneth was dressed so quietly and standing so still behind them that it was almost possible to forget that she was there. Or—no—Kirra realized that Senneth was using deliberate misdirection to make people overlook her. Senneth could, if she wished, actually turn invisible, but she had probably decided with some regret that she had to maintain at least a faint presence here at Amalie's first public appearance outside of Ghosenhall.

Amalie gave her a warm smile. "No, not for years and *years.*"

Eloise laid a hand on Amalie's arm. "Princess, may I introduce you to my friends? Everyone is most eager to meet you."

Indeed, a small crowd had built up around them, not too close, but forming a pretty determined wall around their little island of conversation. Amalie would not be able to take five steps without fetching up hard against a marlord or a clutch of serramarra.

"Of course," Amalie said. "I am most anxious to meet them all."

Almost as soon as she spoke the words, the two royal women were surrounded by nobility. Kirra was left shoulder to shoulder with Senneth, who was scanning the crowd with her usual efficient attention.

Kirra wondered if she had noticed that Romar Brendyn was twenty steps away talking with what she was sure was forced politeness to Mayva Nocklyn and her husband.

They were silent a moment, and then Senneth softly cursed. "This is a nightmare!" she said under her breath. "There are almost forty people in this room! Justin's outside the door but how could he even hack his way through the press of people if one of us screamed? I'm ten paces away from her and I couldn't get to her in time if someone put a dagger through her ribs."

"Who's going to attack her in this crowd?" Kirra demanded. "In front of half the Houses? You might be right to sleep beside her at night, but I can't think she's in danger in such a public place."

Senneth sighed. "I am not used to being responsible for anyone except myself," she said. "I always found it pretty easy to keep myself out of danger. I'm not sure how to protect someone else."

"I think you can relax here."

"Tayse would say a bodyguard cannot relax anywhere."

Kirra made a rude noise to indicate what she thought of Tayse. Senneth smiled and drew back a little to survey her.

"But don't you look lovely!" Senneth said. "I am used to being jealous of you for your beauty, but tonight I can only be awestruck."

"All Melly's work," Kirra said and added, "I like your dress." It was a deep metallic brown cut on simple lines. It offered just enough décolletage to show off Senneth's simple pendant, a gold disk wrapped in a sunburst filigree. "The color suits you."

"I've got a lot of dark tones in my wardrobe for this trip," Senneth said. "My way of appearing unobtrusive."

Kirra grinned. "All you have to do to remain unobtrusive is not set anything on fire."

"I can manage that. I think. If everyone else behaves."

They talked idly for a few more moments, Senneth's attention never straying far from the princess. It hadn't taken long, Kirra noted, for the young men of the gathering to make their way to Amalie's side; already, she was two deep in serramar and their cousins. Not a surprise, of course. She was the most eligible woman on the continent, and lovely besides. Kirra just hoped she was enjoying herself and not feeling overwhelmed by the sudden onslaught of attention. But the expression on Amalie's face was open and friendly. Her smile appeared to be one of genuine amusement.

Valri stood a few feet away, watching Amalie even more intently than Senneth. *What a strange woman,* Kirra thought. *I cannot bring myself to like her.*

A laughing voice sounding almost in her ear had the effect of turning her attention from the queen. "*There* you are!" a woman exclaimed. "I have been wanting to meet you all night."

It was Mayva Nocklyn, dressed in the height of fashion and showing a certain smugness on her round, pretty face. Beside her stood a tall, rather unpleasant-looking man wearing the Nocklyn colors. Kirra was fairly sure Casserah had never met either of them before, though Kirra was well acquainted with the flighty Mayva.

She gave the stiff and formal curtsey that Casserah reserved for the people she didn't like. "I don't think I know you," she said.

"No, indeed, I think you hardly know anybody!" Mayva

replied in her breathless voice. "I'm Mayva. Els Nocklyn's daughter, you know. My father's sick, so I go everywhere in his place. This is my husband, Lowell."

Kirra curtseyed again, and Lowell responded with a polite bow, but that wasn't good enough for Mayva. "Oh, silly, your sister and I are such good friends," Mayva said, taking Kirra's hands and leaning in to give her a kiss on the cheek. "It is so nice to meet you, serra."

Kirra was restraining the urgent impulse to scream as the touch of Mayva's palm brought fire to her hand. Mayva was wearing a moonstone ring and it was searing its way right through Kirra's flesh. Trying to disguise both her pain and her haste, Kirra pulled her hand free and hid it in the folds of her dress.

"Yes. Good to meet you both as well."

Mayva had taken her hand with its dangerous ornament and linked it through her husband's arm. He did not look as if he especially relished her affection. "I saw Kirra not four months ago," Mayva continued with another of her giddy laughs. "What hair that girl has! So gold and curly! But you're dark, like I am. I never saw two sisters who looked less alike."

"We have different mothers," Kirra replied in an unencouraging voice.

"And different—heritages," Mayva said, trying to sound delicate and succeeding only in sounding arch. "It must have been very strange, growing up with a sister who could do magic."

"As long as she didn't practice it on me, I didn't much care," Kirra said.

"And now she's not to be heir," Mayva said. "I hope that didn't make her too unhappy. Kirra was always the most light-hearted girl."

Kirra softened toward her a little, for that was actually kind, by Mayva's standards. Everyone else who had commented about the change in inheritance had seemed to be gloating over it. "She has taken the news very well," Kirra said. "I will always keep a place for her at Danan Hall, of course." She didn't feel like spending much more time talking about Kirra, so she made a quarter turn toward Senneth, who was definitely trying to fade into the background now. With a certain sense of malice, Kirra inquired, "Are you acquainted with Senneth Brassenthwaite? She's here in Princess Amalie's party."

Mayva almost gasped, she was so excited to come face-to-face with the returned serramarra. She dropped her husband's arm and made a deep curtsey, babbling the whole time about how exciting it was to finally meet her. Kirra was more interested in Lowell's reaction. His indifferent expression sharpened to one of narrowed speculation, and after he surfaced from his bow, he kept his gaze on Senneth's face. But, of course, Kirra thought. He was the cousin of Halchon Gisseltess, who wanted nothing so much as a marriage to Senneth. He would be storing up any details of this encounter to report back to the marlord currently under house arrest for possible plans of treason.

They made agonizing small talk about travel and weather until the butler announced dinner. Kirra was ready to offer thanks for her deliverance to the Wild Mother and any other god who might be watching over her. More beneficence: Mayva and Lowell were nowhere near her once they had all taken their seats at the six round tables set up in the room. But neither was Senneth, which was a disappointment.

But neither was Romar Brendyn, which was a relief.

It might be possible to get through the meal after all.

Kirra quickly assessed her own dinner companions: marlord Rafe Storian and his wife, whose name she could not remember, and his son, also unfortunately nameless; Seth Stowfer, cousin to the marlord of Merrenstow, and his two daughters; and Darryn Rappengrass, the youngest son of Ariane Rappengrass. Even Casserah knew Rafe and his family, Storian being the nearest neighbor to Danalustrous, and Kirra gave them all Casserah's version of a warm smile. More polite hellos to the nobles from Merrenstow.

It was an effort to restrain Kirra's real delight at seeing Darryn, a charming and handsome young man with whom she had enjoyed many a flirtation on a ballroom floor. He was seated to her right, while the Storian heir was on her left; the Stowfer girls were placed on either side of the two eligible young men. Eloise had put some thought into her table arrangements.

Darryn turned to Kirra before the first course had even been served and said, "It will break my heart if you tell me you do not remember me, serra Casserah."

Kirra's eyebrows rose in her sister's most common expression of uninterested surprise. "I hate to damage anyone's heart, but you'll have to remind me."

"Two summers ago, there was a ball at Rafe's place. We danced twice. You smiled once. I was in ecstasy."

Even Casserah would have smiled at that. "Then naturally I remember."

Servants came to their table and began to lay portions on the fine plates. Darryn leaned around one of them to ask, "What brings you so far out of familiar territory? You told me you hated to leave Danalustrous."

"My father thought it was time I attempted to be more sociable."

"And is the experience as bad as you feared it would be?"

"So far, about what I expected."

He grimaced. "Not good then. Your hopes cannot have been high."

Kirra lifted her water glass and took a meditative sip. Casserah almost never drank wine. "I find hope inconvenient," she replied. "But let us say I have not been disappointed."

Darryn laughed. Kirra had the feeling he was one of the few people in Gillengaria who would find Casserah genuinely diverting. "Well, let me know if there is something I can do to make your stay less horrible," he said.

"You could," Kirra answered, leaning closer. "Tell me who these people are."

He looked even more amused. "What? All of them?"

"I know Rafe Storian. I cannot remember anyone else's name."

"What about everyone else in the dining hall?"

"I don't have to make conversation with *them*."

So he whispered names to her and she thanked him gravely, and the rest of the meal proceeded smoothly enough. Toland—which happened to be the name of the serramar of Storian—turned out to be impossibly arrogant, a bit loutish, and desirous of a closer acquaintance with his near, powerful, and unmarried neighbor. Kirra would have handled him with her usual laughing ease, giving him no reason to suspect she disliked him, but Casserah was not quite so oblique. So she gave clipped answers to his sallies, refused to smile at his jokes, and offered no innocuous conversation to fill in any awkward moments in their conversation. Casserah was immune to awkward moments.

Most of the time, fortunately, talk at the small table was general. Marlady Clera Storian and the Stowfer girls wanted to gossip about the two most exciting and unexpected women in the room: the princess and Senneth. The topics were both so fruitful that even the men occasionally joined in.

First, Amalie. "Isn't she pretty? Shy, though."

"She looks so frail, don't you think?"

"That's just the color of her hair."

"Do you think the king is trying to find her a husband? That's why he's sending her out to all the balls of the season?"

"Oh, surely he has someone in mind already. Someone from the four corners, wouldn't you think?" The "four corners" always referred to the four most powerful Houses of Gillengaria: Brassenthwaite, Danalustrous, Gisseltess, and Fortunalt.

"Well, he'll *hardly* marry her to anyone in Gisseltess! What with all the fuss Halchon has raised. Though—I don't know—that might be the very thing to keep the peace."

"And there aren't any marriageable sons in Fortunalt or Danalustrous. But aren't one or two of the Brassenthwaite brothers still unwed?"

"Yes, he might be looking toward Brassenthwaite."

Which then reminded them of Senneth.

"I heard she was missing for seventeen years! Practically since the day I was *born*! And yet her brothers have taken her in and named her serramarra again."

"But she's—isn't she—a mystic? How could they possibly trust her? And who would marry her?"

"Yet the king trusts her—"

"These are terrible times. Sorceresses making pacts with the king. Strange women masquerading as queen. And a pale little girl next in line for the throne. It makes me uneasy at night, it does."

"I've begun wearing my moonstone to bed with me. It makes me feel safer."

"So have I! For a mystic can't harm you when you're protected by the Pale Mother."

"Coralinda Gisseltess has the right of it, in my opinion. Turn the mystics out. Burn them, if you have to. Destroy them all."

"That still leaves the problem of the succession."

"The king seems healthy enough."

"He's old. Do you really want to be ruled by that wisp of a girl?"

"There's Romar." That stiff observation came from Seth Stowfer, speaking up coldly to defend his kinsman. He'd been rather hot on the topic of mystics, though. "He will guide her."

Rafe Storian shook his head. "She needs a stronger hand. A good husband who can keep the Houses in order."

A squeal from one of the Stowfer girls. "Oooh, then you think she *is* attending the summer balls to find herself a husband—"

Kirra thought she might go mad if she had to sit there much longer listening to such talk, a mix of intolerance, speculation, and treason. Casserah, she thought, would surely have pushed herself away from the table and left the room.

Darryn caught her eye and smiled, then leaned a little closer to have what would pass for private communication. "Don't let it bother you," he said. "It's all just talk."

She gave him a cool look. "I cannot condone it."

"The same conversation is going on at every table in the room, in every dining hall in Gillengaria. People are uneasy and trying to decide what to do."

"They should look to their own lands and care for their own people. Then there will be no trouble."

"What if trouble comes anyway?" he asked sadly.

She remembered again Rappengrass's unfortunate placement on the southern edge of the continent, next to Fortunalt, not far from Gisseltess. No matter how loyal or isolationist Rappengrass might want to remain, it was likely to be sucked into any conflict.

"Where does Rappengrass stand?" she asked more bluntly than Kirra ever would.

Darryn nodded toward the central table, where Amalie sat. Senneth, Valri, and Eloise, the highest-ranking women present, filled out her table. Romar was beside his niece. Kirra had been doing her best not to give too much attention to that table during the course of the night. "Rappengrass is loyal to the crown," he said in a very soft voice. "But the crown needs to be loyal to Rappengrass in return."

"What does that mean?"

"Prove that Amalie is fit to rule. Make us believe that the crown is strong enough to withstand an insurrection. Show us some strength. Gather allies. Do not just sit back and wait upon events."

Kirra took another sip of her water. "I think that is why the king has sent his daughter and his regent to this place. For just those reasons."

"And is that why you are here as well?" he said, his voice even quieter. "To show solidarity? One never knows with Malcolm Danalustrous what his motives are."

She met his eyes. "Even I could not always tell you that."

He settled back in his chair, smiling a little at the rebuff, but not seeming offended. "My mother is preparing for war— I wonder if your father is," he said. "I think your sister swung by Rappengrass a few months ago to talk strategy with my mother. Maybe I should do the same with your father."

"We are always pleased to see you at Danan Hall."

He smiled again and seemed to forcibly lighten his mood. "And is your sister there? I always enjoy her company so much. One of the most delightful women of my acquaintance."

"She's a mystic," Casserah said flatly. "And haven't you been paying attention? Some of your friends would cut you cold if they thought you called such a woman your friend."

Darryn sighed and slumped a little in his chair. "At this point, I would boast of a friendship with Coralinda Gisseltess if I thought the Silver Lady had any power for healing," he said. "But as far as I know, that's not something the Daughters of the Pale Mother claim."

Kirra tilted her head a little to one side. "Are you sick?"

"Not me. My oldest sister's youngest girl. They think she's dying and there's nothing—" He made a gesture of helplessness.

Even Casserah would have showed sympathy at that. "What's her illness? What cures have you tried?"

"Some strange wasting disease. They call it red-horse fever. And we've had a dozen healers come to the house, but no one can do anything. The feeling is she'll be dead by summer's end."

"Darryn, I'm so sorry."

He nodded. "So, if Kirra were here, I'd beg her to come

visit my niece. I know she's got some magical healing powers in her hands. I wouldn't care if the Pale Mother damned me to some eternal hell if I could only keep that little girl alive."

Kirra felt absolutely wretched—the more so because even if she had been in her own body, she would have been unable to offer him any comfort. "I've heard of this fever," she said. "I have not heard of anyone recovering from it. I'm sorry."

"Small problems in the middle of big ones," he said. "But sometimes they seem to matter more."

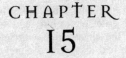

CHAPTER
15

FINALLY, the sad, infuriating, confusing, interminable meal was at an end. The guests slowly rose and chattered their way into a salon just a short hallway from the dining room. Kirra was watching the placement of the guests, so she saw Romar escort his niece into the room, smiling down at her with an obvious affection. Amalie laughed as she talked with him, more animated than Kirra had yet seen her. So Romar Brendyn was kind to his dead sister's daughter. One more thing about him that a person could not help but admire.

They hadn't been in the salon three minutes, however, before Romar was supplanted by younger men, all eager to make themselves attractive to the princess. Kirra found an unoccupied seat beside a Coravann matron, accepted a cup of tea, and continued to watch the drama while pretending to listen to the conversation nearer at hand. Toland Storian seemed to be among the most determined of the suitors, continually elbowing aside less single-minded rivals to position himself at Amalie's left hand. Darryn Rappengrass flirted with her for a few moments and moved on. Maybe seven other young men came and went, or came and lingered, during the thirty minutes that Kirra watched.

It was that long before she thought to look for Senneth, and even then she had to concentrate to locate her standing just outside the circle of eligible men. Pulling that invisibility trick again. So no one would distract her from her primary duty of guarding Amalie, or so she didn't have to engage in the inane conversation that she despised even more than Casserah did? Kirra grinned and sipped her tea.

It was easier to spot Valri, a bit farther from the assiduous beaux but making no effort to hide and very little effort to hold up her part of the conversation with Seth Stowfer. Romar, on the other hand, had disappeared. Surely he had not been rude enough to leave the gathering altogether? No—fifteen minutes later she saw him enter the room again with some degree of stealth, stepping inside through a side door that led, if she remembered her house geography, to a hallway that fed into the garden.

Kirra grinned. Senneth and Casserah and Romar Brendyn should form their own private club of Nobles Who Hate Social Gatherings. They could all sneak out together, enjoy a little night air and a general moratorium on conversation, before slipping back inside to attempt to remain civil for another hour or two of vapid discussion. Surely Amalie could survive that long without any of them watching over her? They might even let Valri join their organization, since her expression clearly showed she wasn't enjoying herself in the slightest and she'd never demonstrated much inclination for meaningless chatter in the past.

Kirra thought she might have more fun at the party if something interesting happened. A fight, perhaps. A raelynx loose on the premises. One of the Riders striding in to accuse someone of treason. She sat there a few minutes, seriously considering what diversion she might create, before concluding that no one, not even her friends, would thank her for making the evening any more difficult.

Instead she made some innocuous comment to the women sitting nearby and rose to get her teacup replenished. Maybe her unspoken prayer for excitement had been granted by one of the capricious gods; maybe she just got careless. When she turned around with a fresh cup in her hands, Romar Brendyn was standing right beside her.

"I've been waiting all night for someone to introduce me, but no one has," he said. "So I thought I would be bold enough to approach you on my own. I'm Romar Brendyn. I believe you're Casserah Danalustrous."

He took her hand and bowed, his dark blond hair tumbling around his shoulders. When he straightened, he gave her a very direct look, making no attempt to hide his curiosity.

She did not allow her hand to rest in his, though she wanted to. She was concentrating very hard on being Casserah. "I am," she said coolly. "Next you will tell me some tale of your great friendship with my sister."

He almost laughed. "I would, except I sense such a comment might be unwelcome."

"It's practically the only conversation I've had all night."

"Would you rather I reviled her? That's not usually how I introduce myself to relatives of people I know, but I can try to accommodate."

Kirra was amused; Casserah would have been, too. "Thank you, but I think I know her faults. Can we choose another subject?"

"I'm not much of a courtier," he said. "Most of my topics tend to be grim. I'd happily hear about Danalustrous, though, if that's something you'd like to talk about."

Kirra smiled. Neatly done. Nothing else could have been better calculated to appeal to Casserah. Slowly they edged away from the tea table and slowly began to walk a circuit of the room. "Why, it is the most beautiful land in the world," she said, her voice almost playful. "No place can compare."

She spoke at length about the architecture of the Hall, the ancient history of the family, the primary trading ventures, the lifestyle contrast between lands along the coastline and estates in the interior farmland, and whatever else occurred to her. She knew she should ask about Merrenstow in return, but she didn't want him to describe his own holdings, mention his wife, reveal his plans for having children and leading a life of domestic bliss.

"I can see you love it very much," he said when she finished up. "I'm surprised your father could convince you to leave."

"He offered me an interesting bargain."

"I hear all bargains with Malcolm Danalustrous are interesting."

She laughed. "I am just as surprised to see you outside the confines of Merrenstow," she said. "But perhaps you have taken extra precautions to ensure your safety this time when you traveled."

For a moment, anger molded his face, fierce enough to make her regret the careless words. But it seemed he was not directing his fury at her. "Yes, I half think the intent of my botched abduction was to make me fearful and uncertain," he said. "And a man afraid is a useless man. I do not intend to be useless."

Their perambulations had taken them to the shadow of a huge plant set on a tall marble base. Its leaves were just at hand height, so Kirra lifted her fingers and began toying with the greenery. "A man afraid is not always useless," she said. "I have seen men accomplish great things even in the grip of fear. The trick is not to let fear stop you."

He smiled. "The trick is not to let anything stop you."

She slipped the wide waxy leaves through her fingers the way she would tease Donnal's ears when he was in dog shape. Strange that she would think of Donnal at precisely this moment. "Nothing?" she repeated. "That's a little ruthless. What lengths would you go to in order to achieve a goal?"

He seemed to consider. "It would depend upon the goal. If it was something I wanted, a personal challenge, a desire to fulfill, I would go to extraordinary lengths. I would be reckless at times, foolish at times, cunning when I could be. But I wouldn't mortgage my future. I wouldn't throw away everything I had or risk the lives and happiness of the people I cared about." His brown eyes focused intently on her again. He had a habit of doing that, as if to check that she was paying absolute attention to whatever he had to say. "But if it were something I believed was right? Something to do with justice or morality or the fate of the kingdom itself? Nothing would stop me. I would jeopardize everything, everyone. I wouldn't care what else I lost."

Kirra dropped her hand and began her slow promenade again. Romar fell in step beside her, his hands clasped behind his back. She liked his specific height next to her own, the bulk and proportions of his body. He was perhaps five inches taller than Casserah, solid, hard-muscled. She was so used to Donnal at her side, so much slimmer, so sleek, almost exactly her height and weight.

"You speak like a passionate man," she said in Casserah's unruffled voice.

"You have passion of your own, though you reserve it for Danalustrous," he said. "I know enough of your father to know there is nothing he wouldn't do for his land. I'm guessing you're cast in the same mold, though you seem so cool."

She couldn't help but smile at that. "It is easiest to care only about one thing," she said. "That way, your choices are always already made."

"Make sure you care about the right thing then," he said.

She stopped right there in the middle of the floor, with no column or potted plant or other physical marker to give them a reason to come to a halt. "You're speaking of Gillengaria," she said.

He nodded. "Don't choose Danalustrous over the kingdom," he said.

"As you would not choose Merrenstow?"

He shook his head. "My first duty is to Amalie."

Her voice was so soft it might be possible he couldn't hear it. "Shouldn't your first duty be to your family?"

But he did. "My wife understands," he said. "I am a regent before I am a husband. At least as long as I am regent."

"Were I your wife," she said, unable to believe the words were coming from her mouth, "I would not be so pleased to be relegated to second place."

"Were I your husband," he retorted, "I could say the same thing."

It was so unexpected that she laughed out loud. Several heads turned as people craned their necks to look in their direction. Kirra couldn't keep her amusement in check. "We have provided the evening's entertainment," she said merrily. "No one else has said anything the least bit funny and now they will all be dying to know what we talked about."

He gave her a little bow; she could tell by that he realized it was time to mingle a little more, not give quite so much attention to one unmarried woman. "We can answer quite honestly," he said. "We talked about the land we love so well."

JUST when it seemed possible the evening might never end, it was over. A clock somewhere chimed the midnight hour, and

Eloise was caught yawning in someone's face. "Forgive me!" she exclaimed. "I think it must be time for me to seek my bed."

Thus released, the whole crowd headed slowly for the halls and began a general dissolution. Kirra, the first of her own group to step through the door, saw Justin still standing there very alertly, ready to leap into action. She did not acknowledge him and he did not give any sign that he knew her, but it wouldn't have been strange if she'd stared. Half the other guests did, noting his sober face, his visible weaponry, and the gold lions splashed across his black sash. Then they leaned over to murmur to someone else in the crowd. *King's Rider. Here to watch over the princess. Can you imagine that Baryn would not think she was safe even here?* But the display of power and wealth impressed them. Those were the two things the aristocracy valued most in the world.

Kirra could not resist peering over her shoulder once to see that Justin had fallen in step behind Amalie and Valri. Senneth, a few paces back, struggled to end a conversation with some lesser lord. Eventually they had thinned down to their own particular party as they climbed enough stairwells and turned down enough corridors to reach the wing where they were all housed. Kirra figured there might be a council of sorts in Amalie's room, so she passed her own door and waited for the others outside of Amalie's.

Tayse stood there on guard. He did not smile as they approached, merely gave a brief nod and said, "Let me check the room before you enter."

Amalie stopped obediently in the hall. "I'm exhausted," Valri said, continuing on toward her own door. "I'll see you in the morning."

Senneth sagged against the wall. "And to think we have dozens more nights like this ahead of us." She sighed. "How will I endure it?"

Amalie gave a shy smile. "I had a good time," she said. "Everyone was so nice to me."

Senneth smiled back. "They would be fools not to be. Was there anyone in particular you enjoyed talking to?"

"Oh—everyone," Amalie said.

Kirra hoped the princess's conversation had been a little more lively when she was interacting with her subjects.

Tayse emerged. "The room is secure. Her maid said no one has come to the door except some servants with fuel and hot water."

"Thank you," Amalie said, and stepped past him into the room.

And screamed.

Kirra had never seen anyone move as fast as Tayse did, plunging back through the door. She and Senneth and Justin were hard on his heels. She could catch a babble of conversation—Amalie's questions, the maid's hysterical responses—but the first thing she noticed when she got inside was that there was no blood. Tayse hadn't killed an intruder. Indeed, the Rider had dropped his sword hand and released all the menace from his pose. He was just staring at the bed.

Where a black dog was sitting on the counterpane, tongue hanging out, tail thumping against the covers.

"Donnal," Tayse said, sheathing his sword. Behind her, Kirra heard Justin do the same. "A very good trick."

"But how did he get in here?" Amalie asked, bewildered. The maid was still crying but no one was paying her much attention. Senneth crossed the room and sat beside Donnal, putting her arms around his neck. She was laughing. Amalie added, "Didn't you just check the room?"

"I did and—"

"What's wrong? What's happened?" The fresh voice belonged to Valri as she burst through the door. It was clear she was instantly puzzled by the casual atmosphere inside. "Why did she scream?"

Senneth spoke. "She was startled by the appearance of the dog. We didn't realize he was in the room."

Valri's attention transferred to Donnal, but she was confused. "Whose dog is that?" She looked around and found Kirra. "Is it yours? It looks like the one who traveled with us from Ghosenhall. Why is it in Amalie's room?"

Oh, Bright Mother burn me, Kirra thought. "He's not a dog, he's a mystic. A shape-changer," she said in a voice she hoped sounded reasonable. "We were trying to decide how safe the princess's room was, and Donnal said he thought it could be breached by a shiftling. And he's just proven that it can."

Valri digested this quickly. She seemed completely

unconcerned with the news about the shape-changer in their midst. "So how do we protect against an assault by a shiftling who means her harm?"

"I will stay in the room beside her," Senneth said. "A Rider will stand guard outside the door. I don't know that we can do more than that." She glanced at Donnal. "I believe I would be able to overcome a shiftling, even in a desperate fight."

Donnal barked at that and wagged his tail again. Kirra interpreted that as meaning *I wouldn't be so sure of myself, serra,* but Senneth merely smiled. "And Donnal agrees with me," she said smoothly.

Valri lifted her hands to her cheeks. It was the first time Kirra had ever seen her distraught. "This is so dangerous," she said. "I wonder if we should go back to Ghosenhall."

Amalie went over and put her arms around Valri's shoulders. Amalie was just of medium height, but Valri was small next to her. Amalie might almost have been an adult comforting a child. "Nothing has happened, Valri," she said. "No one has attacked me. They're only trying to discover ways someone *could* hurt me. I'd rather Senneth found these ways first and considered how to protect me."

"Keep Donnal in the princess's room," Tayse suggested. "He might sense any danger before it comes creeping through the windows." He looked at Donnal. "Or the walls. Or wherever he came from."

"He was probably in the room when you went in to look," Kirra said. "Spider or something small hidden on the bedspread. He can change so fast you can't follow the motions."

Tayse glanced at her. "I remember."

Amalie was gazing rather doubtfully at Donnal. "But—he's really a man? You want him to sleep in my room with me?"

Kirra had to choke down a wild desire to laugh. It was all she could do to keep from exclaiming, "Yes, he'll sleep right beside you on the bed. You'll be delighted at how warm he'll keep you." She was fairly certain that Donnal, and probably Senneth, could read what was in her mind.

"Perhaps not," Senneth said.

Donnal jumped to his feet, gave Kirra one pained look, and melted into a small, round, feathered shape. Hunting owl. Kirra crossed the room to open the closed shutter, and Donnal

sailed soundlessly past her, circled once, and returned to land
on the stone sill of the window. Kirra closed the shutter again.

"He'll guard you all night," she said. "I think you can feel
fairly confident that no one else will slip into your room."

Valri dropped her hands. Her green eyes stood out in stark
contrast to her deathly pale skin. "Thank you. You seem to
have taken very effective measures. Thank you."

Kirra held her arm out to shepherd Valri toward the door.
"Come, majesty," she said. "Time for us all to get some sleep."

Although, Kirra reflected later that night as she lay in bed,
she herself wasn't entirely happy at the turn of events. No
more Donnal to warm her back. No more Donnal to watch *her*
every move, make certain *Kirra* was always safe. She was not
so certain she liked his loyalty being diverted elsewhere; she
was a little surprised that he had so readily agreed to Tayse's
suggestion. Then again, she had been just about to make the
same suggestion herself, and he certainly would have obeyed
her instructions.

She huddled under her blankets and thought the early summer air was a little too cool and wondered how everyone else
fell asleep so easily when they were solitary in their beds.

CHAPTER
16

THE next two days were much like the first one, but worse because there were the daylight hours to get through as well. Amalie was in high demand for breakfasts, afternoon teas, strolls through the gardens, and excursions into the shopping district of the city that bordered the court. She seemed happy to be invited anywhere and to attend any function. Senneth, managing to look both expressionless and grim, naturally accompanied her on any outing, with at least one Rider always trailing. Sometimes Donnal accompanied them in a variety of guises. Sometimes he stayed behind.

On the afternoon of the second day, Kirra found Donnal napping on the floor at Justin's feet, outside the door to Amalie's room. Cammon was sprawled across the hall, telling a story that, to judge by Justin's face, wasn't entirely interesting.

"The princess is sleeping," Justin informed her.

"Do you feel competent to keep her safe for a few hours if I take Donnal somewhere with me?"

Justin just grinned and didn't answer. "I'll stay and help keep watch," Cammon offered.

"Excellent," she said. She toed Donnal awake. He yawned and came to his feet, then stretched his back and legs. "Oh, you're getting used to this life of leisure," she said. "You won't be any good to me at all anymore."

Naturally, he made no answer to that, but his expression fairly closely imitated Justin's grin.

"Let's go for a walk," she said. He followed her down the many halls and stairwells till they were out and rambling through the surrounding grounds. It took some effort to find an area so remote it wasn't patrolled by guards or frequented by visitors, but finally they located a shadowy, tree-lined path that no one else had discovered that day.

"Finally," Kirra muttered. "Hold up a moment."

She stopped and shut her eyes, concentrating for a minute on the details of her body. Arms just so, skin just this weight— but these shall stretch to wings and this shall ruffle to feathers. When she opened her eyes, the world had changed colors and proportions, and her own body was light as a puff of air.

Donnal had changed right alongside her, and now they were both summer songbirds, fashioned of such bright colors and sweet melodies that they seemed constructed of joy. Donnal twisted his head and asked a question in a strange twittering tongue, and she replied, and simultaneously they flung themselves into the rippled blue-and-white sky. Sunlight and motion and the sheer delight of existence buoyed them on their flight. Kirra could not even sense the effort of moving her wings, of gauging the air currents, estimating distances. She merely was, and was happy.

They chased each other through the afternoon, pausing two or three times at one of Eloise Kianlever's ornamental fountains to splash in the water. Kirra spotted a marmalade cat crouched beside one of the fountains, poised to spring, and she let loose an undignified screech and tore into flight again. That would be a scandal, a tragedy, a ridiculous way to end her disorganized life, as dinner for a house cat at one of the Twelve Houses. She had always wondered what would happen to her if she was killed or severely injured while in another shape. Would she revert to her true form or die as she was, incapable of calling up magic? She wondered if the same worry had factored into her father's decision to name Casserah as his heir. *Serramarra Kirra has disappeared. There is no trace of her body anywhere to be found. . . .*

But such dark thoughts couldn't long be entertained in such a small and giddy brain. Donnal dropped to a rosebush and she settled beside him, happy to look for aphids or ladybugs or anything that might resemble an afternoon snack. Song trilled out of her, a few notes that might have meant something, though she didn't know what. Donnal replied in the same language, and she almost understood him. He could have been naming her his soulmate, his lifelong companion. He could have been calling her attention to some tasty grubs wrestling in the dirt. It was all the same. It was all about the present moment, this brief and sun-kissed second of life. She hopped from the bush to the grass below and scratched at the dirt with a dainty claw.

They played all afternoon and it was Donnal who reminded her that there was another life to go back to. One minute he was beside her on a tree limb, chattering inconsequently, the next minute he had dropped to the ground and bulked into a dark, silken, ferocious shape. She was actually startled for a moment and chirped her alarm. Then she realized that he wasn't a bird, he was a dog. He was *Donnal* who was a dog, and she wasn't a bird, either. She was human.

So she opened her wings and drifted down, and the foot that she placed lightly on the ground was human and shod in embroidered leather. She stretched and shivered and extended her arms to remind her of their proper length, then she shook her head to remember the weight of her hair against her back. The dog sat and watched her, its head cocked to one side, a single ear back in a quizzical expression.

"What?" she asked. "Is my hair all mussed? Do I have feathers on my back?"

He barked once, and when she still didn't understand, reared up on his hind legs and put his front feet on her hips. Another bark, then he whined, and nudged at her hand with his cold nose. She giggled and caught his paws so he didn't scratch her.

"Donnal! What is it? You have to be more explicit."

He squirmed in her hold and licked at her forearm. She laughed and dropped him back to the ground. "Casserah would never put up with that—" she started. And then she froze. Reached up a hand to tug on a lock of her own hair.

Gold. Curly. She had reverted to Kirra.

Trembling just a little, she focused, finished the transformation to her sister's shape. She could not remember a time she had ever forgotten the form she was supposed to return to.

Then again, she rarely went so long disguised as another creature, and perhaps her body had simply longed for its own familiar contours. But she knew that wasn't it. She had spent the afternoon playing with Donnal, both of them in a primitive, elemental form. That was what she was used to considering as the constant reality of her life; that was what she envisioned when she had to picture her own soul. She had been Kirra while she had been a bird beside Donnal on a rosebush. She had only changed shapes as she returned to human form. She had not changed who she was.

AMALIE'S door was guarded by one of the Riders she didn't know, so Kirra took a chance and went to Senneth's room. Yes—there they all were—Cammon and Tayse and Justin lounging on the bed and playing a card game; Senneth sitting in the window seat staring out at Eloise's front lawn. Donnal had followed her into the room and plopped down with a sigh on the floor beside the bed. Kirra went to sit beside Senneth.

"What's this?" Kirra said. "You've dared to leave Amalie alone?"

"Valri's with her and they're discussing something highly secret. Also, I think the princess wanted a chance to bathe without me looming over her. I think she's a little shy around me."

"She doesn't realize that you're used to bathing in rivers and streambeds—if you get a chance to bathe at all."

Senneth smiled somewhat reluctantly. "No, I have been much more civilized on this particular jaunt. I've actually combed my hair every day."

"So why do you look so gloomy?" Kirra was just as happy to learn that someone else was having a bad day. It would distract her from her own.

"Thinking. Not sure what to do." Kirra waited and Senneth eventually continued. "I don't really believe Amalie's in danger here. Even if we weren't taking such fanatical precautions, I think she'd be perfectly safe. But I—I would like to make clear how far we would go to protect her. I can't figure out how to do that."

Justin spoke over his shoulder; the room was small enough

that everyone could hear their conversation. "Set someone on fire," he said. "That usually does it."

"Ooh, can it be Justin?" Kirra squealed.

"I would," Senneth said, "but something would have to provoke me."

"Justin always provokes *me*."

Senneth gave her a repressive look from her gray eyes. "You would be more helpful if you took this seriously."

"Seriously, I'd like you to set Justin on fire."

Tayse lifted his eyes from the cards in his hand. "Has anyone behaved inappropriately to the princess?"

Senneth considered. "Most of them have been very respectful. The one I dislike the most, for no real reason, is Toland Storian. He sits too close. He's always touching her—putting his hand on her arm to get her attention or playing with the ribbons on her dress. I asked her, and she said she's not afraid of him, but he's the one I'd most expect to cross the line."

Cammon discarded. "All the housemaids hate him," he said.

There was a short silence while everyone looked at him. He glanced up, surprised. "What? They do. Apparently he's got a history of forcing himself on them when they're in the kitchens or the hallways."

"There's your villain," Kirra said.

"Yes, but I can hardly punish him for overpowering an abigail on the back stairwell."

"Really?" Justin said. "It's just the sort of thing that I'd expect to bring out your vengeful side."

Senneth bit her lip and tried not to laugh. "I meant, and make a point about Amalie."

Kirra pursed her lips and tapped them with her finger. "I wonder . . ." she said. "Maybe I could push him a little."

Now Senneth grinned outright. "I've always thought of Casserah as the type who could defend herself. Mystic or no."

"I might take some other shape. Let me think a minute."

Her hand was still before her face; Senneth reached out and caught her gently by the wrist. "What happened here? Did you burn yourself?"

Kirra let her examine the raised red welt, then pulled her hand away. "Oh, that was Mayva. Her moonstone brushed against my skin."

Now Senneth was concerned. "That's not going to be the

only time someone's going to touch you with a moonstone. Half the people here are dripping with them—which I noticed to my dismay our very first evening."

"I know," Kirra said. "I'm a little worried about it. And tomorrow at the ball—dancing—if a man's wearing a moonstone ring and has his hand at my waist—well, it's a very odd serramarra who yelps every time someone puts his arms around her."

"And you'll look even odder if you're all covered with welts," Senneth added.

"That I can take care of," Kirra said. She made a fist, and the red marks smoothed away. "No one will even notice—unless I make a fuss when I acquire them." She let the magic fade and the marks reappeared.

Cammon stood up, tossed his cards to the middle of the bed, and crossed to the window seat. Falling to a crouch, he took Kirra's blemished hand in his. "Let me see that."

Kirra shared a startled look with Senneth. "So you're a healer now?" she asked.

"No," he said absently and turned her wrist this way and that. Justin and Tayse had put down their cards and twisted on the bed to watch. Donnal sat up and gently panted. "Well, then," Cammon said after a few moments, and frowned as if in great concentration. The rest of them looked at each other, looked at him, tried not to laugh. No one said anything. Kirra could feel a strange sensation dance along her wristbone and up her arm, and for a moment her whole body felt odd, as if she was standing outside just as a thunderstorm was about to pass through. Then all the hair on her body smoothed down again, and Cammon released her. "There you go," he said.

She said cautiously, "There I go what?"

"I don't think you'll feel it now. A moonstone will still scald you, so you need to be careful, but at least you won't feel it when it happens."

Again Kirra looked silently at Senneth. "Well, let's just try that," she said and held her arm out. Senneth stripped off her bracelet and laid it across Kirra's flesh.

Nothing. Cool textures of metal and smooth gem against her skin. Kirra felt a little shiver go up her back. "That's awfully strange," she said, trying to keep her voice normal.

Cammon pushed the bracelet off so it fell into Senneth's

lap. "But be *careful*," he repeated. "See, you're getting a mark already."

Senneth was watching him very closely. "When did you learn this particular trick?" she asked. "I can't imagine it's in Jerril's repertoire. Have you been studying with someone else in Ghosenhall?"

He looked surprised. Kirra thought that surprise was probably the expression most often to be found on Cammon's face. Surprise or happiness. "No, I just thought it was something I might be able to do," he said. "You know, divert her mind."

Senneth continued to watch him. Justin snorted and picked up his cards again. "Good thing *we're* the ones who found him in Dormas," he said. "I'd hate to have him working for the king's enemies."

"What else can you do?" Senneth asked very softly.

Cammon shrugged. "I don't know. A lot of stuff, I guess. Ask me something."

"I will—when I can think of the right questions," she said. "But Justin's right. We need to make sure you're always *our* friend."

Again, surprise on Cammon's face. "Of course you'll always be my friends. I don't even have any other friends."

"You would if anyone knew what you could do," Tayse said. He was sorting through a fresh hand, aligning cards, and he seemed completely unfazed. For a man who, just six months ago, had distrusted mystics with all the considerable force of his personality, Tayse seemed remarkably at ease with them now, Kirra thought. It wasn't just because he loved Senneth. It was because he had decided mystics were just another weapon, like a sword or a bow, and he figured he had a pretty good arsenal lined up. For Tayse, everything came back to strategy and strength.

Justin looked back at Cammon. "So are you playing or not? Since you're our friend, I dealt you in."

Cammon scrambled to his feet and launched himself toward the bed. Kirra and Senneth exchanged glances again. This time, Kirra was laughing. "Hey, you're the one who found him," she said.

"And what a good day that was," Senneth said with a sigh. "So what's your plan? Do you have one?"

"I think tonight. After the dinner. Doesn't Eloise have some game organized where we break into teams and perform skits?"

Senneth rolled her eyes. "I cannot imagine how I will get through that."

"I think Toland Storian might be induced to behave a little too rambunctiously with the princess. You might need to rescue her with sharp words or—who knows?—some kind of display. You might warn the princess that things are going to get ugly."

Senneth was regarding her soberly. "And how exactly are you going to induce him to be stupid?"

Kirra laughed. This was the fun part. It was about time something in Kianlever was fun. "That's my problem. Don't you worry."

In fact, it was ridiculously easy. One of her dinner partners that night was a young lord from Tilt named Raegon, who was about as cocky as Toland Storian. In fact, the two young men were fast friends, and Kirra had seen them taunt each other into disreputable behavior a couple of times during this visit. She—well, Casserah—had not been particularly friendly to Raegon so far, but this night she made an effort to charm him in Casserah's sleepy, beguiling way. She watched him from those wide-set blue eyes, an enigmatic smile on her face, and refused to give him complete answers when he asked her a direct question.

"Red and silver hell," he exclaimed under his breath at one point. "You're the strangest girl. Is it always this hard to talk to you?"

"So don't talk to me," she said, and then she laughed at him. "Though *I* like talking to *you*."

He glanced quickly around the table, as if suddenly remembering their conversation could be audited by six other people. "Maybe you'll be easier to understand when there aren't so many people around," he said.

"Maybe," she agreed, and sipped from her water glass, watching him over the rim. "There's a game tonight. After the dinner. I don't know if it will be that interesting."

He nodded, his mouth pulling back in a wide and rather

frightening smile. Kirra wondered if Cammon would know whether this man enjoyed forced liaisons with the servants, too. "I'm sure it won't be," he said.

So they had a rendezvous out in the gardens, a few hedge-rows over from the windows of the dining hall so no one would witness them. Kirra saw no way to prevent him from kissing her, not if she wanted this little caper to work. As he took her in a clumsy and rather drunken embrace, she spared a moment to hope no one else was wandering the gardens tonight for a little late-night breath of air. Romar Brendyn, for instance, who snuck out every evening for a break from the crowds and the vapidity. She closed her eyes and concentrated on the un-pleasant feel of Raegon's mouth pressing hard against hers, and she ran her hand in a kind of caress along the smooth silk of his jacket.

He pulled back from her abruptly, one hand to his mouth, one hand to his stomach. "Sorry," he mumbled. "I think—damnation—all of a sudden my stomach—serra, I believe I'm going to be sick."

He was, all over one of Eloise's prized rosebushes, and more than once. Kirra fluttered nearby, offering phrases of sympathy and helplessness. She'd never really used her powers of healing in reverse before, making the body turn against it-self in a moment of deep revulsion, and she hoped she hadn't been too enthusiastic. Then again, Raegon had had about a bottle and a half of wine with dinner; it would probably do him some good to expel some of that alcohol.

"I think you'd better go back to your room, ser," she said, trying to sound concerned. "Shall I have Eloise send someone to you? There must be someone at the house with knowledge of herbs and healing."

He wrenched himself upright and staggered toward the door. "No—I'd rather be alone—in my misery," he gasped out. "I apologize, Casserah. I will feel—foolish—tomorrow."

"Just go to your room," she said. "Tomorrow will take care of itself."

He nodded, rested for a moment with his hand on the wall, then stumbled through the door and inside.

It was a matter of a few moments to transform herself into Raegon, silk jacket, insolent smile, and all. Imitating his self-important swagger, she sauntered back into the house, found the salon where the guests were gathered, and looked around.

The diners had already been divided into groups of about ten people, and each group was clustered together, arguing over some plan. Kirra was not surprised to see Toland Storian and three or four other young lords had been assigned—or had appropriated—places in Amalie's circle. Senneth and Valri hovered nearby, watching but not participating. Valri sat in a chair a few feet from Amalie and observed her with that usual unnerving attention. Senneth stood against the wall and practically blended into the stone and brickwork. Kirra grinned. Not for long.

She strolled over to join her supposed friends. "I missed the explanation, whatever it was," she said, her voice a low drawl. "What's the game?"

Toland gave her a grin; the others ignored her. "We need to come up with a skit," he said, "to act out a word. We're trying to decide on our word."

"I think it should be hard to guess," Amalie said. "If no one guesses, we win a prize."

"I think it should be an easy word," Toland said.

"Here's an easy word," Kirra said, still in that sneering drawl. "How about *dance*?"

And she surprised the princess by pulling her into Raegon's arms and twirling her once around. There was a moment when Amalie looked disconcerted, but then her face smoothed out. She freed herself and stepped back. "That one is *too* easy," she said.

"We need a word with several parts," said one of the other young lords. "Like *waterfall*. We could act that out in two sections."

Toland mimed slipping and falling to the floor. "Like that?"

"Yes, but what would we do for *water*?" Kirra asked.

"Maybe we need something that would be really hard to guess," Amalie said. "Like *counterfeit*."

"Are they giving prizes for things that are impossible?" someone inquired.

"I think it should be an easy word," Toland said.

Kirra gave him a nudge. "Like what? Got a word in mind?"

He grinned at her. "Like *drink*." He downed his glass of wine, set it on a table, and motioned a servant to refill it.

"Like *curtsey*," Kirra said, attempting the maneuver while wearing trousers, which caused a general laugh.

"Like *smile*," said Toland.

"Like *kiss*," Kirra suggested.

It was the word they had all been circling around, and there was a nervous, speculative laugh from the men. "Shouldn't it be something harder than that?" Amalie asked.

Kirra was smirking at Toland, poking him in the side. "So? *Kiss*? What do you think? How would we act that out?"

He grinned back, tossing his head a little. "You just want to start trouble."

"I just want to play the game! Asking you a simple question. How would you act it out? Can you think of a way?"

A certain deviltry crept into Toland's expression. "Well, let's see. I'd take someone's hand—" He caught Amalie's fingers in his. Her face registered just a faint touch of alarm. "And I'd pull her closer to me—"

"I don't think I like this word," Amalie said. She put her free hand against his chest and pushed. But Toland was the sort of man who rather liked a little struggle, and her rejection just made him hold her closer.

"And I'd put my hand under her chin—" he said, suiting action to the words and dropping his mouth very close to hers. "And then—"

"Toland, don't," Amalie pleaded. "Everyone is staring."

"Then I'd kiss her."

Then he kissed her.

Then he caught on fire.

Shrieking, he flung the princess away; she stumbled into Valri's arms. Still screaming, he beat at the flames on his chest, his thighs, with hands that were also on fire. Flames licked from his hair, down his spine. He spun from side to side, waving his arms, crying, but all his friends backed away from him, stunned, horrified. Everyone else in the room pressed closer, staring or calling out in panic or covering their eyes and turning away. Kirra didn't even see Tayse drive through the crowd, but suddenly there he was, sword tip held directly to Toland's burning throat.

As abruptly as the blaze had started, it went out. For a moment there was dead silence except for the sound of Toland's hard breathing, edged with a whimper. Kirra could see the singe marks on his shirt and shoes, but his skin looked whole, unharmed. He had not been hurt, merely terrified.

Senneth stood before him, her face cold as dead coals. "Never. Touch. The princess. Again," she said, dropping each word like a separate stone. "You—" She swept her icy gaze around the other men standing nearby, stupefied and blank. "Any of you—" She pulled back and sent a look that covered everyone in the room. "Anyone. If you harm her, if you touch her without her permission, you are dead."

Not a soul in the entire room moved or spoke. Toland stood absolutely immobile, his eyes flicking desperately between Senneth, on his right, and Tayse, inches away from him with a blade to his throat. Clearly he was afraid to even take a deep breath. "I won't," he whispered. "I didn't—I was only playing."

"Find someone else to play with," Senneth said.

"Yes. Serra. I'm sorry. Serra."

Senneth watched him another long moment, then gave a sharp nod. Tayse sheathed his sword, offered a small bow that could have been directed at Senneth, Amalie, or even Toland, and spun around. The crowd parted for him as he strode back to the door.

Senneth gave her own little acknowledgment to the entire room, an abbreviated curtsey. "Sorry to disrupt your game," she said in a cool voice. "Please, continue."

And she stepped back against the wall again and commenced to try for invisibility. Harder to pull off when everyone was still staring at her, but she did manage to look much less dangerous than she had a few moments ago. Toland's friends closed around him in a murmuring circle. By the time Toland thought to look for Raegon a few minutes later, Kirra had already hidden behind a column and transformed herself to Casserah.

She stepped briskly up to Amalie and inspected the girl's flushed face. "That was an edifying scene," she said in Casserah's cool voice. "Would you like to come sit quietly by me for a while? I'm not sure you'll enjoy the rest of the game."

Indeed, Toland and the men of her party had completely turned their backs on the princess and looked unlikely to even speak to her for the rest of the night—perhaps ever. Valri seemed relieved to see Amalie trail off behind Casserah, in every way an acceptable chaperone. The queen turned to ask Senneth a question. Kirra saw Senneth laugh and nod.

Kirra found a few unoccupied chairs grouped together and pulled Amalie down beside her. Everyone sitting nearby hastily cleared out. Kirra smiled; Amalie looked wistful.

"Now no one will even speak to me for the rest of the time I'm here," the princess said. "They'll be afraid of what Senneth will do."

"You're in a difficult situation," Kirra admitted. "But that's something you have to remember. You're not like other girls. You cannot mingle freely. You always have to realize that you're different and you could be in danger."

Amalie gave her a very direct look from those huge dark eyes. "It sounds very lonely."

"I imagine it will be."

"I've been lonely so long. I thought it would be different now."

The words caught Kirra completely by surprise. Had she been herself, she would have leaned in and hugged the woebegone princess. But Casserah would never have done such a thing. "It may yet be different," she said. "You have a chance now to make real friends. But you have to make them with a great deal of care. Not everyone you will meet from here on out is to be trusted. Not everyone will have your best interests at heart."

"How will I ever know?"

"You can always trust Senneth." She smiled, a little ruefully. "You can trust me. You can trust the Riders."

A shadow fell across them as someone pulled up a chair. "You can trust me," said Romar Brendyn. He bestowed a warm smile on his niece. Even Kirra came in for some of the glow. "I'd give you a big hug right now, but I don't want serra Senneth to set me on fire."

"She only does that when she's trying to make a point," Kirra said. Then added conscientiously, "Or trying to kill someone."

Romar gave her a considering look. "I cannot help but feel that whole event was somewhat orchestrated."

Kirra lifted her shoulders in a faint shrug. "Perhaps Senneth was looking for an opportunity to make a display. She has a history of being somewhat—spectacular."

"I could have handled Toland," Amalie said.

"Actually, I'm glad she pulled the stunt," Romar said. "You shouldn't have to try to handle bullies and drunken lords. I'm glad if they're all a little afraid of you. Or afraid of Senneth."

"But no one will ask me to dance tomorrow night!"

Romar laughed. "I will. And I'll wager some of the young men will. They'll just ask most politely."

Amalie sighed, then she visibly tried to force away her despondency. She gave her uncle a playful smile. "It is very hard to be princess," she said.

"It is very hard to be anything," Kirra said in Casserah's driest voice. "The trick is to try to be graceful no matter what situation you find yourself in."

Romar gave her her very own smile for that. "A trick that serra Casserah manages very well," he said. "I hope you will have time to dance with me tomorrow night as well."

Bright Mother burn me, Kirra thought as she tranquilly nodded in acquiescence. "I will dance with anyone who asks," she said.

He laughed at that; perhaps she had not been so graceful after all. "You see?" he said, ruffling Amalie's hair, which caused her to squeal and jerk away. "We will all have a wonderful time tomorrow at the ball."

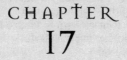

CHAPTER
17

KIRRA was less sanguine about that as the next day unfolded. Because the lady of the house was so involved with the night's preparations, there were no formal events during the day, and the guests entertained themselves pretty much at random. Most of the women kept to their rooms, indulging in beauty treatments that would guarantee they looked their best that night. Just for something to do, Kirra changed to cat shape and slunk around the mansion, Donnal at her side. They stole scraps in the kitchen, chased birds on the front lawn, and witnessed more than one tryst in the gardens. They also overheard an argument between Toland Storian and Raegon, the young Tilt lord, as Raegon claimed to have had no part of the disaster the night before. They would both go to their graves believing the other a liar, Kirra thought. She was a little sorry for it—but not much.

She and Donnal also darted in and out of the stables, watching the grooms clear out space to hold the carriages and horses that would start arriving just before sundown. Eloise had said she expected a hundred guests in addition to those already gathered at the house. These would be her vassals and their families, Thirteenth House gentry invited as a way for Eloise to publicly thank them for their loyalty.

This would be the night something would go wrong, if anything were to go wrong, Kirra thought. So many people moving in and out of the house. So many servants, coachmen, younger sons, ambitious mothers, and jealous lords gathered in one place. It was practically a prescription for trouble—if you were expecting trouble.

When she returned to her room, she found Melly in a rare taking. "Look at you! How am I going to get you dressed up in time for the ball? Where have you been all day? You should have been resting! You should have had compresses on your eyes! Your hair's not even clean. Oh, what the serra would say to me, I can't even guess."

"She'd say, 'Never blame yourself for Kirra's faults,'" Kirra said, stripping quickly. "Come. It won't take so long. I put myself completely in your hands."

In fact, it was nearly two hours later before Kirra was washed, dressed, and styled to Melly's satisfaction. Kirra had to admit that she looked superb as Casserah. She wore a dark red gown with a tight bodice and plunging neckline. The V at the throat, the three-quarter sleeves, and a panel down the front of the dress foamed with antique lace of a pale gold cast. Her dark hair had been drawn back from her face with a profusion of red ribbons and ruby combs; subtle cosmetics added drama to her wide cheeks and large blue eyes. The rouged red of her lips matched the deep color of the Danalustrous ruby that hung just above her breasts.

Kirra watched herself in the mirror, practicing Casserah's languid expression and mysterious half smile. She dropped her eyelids and turned her head to watch her reflection sideways.

"Very beautiful," she approved at last. "I should have a marriage proposal by midnight, wouldn't you think?"

Melly was behind her, fluffing out the lace at the back of Kirra's neck and infinitesimally rearranging the hair. "Maybe, but would your sister accept the offer?"

Kirra laughed. "She *is* very particular."

Melly actually smiled. "You're so much more easygoing. Though I quite adore her, of course," she added hastily. "You are *too* easygoing. You don't care enough."

"Not about ballgowns and jewelry," Kirra agreed. She paused on her way out the door and sorted through small items on her dresser till she found the one she wanted. She tucked it deep inside her neckline.

"What is that?" Melly asked instantly. "What have you done? Have you ruined the front of the dress? Let me see."

It was the small stone lion she had found at the Wild Mother's temple. Kirra had gotten in the habit of carrying it with her when she left the room, slipping it into a pocket or a purse. This outfit offered neither. "I don't think anyone can see it," she said, turning so Melly could make her inspection.

"I take back everything I said," Melly scolded. "You are not easy at all."

Kirra grinned. "You know, if I have to have a maid foisted on me, I believe you're the only one I would be able to stand. Don't wait up for me. The ball will go quite late."

"I'll wait up if I want to," Melly said.

Kirra was laughing as she left the room.

Normally she would have just headed downstairs on her own, but this was the important night; this was the grand event. So she stepped down the hall and knocked on Amalie's door. Valri answered, looking striking in a hunter-green dress accented with black and gold. Her short black hair was pulled back in an utterly severe style.

"Casserah," she said. "We were just about to go down."

Senneth, as usual, was wearing dark colors, a narrow cobalt dress with straight lines and little ornamentation. Someone had spent some time fixing her hair and making up her face, however, because both were quite elegant. Her gray eyes seemed washed with the same blue as the dress; her hair actually curled in tendrils to soften her face.

"I think you'll have a little more trouble disappearing tonight," Kirra commented.

"Doesn't matter," Senneth replied. "Everyone will be staring at Amalie anyway."

Indeed, Amalie could hardly have looked more regal. She wore a stiff, full gown of deepest purple edged at all borders with thin gold ribbons; her red-gold hair just seemed like more glorious ornamentation. Even her brown eyes had a gold cast this night. Around her throat she wore a collar of braided gold chains; from the center, covering her housemark, dangled a single gold charm shaped like the stylized royal lion. Amethysts were set at random in her hair and glowered in two rings on her right hand. On her left hand she wore a gold signet ring carved with the king's crest.

Kirra smiled and made a low curtsey. "The very picture of a princess," she said. "Most excellently done."

"Do you think anyone will ask me to dance?" the princess asked anxiously. "Besides my uncle, I mean."

Kirra silently resolved to transform herself into an attractive young suitor and dance with the princess herself if no one else stepped forward this night. "I'm sure they will," Valri answered. "And they will be honored to do so."

"Then let's go on down," Senneth said.

Kirra was highly conscious of the significance of their little parade as Valri led the princess through the hall and down the stairs. Senneth followed Amalie, and Kirra was in the rear. *Ahead of me are the three most powerful women in the kingdom,* Kirra thought. Each powerful in a different way—and Amalie, who was the most valuable of the three, was in every way the most vulnerable. *Pray to all the benevolent gods that this evening goes well for her.*

IT started off propitiously, at any rate. Romar Brendyn was loitering at the foot of the steps, clearly stationed there to await his niece. A few other lords and ladies had paused casually in the foyer where the great stairwell fed to the bottom floor, acting as if they were engaged in important conversations, but clearly they were there to catch the first glimpse of royalty. A soft little murmur went up from this crowd as Amalie appeared behind Valri, her violet gown in vivid contrast to Valri's sober green. Romar fell into a deep bow from which he did not rise until Amalie's feet pattered across the stone floor and she stood before him.

"Princess," he said, taking her hand and kissing it, "you are exquisite."

She could not keep the delight from her face, though it was clear her stepmother had counseled her to try to appear unmoved by compliments. "Thank you," she replied with a creditable attempt at nonchalance. "You look very nice, too."

Privately, Kirra had been thinking the same thing. He was wearing Merrenstow's black and white, with a checkerboard sash across his chest, but his black waistcoat was embroidered in gold with the royal lion. He had tied his shoulder-length hair back with a black ribbon, and his face looked very stern.

"May I escort you in to dinner?" he asked.

"I would be honored if you did."

Pretty much everyone else in the assembly reacted to Amalie with the same mix of appreciation and formality, from the Kianlever vassals who had not yet had a chance to meet the princess to the Twelfth House serramar who had flirted with her for the past two days. Even during the long dinner, people kept twisting in their chairs to get a glimpse of the poised and beautiful princess sitting at the head table with Eloise, Senneth, Valri, and a few of Eloise's most devoted lords.

"You would not think a ballgown would make such a difference," Darryn Rappengrass murmured to Kirra as they sat together over dinner. "But our shy little princess looks very queenly tonight."

Kirra smiled. "She is nervous, though she hides it. She is afraid no one will dance with her. It would be a great kindness if you could bring yourself to be her partner if you see that she is being shunned."

He laughed outright. "Serra, I will engage to do so, but my prediction is she will not be needing the attentions of insignificant persons such as me. She will be besieged with suitors."

She dropped her lids to half cover her eyes. "Even after last night's demonstration?"

"Even then."

Darryn proved to be right. The dinner finally came to a close and they moved in one untidy body to the ballroom, which had been lavishly decorated with all manner of purple flowers tied up with great gold bows. Eloise had obviously gone to some trouble to inquire after the princess's toilette. The regent led his niece out for the first formal dance, but after that he had no chance to speak to her, as she was surrounded for the rest of the night by eager young lords vying for her hand.

The rest of the young ladies looked rather put out at all the attention focused on the princess. Still, they did their best to appear as if they were enjoying the chance to tell each other diverting stories as they sat in the narrow chairs lining the ballroom and cooled themselves with their elaborate fans. Again, Kirra considered the advantages of changing her appearance, changing her sex, and undertaking a waltz with a few of the neglected women. Some of their no doubt spiteful opinions might be useful to obtain. But the effort seemed too great. Anyway, she was not all that interested in dancing.

While she had been watching Amalie, someone had been watching her. A figure slipped into the chair next to her, and when she looked, Romar Brendyn was lounging beside her. Her heart sped up, just a little, but she managed to mold her face in a dispassionate expression that was worthy of Casserah.

"Your niece is experiencing quite the triumph tonight," Kirra said.

He nodded, pleased. "And to think she was worried she would receive no attention! But she seems to be enjoying herself immensely."

"She might be the only lady who is," she replied somewhat tartly.

His face crinkled in a smile. "Yes, I noticed that the only available men were a few vassals' sons, and our grand serramarra normally would not stoop so low as to converse with *them*. But desperation breeds strange alliances, and I have seen more than one girl from the Twelve Houses accept an offer from a country boy tonight."

"I hope Amalie finds time to partner with some of them as well," Kirra said. "It would make them—and Eloise—very happy."

"I believe it is her intention, serra," Romar said.

Kirra returned her gaze to Amalie, just now engaged in a cotillion with a young man from Coravann. "She is young yet," she said, "but the king surely must be thinking of the next important step. Who shall she marry? Do you see any likely prospects here?"

"Until a very short time ago, the king was not prepared to admit that she was almost an adult who could not be kept hidden away forever like some secret treasure," Romar said gravely. "I'm not sure he can allow himself to think of her as a married woman."

Kirra lifted one eyebrow. "She must wed. If the succession is one of the main preoccupations of our rebellious malcontents, she must give them one less reason to worry. Marry, stop the scheming for alliances, and prove she is fertile."

"Interesting advice," he commented, "from someone who does not look eager to take it herself."

She was so surprised she shut her mouth with a snap.

"Why haven't you married?" Romar continued in a pleasant way. "You *or* your sister, Kirra? Both of you are desirable women not only for your looks but for the connections you offer. I'm surprised Malcolm has been able to sift all the would-be husbands out at the Danalustrous border."

For a moment she wanted to kill him, and then she wanted to laugh. She had to be careful to answer as Casserah would have. "I myself have never been too eager to wed," she said, her voice a little bored. "I think a husband would become tedious after a while." Romar choked and started laughing, but she continued, "I am very opinionated, you know, and I never do what anyone wants me to do. I think some husbands might find me irksome and others might find me cold. And it would be very boring to be constantly having to think of someone else's feelings. Because if I married someone after all, I would not want him to feel wretched and neglected."

Though I imagine that might be how your own wife feels, she wanted to add, but didn't.

"No, indeed!" he exclaimed, strangling his laughter. "You would not want to completely ignore any man you took to husband. But don't you think—if you married for love, or at least for affection—you might actually be interested in spending time with that man? Hearing his thoughts now and then? In fact, considering his feelings?"

Kirra opened her blue eyes very wide. She was enjoying this. "I doubt it."

"So you plan to rule Danalustrous all on your own, with no spouse beside you?" he inquired.

"Ariane Rappengrass and Eloise Kianlever have both managed such a feat quite well."

"Both of them married young and were unfortunate in the early deaths of their husbands," he countered.

"Or fortunate. You might ask their opinions."

He ignored this. "And Eloise's husband died just two years ago. Ariane at least managed to bear five children before her husband passed away. And you must have heirs if you are to be marlady! You can't have children unless you're married."

She was amused. "Can I not?"

He was caught by surprise and for a moment he stared. Then he burst out laughing again. "Indeed, I stand corrected," he said.

"You can. Perhaps you will. Accept in advance my sincere hopes for a happy and prosperous life, however you choose to lead it."

She gave him a little nod. "Thank you, lord."

"So we have disposed of your matrimonial chances," he said cheerfully. "What of your sister? Do you suppose she will ever marry?"

"You'd have to ask Kirra that."

He shook his head, his face gone suddenly abstracted as if he was revisiting a memory. "She is—she was— What a remarkable woman. Fearless. She has this natural elegance, this sophistication that informs every gesture and expression, and yet she is so much more vital and alive than any other woman I have met, in or out of the Twelve Houses. I looked at her and thought that there was nothing she could not do if she wanted to. She could charm a marlord in his hall or kill a bandit on the road. I thought, there is a woman not bound by any convention. There is a woman you cannot contain or predict. I have never encountered anyone like her."

She wished the gods would strike him dumb so he could not say another word; she wished he would keep talking till the music ended, or the night ended, or the world ended. What would Casserah say, if she were sitting here listening to such warm praise of her sister? Casserah would agree with every word. But Kirra was not about to. "Yes, I love her very much myself, but she is not an easy companion," she replied in a dry voice. "You never know where she will be from one day to the next. You never know what unfortunate friends she will bring home with her. She is restless, and odd, and uneven. You can count on her fidelity, for she is loyal as they come, but you cannot count on her for anything else."

"Merriment," he said. "I think you always expect her to show that."

"You're right. And that's a fine quality to rely on when you're in desperate straits."

He gave her a serious look, maybe a bit reproving. "That sounds like how your father must have talked when he was telling you he was going to name you heir."

She refused to be chastised. "Do not lecture me on how to appreciate my sister, lord," she said in a sharp voice. "I value her more than you will ever know how to. But do not be deceived by her bright hair and her laughing manner. She is a shiftling. She cannot stay still. She will make no man a tame and loving wife."

He glanced away, as if afraid to reveal some expression on his face, and then glanced back, utterly composed. "I am not looking for a wife," he said. "And I think it would take a unique man to serve as husband for your sister. I did not expect to rouse your ire by saying so."

"I told you three days ago that I have heard nothing but praise and admiration for my sister," she said, allowing a faint note of petulance to creep into her voice. "I suppose I had thought the subject was closed."

He gave her a slight smile. "Jealousy? From Casserah Danalustrous? I find it impossible to believe."

"Lord Romar," she said, "I think I would surprise you most any day."

"Serra Casserah," he replied, "I am sure you are right."

The music ended and the dancers paused to offer light applause. Young men pacing the borders of the ballroom streamed onto the dance floor to compete for Amalie's hand. Romar rose to his feet, which caused Kirra to feel great relief and great disappointment. He was leaving.

Wrong again. "Would you surprise me again by dancing with me this evening?" he asked. "I promise, we will speak only of you and your many charms."

For a moment, she knew, her expression was dumbfounded. He smiled and held his hand out, bending over in a half bow. "Please," he said. "You are the only lady here to whom I feel free to speak my mind. It is a rare luxury for a man like me, who despises social conventions. You would be doing me a great honor and a great kindness if you would give me one waltz."

Irresistible, no matter how much she wanted to resist. Wordlessly, she put her hand in his and allowed him to pull her to her feet. They glided onto the dance floor just as the music started. Romar's left hand rested with a light pressure against her waist, but she was as aware of his touch as if he had worn moonstones on every finger. She thought she was just as likely to find welts on her skin in the morning.

The music was lovely, sweet and a little mournful; other couples twirled around them in a jeweled pattern of color and motion. Kirra made no effort to speak, as Casserah certainly would not have, and Romar seemed content to dance in silence. He smiled down at her, though, his eyes fixed on her face. She had to school herself to show only Casserah's mild enjoyment bordering on true indifference.

Though she was wishing most passionately that the dance would never end.

It did, of course, with a minor crescendo of music and a last trill on a haunted flute. Romar immediately dropped his hands and bowed to her. Kirra swept him a regal curtsey.

"I enjoyed that," Romar said. "You are a most graceful lady."

"Thank you," she said, unable to come up with anything more witty.

He had crooked his arm as if to lead her off the dance floor, but Darryn was beside them, making his own offer. "I did not realize you were dancing, serra," said the Rappengrass lord. "Will you take a turn with me?"

Yes, with him, with Raegon Tilton, with Toland Storian, with anyone, just so she could end this long conference with Romar Brendyn. The regent bowed again and exited the floor. Kirra arranged herself in Darryn's arms and they dipped into the dance.

That marked her as willing, and for the next hour she passed from hand to hand. Some of the younger lords had finally given up the pursuit of Amalie and were leading other ladies to the floor, but Casserah did not seem to appeal to this contingent. No, it was Seth Stowfer and the fathers of the bachelors and Eloise's oldest vassals who wanted to squire the Danalustrous serramarra around. They were interested in alliances, not romance, and she had no quarrel with that. She let them rhapsodize about the beauties of Danalustrous and inquire after the health of her father and congratulate her on her new position in the household. She noted which ones wore moonstones—though Cammon's magic held and she was not seared by them—and which ones sported only the gems and colors of their own Houses. But none of them asked her outright where Danalustrous might stand in a war. None of them mentioned either Halchon Gisseltess or the king. It was impossible to tell whose allegiances lay where.

Eventually she was able to free herself from Seth Stowfer. She made her way around the perimeter of the dance floor to where Senneth stood near a pair of tall windows.

"Where's Valri?" Kirra asked. "She's usually lurking right next to you, staring at Amalie."

"She's dancing with Heffel Coravann. For the third time this evening. He seems quite infatuated with her."

Kirra scanned the dance floor till she located the unlikely couple, the tiny dark-haired queen and the rather lumbering marlord of Coravann. "Didn't his wife die a couple of years ago? She was small and dark, too. Maybe Valri reminds him of her."

"Maybe Valri ought to be careful of causing any gossip by seeming to favor any one marlord over another."

Kirra raised her eyebrows. "Senneth Brassenthwaite lecturing on propriety," she marveled. "I never thought to hear it."

Senneth offered a reluctant smile. "Yes, but there are a few people who can't afford to make mistakes. And Valri's one."

"The princess seems to be handling herself very well."

Senneth nodded. "*She* doesn't make mistakes. Even little ones. That's something I've been noticing."

"I think under the shiny hair and the cow eyes she's a very smart girl," Kirra said.

Senneth gave her an indignant look for the unflattering description but said, "There are days I almost feel hopeful."

"Let's see how well the trip progresses before we start becoming as rash as all that," Kirra said.

Senneth laughed, and they talked idly for a few more moments. Kirra danced one or two more times, returning to Senneth's side after each one to exchange observations. It was about an hour later and the ball was perhaps half over when Kirra saw Romar Brendyn slip out a back doorway of the ballroom. She smiled to herself; she didn't think he'd made it through an entire evening yet without disappearing for a while. Three minutes later, Amalie twirled up beside them on Darryn Rappengrass's arm, looking flushed and happy.

"Have you seen my uncle?" the princess asked. "Darryn wanted to ask him something."

"He was supposed to give me the name of a swordsmith in Nocklyn," Darryn said. "I'm leaving in the morning."

"He went out the back way, toward the gardens," Senneth said. Kirra was impressed. That was something she would have expected Tayse to notice because Tayse noticed everything, but she hadn't thought Senneth was paying such close attention.

"Well, I'll—" Darryn began, but Amalie clutched his arm.

"Oh, no, dance with me again," she said in an undervoice. "I have been avoiding Toland Storian all night and he's heading this way right now."

Kirra grinned. "I'll go find him," she offered. "You two dance."

It was a relief to step from the overheated, overfull, overlit ballroom into the cool empty darkness of the corridor, and even better to step outside. The air was rich with the scent of summer flowers and thick with the promise of rain. The moon was full and high, but what light drifted through the gardens fell mostly from the ballroom windows. The scene inside was all bright colors and yellow candle flame, a painting of gaiety and grace. Outside, the world seemed mysterious, hushed, alive with secret possibilities.

High hedges separated the gardens proper from the sweeping outer lawn surrounding Kianlever Court. Kirra moved slowly in the darkness, the green walls of shrubbery to her left, the stone walls of the house on her right. The gardens were a maze of flower beds, fountains, statuary, trellises, and follies, and Kirra only knew her way through them because of the days spent roaming with Donnal in animal shape. Where would Romar have gone? Not far, she thought. He might even be walking along the pathways closest to the house so he could glance through the windows from time to time, watch his niece, make sure all was well. . . .

She located Romar at last, pacing slowly along an outer path, head down, hands behind his back, seeming to be working out some great problem. It was hard to see him clearly, but Kirra recognized the shape of his shoulders, the tied-back style of his hair, the faint checkerboard pattern of his sash. He looked like a shadow set with a few blurred, familiar details.

A few seconds after she saw him, she saw the other men.

CHAPTER
18

JUST as Romar passed a stand of ornamental trees, two shadows detached themselves from the thin trunks and came creeping down the path behind him. Kirra could make out the glint of silver in their hands—knives or swords. They deployed, one to the right of Romar, the other to the left and a little behind his companion. Positioning themselves for the first blow and then the second.

Kirra didn't have time to scream, to think of screaming, even to gauge whether they were close enough to the house for Riders to hear her call. The first man charged forward in a silent run and collided with Romar in a blow that sent both men tumbling to the ground.

A scramble, a grunt, a choked cry, and the second man was running forward in a low crouch, weapon out, seeking a place to land a blow. Kirra could see the deadly struggle between the two on the ground—Romar not dead, then—but could not tell who was winning the contest.

She put a hand to her chest, felt the hard knot of the carved lion under her bodice. *Wild Mother watch me,* she prayed, the words coming to her without conscious thought, and eased her body into another shape.

The second attacker had struck twice, hard, and now raised his arm for a third time. His hand never fell. The lion made a perfect spring from the pathway to his shoulders, bringing him down in a thrashing bundle. He screamed once and fought madly to free himself. She raked her claws straight down his face and chest, slicing through cotton and leather and skin. He howled and coiled from side to side in terror or agony, beating at her with his hands. The lion batted him across the face so hard his head slammed into the stones of the pathway. He lay still. She lost interest, turned her head to seek more lively prey.

Three feet away, the two other men were locked in a grim struggle, though the attacker with his hands around his victim's throat had been distracted by the sight of the great cat. Kirra slashed at his exposed rib cage, drawing blood, then darted in and closed her wide jaws over his head. He screamed and fell backward, releasing Romar, who choked and rolled to a seated position. Kirra shook her head with the man's skull still in her mouth, and his body dragged from side to side on the pathway. He was still shrieking. His hands flailed at her as his feet tried to find a purchase on the ground. She could taste blood in her mouth, smell fear in the air.

Romar heaved himself to his feet and staggered, his hands checking his body for wounds. Behind her, Kirra heard halting footsteps weaving away as the other attacker regained consciousness and made a battered run for freedom. She relaxed her jaws and allowed the second man to pull free. Sobbing like a child, he first scrabbled away on all fours, then pitched himself to his feet and ran.

Kirra dropped to her haunches and let him go. Her concern now was the man before her, who looked to be a little steadier on his feet and not suffering from any kind of life-threatening wound. His clothes were ripped and there was a trail of blood down one cheek, black in the moonlight, but he looked neither too dizzy nor too weak to stand. Indeed, he took a few hasty steps after his departing assailants before he realized that they were too fast and too far ahead of him. Then he slowed, and stopped, and spun around to stare at the creature sitting in the garden path, licking her mouth once with her broad tongue to clean away the traces of blood.

He watched her a long time and she held his gaze, her whole body unmoving. He seemed neither afraid nor confused, though his breathing was still hard and he gave every appearance of a man who had been in a desperate fight. But that didn't seem to be what concerned him right now. He came one step closer to the lion and continued to stare.

"I know you, I think," he said at last in a low voice. "Show me your true shape."

She had always been a little vain of her ability to change forms with a sinuous grace. She considered the transformation to be like a flower unfurling or a fist unfolding, something elemental and inevitable and marked with its own ritual. Still, it was a curiously intimate thing, to move from one state to another, essentially recast a life, while under someone else's intense scrutiny. She tilted her head and shrugged her shoulders and felt her bones and muscles realign while all the textures of her body regrouped. She kept Casserah's red gown and ruby necklace and the lion's golden hair and stood there in the garden facing Romar Brendyn as Kirra Danalustrous.

"How many times will I be called upon to rescue the king's regent?" she greeted him, keeping her voice light. "I would have thought you would have grown more careful by now."

He glanced over his shoulder as if to see whether more enemies were arrayed against him. "Who were they? Could you tell?"

She shook her head. "Someone who knew that you walk in the gardens every night at about this time. That could be any of Eloise's houseguests—or anyone who has been spying on the house, watching your habits."

"As you have been?" he asked pointedly. "How did you know where to find me? Why were you looking?"

For this at least she had an easy answer. "Darryn Rappengrass had a question for you. Senneth Brassenthwaite had seen you leave. I volunteered to fetch you." She looked around. "Not knowing I would also be saving your life."

He nodded and then he bowed, very deeply, as if being introduced to Valri or Amalie for the first time. "As you seem to be destined to do, over and over. I am so much at a loss for how to thank you that I do not even know how to act. My mind is reeling. I was not prepared for an assault by enemies, and I was not prepared to see you again."

He straightened and looked at her, coming a few steps closer without even seeming to be aware that he moved. His hands were outstretched; his expression was both wondering and joyful. "Kirra," he said, and without thinking she put her hands in his. "How good it is to see your face."

Her throat was so tight she was not sure she would be able to answer. "Lord Romar," she managed. "Let me say the same."

He peered at her in the darkness, bending just a little to get a better look. His hair must have come loose in the scuffle, because now it fell alongside his cheek, softening its lines. Whatever scrape had been bleeding seemed to have stopped, but a line of blood still made an interesting stripe down one cheek.

"How did you come to be here?" he asked. "When did you arrive? I have had a series of most intriguing conversations with—" He shut his mouth, obviously working it out that very moment. "With you, I suppose," he continued. "Not Casserah at all."

"Don't be offended," she said. "It was a plan my father hatched. He thought she should be here but she wouldn't come. My intent was not so much to deceive as to represent my House."

"I'm not offended. I am impressed by your ability to carry out such a charade. And I confess I am reviewing what I might have said and how foolish I might have sounded."

"Not at all foolish. You have been brave and thoughtful and most complimentary." She could not help a smile for that.

He was thinking back. "Ah. I admit to feeling a bit of anger at Casserah for not valuing you as she should. I see you were playing a deep game. I will strive to forgive Casserah."

Now she laughed. "I spoke much more harshly than my sister would have," she said. "One can hardly sit there and heap praise upon oneself without feeling a bit ridiculous."

He regarded her closely for a moment. "I had the sense—almost—Casserah was warning me away from Kirra. But it was you. Telling me not to be too fond of you. Why would that be?"

It was at that exact moment that Kirra realized he was still holding her hands. She tried to casually pull them away, but his grip tightened. She felt her breath come a little faster. "It was not a warning," she said, trying to keep her voice normal. "I was just talking. Part of the game."

"I've thought about you," he said. "Every day, since you left me at the borders of Merrenstow. Wished I could speak to you again. Wished I could tell you—tell you how much I appreciated—"

Now she did yank her hands free. "Oh, please. No more thanks about the rescue from Tilt," she said. "I was doing a service for my king."

"I wanted to tell you how much I appreciated your conversation," he continued steadily. "Your laughter. Appreciated you. Your voice and your smile have lingered with me all these weeks. It is a bit like being haunted by a very merry ghost."

She was silent a moment, torn between the happiness of hearing the words and the despair of knowing he shouldn't speak them. "No one has ever called me a ghost before," she said. "I will add it to my list of favorite compliments."

His expression shifted; he became even more intent. "I could call you other things," he said. "Use other words."

"You're married," she said baldly.

He nodded. "I am. As soon as I met you, I wished I wasn't."

She took a quick breath. "Foolish talk. You've been overcome by moonlight and the romance of another wild adventure at my side."

"I have been planning to ride to Danalustrous to see you again," he said. "I would have made up some reason to come meet with your father. I have been rehearsing sentences in my head for weeks."

Better and better—worse and worse—Kirra turned her shoulder to him and began pacing along the flagged walkway. Romar fell in step beside her. "Had you come to Danalustrous, you most likely would not have found me," she said. She was determined to keep her manner airy no matter what he said. "I am rarely there. I am rarely anywhere for long."

"I know. But it seemed impossible to me that I would go the rest of my life without seeing you again. So I practiced for the day."

"Lord Romar—" He gave her a swift look of reproach for using his title, but she did not amend. "You scarcely know me. Be careful what you say and what you feel. You are crafting your emotions around the picture of a woman that you have built in your head. The chances are very slim that I am that picture come to life."

"I know that the longer I know you, the more you will astonish me," he said, "but I do not think I have the basic outlines of that picture wrong."

She gave him a quick, sad smile. "It will do neither of us any good if you carry that picture with you in your heart."

"Very well," he said. "I will try not to fall in love with you."

She could not help but laugh in astonishment at that.

"But I would like the chance to become one of your friends—one of your intimates," he said. "One of the people you turn to as you share the random thoughts in your head, one of the people to whom you show your true self—even when the outward form of that true self is in disguise. I would like to be able to know you as few people do. That much you can give me, don't you think, without compromising my honor or your own?"

She stopped abruptly to face him on the path. "I think pacts like that can be dangerous and easily overset," she said.

"Kirra," he said—and then, again, as if the very sound of her name gave him pleasure. "Kirra. Let us just try the business of being friends."

She didn't know how to answer. She had realized, as he probably had, that the structure of the social season was likely to throw them together over the next few weeks, for it was likely that he, too, would be traveling to the other great Houses for the summer balls. And for the past five years, she had spent as much of her time at Ghosenhall as she had spent at Danalustrous, for she was a favorite of the king's. No doubt Romar's responsibilities as regent would bring him to the royal city even more often. There was almost no way they could avoid each other without actually making that a priority.

She knew it was not something she would have the strength to do.

"We are friends," she said.

"Then that is enough for me."

Someone inside the ballroom screamed.

Romar's head whipped in that direction; Kirra felt her entire body tense. Another scream, and then a whole chorus of cries, accompanied by the sounds of shattering glass and falling objects.

"Silver hell," Romar grunted and took off at a dead run for the house. Kirra picked up her skirts and raced beside him, changing her face, changing her weight, resuming Casserah's body as she ran.

They burst into the ballroom a moment later to find it a scene of chaos. Kirra instantly spotted Senneth by the pool of fire in one corner of the room; that meant Amalie was inside the ring, and safe. Everywhere else was a tumble of bodies as hand-to-hand fights threw assailants across the smooth marble floor between overturned tables, smashed vases, and scattered purple flowers. The walls were rimmed with beautiful women in brightly colored dresses, clinging to each other and weeping. Beside them stood dozens of noble men, helplessly watching, not accustomed to battle. But a few lords were alongside the soldiers and guards furiously fighting on the floor. All four Riders were among the combatants, mowing down adversaries with their usual brutal efficiency. More Kianlever guards poured through interior doors even as Kirra watched.

Romar leapt forward to join the fray, but even in the short time it had taken them to run in from the gardens, the battle had pretty much been decided. There couldn't have been more than twenty attackers, and the Riders had accounted for almost half of those. The others were ruthlessly overcome until there were only loyalists left on the dance floor, milling about with swords upraised, bending down to check that each fallen man was truly dead or disabled.

The instant that Tayse sheathed his sword, Senneth's wall of fire came down. Kirra spared a moment to admire their symmetry, then ran across the floor toward Senneth, picking her way around the bodies. Tayse's head turned toward the sound of her footfalls, then he quickly turned his attention to the guards still prowling the ballroom.

"To me, all of you," he called. "Who are these men? Are any left alive to be questioned? What do we know?"

A loose knot of lords and soldiers gathered in the middle of the ballroom to confer. Kirra arrived at Senneth's side. Amalie was seated on a divan, patiently repeating to Valri that she was fine, she was unhurt, she was not afraid. Three women were bending over Eloise, who appeared to have fainted into a plush chair. Kirra saw no one in this particular group who was actually hurt.

"All safe?" she asked Senneth in a low voice.

Senneth nodded. "And you?"

"Yes, but there were two men outside who attacked Romar just as I arrived. Part of this contingent, I suspect."

Senneth raised her eyebrows. "Yes. He escaped?"

"With my help."

A small smile for that. "You have your uses."

"What happened here?"

Senneth nodded toward the dance floor. "As you see. I looked up to find Donnal flying in through the ballroom window, so I knew there was trouble. I pulled the princess off the dance floor just as Tayse and the other Riders came running in, warned by Cammon. The Kianlever guards arrived late."

"Though they should have been the first to fight," Kirra murmured. "In Danalustrous, they'd have all been dead before Danan Hall was breached."

"In Brassenthwaite as well."

For a moment, blue eyes stared into gray as they tried to assimilate this knowledge. "Sabotage?" Kirra breathed.

"Treason?" Senneth replied.

"In *Kianlever*?"

"Maybe we'll learn something from the men left behind."

Indeed, Tayse, Romar, the man who looked to be captain of the guard, and one of Eloise's vassal lords had all clustered in the middle of the room. Kirra saw the captain bending over a man who lay on the floor, bleeding but apparently alive. She considered drifting closer to hear what they might be saying, then thought of sending a spy instead. She looked around, but saw no sign of an owl or hawk.

"Where's Donnal?"

"Back out patrolling. I wasn't sure if there might be a second assault to follow the first."

Behind them, there was a moan and a stir, and Eloise pushed herself upright in her chair. Kirra murmured, "If I was Kirra, I would see if she needed the help of a healer."

"I'm guessing she's not hurt, merely frightened. And horrified," Senneth replied. "This will be hard to explain to Baryn."

Kirra gave Senneth another inquiring look, eyebrows raised, incredulity on her own face. *Did she plan this?* Senneth shook her head. "I just don't know," Senneth said.

Justin was making his way through the bodies toward them. Kirra and Senneth moved forward to meet him so that none of the other ladies could hear their low-voiced conversation.

"Any information?" Senneth asked.

"Kell Sersees says two of the men were at his house three days ago for some ball he had."

Senneth looked at Kirra. "Who?"

"Kell Sersees. The richest vassal in Kianlever," Kirra explained. "He had what Eloise called a—a 'Shadow Ball,' a big event a few days before her own. Apparently, among the Thirteenth House, there's a whole summer season that mimics our own."

"Thirteenth House," Senneth repeated.

Kirra nodded. "Yes. Again. Might clear Eloise, though."

"I don't think we'll learn much from the survivors," Justin said. "They look like common house guards who just do what their commanders tell them. It's not like they'll be carrying letters signed by Halchon Gisseltess saying, 'Go to Kianlever and attack the princess.'"

"If Halchon had anything to do with this," Senneth said.

Justin looked surprised. "Who else?"

"That's the question," Senneth replied. She glanced around the room. "Is it safe to disperse the crowd, do you think? Send everyone to bed? Or will Tayse want to ask them questions?"

Justin shook his head again. "We've already gathered up the people who might be able to answer any questions."

"You take care of Amalie and the queen," Kirra said. "I'll do what I can to help Eloise."

It was another weary hour or so before the ballroom was cleared out. Most of the women were happy to leave, still sobbing into their handkerchiefs or pale with shock, but a handful of hardy souls lingered awhile, fascinated by bloodshed and remembered battle. A contingent of guards carried out the bodies and escorted out the survivors, while the Riders and a few top soldiers continued to debate. It was at least two hours past midnight before servants appeared with mops and buckets and began to wash away the blood.

Eloise was still encircled by a ring of friends, vassals, servants, and the merely curious when the cleanup commenced. Kirra pushed her way through the group with her sister's unself-conscious determination. "Time the marlady was in bed," she said, pulling on Eloise's elbow. "And the rest of you, too. I'll see her to her room."

Eloise looked grateful at the rescue and actually leaned on Kirra's shoulder as they climbed the steps to her suite on the second story. But her gratitude turned to apprehension when, once inside, Kirra pushed her to a seat and then pulled a chair up beside her.

"You must realize this looks very bad," she said.

Surprise, comprehension, and wretchedness chased each other in quick succession across the marlady's face. "Casserah— you cannot believe—surely the princess cannot think—I had any remote association with the scoundrels who broke in here tonight!"

Kirra raised her hands in an equivocating gesture. "No one knows what to think. But it *is* your house, and it was not adequately defended. Two among the princess's own party were the first to raise the alarm, and it was Senneth and King's Riders who kept her safe. Baryn will not be happy. You may not have planned this, but someone in your household allowed it to happen. Someone with knowledge of your grounds and your guests plotted the assault. Guards were bribed or looked the other way. If you were not responsible for this, who was? You must start asking questions so that you can answer the questions the king will pose to you."

Eloise buried her face in her hands. "I'm so tired," she said. "All I wanted was to have a party. To show the princess special honor. And now you think I'm a traitor."

"I don't. But it looks bad. You must search for trouble in your own ranks. Among your guards or your vassals."

Eloise lifted her head. Her face was already red with worry and weeping. Kirra was betting she would have a bad night of it. "My vassals?" she repeated.

Kirra made that gesture of uncertainty again. "Some of the men who attacked tonight appear to be members of the Thirteenth House. Kell recognized them. There is unrest among the lesser nobles, Eloise, or had you not heard? Turn to the ones you trust and find out what you need to know."

Eloise stared at her a long moment, her face so blank Kirra was not sure she had actually understood. At last she said, "Casserah. You must believe me. I would never betray my king. I would throw all of the resources of Kianlever behind the throne if it came to a war. I will investigate most thoroughly, and I will do what I must to make sure such a thing never happens again."

Kirra nodded. "Good. Now I believe it is time you went to bed."

Eloise shrugged hopelessly. "Why? I won't be able to sleep."

Kirra rested a comforting hand on Eloise's shoulder and contrived to send a tendril of healing magic down through the muscle and bone. *Relax now and be at peace.* "Just try," she said. "Lay yourself on your bed and close your eyes."

"I'm so tired," Eloise said again.

Kirra stood and beckoned to the maid, who had hovered in the shadows this whole time. "We will see you in the morning before we leave," she said. "Think over what I said."

She had barely made it to the door before Eloise had thrown herself on her bed. The maid was going to have a time undressing her before Kirra's magic took effect. Still, Eloise's problems would look just as grim by daylight; Kirra did not envy her.

She was exhausted herself, and the long walk back to her own room seemed to take an inordinate amount of time. It was while she was climbing the second stairwell that she felt a shape materialize behind her. She turned to find Donnal climbing the steps at her back. Donnal in human shape, looking very dark and serious.

It felt like weeks since she had seen him, Donnal himself, and she was irrationally pleased. "There you are," she exclaimed, stopping one step above him and placing her hands on both his shoulders. "I hear you were the hero tonight, warning Senneth of approaching danger."

He nodded, but his expression didn't change. "You weren't in the ballroom," he said. "I wanted to make sure nothing had happened to you."

She nodded. Like the princess, she had practiced nonchalance. "Amalie wanted her uncle, and Senneth had seen him go to the gardens. I went to find him—just as two of tonight's attackers came after him. We had our own little skirmish among the flower beds and statuary, but no one was hurt. Even the attackers got away."

"This isn't as easy as we thought it would be," he said.

"I'm not sure Senneth or Tayse ever expected it to be easy," she said, "but I certainly wasn't prepared for this. I've never heard of such a thing happening—an assault on a party at one of the Twelve Houses!"

"Are you afraid?"

She smiled at him. "Not with you and Cammon on guard," she said. "Though I admit I am a little jealous of Amalie right now, since you are watching her instead of me."

"I am always watching you," he said quietly. "I would never give anyone else so much of my attention that there was none left for you."

She was humbled by the words, the more so because, after tonight, she was fairly sure she could not say the same thing to him. "I know," she said. "The thought alone keeps me safe."

"Any time you ask, I'll leave the princess's room to come back to yours."

She managed a small smile. "Her life is more important than mine."

"Not to me."

She lifted a hand from his shoulder to touch his cheek, smooth down the dark beard. "Do as you have been doing," she said. "Guard us both."

They went together to Senneth's room, set up as war headquarters now. It was crowded with all four Riders, Romar, Cammon, Senneth—and the princess herself. Valri, who always followed Amalie like a relentless shadow, sat in a chair in the corner of the room, bolt upright, hands clutching the armrests. Everyone else seemed marked by a deep fatigue—though none of the Riders, Kirra noticed, looked remotely relaxed. All of them wore their weapons belts, and their hands hovered near the hilts.

Except for Tayse. He stood behind Senneth, his arms loose around her waist. She leaned against him, a column of weary blue. Her hands were folded over his forearms and she looked rested and secure, as if she had found a momentary haven. There was such a tenderness to their casual pose that Kirra felt a tiny spasm of jealousy, or perhaps it was longing. She wanted to lean into just such an embrace, to feel, for a moment, just as cherished. She pushed the thought aside.

"What do we know?" she asked, closing the door behind Donnal. She nodded at Romar, who had managed to wipe the blood from his face and change into a fresh shirt; he didn't look like he'd recently been in a fight for his life. His eyes went from her face to Donnal's before he turned his attention to Tayse, who was speaking from behind Senneth's ear.

"Kell Sersees recognized four of the dead men. Two from Kianlever, one from Nocklyn, one from Fortunalt. All Thirteenth House. Unfortunately, the ones who lived all appear to be hired men with no ties to any of the Houses. Kell himself claims to have had no knowledge at all that such an attack was planned."

"I believed him," Cammon said.

"Cammon believed him," Tayse repeated, the smile so faint that it was possible to miss, "and so I believe him as well. He promised to interrogate family members and associates of the fallen men and see if he could uncover any other threats or alliances. I don't know how quickly we'll learn anything."

"We've learned that Amalie is in danger," Valri said. "We should consider returning to Ghosenhall without delay."

"We've also learned that we are equal to defending her," Tayse replied gently.

"Once," she said grimly.

Senneth spoke from within the circle of Tayse's arms. "We have to ask ourselves why these men launched the attack. Was it to hurt Amalie? To discredit Eloise? Were they merely trying to drive us back to the royal city, to make the king look weak? If we return to Ghosenhall, will we be giving them what they want?"

"I don't care how we look as long as Amalie is safe," the young queen snapped.

Kirra stepped farther into the room. "I think Senneth is right," she said. "Unrest in the realm and worry about the succession have made it imperative that Amalie become more visible. If we run back to hide in Ghosenhall, we just heighten everyone's fears. There will be more questions about whether Amalie will be fit to rule. There will be more people willing to try to hurt her."

"But *if* they hurt her—" Romar began.

Amalie cut in. Her voice was so soft and unassuming that Kirra was amazed by her ability to hold their attention. "I'm not afraid," she said. "I know that Senneth and the others can protect me. I feel safe when they're nearby. I believe we should continue on to Coravann."

"I agree," said Senneth.

"And I," Kirra added.

Valri came to her feet. "You have no idea how valuable she is," she said in a rapid voice. "You have no idea what it would mean to lose her. She is too young to make this decision for herself! Don't encourage her in foolish choices."

Romar looked at her. "She is old enough to be queen and must be ready to take a queen's risks," he said sadly. "She cannot be seen as frail or she will not be trusted. I vote that we go on to Coravann."

Amalie stood, shaking out the folds of her purple dress. "Then that's settled," she said. "Do we leave in the morning?"

"As soon as you're ready," Senneth said.

"I'm riding with your caravan," Romar said. "And I have twenty men to augment your numbers."

"Excellent," Kirra said. "Perhaps we'll be able to keep you safe as well."

There was a moment's silence, while Romar looked outraged and the others looked shocked, and then Justin and Cammon started laughing. Even Tayse smiled.

"We will be glad to have you, lord," Senneth said, managing to sound serious. She pulled herself reluctantly from Tayse's arms and held her hand out to Amalie. "Come. Time to get you to bed."

Tayse glanced at each of the Riders in turn, silently confirming for them some previously made assignments, Kirra guessed. When he looked Donnal's way, the smaller man nodded and followed Amalie and Senneth out the door. Kirra sighed.

"I'm too agitated to sleep," she said, settling on the bed between Justin and Cammon. "Anyone up for a game of cards?"

CHAPTER
19

DESPITE the increase in their numbers, the party from Ghosenhall managed to achieve a tidy exit in the morning. Eloise made sure to be at the front door to offer her profuse apologies to the princess and beg Amalie not to question her loyalty. Amalie gave the older woman a spontaneous hug and said, "I would not doubt you." A nice gesture, Kirra thought. They were on their way very quickly after that.

Travel between Kianlever and Coravann was easy. The two Houses had a long history of friendship and commerce, so the roads between major towns were excellent. The weather was so fine that Kirra could not stand the idea of being cooped up in a carriage, so she spent the first day riding a spare horse. Donnal, still in human shape, rode beside her part of the time, yielding his place now and then to Cammon. And once to Romar.

She greeted the regent with offhand friendliness. "How are you this morning?" she asked. "Any lasting damage from last night's encounter?"

"Nothing but a bloody shirt that I left behind in my room. Eloise's servants may wonder what sorts of activities I engaged in during my stay."

"Oh, I'd guess you weren't the only visitor to leave behind ripped and bloody clothing. Very unsettled days at Kianlever Court, to be sure."

"I find it hard to believe Eloise had a hand in the attack," he said abruptly. "And yet—"

"And yet no one feels safe," Kirra finished. "But I agree. I think Kianlever was the stage, but someone else produced the play."

"We'll have to expect more of the same in Coravann."

Kirra nodded a little absently. She was thinking something over. "Have you ever heard of something called a Shadow Ball? Does your cousin have such things in Merrenstow?"

"Yes. It is considered quite an important event for the lesser lords. I go anytime I'm in the vicinity, as does my cousin. His vassals appreciate our presence—and, frankly, the events are often more fun than the ones to be endured at Merren Manor."

Kirra grinned. "I don't believe the tradition exists in Dana-lustrous. I'll have to ask my sister. But I'm wondering—" She frowned a little.

"Wondering what?"

"If I might somehow find a way to attend this shadow event at Coravann. I think I might learn something. If all this trouble is originating from the Thirteenth House—"

Romar looked intrigued. "An interesting plan."

"I'm sure some of my father's lords have been invited. I would disguise myself as one of them, except I don't know who might be there and who might not! Very awkward if there were two of us at the same ball on the same night."

Now he laughed. "I have a better idea. Come with me." She sent him a look of inquiry. "I've been invited. I was invited to the one at Kianlever, too, but I failed to make it. I think it might please the lesser lords to have the regent attend their affairs." He glanced over at her with a smile. "Perhaps if I demonstrate amiability they will have less desire to murder me."

She laughed. "Or find it easier to do once you're in their midst," she pointed out. "Will you feel safe at such an event?"

"I'll bring Colton and my men."

"Thus contradicting your claims to amiability."

"Surely a man who has been recently attacked can be excused for showing a little caution, even if he's trying to appear friendly."

"You might bring one of the Riders as well."

"No. I want them by Amalie's side. I had seen Justin in action before, of course, but I could not imagine that all Riders were so skilled. Now that I have watched them all fight, I feel certain she is safe in their hands."

"That's something I've come to admire about the princess," Kirra commented. "She has said more than once that she's not afraid. I don't believe she is. She's not stupidly unaware of danger, she's—fearless. Or very good at judging who can protect her."

"And lucky to have such protectors at her side."

"Senneth and Tayse are a formidable combination," Kirra said. "Add to them the skills that Donnal and Cammon bring, and they are even more impressive. Prescience, strength, and magic. Very hard to counter that."

"Your own gifts are spectacular," he said. "I will feel quite safe if you're the one to accompany me to the Shadow Ball at Coravann."

She laughed. "I would love to attend," she admitted. "But in what guise?"

"Why not go as you are now?" he said. "Is Casserah Danalustrous too good to be seen at such a function?"

She smiled a little. "Indeed, no, Casserah is unimpressed by class distinctions. But she hates all social events, so she would be unlikely to attend. However, the Coravann gentry are unlikely to know that. Perhaps I could go as myself after all."

"That would be even better," he said.

It took a moment for her to realize what he meant, and then she shot him a glance of irritation. He was laughing. She demanded, "Are you, in fact, the sort of man who can be entrusted with a secret?"

From horseback, he swept her a grand bow. "Serra, I can be trusted with anything you care to bestow on me."

She tried not to think of what that list might include—*my confidence, my heart*—and made her face stern. "Prove yourself first."

"That has been my goal since I met you."

IT took them two and a half days to make it to Coravann Keep, passing through landscape that was increasingly hilly and harsh. The Keep itself was a dour fortress within view of the Lireth Mountains. Kirra had not remembered how close it was to the Lirrenlands, if you discounted the effort it would take to cross the inhospitable Lireth range. She remembered the strange, cautious men she had seen on the streets of Kianlever Court and thought they might see even more of the Lirrenfolk here at the Keep.

Although they were not, at first, particularly evident. As if to make up for the grimness of its central feature, the city surrounding Coravann Keep was a joyful little place of small, pretty buildings, wide boulevards, and excessive flowers. Someone had gone to some trouble to anticipate the arrival of their party, for as soon as the procession passed through the city gates they were greeted by cheering crowds lined up on both sides of the main street. Children threw rose petals before the wheels of the lead carriage and young boys climbed each other's shoulders to watch them pass by. Kirra caught music from a dozen different sources as individual choirs greeted them with snatches of melody. Up and down the double line of the throng, the chants rose up: "Amalie! Amalie! Amalie!"

"Oh, this is delightful," Kirra said to Melly as she stretched out the window to see as many of the faces as she could. Up there was a juggler; over there, someone who looked like an acrobat. She could smell meat frying and beer heating up in the sun. "It's like a fair day. The Festival of Amalie."

"I'd be frightened to have so many people calling out to me like that," Melly said.

"The princess doesn't seem to scare too easily."

She was not surprised when her carriage halted behind the other two coaches as they came to a stop. "She's getting out," Kirra guessed. "So am I, then."

Indeed, her feet had barely touched the cobblestones before she saw Amalie, Valri, and Senneth disembark from the lead carriage. Valri looked unhappy about the decision, but as she joined the others, Kirra saw a faint smile on Senneth's face. They waited until the four Riders dismounted and formed a rectangle of protection around Amalie, then the eight of them moved to the very front of the procession. There was a great cheer when Amalie first stepped into view and waved at the crowd. No one surged close enough to try to touch her, though, no doubt discouraged by the upraised swords held in the Riders' hands.

They proceeded through the winding streets of the Keep city, encountering residents at every corner. Amalie and the

Riders stayed in the lead, Valri a few paces behind, Senneth and Kirra side by side behind her. Now and then Amalie paused to kneel on the stone road so a little girl could run up and throw a garland over her head. Twice she accepted gifts from boys who darted past the Riders to press something in her hand. No adults approached her; no apparent danger lurked in the open doors and windows of the buildings fronting the road. But Amalie's guards were ready for it if it were to come. Kirra gradually became aware that she was starting to sweat from a reaction to warmth much greater than the summer day would seem to warrant. Only then did she realize that Senneth was generating waves of heat, her body at a fever pitch to deliver fire if fire was suddenly called for.

She glanced up and spotted Donnal overhead, gliding above them on outstretched wings. "Hawk," she said to Senneth with a note of satisfaction.

Senneth nodded. Her eyes never left Amalie's back. "Won't protect her against an arrow," she said. "I'm hoping Cammon can do that. One cry from him and Tayse hauls her to the ground."

"I don't understand this girl," Kirra said, "but I'm starting to really like her."

A smile for that. "I feel exactly the same way."

By the time they finally reached the Keep, Kirra was feeling hot and just a little grumpy. It did not exactly cheer her up to pass between the spiked metal gates and stride up to the fortress itself, built entirely of a charred-looking black stone that had probably been quarried in the Lireth Mountains. Still, the reception at the doors was gratifying. Heffel Coravann was there to greet them, bowing low to Amalie, taking Valri's hand in a warm clasp, thanking all of them for coming. His servants distributed themselves efficiently among the party, taking charge of luggage, offering to lead travelers to their rooms.

"Welcome to Coravann!" Heffel called out, turning away from Valri to include the whole lot of them. He was big, somewhat bearlike, somewhat clumsy, with a florid face and dark hair just beginning to gray. A powerful man starting to show his age, Kirra thought. She knew that her father liked him. This made her believe he was much more astute than he might first appear. "I am very glad to have you here."

• • •

To Kirra's surprise, Senneth was not entirely pleased at the idea of her attending the Shadow Ball. "It seems dangerous," Senneth said. "If there are indeed malcontents gathering at these events—"

"Then I'll get a firsthand look at them."

"They are hardly likely to draw you aside and confide their plans for insurrection," Senneth retorted.

"They're hardly likely to pull me aside to kill me, either."

"No, but Romar might not be so safe."

"He'll bring his men."

"I wonder if Justin should go with you."

"Romar would rather have all the Riders watching Amalie."

"I'll see what Tayse thinks."

Tayse didn't share Senneth's concerns, or if he did, he considered both Kirra and Romar expendable, because the very next night, Kirra was dressing to attend the Shadow Ball. Melly was horrified that Kirra would waste her time attending such an inferior event and refused to let her wear any of her best gowns, but Kirra thought Casserah looked striking anyway in a dress of muted gold. She wore her ruby pendant and a simple hairstyle and decided she would be the equal of any lady at the gathering.

She had not really considered the logistics of the trip until she met Romar in the great, gloomy foyer of the Keep and glanced out at the courtyard. Yes, of course; they would need to take a coach to cover the ten or fifteen miles to the estates of Bat Templeson, where the ball was to be held. It was still daylight now, which would cut down on whatever romance the situation might inspire, but it would be well past midnight by the time they were traveling back.

She hadn't thought about that. Whether or not Senneth realized it, this might be the real reason the Shadow Ball was not such a good idea.

"You look lovely," Romar said, acknowledging her with a bow. "Shall we go?"

The trip out, at least, was passed in comfortable conversation. They watched the unfolding countryside and commented on any features that caught their eyes—attractive estates, roadside taverns, a field green with some crop neither of them could identify. Behind them on the road Kirra could occasionally catch the sounds of twenty men and horses as Romar's guards followed. She was surprised to find herself, even so, just a bit nervous about their safety should they actually be attacked on Templeson's lands. She did not think any soldiers could be matched alongside Tayse and the other Riders. And, after all, Merrenstow men were the ones who had yielded Romar up to abductors on the road to Tilt. No, she did not feel particularly well defended—but then, she was perfectly capable of defending herself.

It was close to dark by the time they arrived at the Templeson estate, a large, well-built mansion just now overflowing with light and music. Romar helped Kirra from the coach and kept her hand linked through his elbow as they approached the front door, where three men waited. Two were servants, poised to answer any need; one was their host. Both Kirra and Casserah had actually met Bat Templeson a couple of times, for he had been to Danalustrous. He was a short, good-looking, voluble man who seemed to possess inexhaustible energy. He had always seemed bent on proving himself to be an invaluable ally.

She imagined nothing could have made him happier than the regent's appearance at his door.

"Lord Romar! Such a pleasure to see you! My humble house is most honored by your presence!" His bow would have been acceptable to the king. "Bettany! Come see who has graced our ball."

The lady of the house hurried over, a small dark-haired woman who seemed to have energy to match her husband's. "Lord Romar! We were so pleased to get your note yesterday. Everyone is looking forward to meeting you. Let me take you in and make some introductions."

"First, I would like to present my companion," he said, resisting the lady's attempt to devour him on the spot.

Kirra held her hand out to Bat. "You know me, I think, though it has been a while since you were in Danan Hall."

"Serra Casserah!" he exclaimed, shaking her hand with great vigor. "No one told me you would be here."

"Perhaps Lord Romar omitted me from his note."

"Oh, but there are others here who could have spread the word. Erin Sohta is here tonight, and Berric Fann. They did not so much as mention your name!"

Kirra laughed at that while she mentally reviewed whether

she would have to avoid the people she knew. No; there was no disgrace to attending the ball, and neither Erin nor her uncle should have any reason to know that Casserah was safely back at Danan Hall. "I have been traveling casually and choosing events as they suited me," she said. "They did not know I would attend."

"Besides them, do you have friends here? Do you need me to make introductions?"

"I am able to fend for myself, thank you. You have other guests even now arriving at your door."

"Yes—well—look for Bettany if you find yourself at a loss," he said. "She will match you up with someone you will like."

At the moment, however, the lady of the house seemed more determined to promenade around the room with the regent on her arm. Kirra slipped away from the two of them and eased herself into the ballroom alone. She took a moment to glance around at the furnishings and decorations and found them understated and pleasing, all soft hues and summer flowers. The ladies on the dance floor were dressed as exquisitely as any serramarra, and they all wore jeweled pendants sized as if to cover housemarks, which none of them had. She could not help but notice that a high percentage of the pendants were moonstones and that a disproportionate number of the men wore the black-and-silver colors that Coralinda Gisseltess had appropriated as her own. More than a few also sported pieces of jewelry shaped like small red flowers. The crest of Gisseltess. Apparently a few of Halchon's vassals had chosen to attend the Shadow Ball in Coravann.

She could hardly start pacing around the ballroom, introducing herself at random, so she looked for one of the people she knew. Erin Sohta was immediately visible half a room away, her dark hair splendidly set off by the Danalustrous red of her gown. She did not spot Berric, and there was no sign of Beatrice, who might not have accompanied him anyway. She was surprised Berric was here; he was not overly social. But perhaps he had some connection with Bat Templeson. Or perhaps he had been in the mood to mingle.

Before she could cross the room to catch Erin's attention, she felt a hand on her arm. "Serra Casserah? I didn't know you were coming here tonight."

It was Heffel Coravann's daughter, a rangy girl with her father's height and darkness but a rather sharper set of features. "Lauren." Kirra greeted her with a smile. "I accompanied the regent, who wanted someone to make him look respectable. I didn't know anyone from the great House would be attending."

"My brother and I are both here. My father thinks it is an important gesture of goodwill, and I agree. But my brother is—" She compressed her lips and tried to smooth a look of fury from her face.

"Your brother is behaving badly," Kirra guessed. "Drinking too much, perhaps?"

"Yes! I'm so angry with him I don't know how I'll stand to ride home with him tonight."

"Worry about that later," Kirra suggested. "Try to enjoy yourself for now. Introduce me to a few of your father's favorite lords."

So that was pleasant enough, circling through the ballroom in company with someone who was clearly much beloved. It was always a good sign, Kirra thought, when the vassals felt a fondness for the heirs of the House; it generally meant the marlord's rule had been benevolent. More than one of them used their brief moment in Lauren's company to bring up a business matter or air a minor complaint, and Kirra was impressed with the girl's quick and competent answers.

She was surprised to be introduced to three men and two women who bore a curious resemblance to each other, who were dressed in clothes of very expensive fabric but extremely plain design, and who made almost no attempt at conversation. Both women wore their hair in tight rolls pinned at the base of their skulls; their demure gowns were ornamented by fine brooches set with black opals. Each of the men, dressed in even more somber colors, wore weapons belts hung with knives or swords. They all sized Kirra up with frankly measuring eyes. She could not tell what verdict they passed on her before they gave small bows and walked unceremoniously away.

"Well!" she exclaimed in an undervoice. "That was very odd."

Lauren glanced at her. "Don't be offended. They don't like strangers. But they consider it an honor to be invited to these events and assume it would be a great rudeness to refuse, so they make some effort to attend. They will be at my father's ball in two days as well."

"Are they—I'm not sure—are they from the Lirrens?"

Lauren nodded. "My father has established trading partnerships with a few families on the other side of the mountains. He works very hard at maintaining them because the business is lucrative, but he says no one else is as difficult to deal with and he is always afraid he will make a mistake. It was easier when my mother was alive, of course."

Kirra was at a loss. "Because—?"

"My mother was a Lirren girl."

Kirra felt her eyebrows spike. "I thought Lirren girls never married outsiders. I thought if they took a lover from over the mountains, that their fathers and brothers would hunt that man down and kill him."

A very small smile came to Lauren's lips. "Yes. And there's truth to that. Someday see if you can get my father to recount the tale of my mother's wooing."

"And do you know any of your mother's relatives?"

"Many of them, in fact. Uncles, cousins, second cousins—there is a whole vast clan network, but it would take me a day to explain to you how all of them are related."

Kirra laughed softly. "And I thought my own family was strange."

Lauren was still smiling. "Every family is."

They continued their circuit through the room. Those wearing moonstones and Gisseltess heraldry remained aloof as they were introduced to Kirra. Everyone else seemed delighted that another serramarra had attended their gathering. Lauren was pulled into yet another conversation about some tithing problem, and apologized to Kirra with her eyes as the grievance ran long.

Kirra touched her on the arm. "I see someone I know," she said, and slipped away.

Berric was standing by himself near a refreshment table, his heavyset body straining at his fine jacket and waistcoat. His face was drawn into a frown, but he didn't appear to be focusing his displeasure on anyone or anything in particular. Rather, he looked as if he was mulling over something and was not sure he liked his conclusion. Kirra grinned. Beatrice always claimed Berric was as grouchy as a water-soaked cat, but it was a side he rarely showed to Kirra. He was always pleased to see her, and she was delighted to encounter him in this unlikely place.

She snagged a glass of wine for him and water for herself and held out the wine to him as she approached. "You look deep in distressing thought," she said gaily. "Perhaps this will clear your mind."

His hand automatically reached for the glass, but his face did not, as she expected, miraculously clear. "Serra," he said in a flat voice. "This is the last place I would have expected to see *you*."

She was so surprised that she nearly dropped the goblet before he could take it from her fingers. She almost exclaimed, "Uncle! What's the matter?" before she remembered.

She was not Kirra. She was Casserah.

Berric and Beatrice hated Casserah.

She never made mistakes like that. Never.

She sipped from her water to cover her momentary confusion. "Perhaps you did not know that I have been traveling for the summer season," she said at last, her voice now as cool as her sister's would have been. "Part of my father's plan to renew friendships between Danalustrous and the other great Houses."

"And to allow everyone a chance to comment on your elevated status," he said. "Serramarra. One day to be marlady. You are to be congratulated."

Well, if this was how he always treated Malcolm and Casserah, no wonder they held him in some dislike. Kirra wanted to laugh, but she did not want to give herself away. "It is a difficult and consuming business to govern a realm," she said instead, her voice very serious. "I shall strive to be a steward every bit as good as my father."

"Or even better," Berric replied.

Really, just the edge of an insult there. She could hardly take offense since it was clear he was still enraged on Kirra's behalf. "But what brings you to Coravann?" she asked. "My sister told me you were injured when she saw you last. Are you well enough to travel so far?"

"Yes, my leg no longer pains me, thanks to Kirra's magic," he said, his voice warming as he said her name. "And I came for much the same reason you did—to improve relationships. I have many friends in this part of the country. I would hope to make more."

"I can introduce you to one man, if you have not already

met him," she said. "I was escorted by the regent, who is also bent on making friends. Do you know him? Would you like to?"

His eyes went past her to a figure across the room. "Romar Brendyn," he said in a considering voice. "No, I do not know him, and yes, I would very much like to. That would be a kindness, Casserah."

"Let me take you to him."

He offered her his arm, which she thought had to cost him something, and they made their way through the crowd. Kirra noticed that virtually everyone in the room acknowledged Berric with a bow or a friendly greeting. She had not realized her uncle had such an extensive network of contacts outside of Danalustrous. Perhaps that was because everyone else in Danalustrous, particularly her father and sister, seemed so insular that it never occurred to her that lesser lords would enjoy contact with outsiders. Even the visitors from Rappengrass and Helven knew him; even those from Gisseltess and Nocklyn.

Romar was just bowing his way to the end of a conversation with a very attractive older woman when Kirra and Berric fetched up beside him. He smoothly turned away from the woman and toward them, sketching another small bow. "Serra. I see you've made friends among these strangers."

"Ah, this is not a stranger. This is Berric Fann, my sister Kirra's uncle. One of his sisters was Kirra's mother, and Kirra has always been very close to him and to his other sister. Lord Berric, Romar Brendyn."

It would have seemed like a torturous introduction except the nobility were always obsessed by bloodlines and could follow complex genealogical charts in their heads. "I met serra Kirra a couple of months ago," Romar said. "I found her a most intriguing lady. I cannot remember the last time I liked anyone so well on short acquaintance."

Whether he said that to please Berric or annoy Kirra, it achieved both ends. Berric positively glowed, and Kirra glowered. "I have never met anyone I would consider her equal," her uncle replied.

That was certainly aimed at Casserah. "Yes, she is quite dear," Kirra drawled, boredom creeping into her voice. "Too bad she is not with us this very night."

Now Berric was annoyed and Romar was amused. "I am quite content with the company at hand," Romar replied.

Berric decided to ignore Casserah and subtly turned his shoulder to her. "What brings the regent to a humble ball in Coravann?" he asked.

Romar let his eyes wander around the fine decorations and the elegant dancers. "Would you call it humble?" he asked. "I think it an impressive display of prestige and power."

"Power?" Berric repeated. "I think most of the men and women in this room would say they have very little of it."

"And that makes them unhappy," Romar replied swiftly.

Berric shrugged. "Some of them. I think most would be easy to mollify. Some concessions here, some recognition there . . . They do not seem like unreasonable men to me."

"The king and his daughter are both desirous of maintaining excellent relations with the lesser lords," Romar said. "Perhaps sometime there could be a conference of sorts to discuss some of these—concessions."

Berric gave a little bow. "That would be most welcome," he said. He glanced around the room. "Though this is hardly the time."

"No," said Romar, smiling. "This is the time I would like to dance with serra Casserah."

Berric flicked her a look and Kirra almost could not prevent herself from adding, *Since her superior sister, Kirra, is not here for him to dance with instead.* Really, she'd had no idea Berric could seem so spiteful. And she certainly hadn't expected him to take up the cause of the Thirteenth House the minute he laid eyes on Romar. She felt she had missed all the interesting conversations of the night, which had probably occurred in darkened corners and back rooms and consisted of a lot of grumbling about the marlords and the great Houses. Not such a fun party after all.

"I will be happy to dance," she said, accepting Romar's extended arm. "Berric. So good to see you. Give my regards to your sister when you return home."

She was just as glad to be whirled away into the gaiety of a romping waltz, though she instantly realized she had traded one form of unease for another. Romar held her rather closer than propriety dictated and smiled down at her with satisfaction he made no effort to conceal.

"It looks like the same woman in my arms, but somehow it

feels different dancing with her when I know who she is," he murmured. "I will look forward to Heffel's ball."

"There will be nothing to look forward to if you do not behave with some decorum here," she said. "I seem to remember that all of my dances are already bespoke."

"Nonsense. Casserah is too cold to have all the young lords throwing themselves at her feet," he replied. "I predict you will sit out more than one number if I do not look after you."

"Casserah is not cold," Kirra argued. "She's—disengaged. Unless you happen upon one of the very few topics that interests her."

"Your uncle doesn't like her much."

Her laughter bubbled over. "No, wasn't that funny? I've never seen him so ill-behaved. He treats me with the utmost affection. He always hated Casserah's mother, you know, for displacing his sister. And now he hates Casserah for displacing me. It's hard to convince him that I don't mind." She sighed. "It's hard to convince anyone."

"I'm convinced," he said. She looked up at him, trying to read what lay behind that answer, and he smiled. "I think you would have hated being tied to Danan Hall. I think you would have tried your best to be a good marlady, and all your vassals would have loved you, and all the tenant farmers, and everyone who crossed the borders. And you would have done everything in your power to please them and keep the House strong, and you would have given up everything that you cared about, and you would have lived a frantic, hard, and wistful life. No one would have suffered but you. And I am glad your sister will be marlady instead, because I would rather that you be happy."

Almost impossible to make a reply to that speech. He had caught it precisely, of course. Everyone else had realized that Danalustrous could do much better than to have Kirra for its leader; only Romar seemed to have realized that Kirra could hardly do worse than to have Danalustrous as her responsibility. "I do love Danalustrous," she said in a low voice. "I need to be there from time to time, in order to feel whole, in order to—understand myself. I miss my father and my sister when I am gone from them too long. But they only hold pieces of my heart. The rest of the pieces are scattered across Gillengaria.

But Casserah—her heart is whole, and it is rooted in Danan Hall."

"My cousin is much the same way," Romar said. "He would rather be at Merren Manor than anywhere else in the world. And it's a fine place, a lovely hall, but it's only a building. It's only a plot of land. I feel the same about my own estates. I care for them, I want them to prosper, but I could let them go without too much distress. If I have to give them up in order to serve as regent, I will do so. Gillengaria matters more to me. My life does not center on a plot of land."

"So we have that in common," Kirra said.

He nodded. "As we have so many things."

She decided not to question that and let the dance come to its energetic conclusion without any more conversation. Indeed, she realized shortly, the event itself was almost over. People had already begun to leave in small groups, and Bettany was stationed at the door to offer formal farewells.

"We've got a long ride back," Romar said. "It might be time to call for the carriage and the guards."

Kirra nodded. "I have one more person to talk to. I'll meet you as soon as I can."

It took her a few minutes to locate Lauren, standing with her Lirren relatives on the far side of the room, and Kirra actually hesitated before going forward to join the conversation. But none of the Lirrenfolk looked actively hostile as she approached, and Lauren smiled at her.

"The regent and I are returning to the Keep now," Kirra said. "I wondered—if your brother is indisposed and not fit for travel—would you like to ride back with us? Your own carriage could remain here to bring him in the morning."

Lauren's dark face lit with relief. "Oh, yes! I would be so grateful. Let me just tell Bat—and my brother—what we've decided, then I'm ready to go."

It was possible Kirra surprised a look of approval on the face of the Lirren aunt, but it was possible the arched eyebrows signified nothing at all. Kirra gave them all a mute curtsey and turned away, meeting Romar near the front door to tell him she'd added a passenger.

She'd thought the news might annoy him, but instead he looked amused. "Shall we call ourselves her chaperone?" he said. He did not suggest the alternative, the truth, but clearly he understood Kirra's intent.

"I try to never overlook a chance to do a simple kindness," she said instead. "It will be no bad thing for Lauren Coravann to think well of Casserah Danalustrous."

There was a tedious wait while the departing guests jostled at the front door and dozens of carriages clogged the great driveway, but eventually their coach arrived and they were settled inside. The night air was still warm enough to be welcome, so they kept the windows open. It was always easier to talk in the dark, so the three of them exchanged observations and idle thoughts until exhaustion gradually made them lose interest in conversation. Kirra could tell, by his restless movements, that Romar was wide-awake for the duration of the drive, but Lauren fell asleep with her head against Kirra's arm when they had been in motion for about an hour. Kirra pretended to sleep a few minutes later.

And so the trip back offered no chance for flirtation or confidences, and they pulled up to the Keep having said nothing that the whole world could not overhear. Kirra could not decide if she was relieved or disappointed. She shook Lauren awake, and the three of them stumbled out of the carriage and into the shadowy foyer. Lauren was instantly whisked away by some female servant, and Kirra and Romar said brief goodbyes as they separated on the first landing.

Melly was asleep when Kirra let herself into the room, and Donnal was nowhere in sight. Probably outside in some avian shape, guarding Amalie's room. As Kirra swiftly undressed and slipped between the cool sheets, she wondered, once again, if Donnal's absence left her disappointed or relieved.

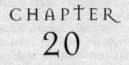

CHAPTER
20

AMALIE was enjoying herself in Coravann. Valri and Senneth were less enthusiastic. The princess had taken an instant liking to serra Lauren and her scapegrace brother, and the three of them began meeting in the morning to go horseback riding before the air grew too hot.

"I can see why *you* feel compelled to saddle up and ride out behind her, but I don't know why *Valri* feels she has to spend every waking moment in Amalie's company," Kirra said when Senneth wearily reported the details of another very early morning. They were sitting in Kirra's room drinking hot chocolate while Amalie took a bath in private. Kirra was not yet out of bed. It was the day of the great ball and she had decided to sleep as late as her body allowed and then do nothing until the evening rolled around. She was not accustomed to such laziness, but the idea seemed appealing.

"No, I don't understand it, either, but Valri seems bent on not allowing Amalie out of her sight, even for half an hour. She'll sleep apart from her if she feels Amalie is safe, but once Amalie's eyes open, Valri wants to be in the room."

"It's a little sinister," Kirra said, wrinkling her nose. "Does Amalie seem to mind?"

Senneth shook her head. "No. Even stranger, she seems— it's as if Amalie feels like *she* is the one protecting Valri. She can tell it soothes Valri to be near her, so she is very gentle with the queen. Whereas I," she added with asperity, "would have shoved her out the door and locked it in her face weeks before this."

"First setting her on fire."

"Contrary to what you and Justin think, I have not set that many people on fire."

Kirra sighed. "Well, that's a disappointment."

"Anyone you'd particularly like to see burn?"

"No, this has been a most sedate gathering. Even Toland Storian, of whom I had high hopes, has behaved with great circumspection. It's been a dull party all in all."

"That's the kind I like," Senneth said.

"I saw you talking to those odd people yesterday at dinner," Kirra said.

Senneth grinned. "Which odd people would those be? How can you choose among them?"

"Heffel's in-laws, I suppose. The people from the Lirren-lands. When *I* was introduced to them, they had nothing to say to me, but *you* were chatting away with them like you were old friends."

"I've never met them, but I know some of their kin connections, and family relationships are the single most important part of life in the Lirrens," Senneth replied. "They were friendly to me because I'm practically a sister. Or maybe a cousin."

"I always forget you lived in the Lirrens—all those years ago."

Senneth grimaced. "Seems like a different life. Before I became respectable. Before I became bodyguard to the king's daughter."

Kirra sipped from her chocolate. "And have your duties as bodyguard allowed you *any* time to spend with Tayse?" she asked in a soulful voice. "Or have you had to content your-selves with longing looks from across the ballroom?"

Senneth gave her a cool look from those gray eyes. "You're entirely too interested in the specifics of my love life. Perhaps you should develop one of your own instead."

"You might not approve of my choices."

"I imagine most people disapprove of many of your choices."

Kirra couldn't help giggling at that, but she protested. "I am not as reckless as people think. I am no wilder than you are incendiary."

Senneth was smiling. "Maybe it's just that people see the potential in us all the time and it makes them distrust us."

"They must lead extremely boring lives if watching us is their only entertainment."

"Oh, I don't know. I'd count my life as fairly adventurous, and yet I always get some amusement from watching you."

Kirra thought about throwing a pillow at Senneth's head, but didn't want to risk having chocolate spilled all over the bed. "So? You and Tayse? All is well with you?"

"Yes, serra. All is well with us."

Now Kirra's sigh was one of happy contentment. "Then who cares that this is such a dull party? As long as there is love in the world, that should be enough for all of us."

SHE dressed for the night in another red gown; the color was clearly Casserah's favorite. This one was a fat satin embroidered all over with clumped gold flowers. Warm for summer wear except that the sleeves were crafted of translucent tulle that glittered with a wash of crimson. Melly coiled her hair tightly to the back of her head, allowing only a few tendrils to escape around her face. Appraising herself in the mirror, Kirra thought Casserah looked a bit forbidding but very beautiful. Not at all wild. Anyone who wasn't afraid of her would likely decide she could be trusted.

Accurate enough. Anyone who earned Casserah's loyalty would have an ally for life. But it was not an easy thing to obtain.

She joined the other women in Amalie's room and exclaimed over Amalie's ivory dress and braided hair. Valri was in her usual green, Senneth again in bronze. "Soon people will be able to pick us out of the crowd merely by our colors," Kirra observed.

"It is not inappropriate to have a signature style," Valri replied.

Though this is not mine, Kirra thought. "Shall we go down to dinner?" she said instead.

For the past three days, their meals in the gloomy dining hall of the Keep had been cheerful and casual enough to counteract some of the pall cast by the black stones of the fortress, but tonight the atmosphere was of chilly formality. Eight long linen-covered tables were set with twelve places each, and it was difficult to talk with anyone but a near neighbor. Kirra thought the sounds of china and silverware were louder than the hum of conversation as everyone succumbed somewhat to the oppressive atmosphere. She was seated between two older lords she knew only slightly, and she couldn't feel that Casserah would exert herself much to charm them. So she concentrated on her food, eavesdropped when she could, and was much relieved when the meal was over.

The ballroom was much more festive, lit by four great chandeliers and dozens of candelabra. Inset into the marble floor was a huge replica of the Coravann crest, a six-pointed white star inside an oval of lapis lazuli. Sprays of deep blue flowers had been placed in white bowls throughout the ballroom, and curtains of the same colors hung at the ceiling-high windows along the western wall.

"How lovely this room is!" Kirra exclaimed to Lauren, who happened to be entering at the same time. "I can't imagine that you don't spend all day every day dancing, just to be in here."

Lauren smiled but was quickly called away. Kirra passed a moment hoping Romar had been wrong in his prediction that no cavaliers would seek out the cold-hearted Casserah, and soon enough, Darryn Rappengrass was by her side.

"I always look first for Danalustrous red, and there you are," he said. "Come dance with me. That will give me the strength I need to approach the hideous old dowagers that my mother insisted I court while I was here. But beauty first! Then duty."

So that was fun. Kirra had decided that even Casserah would not have been able to resist Darryn, so she always allowed herself to enjoy his company. After that, she was approached by a succession of partners, some young and shy, some old and purposeful, all of them desirous to prove themselves worthy of a Danalustrous partnership. Kirra thought again of her threat to find Casserah a husband while she was making the summer circuit. So far she hadn't made any progress. There wasn't one of these men she would marry herself.

Well, one perhaps. No use thinking of him.

Romar did dance with her—twice—but flirted with her no more than he might have with any other serramarra that he did not know particularly well. This depressed her, though she tried to pretend it didn't. Later she saw him lead first his niece onto the dance floor, and then Valri, which surprised her. She had never seen him exchange any but the most cursory conversation with the dark-haired queen. Then again, perhaps he had noticed, as many people had, that the only other man to ask Valri to dance was marlord Heffel Coravann. Romar had no doubt decided that things would look better if Valri did not seem to be granting all her favors to one man.

The ball was about two hours old when Kirra was approached by a stranger, a slim, beardless young man with light brown hair and an unaffected smile. He wore no immediately identifiable jewels or colors and looked like he might be a third or fourth son. Nobody important. Still, she liked the way he bowed to her, with an old-fashioned correctness, and his voice was strangely musical and pleasing.

"Would you do me the honor of a dance, serra?" he asked formally.

"I would. Thank you," she said, and slipped into his arms.

It was the best dance of the evening. Perhaps the music was especially good for this one number, or perhaps this young man, who looked so unprepossessing, was simply extraordinarily skilled at putting his partner at ease. He moved with the grace of an athlete or a fighter, someone intimately acquainted with all the poses of his body, and he anticipated her every shift as if he could scan her mind. But there was nothing flashy or outrageous about their dance. Merely, it felt like they had discovered the pure joy of motion and were able to share it; it was as if they were extensions of the music, drumbeat for heartbeat, flute for breath. Kirra felt her delight showing on her face, and once she laughed out loud as he spun her with particular dexterity out of the way of an inept oncoming couple.

"You are a very good dancer," she said, though they had accomplished most of the number in silence.

"With certain partners," he replied.

"I have not seen you before tonight."

A smile for that. "I am easily overlooked."

"I am glad you decided to show yourself to me."

The music came to a flourishing conclusion. He twirled her around once and then presented her with a deep bow. "To you and to no one else, serra."

And then she knew. "Donnal," she breathed.

He was laughing as he straightened up. "Serra," he repeated.

"Oh, let's do that again! It's been years since my father made us take dancing lessons! I'd forgotten how much fun it was."

He glanced around the room. "There are others who have more claim on your attention tonight."

But her hand was on his arm, insistent. The music was starting up again. "One more. Please? And then you can turn yourself back into a bat or a butterfly or whatever you were to slip into the ballroom without a card of invitation and with a face no one would recognize."

She knew he would not be able to resist her. If she asked him to, he would stay beside her all night or lurk in the shadows until she was free to grant him another five minutes of her time. She should perhaps send him to Amalie. The princess liked Donnal and would no doubt enjoy a respite from the fawning attention of all the ambitious lords.

No. She would keep Donnal beside her and not share him with anyone.

He bowed to her again and they slipped into the next dance—and then, when that one ended, a third. Anyone paying attention to serramarra Casserah would be starting to wonder about her strange partiality for an unknown suitor, but Kirra didn't think it would hurt her sister's credit any. Senneth had probably figured it out already and Romar—well, he might not have even noticed. Or cared if he had noticed. And Casserah was contrary enough to dance as long as she liked with whomever she pleased, be he the most eligible serramar in the Twelve Houses or the brother of the scullery maid. No one would think it strange.

But Donnal was more careful of her reputation than she was. After their third dance, they stood on the edge of the ballroom, catching their breath. "This should probably be where I leave you," Donnal said.

"Oh, no, not yet! One more!"

"You're supposed to be ensnaring potential allies for Danalustrous," he reminded her. "Not spending time with me."

"If it's a waltz, you have to dance."

"I don't think I should."

"Please."

He never could refuse her. She could see the helplessness in his eyes and felt an ignoble spurt of satisfaction. "Only if it's a waltz," he said.

"Or even a polonaise," she said.

But she had lost his attention. His predator's instincts had swung his head around to track a running shape that darted through the great door and dove through the elegant crowd like a slim fish through colorful waters. Beside her, Kirra felt Donnal tense, then relax, as he recognized the figure. "Cammon," he said. The boy headed straight for Senneth and whispered something in her ear.

"What's wrong? Can you tell?" Kirra whispered. Across the width of the room, she watched Senneth spin toward the door and stand there waiting, her face grim, her hands curled into fists. "She doesn't look afraid," Kirra said. "Angry, maybe."

"Senneth never looks afraid."

Kirra could not help a slight laugh at that. "Even so, maybe I should go wait with Senneth."

"No time," Donnal whispered.

Suddenly, it was as if all the candles in the room guttered at once. An unseen wind sucked all the flames from the chandeliers and sent a gust of cold blowing across the room. There was a murmur of surprise from everyone in the ballroom as couples relaxed their embraces and fell apart, and matrons leaned over to ask each other questions. Then the candleflames reignited, burned several degrees higher; the whole room glittered with light, though the temperature remained oddly cool. Kirra, who had cast her eyes around to try to determine the source of the strange breeze, looked again at the huge doorway.

Now filled with a small cadre of women.

In the lead was a shortish, square-faced woman dressed entirely in black. Moonstones gleamed around her throat and on every finger as if to lighten the effect of her dark gown and her graying black hair, but in fact they only accentuated the deepness of the colors. Her bearing was so self-assured that it made up for her lack of height. She stood quite still at the entrance to the room and looked around her as if surveying a collection of her own serfs and vassals—people she knew, people she owned.

"Coralinda Gisseltess," Kirra whispered.

Behind her stood a half dozen young girls dressed all in

white, seeming to cast light against Coralinda's darkness. They all stood demurely, hands before them pressed palm to palm, eyes downcast, unsmiling. "And a few of her novices," Donnal replied.

For a moment, no one moved, no one spoke, not the guests in the ballroom, not the visitors at the door. Then a lone figure cut through the gaping couples, arrived before Coralinda, and gave her a respectfully deep bow. It was Heffel Coravann.

"Serra," he said in his gruff voice. "Welcome to my house."

Then there was a ripple of movement throughout the room, as if all the people present suddenly shook themselves awake from a moment of aimless dreaming. Maybe a quarter of the guests surged forward, toward the door, as if to greet the new arrival. The rest broke into small groups and backed toward the walls, whispering. The room was filled with a low buzz of conversation and that persistent, creeping chill. The orchestra sounded a few tentative notes but did not launch into another melody, apparently convinced no one would take to the dance floor again.

"I have to talk to Senneth," Kirra said, and plunged across the room. Donnal followed.

Senneth was standing very still, exactly as Kirra had seen her last, except that she was turning her body infinitesimally to track Coralinda's movements. Valri and Amalie stood behind her as if using Senneth's body as a shield. Valri had taken the princess's hand and clutched it in a grip that Kirra imagined must hurt. Valri's normally pale face looked even whiter, almost frightened, but Amalie's foremost emotion appeared to be curiosity. She stood on tiptoe and craned her neck and tried to peer around Senneth to get a better look at the woman who served the Pale Mother with such devotion. Cammon stood halfway between Senneth and Amalie, poised as if to leap to either one's assistance. The notion made Kirra smile; he was such a slight boy, not much of a fighter. But his flecked eyes blazed with excitement. Clearly he thought this might be an evening of rare drama.

Senneth flicked Kirra a look as the other mystic arrived. "Now this was something I had not anticipated," Senneth said, and her voice was composed though she still looked angry. "The woman is bold."

Kirra turned so she could stand beside Senneth and watch

the scene before her. Coralinda was progressing majestically into the room, one arm linked with Heffel's. Her other hand was extended to press the fingers of all the people lined up to greet her, their own arms stretched out to touch her. "As is marlord Heffel," Kirra said. "I would not have believed he would have invited her here."

"She has not been interdicted. Only her brother," Senneth replied. "There is no quarantine keeping her at Lumanen Convent."

"There should be," Cammon said darkly.

"Why? What has she done?" Amalie asked, still twisting to see around Senneth's body. Kirra wondered how much her father had considered wise to tell her.

"Very little that can be traced to her," Senneth said over her shoulder.

An inarticulate exclamation from Cammon. "She took Tayse! She was going to kill him!"

"We have no proof of that. At any rate, she didn't harm him."

"She is guilty of other crimes," Valri said in a low voice.

"Yes, but what?" the princess asked.

Donnal answered. He had taken his own shape by now and no one in this particular group seemed surprised to see him at Kirra's side. "She is recruiting an army of malcontents and fanatics. They guard her and her growing band of converts at the Lumanen Convent, not far from here. There is also some speculation that she sends them out to harass and eliminate mystics, whom she considers abominations. And she is trying to convince the rest of Gillengaria to fear and hate those with any claim to magic. She is a danger to those of us who are mystics, but it is hard to know what other threat she poses."

"So far she has not spoken out against the king," Senneth said.

"Except to say he endangers the kingdom by tolerating mystics," Valri added swiftly.

Kirra spared the queen one quick look. Yes, the rumors persisted that Valri herself was sorcerous. Kirra had never seen her display the faintest trace of power, but perhaps she was very careful. In any case, she only had to enchant one man—her husband—to be considered lethal by those who feared magic.

"I wonder what she plans to accomplish by coming to Coravann," Senneth said.

"We must keep Amalie away from her," Valri said.

Senneth was quiet a moment. "Or make sure to introduce her."

"Coralinda Gisseltess cannot be trusted!"

"I'm not afraid," Amalie said. As she always said. Kirra was beginning to think it was actually true.

Senneth turned to give Amalie a long, thoughtful look, and Valri a quick one. "Coralinda can hardly do anything to the princess while we are standing here watching."

"She's *evil*," Valri said intensely.

Senneth nodded. "So I believe. But Amalie is safe with us. Here and now."

"I think I should introduce myself," Kirra said suddenly.

Senneth glanced at her, that faint smile on her face. "Has she never met you, serra Casserah?"

Kirra shook her head. "No, never. Don't you think she'd like to? My father knows her, of course."

"Bring her here when you've finished making polite conversation," Senneth said.

"It's not safe," Valri insisted.

Senneth didn't even turn her head. "Cammon. Go fetch Tayse."

There was a grin in Cammon's voice. "All right." A rustle of ragged clothing and he was gone.

Kirra was smiling. "Let me go make myself known to our unexpected guest."

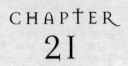

CHAPTER
21

KIRRA made her way across the dance floor, mostly empty by now as people clustered in small groups against the walls. The orchestra had given up any notion of playing dance music and now offered a muted score of soft strings and wistful reeds. Servants were circulating through the room, carrying wine and other refreshments. Kirra snagged a glass of water from one tray, drank it all down, and handed it to the next servant who passed.

By this time she was on the outskirts of the group still gathered around Coralinda Gisseltess. Worthwhile to take note of those who were fawning over the woman who headed the Daughters of the Pale Mother, and those who had gathered in the corners of the room to scowl at her. But the quick tally did her no good, for it seemed that some members of the Twelve Houses could be found in either camp. And she herself, representing Danalustrous, was carefully pushing herself through the crowd, impatient to introduce herself—and all the gods knew that she was no fan of any of the heirs of Gisseltess.

"Excuse me," she murmured, slipping between two women who wore moonstone pendants over their housemarks and who watched the newcomer with reverent eyes. "I beg your pardon." Her left hand was deep in a hidden pocket of her red gown, closed around the small, smooth shape of the striped stone lioness. Just the feel of it gave her courage and strength. *Wild Mother watch me,* she thought, and broke through the final circle of bodies surrounding Coralinda.

She found herself side by side with Heffel Coravann, who looked down from his superior height to give her a rather silly smile. "Serra," he acknowledged. "Would you like to meet the Lestra?"

She felt her eyebrows arch in what surely would have been Casserah's most supercilious expression. "The 'Lestra'?" she repeated.

He nodded. "The title accorded the woman who leads the Daughters," he said.

She remembered now; Tayse had returned from Lumanen Convent with that name upon his lips. "A self-proclaimed title, I assume?" she said coolly. Heffel looked scandalized.

"No, no, she is a most devout lady," he said. "Come, let me introduce you."

Coralinda finished some conversation with a fatuous-looking older man, who bowed deeply and touched his right hand to his left shoulder. Kirra was a little shocked; that was a gesture that the Riders commonly used to acknowledge their king, or vassals used to honor their marlords. She had never seen anyone use it to express reverence for a religious figure. Coralinda nodded to him and turned away, her eyes searching the crowd for the next supplicant.

Heffel immediately caught her attention. "Lestra," he said. "May I present another admirer? Serramarra Casserah Danalustrous, who is most desirous of meeting you."

Coralinda was shorter than Kirra, yet Kirra still had the sense of looking up into a face some immense distance away. That the face showed a certain surprise was gratifying. "Serra," Coralinda repeated. "I am pleased to meet any admirer from the House Danalustrous."

She extended her hand, wrist and every finger clenched with moonstones, and Kirra held her breath as she laid her own hand against Coralinda's. Cammon's magic held, but barely; she felt a jolt run up her wristbones and quiver all the way down her spine. She squeezed the lioness in her pocket even more tightly, and the trembling ceased.

"Serra," she drawled in turn, because she was not going to flatter the old hag by offering made-up titles. "I never would have expected to find you at such a frivolous event. My father has given me to think you are the most serious of women, but here you are, come to dance with the rest of us on a summer's night."

The frostiest smile crossed Coralinda's face. "Not at all," she said. "I came to see my friends among the Twelve Houses, conveniently gathered in one place."

"I had not realized you had so many," Kirra said.

"There is much that Danalustrous does not seem to realize," Coralinda replied.

"Is that so?" Kirra said in a musing voice. "And yet, my father is a very observant man. I have never found much that escaped his attention."

"Your father makes dangerous choices."

Kirra opened her eyes very wide. "Dangerous? How? Are there armies even now headed for the Danalustrous borders? Let me know, and I will send word to my father."

The Lestra was not amused. "He endangers his soul, Casserah. He starves it. And he feeds it instead with a diet guaranteed to make him sick."

"You talk in riddles, serra."

"I am not averse to plain speaking," Coralinda replied. "Your father allies himself with mystics and offers them safe harbor. Such sorcerous association will sear his soul."

"You speak of my sister?"

Coralinda nodded. "Your sister and others whom Malcolm has befriended. He does not realize the danger he puts himself in—himself, his heirs, and his realm."

"I do not feel endangered."

Coralinda leaned forward, suddenly intent. Kirra felt herself sparkle with chill, as if the Lestra herself exuded an icy air. "You are opaque," she murmured. "You are the strange, dark daughter that no one has been able to penetrate, and even I cannot read you. But I would be glad to know you better. I would be glad to explain to you some of the glories of the goddess—and some of the perils of your own path. Come to me—tomorrow or the next day. I will visit here awhile. I will propound to you on the mysteries of the true faith."

Kirra felt her heart pounding. She could imagine few things she was less interested in doing than having an exclusive audience with Coralinda Gisseltess to discuss the Pale Mother. But Casserah would not have hesitated; Casserah would not even have been alarmed. "Perhaps, serra," she said. "If my party and I stay another day or two, I can take you up on this generous offer. I am interested to learn what you are so eager to teach."

Coralinda reached up one of those bejeweled hands to trace the curve of Kirra's cheek. Kirra felt the moonstone etch a line down the bone, barely concealed by the mortified skin. "You are young and beautiful and intelligent," Coralinda murmured. "It is so important that the ones like you do not go astray."

It was actually rather difficult to speak calmly. "There are others here even more young and beautiful," she managed. "Would you like to be introduced to the princess? She is across the room and most agog to meet you."

Coralinda's square face sharpened with interest and she dropped her hand. "Amalie is here? Her father has released her from the prison of that walled city?"

"I do not think she considers it a prison, but yes, she is traveling. She is here now. Let me take you to her."

"I would like that very much," Coralinda said. Taking Kirra's arm, she paced forward across the white star in the lapis oval, heading in Senneth's direction.

Kirra felt heat flash up through her bones and turn her whole body into an inferno. She had the quick, irrelevant thought that this must be what it was like to be set on fire by Senneth's magic. She actually stumbled, the pain was so intense, and Coralinda gave her an inquiring look.

"Turned my ankle," she gasped. "My heels are too high."

"Something else we must talk about," Coralinda said. "The hazards posed by ridiculous fashions." She squeezed Kirra's hand in a friendly way, and Kirra felt her wristbones kindle within her skin.

Across the room, Cammon glanced up, looked straight at her. He murmured something to Senneth, then hurried across the dance floor to intersect with Kirra.

"There are chairs over by that wall. Let's go sit there," he said, guiding them in the proper direction by laying a hand across Kirra's back.

The agonizing knife of fire throughout her body cooled into smoke and drifted away. Just with the touch of his hand on her body. She could not keep herself from sending him one quick, marveling look. He kept his eyes straight ahead, urging them forward, but she saw a tiny smile play around his mouth.

Now that was frightening. That was almost as frightening as seeing Coralinda Gisseltess at Coravann Keep. From thirty yards away, Cammon could sense her pain, and as soon as he touched her, he could make it vanish. She had never heard of anyone with power like that.

They made their way not entirely smoothly across the room, interrupted at frequent intervals by lords and ladies approaching Coralinda for a benediction. Finally, finally, they arrived at a cluster of chairs and sofas that seemed designed for some kind of intimate conference. The others, unimpeded by well-wishers, had arrived before them—not just Senneth and Amalie, but Valri, Donnal, Tayse, and even Justin.

And Romar, come to defend his niece from danger. He looked fierce, serious, and handsome, but he was not even wearing a dress sword. Kirra thought if she were making wagers on who in this group might keep Amalie safe, it would be Senneth and the Riders.

And Cammon, if the touch of moonstones burned Amalie's skin.

Coralinda dropped Kirra's hand and very properly curtseyed, as any serra would to royalty. Kirra took a deep breath and refused to look down at her disguised flesh, but she knew that in its proper shape it would be crisp with red welts. Amalie responded to Coralinda's curtsey with a dignified nod. Though they had purposefully gathered around this arrangement of furniture, no one sat.

"Do you know all my friends?" Kirra asked, dying to introduce Donnal and Cammon as well as the high-ranking individuals, but deciding that even Casserah would not be so audacious. "Senneth Brassenthwaite, of course. You remember her." Coralinda was unlikely to forget. "Queen Valri. Lord Romar Brendyn of Merrenstow. And Baryn's daughter, Princess Amalie."

Coralinda did not bow again, but she gave quick nods of recognition to everyone except Senneth. Her eyes moved beyond the circle of nobility to settle on the big Rider standing just a pace behind.

"Tayse," she said, her voice sorrowful. "I am sorry to see you here among these fellows."

"Lestra," he replied. His face was absolutely expression-less, but Kirra would swear he was amused.

"I had hopes for you," Coralinda continued. "You have such strength. I hate to see it corrupted."

"I am happy where I am."

Senneth spoke, her voice edged. "It is hardly my place to teach you manners, but you would more profitably direct your attention to the princess," she said. "Who is most eager to make your acquaintance."

Coralinda transferred her gaze to Amalie. Kirra had a strange moment of blurred vision when it seemed her eyes could not take in both of them at once, the dark, malevolent Lestra and the red-gold princess, hair and dress softly gleam-ing in the unreliable candlelight. Beside her, she heard Cam-mon take a deep breath. Senneth's face showed a moment of confusion. Then Amalie moved and the illusion was broken and everyone looked ordinary, if a little grim.

"I am charmed to meet the princess," Coralinda said. Her voice was surprisingly beautiful; she must be hypnotic when she told a story or explained a metaphor. "You are quite beautiful."

"And you are most impressive," Amalie replied in her demure way. "I am glad to finally get a chance to see you face-to-face."

"But I cannot stand here and merely mouth platitudes," Coralinda said, and everyone standing nearby stiffened with outrage. She leaned forward but did not get so close to Amalie that the Riders put their hands on their swords. "You are in danger, princess. Take care."

Romar made a sudden movement, as if to throw himself forward and shield Amalie with his body, but Senneth flung out a hand to hold him in place.

Amalie did not seem alarmed. "What danger? Where? Only show me and I will prepare," she asked in her soft voice. Kirra thought suddenly, *Have I been underestimating her all along because she speaks so quietly? Listen to what she says! And how she says it!*

Coralinda's voice dropped almost to a whisper, intense and persuasive. "You are surrounded on all sides by mystics, majesty. They are not to be trusted. They will harm you delib-erately if they can—and even if they leave you whole, they will destroy you. They will leach away your soul. They will poison your heart. They will turn your sweet blood to black tar as it moves through your veins."

Amalie did not look dismayed in the slightest. "I wonder why it is you have such fear of mystics, serra," she said politely. "Have they ever harmed you in any way?"

Coralinda flinched back. "Harmed me! No. I am impervious to magic. But they have great influence with the weak and the simple-minded."

"And you think I am weak and simple-minded?"

Absolute silence at that. No one could quite believe Amalie had said it. Senneth's face did not change by so much as a muscle, but Kirra could almost hear her laughing. Very slowly, very carefully, Romar turned his head to give his niece a speculative appraisal.

"I do not know," Coralinda replied somberly. "But you are practically a child still. You are easily swayed by the people around you who appear to love you and mean you well. Trust me when I say these folks are a chancre in your heart, and they will eat you from the inside."

"What reason do I have to believe *you* mean me well, Coralinda?" Amalie said, and she appeared to be genuinely asking for information.

"I serve the goddess, who offers only light," the Lestra immediately replied. "She can guide you to the true path."

"You mean you can guide me."

"I do."

"I don't trust you," Amalie said.

There was another profound silence.

"And I don't, in fact, believe you mean me well," the princess continued in a conversational voice. It was as if Coralinda had proposed that she wear a blue gown to her next ball and Amalie was deciding against it for rather trivial reasons. "You are very ambitious and you are very interested in power. I cannot trust ambitious people when they are trying to claw their way closer to the throne."

"And this lot, these adventurers and schemers you have surrounded yourself with?" Coralinda shot back. "You think they are not ambitious as well? You think they have not allied themselves to you because they are interested in power?"

Amalie actually laughed. The rest of them were frozen. "Valri is so little interested in the crown that she would disappear from the ballroom right now if she felt free to do so," Amalie said. "Casserah would rather be in Danalustrous than anywhere else you could name, including Ghosenhall. And even you must realize that the only thing Senneth would do with temporal power is throw it away. These are not people who would steal my throne from me. They don't want it."

"And Romar Brendyn of Merrenstow?" Coralinda asked in a very low voice. "The regent is not interested in the throne?"

Kirra felt herself grow cold all over.

Could Coralinda Gisseltess be behind the attacks on Romar? Could that be why they had seemed so random, so disorganized, so unlike Halchon's usual cruel efficiency? Because they had been carried out not by his ruthless and well-trained troops but by scattered individuals loyal to the Lestra and acting on her ill-defined charge? *Rid me of this regent, any way you choose.* It was certainly possible.

Romar answered the accusation. "No, serra," he said. "I would not take the throne from my sister's child. In fact, I would give my life to see that she attains it."

"If she attains it with the aid of mystics and charlatans, she will not sit there long," Coralinda prophesied.

"And would you be the one to try to dislodge her?" Senneth asked coolly.

Coralinda gave her a look of such hatred that even Senneth looked surprised. "I would use every means in my power to make sure she held the throne without people like you at her side."

Senneth nodded. "So you threaten me, not Amalie. You think that sounds less like treason."

"I do not speak treason at all. I carry the goddess's word through Gillengaria. And the goddess abhors mystics. And mystics will all be dispersed or destroyed. And anyone who clings to mystics is likely to find her own world destroyed as well."

"I wonder what you are so afraid of," Amalie said.

Coralinda gave her a look of frigid fury for that. "I am afraid of nothing! Except seeing the kingdom fall into the hands of soulless men and women. Majesty, they surround you, but I can free you from their coils. Come to me at Lumanen. You will be safe there."

And she reached out to clutch Amalie's arm.

For a moment, Kirra's vision wavered again. Shadows seemed to swoop in from all sides, and her whole body grew cold. Either she closed her eyes for a moment or someone moved too quickly for her to follow, for when she could focus again, Coralinda had been shoved two paces back from Amalie—and Valri was standing with her body between the women.

Valri. Not Senneth or Tayse. And her perfectly white, perfectly shaped face was strained with rage.

"Never touch her," the queen spat out. "*Never* lay your hand on the princess again."

"You're a fool," Coralinda said in an icy voice. "I want to save her, not harm her."

"I am safe where I am," Amalie said, completely unruffled. "But I think you antagonize my friends. If we are to talk again, it must be some other place and time."

Thus with utter composure dismissing such a dangerous and angry foe! Kirra briefly lifted her gaze from Amalie's face to meet Senneth's eyes. "Perhaps someone can escort the Lestra back to the marlord," Kirra suggested.

"Cammon," Senneth snapped, and the boy stepped forward.

Coralinda made a deep, slow curtsey and surfaced, looking straight at Amalie. "Remember what I told you," she said. "Come to me at any time."

Amalie inclined her head. "Thank you for the offer."

And she watched—they all watched—in silence as Cammon offered Coralinda his arm and accompanied her back across the ballroom.

"That's the most terrifying woman I've ever met in my life," Senneth said at last, breaking the silence that held them all speechless. "I can't figure out what makes her so frightening— I can't see how she can hurt any of us. Here. Now. And yet just seeing her makes my body tense for battle."

Valri had moved a step away from Amalie. Kirra still couldn't understand how she had moved so fast. "I told you. She's evil," the queen said.

Senneth nodded. "Oh, yes. And the more so because she believes she's good."

"If it makes you feel any better, she's afraid of you, too," Amalie said in her soft voice.

Senneth turned to look at her. They all did. "What I don't understand is why *you* aren't afraid of her," Senneth said slowly. "Or were you just pretending?"

Amalie looked surprised. "Why would I be afraid? What

can she do to me? Especially with all of you standing right here?"

Senneth still watched her, puzzlement on her face. "I don't know," she said. "I don't know."

"Speaking in more practical terms," Kirra said, "did anyone think she was threatening Lord Romar? She all but came out and accused him of coveting the throne."

"I don't think she's very interested in me," Romar said. "It's the rest of you she wants to see disposed of."

"I'm not sure she's too particular," Tayse said. "I think she'd like to chip away at the entire circle protecting the princess. I think she'd like to see the princess completely vulnerable and friendless—with only herself as an ally."

"That plan seems destined to fail," Romar remarked.

A small smile from Senneth. "Indeed. She does not seem to realize how deep both our devotion and our resources run."

"Two swords and a woman who manufactures fire," Valri said in a contemptuous voice. "Forgive me if I don't think those resources so vast."

To everyone's surprise, Amalie laughed. "Oh, Valri. If any harm had threatened me, Justin and Tayse and Senneth would have beaten it back, while Donnal changed himself into a bear or a great hunting bird and carried me off to safety."

The words gave Kirra a peculiar start. She had not realized that Amalie felt so comfortable around Donnal that she would trust her person to him in whatever guise he took. Tayse himself put his hand to his left shoulder, bowing, and Justin followed suit.

"Yes, majesty, I believe we can protect her from the foes she might find here," Tayse said in a serious voice. "She has many enemies, and they are not all in this room. But we will not fail her father, and we will not fail her."

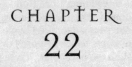

CHAPTER
22

THEY left Coravann in the morning, though Kirra insisted she could not leave without confronting their host. She was more subtle about it when she actually tracked him down in his den, arguing with his steward. He dismissed the other man and greeted her with his usual lumbering charm.

"Sit, sit," he invited, sinking to a plush leather couch and waving her to a chair. "What did you think of the ball last night, eh? Quite a turnout, I thought."

"Even your in-laws from the Lirrenlands were there," Kirra said. "Though not particularly friendly."

He snorted. "That *was* friendly, for them."

"Even the Lestra from the Lumanen Convent."

"An amazing woman," he said earnestly.

Kirra toyed with her ruby pendant, this morning worn over a high-necked traveling gown. "You realize she has set herself against the king," she said in a soft voice.

Heffel looked astonished. "Coralinda! No. She has no interest in politics—though her brother, now, he's a different story. Coralinda cares only for serving the Pale Mother."

"Not entirely true," Kirra said.

He blustered a bit and she waited him out till he finally looked at her with a frown on his face. "Why are you bringing this up? What are you worried about?" he asked.

"Coralinda despises mystics and is on a campaign to abolish them. The king welcomes mystics and has invited many into the highest circles of his court. The question is: How do *you* feel about mystics? Which side would you choose, if sides were to be chosen?"

"I am so tired of talk about a stupid war!" he exploded. "Who will fight whom—who sides with what House. Let it be! There should be no war! Let us all live in peace—mystic, marlord, Lestra, Lirrenfolk, and ordinary men!"

"Fine in theory," Kirra said. "But if war comes, who will you support?"

He looked at her a long time, his eyes watery in his crumpled, aging face. Easy to write him off as a big, ungainly man too simple to know when the realm faced danger. But suddenly he did not look at all stupid to Kirra. He had married a Lirren girl, something that literally never happened, and for years he had run a vast and wealthy House with no hint of turmoil or scandal. "I will not go to war," he said at last. "I have no quarrel with mystics, though I worship the Pale Mother and I find she gives me a deep sense of peace. I honor my king and I would not fight against him, so you can be sure I would not join any ambitious rebellion. But I will not send my vassals into war. I will not ask my tenant farmers to put down their plows and take up swords. If war comes, it will come without Coravann."

"Easy to say," Kirra said. "Not so easy to achieve when your near neighbors come tramping through your farmers' fields."

"They will not come through *my* fields," he said.

She sighed and stirred on her chair. "You sound like my father."

"That's a compliment."

She came to her feet. "But I find myself more cynical than either of you. I do not think it will be so simple to sit back and watch the kingdom be ripped apart, whatever your intentions now."

He stood beside her, reached out to take her hand in one of his great, warm paws. "You need not worry for your sister's safety, serra Casserah," he said. "At least not at my hands. I will lift a sword against no one, and everyone is welcome at my gate."

"I cannot quarrel with your sentiments, but I wish you were a little more discriminating in your friends, marlord," she said, sinking into a graceful curtsey with her hand still in his. "But as long as you do not plot against us, I consider myself lucky. Thank you for a most enjoyable party."

He kissed her on the cheek and she left. Back in her room, she found that Melly had finished packing everything and was directing servants in how to load the carriage. No time to visit with Coralinda Gisseltess, for which she was just as glad. She wrote the Lestra a brief note, doing a fair imitation of Casserah's handwriting, and expressed her regret that their interview would have to be postponed. Then she hurried downstairs to see if the carriages were pulled up to the door. She found she was eager to move on, to leave Coravann Keep behind.

BUT the journey itself was odd, askew, though it took Kirra a day or so to sort out why. The weather was unexpectedly hot and the carriages were stifling. It didn't help that their pace was so slow, for the main road between Coravann and Nocklyn was narrow, picking its way alternately through tall forests and flatlands of dense, prickly shrubbery. In addition, their party was so large: three carriages, a half dozen packhorses, Romar's men, the Riders, the palace soldiers, and the primary members of the traveling party themselves. Romar's captain, Colton, had become de facto organizer of the whole mess, setting the pace, determining who rode in what order, and essentially keeping them all together in a relatively efficient way.

The Riders had made it clear they were in charge of defense. Tayse always rode fifty or a hundred yards ahead of the others, returning from time to time to check that no one had died in his absence. Justin rode just about as far in the rear to make sure no one came from behind by stealth. The other two Riders—Kirra had finally learned that their names were Coeval and Hammond—kept to either side of Amalie's carriage, watching her no matter what the distractions.

That first day, the first distraction was the heat. Well before noon, Kirra had decided she couldn't stand it anymore. When they came to a halt to clear a fallen tree from the road, she hopped out of the coach and found a spare horse and saddle. Within minutes, she was mounted and trotting next to Donnal, who was still in human shape and on horseback himself. She felt instantly more cheerful.

Her example inspired Amalie and Senneth, who soon found horses of their own. Valri kept to the carriage and said she didn't mind the heat, and nothing would induce Melly to ride if she could lie on a cushioned seat in a carriage and drowse.

When they halted for the lunch break, the women sat together and discussed which items of clothing they might be able to remove and still look royal or at least respectable. There were a few giggling retreats to the closed coaches while undergarments came off and lighter-weight skirts were substituted for current items. Kirra, at least, felt better afterward, and judging by Amalie's laugh and Senneth's smile, both of them were cooler and happier as well.

Though Senneth's skin was never actually cool to the touch. And, in fact, she never seemed to mind the heat. But she seemed to be enjoying herself anyway.

Even Valri chose to ride for the second half of the journey, settled on the back of a night-black mare with all the unconscious grace of someone who'd grown up in the saddle. Another small piece of the puzzle Kirra was assembling about the mysterious young queen. Not a lord's daughter, most likely; most noblewomen were only indifferent horsewomen, as they spent more of their time on other pursuits. Kirra had gained all her ease on horseback in the last eight years as she went off on her wanderings.

Romar Brendyn said as much as he ranged up beside her. "I am surprised to see that Casserah Danalustrous is an excellent rider," he said. "She must spend more time in the saddle than most ladies I know."

Kirra laughed. "No, in fact, I am not being quite true to my role at the moment. But it is very hard to pretend to be awkward in the saddle when in fact you feel quite comfortable there."

"And look superb."

"Thank you, my lord," she said, and changed the subject. "I talked to Heffel this morning. He says he won't take sides if a war comes. Do you think we can believe him?"

"I think we don't have a choice. But I think he'll find his principles hard to stick to if war actually arrives on his doorstep."

"If he must choose sides, I think he'll take ours."

"I hope so," Romar said, "for he is a key ally." Kirra sent him an inquiring look; she was not used to thinking Coravann particularly strategic. "Because of the Lirren connection," he added. "He has friends across the mountain. Does he have any influence with them? Can he convince them to ally with us? Perhaps not—but perhaps. I would not like to lose that link."

"I would not think the Lirrenfolk are likely to be drawn into any fight between Houses."

"Perhaps not. But they might think that an aggressor, once used to the idea of conquest, could start looking around for new lands to take over. That's what I'd think, at any rate, if my near neighbors started annexing property."

"I just wish I knew for sure," she said, "what House would take what side."

They debated that topic for a while, arguing loyalty, history, ambition, and tolerance for mystics. Kirra noticed that, no matter how deeply they got into their own discussion, Romar's attention was never entirely on her. He was watching the road; he was listening to the hoofbeats of the riders behind him; he was observing his niece and the other members of their party. His eyes returned again and again to the riders in front of them, and finally he shook his head and laughed.

"What can *they* be talking about?" he wondered.

Kirra let her gaze rove over the other pairs of riders, which was when she realized that no one was with the right partner this afternoon. Amalie and Donnal rode side by side, the princess talking with great animation while Donnal courteously angled his head to listen. When had they become friends? While he perched in owl shape on her windowsill at night? That seemed unlikely. So when? And what was she telling him that he found so captivating? Donnal could be an excellent listener, since he rarely had any inclination to talk, but the expression on his face was usually far more neutral than this look of crinkled amusement. Kirra wouldn't have thought the sheltered princess would have had too many funny stories to tell. Clearly she was wrong.

Behind Donnal and Amalie rode an even less likely couple: Cammon and the queen. Their conversation appeared to be more balanced and a little less animated. By the intent expression on Cammon's face and the thoughtful expression on

Valri's, Kirra had to guess he was asking questions—about what, only the gods would know—and Valri was giving measured answers.

But Romar had been referring to neither of those strange pairs when he asked his question. He was watching Senneth interact with Colton, a conversation that appeared to be another give-and-take between equals. "He is not the kind of man who usually strikes up friendships with serramarra," Romar continued rather blankly.

"Maybe he doesn't realize who she is," Kirra suggested. "Senneth has spent the last seventeen years roaming the country—and other countries as well. Maybe she's telling him about some of her adventures. Maybe he thinks she's just a hired sword."

"Maybe," Romar replied, sounding unconvinced. "But Colton tends to be shy of women. He is not even comfortable having a conversation with my wife."

The word hit like a blow. Kirra rode on a few moments in silence, trying to think of something else to say. Romar glanced over at her and she saw his face twist.

"Sorry," he said. "I've tried to be careful."

She could not even shake her sister's dark hair and pretend she didn't know what he meant. Instead she asked, in a quiet voice, "Why don't you tell me about her? What's she like? When did you decide to marry? It might be useful for me to have an image of her in my head."

He nodded and seemed to think it over. "It was my mother's idea that I marry," he said at last. "By the time I turned thirty, my younger brother already had a wife and two children. Both girls, neither so steady and serious that you'd instantly think, 'Ah, she'd be a good one to leave the property to.' And I was the heir, after all. It behooved me to try to get an heir of my own."

"And you didn't already have your eye on some exquisite young lady who could run your household at your side while bearing you a multitude of blond young sons?"

He grinned briefly at the picture. "Strangely, no. I hadn't been much of one for the social circuit—as you might have guessed, seeing how I despise the events we've been forced to attend. So, I had only met a handful of eligible young women and none of them had—I hadn't—it is not such an easy thing to look at a person and say, 'Yes, that's the one I want to spend the rest of my life with. That one and no other. I can stop looking now.' Because it's not just that she'll be helping you run the household and interviewing for a new head cook and training your sons how to be courteous to their elders. I could think of a handful of young women who would have been highly skilled at those tasks. But it's that you have to wake up in bed next to her—for the next thirty or forty years. That makes it harder to choose."

Kirra couldn't help giggling, though she knew she shouldn't. "But then you stumbled upon a paragon—"

He hesitated, then shrugged his shoulders. "I looked for a while. Two years, I suppose. I went to Ghosenhall and the balls of the northern Houses. I saw no one who appealed to me so much I was moved to offer her my heart." He glanced over at her again. "I don't remember seeing you *or* your sister at any of these events."

"No, Casserah rarely leaves Danalustrous. I leave it all the time, but I do not always go to—" She made an elaborate gesture. "The places you might encounter the nobility."

"So I lost interest in the notion of marrying for love, but I still had to marry. I allowed my mother to suggest a few names. She was most enthusiastic about Belinda, whose father owned property not far from ours. I'd met her a number of times over the years, of course. Now I began to view her in a new light, evaluating her strengths, judging how I might tolerate her if I had to spend unbroken days in her company. She's a very—how to describe her—a very soothing person. She is small and dark-haired and restful. She doesn't fret. She's not easily overset. She's efficient and thoughtful, and she likes to solve problems. She treats everyone she encounters with the same simple kindness so that everyone, from the lowest footman to the king himself, feels comfortable with her. Anyone could look at her and see she would be an excellent mother. And I was sure she would make me an excellent wife." He looked over at Kirra again, very briefly. "And she has."

Kirra felt even more miserable, though she tried to conceal it. "I thought you had no children."

He shook his head. "No, not yet. It is a source of some concern to Belinda that she has not conceived during this first year. But both my mother and hers say that babies take their own time and she shouldn't worry. Meanwhile, she has her

"Are you going to start looking now?"

Now that you've met me, he implied. *Now that I've made you examine what it might feel like to be in love.* "I will go on as I always have," she said. "I don't know yet what has changed."

"Everything has changed," he said.

"And nothing," she said. "Not the way I live my life, not the way you live yours. We both go on as before."

"We go on," he said, "but I am a different man."

hands full enough handling the estates now that I am gone so much. I don't know that she expected to marry the regent of the realm and to become so responsible for duties that should be mine. But she has not complained. In fact, she has done a remarkable job."

"Indeed, she sounds most—most estimable," Kirra replied, stumbling over the words. Belinda Brendyn sounded like a woman it would be impossible to hate. Bad news for Kirra.

He turned his head again to look at her, his face sober. "Since I have met you, I have wished every day I had not married her," he said deliberately. "I find myself wanting to ask you, Where were you, Kirra Danalustrous? Why did you not come to Ghosenhall two seasons back? Where were you when my cousin hosted his own summer ball? I would have seen you, I think, the minute you entered the ballroom. I would have come across the floor to learn your name. After one dance with you I would have known what I had found. What I wanted. So where were you all that time?"

Her throat was so tight it was an effort to talk. "I was crossing the northern borders of Tilt, shaped like a lion. I was swimming the ocean off Fortunalt like some great fish of the sea. I was camping on the road between Helven and Rappengrass. I was exploring the world. I didn't know anyone was looking for me."

"I wish I had kept on looking," he said.

"I wish I had kept on traveling," she replied. "For this is proving to be too hard."

"I don't know how to change that," he said. "I could offer to turn back now—let you go on to Nocklyn and Rappengrass without me. But what good would that do? I will see you again and again. In Ghosenhall. In Brassenthwaite. In Danalustrous. You know our paths will cross. Now that I know you are alive, I will suddenly find you everywhere. Or I will make some excuse to go to the places where I think you'll be. I will try not to, if you tell me that's what you want, but I don't think I'll be able to stop myself. I don't know how I'll be able to forget about you."

She felt suddenly dreary. "Then it will be up to me," she said. "To make sure I am not where you think I will be."

"To avoid me?"

"If I have to."

"Do you want to?"

She almost couldn't speak. "No," she said at last.

"Then don't. Not now. Not yet. Not ever."

"Well, I can't just at the moment," she said with a little sigh. "For there are Nocklyn and Rappengrass to get through, and I don't see either of us heading for home just yet. But I do not think the rest of this trip will be an easy one for either of us."

"Just do me a favor. When we're in Rappengrass, be cool to Darryn. Treat him with disdain. Don't invite him back to Danalustrous."

She couldn't help laughing at that, though the laughter felt as if it scrabbled up past hollow ribs in a painful chest. "Why not? I have been wondering if I should try to induce him to come courting Casserah."

"Because every time I see him flirting with you I want to run him through with a sword. And I don't think the rest of my tenure as regent would go so well if I start off by murdering serramar."

She laughed again, a little more naturally. "He's flirting with Casserah, not me."

"You might be shaped like Casserah, but when I look at you, all I see is Kirra."

"I shall have Donnal take Casserah's shape some day and see if you can tell us apart. I think you will find yourself confused. I think you might then start to question some of these rash emotions."

"I think I will know you no matter how you present yourself," he retorted. "Go ahead. Come to me in some other guise and see how quickly I recognize you."

She shook her head. Her smile was rueful, but at least she managed a smile. "Don't tempt me," she warned. "You have no idea how reckless I can be."

"Yes, I do," he said. "I saw you on the road to Tilt."

She widened her eyes. "I think I was most circumspect on that particular journey!"

"You hazarded your life multiple times."

"I never felt anything but safe."

"I cannot believe you have lived long enough for me to meet you, even this late."

She laughed again. "I think you must have led a very tame life in Merrenstow."

He laughed, too, but almost instantly his expressi[on] serious. "Why haven't you ever married, Kirra?" he as[ked].

For a moment there was no air. Finally, she found a [way to] breathe. "I'm only twenty-five—twenty-six this fall," sh[e said]. "Plenty of time to charm a young lord with a sense of [adven]ture. If I can find one, that is. The serramar I know are [all] quite sedate."

"And ugly," he said. "I wouldn't think you'd like the[m.]"

"You're right," she agreed. "Perhaps I'll run off w[ith a] Rider, as Senneth has, or someone equally unsuitable. A ta[vern] keeper. A sea captain. A smithy."

"Your father will be shocked."

"Nothing shocks my father."

"Your sister, then."

She laughed. "Even less likely."

"You'll break my heart."

"So you can marry and I cannot?" she said. "That seem[s a] little hard on me."

"Marry wisely, then," he said. "Someone I would approve of[.]"

She was irritated. "Should I let you shop for my groom?"

"That's a good idea," he approved. "But I have to warn yo[u] it might take years before I find someone suitable. Decade[s,] even."

She laughed. "I think I shall take care of my own matrim[o]nial plans, thank you."

He gave her another serious look. "But why? Truly? W[hy] haven't you married before now?"

People had asked her this question often in recent we[eks]. She always found herself at a loss, not least because she tho[ught] it was a stupid question. She was happy as she was; she wa[s re]sponsible for no one but herself. Her life was crammed [with] travel and excitement and a long parade of people. She d[id not] feel a lack. And now that Casserah had been named hei[r, she] didn't even have the pressure to marry for the sake of Da[nalus]trous. She only had to suit herself.

"I never thought about it," she said finally. "It nev[er oc]curred to me that I could only have a good life if I was [sharing it] with someone else. My life is full as it is." She flashed h[im a] quick glance and looked away. "And I had never met t[he man] who made me say, 'Now. This one. Stop looking.' I was[n't] looking."

hands full enough handling the estates now that I am gone so much. I don't know that she expected to marry the regent of the realm and to become so responsible for duties that should be mine. But she has not complained. In fact, she has done a remarkable job."

"Indeed, she sounds most—most estimable," Kirra replied, stumbling over the words. Belinda Brendyn sounded like a woman it would be impossible to hate. Bad news for Kirra.

He turned his head again to look at her, his face sober. "Since I have met you, I have wished every day I had not married her," he said deliberately. "I find myself wanting to ask you, Where were you, Kirra Danalustrous? Why did you not come to Ghosenhall two seasons back? Where were you when my cousin hosted his own summer ball? I would have seen you, I think, the minute you entered the ballroom. I would have come across the floor to learn your name. After one dance with you I would have known what I had found. What I wanted. So where were you all that time?"

Her throat was so tight it was an effort to talk. "I was crossing the northern borders of Tilt, shaped like a lion. I was swimming the ocean off Fortunalt like some great fish of the sea. I was camping on the road between Helven and Rappengrass. I was exploring the world. I didn't know anyone was looking for me."

"I wish I had kept on looking," he said.

"I wish I had kept on traveling," she replied. "For this is proving to be too hard."

"I don't know how to change that," he said. "I could offer to turn back now—let you go on to Nocklyn and Rappengrass without me. But what good would that do? I will see you again and again. In Ghosenhall. In Brassenthwaite. In Danalustrous. You know our paths will cross. Now that I know you are alive, I will suddenly find you everywhere. Or I will make some excuse to go to the places where I think you'll be. I will try not to, if you tell me that's what you want, but I don't think I'll be able to stop myself. I don't know how I'll be able to forget about you."

She felt suddenly dreary. "Then it will be up to me," she said. "To make sure I am not where you think I will be."

"To avoid me?"

"If I have to."

"Do you want to?"

She almost couldn't speak. "No," she said at last.

"Then don't. Not now. Not yet. Not ever."

"Well, I can't just at the moment," she said with a little sigh. "For there are Nocklyn and Rappengrass to get through, and I don't see either of us heading for home just yet. But I do not think the rest of this trip will be an easy one for either of us."

"Just do me a favor. When we're in Rappengrass, be cool to Darryn. Treat him with disdain. Don't invite him back to Danalustrous."

She couldn't help laughing at that, though the laughter felt as if it scrabbled up past hollow ribs in a painful chest. "Why not? I have been wondering if I should try to induce him to come courting Casserah."

"Because every time I see him flirting with you I want to run him through with a sword. And I don't think the rest of my tenure as regent would go so well if I start off by murdering serramar."

She laughed again, a little more naturally. "He's flirting with Casserah, not me."

"You might be shaped like Casserah, but when I look at you, all I see is Kirra."

"I shall have Donnal take Casserah's shape some day and see if you can tell us apart. I think you will find yourself confused. I think you might then start to question some of these rash emotions."

"I think I will know you no matter how you present yourself," he retorted. "Go ahead. Come to me in some other guise and see how quickly I recognize you."

She shook her head. Her smile was rueful, but at least she managed a smile. "Don't tempt me," she warned. "You have no idea how reckless I can be."

"Yes, I do," he said. "I saw you on the road to Tilt."

She widened her eyes. "I think I was most circumspect on that particular journey!"

"You hazarded your life multiple times."

"I never felt anything but safe."

"I cannot believe you have lived long enough for me to meet you, even this late."

She laughed again. "I think you must have led a very tame life in Merrenstow."

He laughed, too, but almost instantly his expression grew serious. "Why haven't you ever married, Kirra?" he asked.

For a moment there was no air. Finally, she found a way to breathe. "I'm only twenty-five—twenty-six this fall," she said. "Plenty of time to charm a young lord with a sense of adventure. If I can find one, that is. The serramar I know are usually quite sedate."

"And ugly," he said. "I wouldn't think you'd like them."

"You're right," she agreed. "Perhaps I'll run off with a Rider, as Senneth has, or someone equally unsuitable. A tavern-keeper. A sea captain. A smithy."

"Your father will be shocked."

"Nothing shocks my father."

"Your sister, then."

She laughed. "Even less likely."

"You'll break my heart."

"So you can marry and I cannot?" she said. "That seems a little hard on me."

"Marry wisely, then," he said. "Someone I would approve of."

She was irritated. "Should I let you shop for my groom?"

"That's a good idea," he approved. "But I have to warn you, it might take years before I find someone suitable. Decades, even."

She laughed. "I think I shall take care of my own matrimonial plans, thank you."

He gave her another serious look. "But why? Truly? Why haven't you married before now?"

People had asked her this question often in recent weeks. She always found herself at a loss, not least because she thought it was a stupid question. She was happy as she was; she was responsible for no one but herself. Her life was crammed with travel and excitement and a long parade of people. She didn't feel a lack. And now that Casserah had been named heir, she didn't even have the pressure to marry for the sake of Danalustrous. She only had to suit herself.

"I never thought about it," she said finally. "It never occurred to me that I could only have a good life if I was paired with someone else. My life is full as it is." She flashed him one quick glance and looked away. "And I had never met the man who made me say, 'Now. This one. Stop looking.' I wasn't even looking."

"Are you going to start looking now?"

Now that you've met me, he implied. *Now that I've made you examine what it might feel like to be in love.* "I will go on as I always have," she said. "I don't know yet what has changed."

"Everything has changed," he said.

"And nothing," she said. "Not the way I live my life, not the way you live yours. We both go on as before."

"We go on," he said, "but I am a different man."

CHAPTER
23

LATE in the afternoon there was an ominous crack from the lead carriage. It canted over to one side and halted in the road, the horses neighing and tangling in the lines. The driver of the second coach, drowsing in the sun, yanked his own team to the left, but not in time to avoid ramming his side door against the rear of the other coach. The third driver was more alert and halted without contact, but it was instantly clear that they were faced with a real problem. The lead carriage had broken an axle and the second one had lost a door.

They were going to be here awhile as repairs were made.

Colton, the captain of the Merrenstow guard, seemed to be the one taking care of all logistical problems. He immediately began to sort through the ranks of soldiers to find those with carpentry skills. Romar jogged up to check on Amalie and Valri. Kirra dismounted and looked around, instantly finding what she'd expected: Senneth, Tayse, Justin, and Cammon on foot in a loose huddle, discussing their options. Donnal was on his way to Kirra's side. She nodded toward the others, and they arrived together at their small knot of friends.

"Good thing Amalie was out of the carriage," Kirra observed.

"Colton's checking to make sure it was an accidental break," Senneth said briefly.

Kirra felt a flash of astonishment. Or possibly fear. "You mean—you think someone—"

Tayse shrugged. "Easy thing to do to cut partway through an axle and then let the motion of the journey do the rest. Could have been worse if we'd been traveling faster."

"Or on a bridge. Or fording water," Justin added.

Donnal had his eyes on the crews starting to overhaul the carriages. "This work won't go fast," he said. "We'll still be here by nightfall."

Senneth and Tayse exchanged glances. "Camp out overnight?" Senneth said slowly. "With the princess and the queen?"

"Terrible idea," Kirra said. "We've got one carriage left. Melly can ride a horse, though she doesn't like to. I'm assuming the royal servants can as well, and so can you and I. Put Amalie and Valri in my carriage till we get to the next town."

"We could do that," Senneth said. She sounded uncertain.

"Everyone knows when we left the Keep," Tayse said. "Everyone knows how far we're likely to get tonight. If trouble was to come after us, it might go looking in—" He paused, trying to remember the name of the next market town on their route. "Loben."

There was silence while they all digested this. "But are we any safer camped out on the road?" Kirra asked. "If someone is truly interested in harming Amalie, she's in just as much danger out in the open countryside."

Tayse gave her one of his rare smiles. "I think between us we can manage to protect her," he said. "Don't you?"

She laughed. Her concern was starting to give way to her sense of adventure. "You'll never convince Valri to sleep on the ground."

"She and Amalie can lie in the carriage," Senneth said. "Melly can sleep out with us. We'll put the Riders in a circle around the carriage, and the soldiers in a circle around the Riders. Cammon at one end of the camp, Donnal at the other. Hard to believe anyone could penetrate those defenses."

Cammon spoke for the first time. "Raelynx," he said.

They all looked at him.

"We're not far from the Lireth Mountains," he said. "Raelynxes cross from the Lirrens into Coravann from time to time, the queen told me."

"Is that what you and Valri were talking about this whole time?" Kirra demanded. "I couldn't imagine *what* you were saying to her—"

Cammon seemed surprised. "I asked her about my raelynx, back at the palace." It was hardly *Cammon's* raelynx, Kirra reflected. Senneth was the one who had caught and half-tamed the wild red cat. Though they'd been lucky it was still almost a baby when they found it. Adult raelynxes were so large, so ferocious, and so indifferent to weapons that they could almost never be captured or killed. Cammon went on, "Valri's the one who's been taking care of him, you know, and with her being gone so long, I was worried. But she's got someone to make sure he's fed and healthy. And then we just got to talking." He shrugged. Cammon didn't have much sense of class distinctions. "But she's the one who mentioned that we might see a raelynx on this part of the trip."

Senneth had a palm over her face, probably hiding a laugh. "Bright Mother blind me," she said, dropping her hand with a sigh. "I don't know that I can control a full-grown raelynx that jumps out on us by night."

"I can," Cammon said, and they all stared at him again. Again, he showed surprise. "Really, I can. And I think Valri can, too."

Kirra and Senneth exchanged glances. More and more mystery about the dark little queen. "Well," Senneth said. "I don't know that we want to make the experiment. I might just set up a ring of fire around the whole campsite to scare off whatever night creatures get curious."

"Pretty big signal to anyone looking for us," Justin observed.

Senneth nodded. "We'll be hard to overlook in any case. If we can only have stealth or safety, I'll opt for safety."

They dispersed to spread the news through camp. Kirra followed Senneth as she made her way toward royalty, and was amused to find that Amalie was charmed by the idea.

"Camping out? Cooking our food over an open fire?" Amalie exclaimed. "That will be so much fun!"

"Spiders in your hair by morning and nowhere to wash up," Kirra said. "Not as much fun as you think."

Valri did not look as horrified as Kirra had expected. The

queen turned a searching look on Senneth. "Do you think we'll be safe here?"

"I think that's why we travel with so many soldiers around us," Senneth said. "And we have ways to protect ourselves."

"It might be a good idea to change our schedule unexpectedly," said Romar, still lingering at Amalie's side. "I approve."

The whole caravan was already engaged in the business of making camp as efficiently as possible. Colton had moved the main group off the road, where soldiers had already trampled out a clearing big enough to hold the men, the horses, and all three carriages. Now some went foraging for fuel, some for water.

"The men have enough dried rations to last a few days," Colton said, reporting to Senneth. "But what about the princess? Should we make her a meal from the items we can throw together?"

"We'll have game. Donnal's hunting," Senneth said. "And I might send serra Casserah off to look for edibles. I'm sure she's had much practice in such an activity during her soft life in Danalustrous."

Kirra had to restrain herself from making a face. In fact, Casserah never spent time in the wild, but Kirra had wide experience scavenging for berries, roots, and nuts, and she could live off the land for a long time if she had to. Longer in animal than human shape.

"Let me know if you need any contributions from the men of Merrenstow," Colton said, and went off to review everyone's progress.

Kirra checked in with Melly, to find her unenthusiastic about the prospect of camping overnight but resigned to the thought. She even volunteered to go foraging with Kirra. "And I can cook, too, venison or pheasant or whatever your man brings back," Melly said. "As long as we're stuck here, I may as well make myself useful."

They were gone about an hour and came back in early golden evening to find a cozy sight: smoke rising from four fires, blankets laid like tablecloths along the ground, the coaches pulled off the road and arranged in a line, soldiers deployed in tidy rings around the whole encampment. Kirra and Melly had stumbled across a stand of wild apple trees, so they had picked anything that looked halfway ripe, and they distributed the extra fruit among the soldiers. Melly had also dug up some kind of tubers that she said would roast well among the coals and taste like rather mealy bread, so they had returned with a basket of these as well. Donnal had brought back four grouse, and Justin had matched him in squirrels, and so they had more than enough for their own particular group of diners.

"Squirrel stew," Kirra said with a sigh, dumping all her treasures beside the central fire. "I can hardly wait."

Much to her surprise, Valri was kneeling before the fire and already stirring up a base in a cookpot that Colton or some other kind soul had lent the royal party. Since when could the queen cook rough fare on the open road? Valri exclaimed in pleasure when Melly handed her a fistful of limp leaves snatched from a wild patch of herbs.

"This will be tastier than you expect," Valri told Kirra. "You're actually going to like this meal."

Indeed, they all had a splendid time. The fresh air or the extra work or the necessity for improvising had given them all huge appetites, and there was a certain air of gaiety generated by the very unexpectedness of their situation. A congenial group gathered around their own fire—Senneth, Kirra, Donnal, Justin, Tayse, Cammon, Romar, Amalie, Valri, and Melly—and no one seemed too worried about rank or protocol. The food was excellent and everyone said so, eating additional portions until the pot was emptied. No one was eager to leave the campfire once the meal was over, so they lingered, talking idly in divided groups. Valri and Melly discussed recipes that could be made from game and roadside spices. Justin showed Romar a few tricks he'd learned with the knife that the regent had given him. Senneth sat with her back against Tayse's chest, her head half turned so she could smile up at him when he spoke to her in a low voice that no one else could overhear. Kirra, Amalie, Cammon, and Donnal played a card game and argued over who might be cheating. Kirra sat so close to Donnal that her shoulder rested against his and she could, if she wanted to, read every card in his hand.

"I think it's the princess who's cheating," Donnal said. "Everyone thinks it's Cammon because he can read minds, but I think the princess considers it a royal right that she win the game."

Amalie was not at all offended by the accusation. "Well, I

think it would be *kind* of you to let me win, but I'm not cheating. I don't understand the game well enough to even try!" she said. "But can Cammon really read minds?"

"No," Cammon replied.

"Yes," Kirra and Donnal said in unison.

Amalie made her face very serious and pointed at him with a regal finger. "Explain. Your princess commands you."

"I *can't* read minds," he said. "But sometimes I can tell what people are thinking. Especially when they're feeling strong emotions like rage or fear. Then it's like someone's shouting at me. But it comes through as—as—" He gestured broadly. "It's like someone's standing on the other side of the room waving a brightly colored flag. It's not like I hear words. It's not like I hear someone's voice in my head. Not yet, anyway."

"Not yet?" Kirra repeated. "Not *yet*?"

"That's something we're working on. Jerril and Areel and me."

"Those are his magical tutors in Ghosenhall," Kirra informed Amalie.

"We're trying to learn to communicate words without speaking them out loud. But so far we're not having much success. The most that comes through is a sort of feeling. Like, I don't *hear* Jerril tell me 'run,' but I have a sudden urge to go dashing through the house."

"And can you send the same thought to Jerril?" Donnal asked.

Cammon nodded. "Usually. But Jerril is more sensitive than anyone I've ever met. I don't have as much luck with Areel."

"Can you send some kind of thought to me?" Donnal asked.

Cammon considered. "I don't know. I could try."

"Is it more likely to work because Donnal's a mystic?" Amalie asked.

"I don't know that, either," Cammon said. "I can usually read Tayse's and Justin's moods, and they're not mystics. But I don't know if I could send thoughts to them. I haven't tried."

"I can't see Justin enjoying that much," Kirra said.

Cammon laughed. "Oh, Justin's coming around. Once he starts to think magic is useful, he doesn't mind so much if it intrudes on him."

"Come on," Donnal said. "Tell me something without words."

They all fell silent and waited expectantly. Kirra could feel Donnal sitting beside her, all muscles relaxed, open and ready for anything that might come his way. Cammon sat across from him, face furrowed in a frown, looking down at his hands. Kirra glanced up to find Tayse, Senneth, Justin, and Romar all watching this little exercise with interest. Romar appeared bewildered, but the other three were intent. They had seen some of Cammon's magic before.

After about five minutes, Donnal straightened enough to make Kirra pull away. Casually he began to whistle, a soft little tune that Kirra couldn't identify. The expression on his face was inquiring, as if to say, *Have I got it right?*

Cammon laughed, half pleased and half rueful. "I wanted you to sing," he said. "But that's pretty close."

Donnal quit whistling and started smiling. "That was a strange feeling," he said. "I just had this odd thought in my head. 'Now would be a good time to make music.' Just wandered in and sat there with all my other less-interesting thoughts. I was pretty sure it wasn't my own idea."

"'I lost my love to the southern sea,'" Amalie said.

Everyone looked at her, even the four sitting a few feet away. "What?" Kirra said.

"'I lost my love to the southern sea,'" Amalie repeated. "That's the song Cammon wanted you to sing."

"I don't know any song like that," Donnal said.

Kirra was struck by the look on Cammon's face. Astonishment. Spiced with excitement. "I did have a song in mind," he admitted. "But I don't know the name of it. It's just a tune I used to hear when we were crossing the ocean from Arberharst."

"That's the first line," Amalie said. Completely without self-consciousness, she began singing in a soft, sweet voice. "'I lost my love to the southern sea/One night when the moon sank low/I lost my love and I'll never be/The man you once used to know.'"

"That's it," Cammon said, and now his odd, speckled eyes snapped with eagerness. "That's the melody."

"I heard you," she said. "I heard it in my head."

Kirra looked at the princess, looked at Cammon, and then

turned her head a little so she could see Senneth, whose face
was expressionless. But Senneth wasn't paying attention to
Kirra; she was watching Valri.

Whose green eyes were wide in her pale white face and
who showed fear in every line of her tightly clenched body.

SUMMER dark came late, and they were all ready to seek
their beds. The queen and the princess took shelter in their
own carriage, whose axle had been repaired just as true dark
fell. Colton's impromptu carpenters had found no evidence of
tampering with the rods or wheels, but they admitted they
might not be able to tell now that the frame had splintered. In
any case, it was safe for the two women to climb inside,
though Amalie had expressed an interest in sleeping on the
ground before the campfire. Valri vetoed that without hesitation, and Amalie meekly ducked her head to follow the queen
into the coach.

Cammon and Donnal headed to the points Tayse had assigned them, the Riders fanned out around the carriage, and
the others arranged themselves as suited them best. Kirra was
relieved to see that Romar planned to spend the night alongside the Merrenstow soldiers. She and Senneth and Melly un-
rolled their blankets around the central fire, though Kirra had
a suspicion Senneth might end up lying by Tayse as he guarded
the princess's sleep. She could even argue that she belonged
there, close enough to Amalie to leap to action should danger threaten.

Though such an event seemed unlikely. Senneth had
warned the whole assembly, then generated a thin, flickering
wall of fire that snaked around the entire campsite with red-
and-gold protection. *Danalustrous colors,* Kirra thought. She
heard more than one soldier gasp or curse as the flames went
up, saw a few of them creep close enough to touch. Yes, it was
hot; it scorched unwary fingers. But it would not burn the soil
or the grass or the trees nearby, and it would last all night, even
while Senneth slept. So operated the magic of the most powerful mystic in Gillengaria.

Melly was sighing as she curled up on her thin blanket, too
warm on this summer night to want to cover herself with it.
"'Go work in the marlord's house. You'll lead a soft life,'" she

muttered, clearly quoting someone's advice. "'You'll dress in fine clothes and wait on the serramarra and never have to eat squirrel stew again.'"

"You picked the wrong serramarra to wait on if that's what you wanted," Kirra said cheerfully. "Or maybe you picked the right one. You just got unlucky on this particular trip. I'm sure this will never happen again if you stay with—with my sister."

"And I will stay with her, even if it does," Melly said with another sigh. "Goodnight, serra."

"Goodnight."

But Kirra found she could not get comfortable—and once she was comfortable, she could not fall asleep. Too many nights in plush beds in palatial homes ruined a woman for the simple pleasures of life on the road. She thought about her conversation with Romar. She thought about the expression on Valri's face when Amalie proved susceptible to magic. She thought about the look of sheer contentment that Senneth wore when she had even five minutes to lean against Tayse and feel his arms secure about her. She thought about this upcoming visit to Nocklyn and what unpleasant experiences might unfold there since, so far, none of their stops on the social circuit had passed without incident.

She spent some time trying to picture Belinda Brendyn, so quiet and unassuming and efficient and dull—but kind and good and pleasant. No doubt in love with her restless and handsome husband. No doubt hoping that she would conceive his child one day soon, attach him to her with the unbreakable bond of shared parenthood, give him the one thing he could not manage on his own. Belinda's devotion to domesticity— wife, mother, de facto head of household with her husband's prolonged absences—made Kirra feel even more wild, more reckless. She wanted to change into a lioness, right here on the ground between Melly and Senneth. She wanted to transform herself into a white owl and go screeching into the dark. She wanted to melt into a mouse or a mole and go running into the night.

Instead she turned to her side, flipped to her back, turned to her other side, and gave up. Coming to her feet, she threw her blanket across her arm and set off through the camp. Moving carefully and noiselessly, she picked her way past curled bodies and piles of gear, tiptoed around the looming bulk of the

carriages, and aimed for the easternmost corner of the wall of
flame. She had almost reached her destination when she saw a
shape solidify from the undifferentiated shadows and head in
her direction. Her heart gave a sudden bound of fear before
she recognized Tayse. He came close enough to whisper.

"Anything wrong?"

She shook her head. "What are you doing up?"

"Just patrolling. Checking on everyone. You?"

She smiled at him. She had always assumed he could see in
the dark; he could do everything else. "Lonely," she said. "I
couldn't sleep."

He nodded and moved off. She continued another few
yards until she came across Donnal stretched out on the
ground, head lying on his paws, nose pointed straight toward
Senneth's magical blaze. An extraordinary wolf, one that was
not afraid of fire.

Spreading her blanket on the ground, she lay down next to
him, close enough to feel the solid heat of his body against her
back. It was summer, and the fire warmed everything a few
more degrees, and she hadn't been cold to begin with. But
only now did she feel right. Only now was she able to close her
eyes and let herself slide into dreaming.

CHAPTER
24

THEY got back on the road somewhat later than they should have the next morning, as everyone was a little stiff from the unconventional night's sleep. Well, Kirra thought, perhaps the soldiers weren't, and Donnal was certainly none the worse for wear the next day, but she felt achy, hungry, and crabby. They ate a cold, unappetizing breakfast and set out again on the road for Nocklyn.

"And the worst of it is, I can't look any better than Casserah would after such a night," she groused to Senneth. "I know how to keep my hair tidy and my face clean, but Casserah doesn't have such tricks available to her."

"And all the extra water's gone to Amalie and the queen," Senneth said, amused. "But you don't look so bad. Braid your hair back and shake out your clothes. We can stop at the inn in Loben and wash up."

"And get the door to the servants' carriage repaired," Kirra added. "The other women are riding in my carriage with Melly. They're afraid the coach will hit a bump and they'll fall out."

"I don't think the night on the road did us any harm," Senneth said. "We might be a day late into Nocklyn, but we won't miss the main event. And frankly, I'm not so sorry to be spared even a single night at yet another of the Twelve Houses. I can't imagine whatever possessed me to tell Baryn I'd squire his daughter around as she made her debut."

"Oh, but it's been so much fun so far," Kirra said. "You have to wonder how Mayva Nocklyn will be able to top Heffel Coravann."

Senneth laughed. "I'm hoping she won't even try."

It was almost noon before they were close enough to Loben to realize there was trouble, and Cammon was the one to sense it. Donnal, loping along in wolf shape alongside Kirra, showed no alarm, even when Cammon suddenly reined in his horse and dropped back to where Senneth rode beside Kirra. His face was puckered with worry.

"What?" Senneth said instantly. "Is someone coming?"

He shook his head, his expression perplexed. "No, I— It doesn't seem like we're in danger. But something's wrong. In Loben."

"Should we stop? Should we go another way?"

"I don't think so. It's just—something bad lies ahead. Or something bad already happened. In Loben."

Kirra glanced at Senneth then back at Cammon. "Illness?" she asked.

"Attack?" Senneth guessed. "Massacre?"

"I can't tell. But people are sad."

"Let's go tell Tayse."

Senneth and Cammon cantered off, past the carriages and units of soldiers, seeking the Rider in the lead. Kirra pulled her horse to a walk, allowed the other soldiers to pass her, and then retraced the back trail till she came across Justin, solitary in the rear. She noticed how straight he sat in the saddle, how closely he listened to the sounds around him. He spotted her immediately and spurred his horse forward.

"What's wrong?"

"Not sure. Cammon says something happened in Loben. I'm guessing Tayse is going to want you with everybody else."

He nodded and instantly urged his horse to a run, not even waiting for her to catch up. She rolled her eyes and followed more sedately until she had rejoined the main group. The whole party was still moving forward, but at a slower pace. Senneth, Cammon, and the four Riders were in a line before the lead carriage, conferring. Romar rode beside the first coach, apparently conversing with his niece through the open window. Donnal picked his way through the various riders to trot alongside Kirra again. The expression in his amber eyes was inquiring.

"Don't know yet," she said. "But it looks like we're going on."

It took an hour of cautious travel before they finally made it to Loben, a small, picturesque market town with a decent array of houses and small shops lining the main road. They were barely past the first tavern on the edge of town when Kirra caught the acrid scent of recent fire, and she lifted her head to try to track the source. But nothing appeared to be burning right now; the only smoke rising above the chimneys was white and lazy, curling up from kitchen cookfires.

They drew some attention as they traveled down the street, but not as much as they had in other small towns they'd passed through. The few people who were out were hurrying along as if determined to finish important errands. Some merely looked down at their feet as if they were too weighed with their own cares to wave to the passing princess or gawk at the sight of so many soldiers. The whole feel of the town made Kirra uneasy, as if she waded through the aftereffects of grief. She wondered how much more sharply Cammon was experiencing the emotions that even she was picking up.

When they reached the juncture where the main road was crossed by a secondary street, they came across the charred ruins of a fairly sizable building. Here the smell of smoke was strong enough to make Kirra gag, and she lifted a handkerchief to her mouth to filter out some of the scent. She couldn't tell what the structure had been, but all that remained were foundation stones, part of a fence, a green corner of lawn, and blackened timbers. At least twenty people milled around in what used to be a courtyard. A small knot of mourners stood in one corner of the lawn and wept.

For some reason, Kirra felt even more uneasy. Senneth flung up a hand and their whole caravan came to a disorganized halt. Kirra pushed her way past the horsemen ahead of her, trying to get to Senneth. Amalie poked her head out the window and the noon sun turned her hair into a fiery halo.

"Casserah. What's wrong?" the princess asked as Kirra rode by.

"I don't know. I'm going to find out."

Senneth had motioned one of the onlookers over, and he

arrived at her side just as Kirra did. His sober eyes took in Casserah's fine clothes and Tayse's fine weapons, but Kirra could tell he didn't really register anything as he stood in the street and stared up at them.

"What building burned here?" Senneth demanded.

"My brother's inn," the man replied.

Inn? Kirra's hands tightened so suddenly on the reins that her horse whickered and backed away. She nudged it forward again, listening.

"What happened? Did a fire start in the kitchen?"

The man shrugged hopelessly. "I don't know. It was the middle of the night. Both the cooks were asleep. Maybe the fire started in the kitchen. Maybe it started in the parlor or one of the upstairs bedrooms. By the time the alarm was raised, it seemed like the building was on fire in three or four places. Even the roof was burning. We called out the bucket brigade, but there was no use. It had spread too far. The whole building was lost."

"And the people inside?"

Now his face showed real pain. "Most of them dead," he whispered. "My brother and his wife and his two girls. Dead. We think there were five guests staying on the upper floors, but we cannot find all the bodies. One of the cooks survived, and the downstairs maid, but they are both so badly burned we do not know if they will live till nightfall. It's so terrible—so terrible—" His voice shook and he had to stop to try to compose himself.

Senneth waited a moment then spoke again. "And this happened last night?" He nodded and she continued, "I am sorry for your loss."

"I don't know what I'm going to do," he said, clearly no longer talking to Senneth, nor to anyone but himself. "I don't know what I'm going to do without him. We spent every day together. I worked beside him at the inn. How am I going to feed my own wife and my own daughter? How am I going to get by without my brother?"

A woman came up and put her arms around him. She was crying, too, her face red with tears, but she offered him what comfort she had left. Kirra felt her stomach harden with sympathetic despair. She could not imagine how she would feel if this had been Danan Hall and Casserah's body lay inside.

Light flickered beside her and she glanced down to see Amalie out of the coach. The princess's hands were extended; her own face was a study in woe. "I am so sad for you," she said in her soft voice. "What a dreadful day."

The man continued sobbing in his wife's arms, but the woman turned to look at Amalie, and her eyes widened. She could not curtsey while she held her husband, but she bowed her head and dropped her eyes. "Majesty," she whispered.

Amalie pulled something off her left hand and Kirra saw a ring sparkling in her palm. A diamond as big as a man's thumbnail was clasped in a heavy circlet of gold. "Here," the princess said. "It cannot buy back any of the people you love, but it will feed you for a while and pay for some rebuilding."

The woman seemed too stunned to even protest. She put her hand out and let Amalie close her fingers around the jewel. "Thank you, majesty," she said, her voice even more dazed.

Amalie looked up at Senneth. Her sweet face looked incredibly sad and incredibly determined. "Is there anything else we can do?" she asked.

Senneth glanced back at Kirra and seemed unsure of how to phrase her next words. "Apparently two women have been injured in the fire. I don't know if anyone in town is a healer."

The innkeeper's sister-in-law spoke up. "No. We have a healer, but he left a few days ago to visit his mother. He's a three-day ride away. I don't believe they will live that long—" Her voice broke, and she stopped trying to talk, just rested her cheek against her husband's head.

Kirra was already sliding out of the saddle. No one in Loben would recognize her, and Amalie could not know how useless Casserah was in a sickroom.

"My sister is a healer, and I know something about nursing," she said. "If someone takes me to these injured women, I will do for them what I can."

Two other men had come up, impelled by curiosity and not seeming quite as grief stricken as the innkeeper's relatives. "They're over at Lawrence's. By the tavern," one of these newcomers volunteered. "Sukie's watching them, but she doesn't know any medicine."

"I'll do what I can," Kirra repeated. "Take me there."

"We'll both go," Amalie said.

• • •

So that was another strange interlude in a trip that had already been altogether too odd. Where Amalie went, of course, the queen must go, and so must Senneth and the four Riders; and Cammon clearly did not want to be left behind; and Donnal, appearing respectable enough to pad through town as a large black hound, came as well. Lawrence proved to be a wealthy-looking merchant with what was probably the biggest house in the district. It seemed to have been a philanthropic gesture for him to take in the two injured women, so Kirra had to suppose he was either a kind man or running for civil office. She didn't have time to talk to him. She was following his housekeeper up a narrow flight of steps and down a dim hallway to the room at the back of the house where the infirmary was set up. Amalie and the entire retinue were hard on her heels, but only Amalie, Senneth, and Valri entered the room behind her.

"Stay here by the door," Kirra instructed the others, and Senneth nodded. She would make sure Amalie did not come close enough to watch Kirra work.

The two employees from the inn were badly burned, and the two women tending them had both been weeping. Kirra nodded silently at the watching women and knelt beside the first bed, gently pulling back the covers. Yes, she could do something about this; this was a condition her hands and her magic had encountered before. Concentrating closely, she allowed the rest of the world to fall away from her while her fingers played down ruined flesh and smoothed it out, while her palms lifted lingering heat from the stressed body. She wound up skeins of white infection like so much poisoned yarn and drew them from the tortured skin, and she wiped the lungs clean of soot and inhaled toxins. The injured woman sighed and turned over, tucking her hands beneath her cheek.

"She'll mend," Kirra said to herself, and moved to the second bed. This woman was older and more frail, so the ministrations took longer but were essentially the same. This patient, too, sighed with relief as the pain and poison left her body, but she did not slip into a sounder sleep. Instead, her eyes opened, and she gazed straight up at Kirra.

"What have you done?" she asked in a wondering voice.

"I have some skill with my hands," Kirra answered.

The woman lifted her own hands, turned them this way and

that. Her skin was still reddened, but the blisters and lesions had healed; she might have some scars, but they would be slight. "I don't hurt anymore," the woman said in a low voice. "Am I dying?"

"No. No, you will be well in a few days. You may not be as hale as you were before the fire, you might have some aches and imperfections, but you will mostly recover."

The woman watched her now with a close attention. "You're a mystic," she whispered.

Kirra hesitated, but Amalie was over by the door, speaking in a low voice with Senneth and the queen. The only people listening were this woman and the two who had been caring for her. "Yes."

The patient closed her eyes, but Kirra waited. Clearly she was not done talking. "I have always hated mystics," she said, still speaking in a low, strained voice. Kirra felt her stomach knot again. So deep in the southern territories, she should have been more careful before flaunting her magic. If either of the nurses went running from the room with such news, this situation could turn ugly fast.

"I'm sorry," Kirra said, rising to her feet. "I'll go now."

"Wait." The first word came swiftly; the others followed with an effort. "Thank you. I did not realize—I could not have expected—thank you for your kindness. I will never curse your people again."

How to answer that? "Mystics have never done anything to hurt anyone," Kirra said quietly. "No one has any cause to fear us."

The woman opened her eyes. "I will do a kindness someday for a mystic if I can."

"Then I am repaid."

One of the nurses, older and heavyset, had been standing close enough to audit this whole conversation. Deliberately she lifted her hand to show Kirra the moonstone ring she wore, the gem not even half the size of the diamond Amalie had bestowed on the grieving brother. Deliberately she drew it from her finger and threw it across the room.

"You have saved my sister's life," she said. "I will try to repay you as well."

"Then there has been much good accomplished this afternoon," Kirra said.

She gave them both an abbreviated curtsey and joined the others standing near the door. "We have lost a good portion of the day here," she said. "I think it is time we moved on."

Senneth's eyebrows rose slightly as if to ask a question. "The merchant Lawrence has invited us to stay for lunch and use his house to clean ourselves up," Senneth said. "Do you think we should not?"

"Does our host know you are a mystic?" Kirra replied. "My latest conversation leads me to believe such folk are not welcomed in this town."

Senneth glanced back at the four women, the two patients and the two nurses, and clearly understood the gist of it. "He need not know," Senneth replied. "The princess would like to stay."

"Then by all means, show me to a room and allow me to wash my hands and face."

THE meal was tedious but endurable; they were all anxious to get back on the road by the time they were finally on their way again. Colton had allowed the soldiers to draw their own refreshment at the town's three taverns, so they were all rested and fed by the time they were on the move. A whole day lost, though. If they squandered much more time on the road, they would not be in Nocklyn before the great ball.

They were finally clear of Loben and settled into a steady pace before Kirra managed to maneuver her horse next to Senneth's.

"Does the princess realize how close she came to death last night?" she asked in a low voice. "For we should have been sleeping in that inn when it caught fire."

Senneth glanced back at Amalie's carriage. "I'm not sure she put it together. Romar did, and he was quite concerned. Valri, of course, begged us to turn back for Ghosenhall. But I don't think Amalie would agree to that even if she realized that the fire was probably set to catch her."

Kirra felt her face relax into a tiny smile, the first one since they'd ridden into Loben. "I can't help wondering," she said softly, "if the fire would have been quite so devastating if you had been sleeping under that roof."

Senneth's answering smile was also small. "Oh, I'd have been able to control it," she said. "Assuming I woke in time—but I think I would have. Or Cammon would have roused me. I think we would have survived the trap. Which now makes me wonder if we might not have done better to press on last night. Stayed at the inn ourselves, and saved all those lives. I am not sorry Amalie was not endangered, but I regret the price that others paid."

"You think the fire was set on purpose?"

Senneth nodded. "From the way it was described, yes."

"Someone knows our schedule and our route."

"Which means perhaps we should travel unconventional pathways when we leave Nocklyn."

"Valri might be right," Kirra said. "It might be time to return to the royal city."

Senneth turned her head to give Kirra a serious look. "Do you think she will be safe even there?" she said softly.

Kirra felt her shoulders sag; she was suddenly tired. "Then this is to be her whole life? Assassination attempts from hidden enemies? Do we dedicate our own lives to keeping her safe? How can she live like this? Afraid every minute that someone wants her dead?"

Senneth glanced back over her shoulder at the carriage behind them. "She doesn't seem to be afraid," she observed. "And I can't tell if it's because she doesn't understand she's in danger—or if it's because she doesn't care."

"Or if she just trusts us."

"Or if she really is not afraid."

"*I'm* starting to be afraid," Kirra said. "And very little frightens me."

"A great deal frightens me," Senneth retorted, "and I have been afraid from the beginning."

"But we continue on."

"We have to," Senneth said. "I agree with Romar Brendyn. A few days ago, he said that she could not show fear or her enemies would destroy her. I think he's right. If she is to be queen someday, she cannot run away now."

"Well, then," Kirra said. "On to Nocklyn."

CHAPTER
25

Nocklyn Towers was a grand old mansion set on a sweeping expanse of yard just outside the bustling town that went by the same name. The city was nearly as large as Ghosenhall and about as sophisticated, and Kirra wished she could take a day or two to go browsing through its cosmopolitan shops and dining at its fancy restaurants. However, they had arrived only a day and a half before the ball that had been their whole reason for coming here; they would have little time for minor diversions.

And yet, she was soon to find out, a few people in their party were able to snatch at the city's treasures during their brief ride through. They had just cleared the back gate of the city and were on the long, steep rise toward the manor house when Romar brought his horse alongside hers.

"Candy?" he said, offering her a small gold-lined box. She stared at him in wonderment and he laughed. "I bought some for Amalie as we were crossing the main road. She loves sweets. And I thought you might like a few pieces as well."

"Oh, I would *love* some," she said, helping herself to a handful of round, sugary treats. She popped one in her mouth and savored it. "Especially divine after squirrel stew," she added.

"But it was very good squirrel stew."

Kirra ate another candy before speaking again. "So have

you been invited to the Shadow Ball at Nocklyn? Or is there to be such an event here?"

He nodded. "I was invited, but we missed it. It was last night. I am sorry for it but—" He shrugged. "I will find some other way to show myself accessible to the Thirteenth House lords."

"I think we must work first to show ourselves agreeable to the Twelve Houses."

He nodded toward Nocklyn Towers, looming above them with flags flying at all turrets. "This House, at least, seems agreeable," he said with a smile. "I've always thought it one of the prettiest of the twelve."

"Not to compare with Danan Hall, but appealing in its own way," Kirra said.

He laughed. "I was going to add that I was not sure the interior would be as friendly as the exterior."

"It used to be, when Els Nocklyn was well," Kirra said. "But he's been sick, and his daughter, Mayva, and her husband run the House now. Or—well—Mayva's a silly and useless sort of person. Lowell is really in charge these days—and he's not a man who inspires great trust."

"I don't know him. Who is he?"

"Halchon Gisseltess's cousin."

"Ah. Then we need not ask where Nocklyn's loyalties lie."

The grand gate leading to the mansion was already opened for them; soldiers saluted and waved them through. Kirra realized she should have been back in the carriage by now so that she could emerge in a stately fashion, as Casserah would have. But perhaps Mayva would not notice. She didn't seem to notice much.

Indeed, the flighty, dark-haired serramarra waiting at the front door gave all her attention to the princess and the queen as they disembarked from their own coach. "Majesty! We have been so worried about you!" Mayva exclaimed, running forward with her dainty hands outstretched. "We expected you a day ago. Was there trouble along the road? Are you unharmed?"

Amalie permitted Mayva to take her hands and flutter around her. "Everyone is fine," she replied in her quiet voice. "One of the carriages broke down, so we lost some time repairing it. And then we ended up stopping in Loben for nearly a day. Everything took longer than we thought. I'm sorry you were concerned."

"Are you tired? You must be tired. Let me take you to your room." Mayva glanced over at the rest of them, wearily pulling their personal items from carriages or saddles. "All your rooms."

Senneth had glided up soundlessly beside Amalie. Her white-blond hair was ruffled from travel but her gray eyes were calm. She tilted her head in acknowledgment of the mistress of the house. "Serra Mayva," she said. "You remember we talked in Kianlever? I trust you have arranged the chambers as I requested."

"Yes, yes, and after what happened there—! I want you to keep the princess absolutely safe. There is a suite across from hers that will accommodate your Riders."

"Thank you, serra."

They made their way through the airy, light-filled hallways of the Towers to a collection of charming and well-furnished rooms. In the chamber assigned to Kirra, Melly investigated armoires and vanities and proclaimed herself pleased. "She seems like a nice one," the maid observed.

Kirra was amused. "Mayva Nocklyn suits your notions of a proper marlady?" she said. "Well, she certainly typifies the breed. Friendly, frivolous, and not too bright."

Melly shrugged and began unpacking. "But nice," she repeated.

Kirra let it go. She supposed that counted for something. Though in the coming days of conflict and opposition, she expected *niceness* to be trampled by ambition and greed. Mayva seemed too flimsy and fragile to survive.

There was no time to go exploring the house or the grounds; there was barely enough time to take a real bath and dress for dinner. Tonight's gown had been chosen to showcase Casserah's eyes, not her heritage, so she wore a velvet gown of deep blue that gave her face a whole different set of shadows and contours than the usual red.

"I like this," Kirra said, turning her head back and forth and watching her cheekbones in the mirror. "Casserah should wear blue more often."

"She prefers red. That's what you'll wear tomorrow night, of course, for the ball."

"Of course."

"I've made a little pocket for you," were Melly's next unexpected words. "I've been working on putting one in all your dresses. I can't match the fabric perfectly, but the seam is so fine I don't think anyone will notice."

Kirra stared at her in the mirror. "A pocket?"

Melly nodded. "So you can carry that little carving. The one you like to have with you. The pocket's deep enough that it won't fall out."

Kirra bit her lip and turned away from the mirror. She had never appreciated how much information a servant could gather about an individual, how much of the maid's life had to be utterly dedicated to the whims and desires of the mistress. It would never have occurred to her that Melly would care about such a thing.

"Thank you," she said at last. "I am most grateful. You're right. I don't like to be without it."

At that, Melly handed her the little lioness figurine, having no doubt scooped it up from the drawer where Kirra had laid it. "It's pretty," the maid said. "But strange. Does it have something to do with magic?"

Kirra located the tiny slit in the left side of the dress and dropped the lioness into the soft pouch. "I'm not sure. Donnal and I found it in an old shrine that appeared to be dedicated to the Wild Mother. Who knows if the gods had magic?"

"I never heard of the Wild Mother," Melly said.

"Most people haven't. That doesn't make her any less powerful."

"Casserah doesn't pay much attention to the gods," Melly observed.

That's because Casserah has Danalustrous, Kirra wanted to say, but she didn't. "Thank you for making the pockets," she repeated. "I can't think anyone could have a better maid."

When her toilette was finally done, Kirra stepped into the corridor. Amalie and Senneth were in the room right across the hall. Justin stood before their door, face impassive, eyes alert, hand on his sword hilt. He saw her and gave an infinitesimal bow before he realized who she was. Then he cocked his head to one side and surveyed her.

"You look good," he said. He sounded surprised.

Kirra laughed and did a little pirouette. "My sister spares no expense when it comes to clothes. She has a taste for luxury—and she's a beautiful woman."

Justin shrugged. "Not as beautiful as you are."

She was astonished. "Justin! Did you just pay me a compliment?"

He grinned. "It's not a compliment. It's the truth. But there are plenty of worthless beautiful women."

Now she was giggling. "Oh, please. Stop my world from reeling and tell me I'm one of those. I can't get past the idea that you think I'm beautiful. I'll be off balance all night."

His smile was broader. "You have your uses, though it's hard to remember them most of the time."

"Try not to get injured anytime soon," she advised him, knocking on the door. "Because I won't come heal you."

He nodded. "Thanks for the warning. I shall do my best to cleanly win any fight I may get into for the next few days."

"Ever," she said, and slipped inside Amalie's room.

The others were already gathered there, all of them wearing darker colors this evening. Senneth was statuesque in bronze, Valri brooding in black. The princess wore a shiny metallic fabric that seemed to change colors from a glittering blue to a jewel-like green.

"Don't we look sober," Kirra observed.

"Everyone reserves their brightest colors for the ball," Valri said. "So I've been told."

"The night of gaiety." Kirra nodded. "But tonight—people hold whispered conversations with their neighbors or discuss potential alliances. The dinner the night before the ball is a very important function."

Senneth looked at the rest of them and sighed. "Oh, yes. Here we have a princess who has rarely left her castle, a serramarra who has not been to a ball for seventeen years, a queen who is ill at ease on the social circuit, and a woman pretending to be—" Senneth caught herself before finishing the sentence as she probably intended. *Pretending to be someone else.* "Pretending to be interested in anything except Danalustrous," she ended lamely. "We are rather ill-equipped to make deals and carry on intrigue."

Kirra and Amalie were laughing; even Valri was smiling. "I think we have all done very well despite our handicaps," Valri said.

"I have had a wonderful time!" Amalie exclaimed.

"And surely tonight will be a simple enough event," Senneth said. "Are we all ready? Let's go downstairs."

Servants in the foyer directed them to a large, pretty salon where most of the other guests had already gathered. Kirra thought there might be a hundred people in the room, which meant double that number would attend tomorrow's ball. A coup for Mayva and a compliment to the princess.

Mayva and her husband, Lowell, were stationed just inside the room, awaiting the late arrivals. Tayse was standing in the hall, as impassive as Justin and looking even more menacing. Kirra had to wonder how all the other guests tonight had felt about stepping past him to enter the receiving room, enduring his cool, assessing gaze. It almost made her nervous, and she had nothing to fear from him.

Mayva nearly clapped her hands together when the royal party came through the door. "Oh, majesty, don't you look lovely!" she exclaimed. "And the rest of you, as well. Serra Casserah, I don't believe I said hello to you this afternoon when you arrived."

"Hello," Kirra responded coolly. She spotted Romar lurking nearby, obviously waiting for them as well, but he hung back while their host and hostess greeted them.

Mayva laid an impetuous hand on Amalie's arm. "There are so many people here I want you to meet! Come with me quickly, before dinner is announced."

Amalie obediently responded to the pressure of Mayva's fingers. Valri stepped right after her, and Senneth made as if to follow. Lowell pushed himself forward to block her way. Again, Kirra felt a surge of dislike for his wary, watchful face.

He bent a little, for he was even taller than Senneth, and said, "There is someone else here who would like to meet you, serra Senneth. The princess will not set foot outside this room. You can safely leave her with my wife."

Kirra swiftly looked at Romar, close enough to hear, and then flicked her eyes toward Amalie's retreating figure. He nodded, and elbowed his way through the crowd to catch up with his niece. Senneth watched him go and turned her attention back to Lowell.

"Someone who wishes to speak to me?" Senneth repeated, very slightly accenting the last word. "I am not much sought after."

A wintry smile on that calculating face. Kirra liked him less and less. "You undervalue yourself, serra," he replied.

"I will meet whomever you like," she said, and took his arm when he extended it.

Kirra, not about to be left behind, tripped along right after them. She was tempted to lapse into meaningless chatter, just to fill the unnerving silence that seemed to wrap around Lowell, but Casserah was not the type, so she followed them without saying a word.

He was leading them to a small knot of people, three men and two women, who were all somberly dressed and appeared to be deep in a serious discussion. The four whose faces she could see were all strangers to Kirra. The fifth one, a stockily built man with shoulder-length black hair, had his back to her. But something about his shape seemed unpleasantly familiar. Tendrils of dread were already uncurling through her blood before Senneth came to a dead halt a few feet away from the group.

"No," Senneth said in a flat voice, and dropped her hand from Lowell's arm. Kirra came up on her other side and was astounded when Senneth actually reached for her arm instead. She felt the heat of Senneth's fingers through the thin material of her gown. "What is he doing here?"

The sound of her voice must have caught his attention, or maybe someone in his group was staring past him and he wanted to see what interesting sight lay behind him. But the dark-haired man turned to face them in one complete, graceful movement, and Kirra found herself staring at Halchon Gisseltess.

All sorts of thoughts chased themselves through her head in that first numb moment. *What was he doing here? How had he escaped the king's guards deployed around Gissel Plain to contain him? How did Mayva Nocklyn have the nerve to invite him to her home, knowing he was interdicted? How had he gotten into this room without Tayse seeing him? Tayse would have said something, made some gesture, given them some kind of warning. How had he eluded the Rider?*

But most important, of course, most terrifying: *Could he hurt Senneth?*

She wanted to scream, to call Tayse into the room, but she could not bring herself to do anything so spectacular. They were here to set up diplomatic relations, not start brawls at every House they visited. Still, it was petrifying to be the only one besides Senneth to know that their greatest enemy was in the room, and smiling at them with a cold and feral satisfaction. She wished she had Cammon's magical power of communicating without words and across distances. She wished she could alert the Riders, tell Donnal, that they did not have to watch for trouble creeping up to the Towers by stealth. Trouble was already inside the doors.

Halchon came a step closer, that smile still warming his square, intent face. For a moment, Kirra felt a faint wash of his strange energy, his odd ability to dampen or disarm magic. Around him, Senneth could not call fire. Around him, Senneth became mortal and powerless and weak. Even the palm of her hand seemed to cool on Kirra's arm, though her fingers still clutched so tightly Kirra could feel a bruise forming.

"Senneth," Halchon said, speaking with real pleasure. That was something else Kirra had forgotten: how beautiful his voice was, resonant and low-pitched. Hypnotic. As beautiful as his sister's. "I am delighted to see you again."

And he reached his hand out as if to take hers.

Senneth flinched and stepped back, pulling Kirra with her. "What are you doing here?" Senneth demanded in a hard voice. "You are under the king's arrest and confined to your house."

Halchon glanced first over one shoulder and then the other. "Apparently not," he said. "I am free."

"You skate very close to treason."

Halchon laughed softly. "So close, my dear, that I call that country my own."

"What are you doing here?" she repeated.

He allowed his eyes to roam expressively around the room. "Meeting with my friends. Enjoying the social season," he replied. "Isn't that why you're here as well? Though I did not expect to see the long-missing serramarra of Brassenthwaite in such lighthearted pursuits. You must be spending all your time renewing old acquaintances. Have you found that people missed you, Senneth? Have they welcomed you back in their midst?"

"I am not here to make friends," Senneth replied. "I am here to lend my strength to the princess Amalie as she makes her public debut. But you knew that. You are not surprised to see me."

"I am surprised to learn that *you* could be considered enough to protect her," he said, almost purring the words. "For you are powerful indeed, in some circumstances. But I confess I have never found you—shall we say—impossible to overcome."

Kirra felt Senneth flinch again, but her voice was steady and unyielding. "I am not the only one assigned to protect the princess. If I were to fail, she would still be safe."

"Oh, yes, I've heard. Riders in your train. The very thought of tangling with them must make any man quiver with fear."

"Riders were strong enough to best you once," Senneth replied.

"But even the king's army is not threat enough to keep me tamely on my estates," he replied. "You must realize you are dealing with no ordinary man, serra. You must realize I am unique."

"Dangerous."

"But always friendly to you," he said, and reached for her again.

Kirra knocked his hand away.

For a moment, it seemed as if all noise and conversation in the entire room came to a halt. Kirra's head was ringing with the pressure of the marlord's astonishment and displeasure, turned full force on her. Or maybe it was the aftershock of slapping his hand. Maybe Senneth was not the only mystic who was not able to endure his touch.

"And who are you to display such reckless disrespect?" he demanded in an ominous voice.

Kirra was unnerved, but Casserah would have been wholly unmoved. "Casserah Danalustrous," she replied. "Keep your hands off of Senneth."

Now his face lit with a mixture of amusement and speculation. "The reclusive serramarra recently named heir!" he exclaimed. "Everyone has been anxious to meet you! Have you treated them all with such contempt?"

"Only those who deserved it."

"Oh, that's very good. That lovely sneer—that bone-deep arrogance—that will win you many friends in the Twelve Houses."

"I don't need that many friends," she said politely. "I'm not trying to organize a rebellion."

He laughed softly, but his black eyes narrowed and he was no longer amused. "A marlady always needs friends," he said. "And a beautiful young marlady needs a husband."

She laughed out loud at that. "That would temper my arrogance for certain," she agreed. "Perhaps you can suggest a candidate to my father?"

"I am more interested in finding a match for Senneth," he said suavely. "I always have been."

Again, Kirra felt Senneth recoil. Taking a shot wholly at random, Kirra said, "But aren't you here with your own wife tonight, marlord? Isn't she right there behind you?" The Wild Mother was kind to her; the woman's name, wholly forgotten until this moment, slipped into her head. "Sabina, is that you?"

One of the women in the group nearby turned at the sound of her name. She was small and pretty, with very fine blond hair pulled back in a tight braid, leaving her fragile, haunted face wholly exposed. Her blue eyes were huge; her full mouth was pushed into an attempt at a smile. "Yes?" she said in a nervous voice.

Only the faintest look of annoyance crossed Halchon's face. He reached out a hand and pulled her into their conversation. "Sabina, my dear, here are a couple of serramarra you do not often get a chance to meet. Senneth Brassenthwaite and Casserah Danalustrous."

The hand she extended was cold and thin. Kirra felt an irrational impulse to go fetch a shawl and draw the woman over to a fireplace. Sabina was a few years older than Senneth, so hardly a helpless child, and yet there was an air of complete vulnerability about her. Or perhaps Kirra was pitying her too much for being married to her husband.

Even Senneth shook Sabina's hand, holding it a moment or two longer than necessary. Kirra wondered if Senneth was trying to infuse some of her own body heat into the marlady. Senneth was even easier to rouse to sympathy than Kirra, and Senneth had greater reason to hate Halchon Gisseltess.

"I don't believe I've actually met either of you before," Sabina said in a wispy voice. "How delightful that you are here tonight." She turned her eyes toward Senneth. "I am acquainted with your brother."

"Kiernan? I do not envy you," Senneth said with a smile.

"Yes, of course, Kiernan, too, but I meant Nate."

"Ah, my *other* outspoken, overbearing brother," Senneth said.

Sabina actually laughed. "I thought they were both very kind."

"Then you have seen a side of them mysteriously hidden from me! But I'm glad they treated you well."

Sabina now attempted to make small talk with Casserah. "Are you enjoying your travels? I understand you do not often leave Danalustrous."

Even Casserah would have been gentle with this poor woman. "Yes, each House has been more interesting than the last," she said. "I find myself wondering if Danalustrous should not have its own grand ball and invite the Twelve Houses." Casserah would find herself wondering no such thing, but Kirra couldn't help being amused at putting the words in her sister's mouth. She was tempted to add, *Your husband wouldn't be invited, of course, but you'd be welcome.* Better not.

"We are—we are not having a ball at Gisseltess this season," Sabina said wistfully. "But perhaps, if we arrange one next year, you would be able to come?"

Casserah would never forgive her for promising that. "I would be delighted to receive an invitation, my lady."

"And we'll make sure to include Senneth, too, shall we?" Halchon murmured.

Senneth lifted her eyes to his face. "I am not much of one for the social circuit," she demurred. "It is unlikely you will ever find me at Gissel Plain."

"Well, then," he said, his voice quite cheerful, "I shall just hope to see you again one day in Ghosenhall."

Kirra was chilled by the threat implicit in those words—or the unspoken ones that came after. *When I am installed as king, and when I have discarded this pathetic creature and made you my bride.* Impossible as it seemed, Sabina wilted a little more. Senneth said nothing. Even Kirra could not think of a reply. Fortunately, the dinner bell rang just then, and they all turned with some relief toward the dining hall.

Tayse was standing right there.

Kirra gasped and dropped Senneth's arm, and everyone in Halchon's party offered up cries of varying degrees of intensity. How had he crossed the room with such absolute stealth? How had everyone in their own small group failed to see him?

Kirra knew he could move silently when he chose, but he was a big man in dark colors in a well-lit space. How long had he stood there, unnoticed, listening to their conversation?

Halchon Gisseltess was almost hissing in dislike, but he would not speak directly to Tayse. "So," he said to Senneth. "I see your tame Rider still follows you like a dog."

Tayse stepped forward so close, so fast, that Halchon backed up a pace. Sabina gave a little cry and put a hand to her throat. Tayse and Halchon both ignored her. "If you ever lay a hand on her again, I will kill you," Tayse said.

"You would be instantly dead," Halchon scoffed.

"But not before the blade went home."

"I am not afraid of a King's Rider," Halchon said, swinging his attention back to Senneth. "Or a mystic with unreliable powers."

Kirra found her voice and made it sound breezy. "But are you afraid to incur your hostess's wrath? The dinner bell has sounded, and everyone else has gone in to eat."

In fact, the room was only about half empty, as dozens of Mayva's guests lingered to gawk at the little drama being played out at one end of the room. Mayva herself was one of them, standing at the door between the rooms, wringing her hands, and appearing to argue in a low voice with her husband. Kirra had no idea how long Lowell had stood beside Senneth, listening to her trade insults with Halchon Gisseltess. She had not noticed him leaving. She had had no attention for any but the principal players.

Halchon took his wife's hand and laid it on his arm. "Indeed, yes, let us go in to dinner, Sabina," he said. "Senneth. Casserah. I am sure I will have the pleasure of talking with both of you later. Perhaps you will each save me a dance tomorrow at the ball."

"I won't," Kirra said.

"I don't dance," Senneth said.

He gave them both a savage smile. By the expression on Sabina's face, his fingers had just tightened painfully over her hand. "Then we will have to content ourselves with more pleasant discourse," he responded. "I will look forward to the hour."

Finally, finally, he stepped away from them, trailed by the three other members of his party, who looked dazed and a little worried. Kirra blew out her breath in one long, unladylike whuffle and turned to share her astonishment with Senneth.

And found herself even more astonished. For there, in the middle of Nocklyn Towers, in full view of twenty or thirty exalted guests, the serramarra of Brassenthwaite had melted into the arms of a King's Rider and was allowing him to hold her as if he was the only thing keeping her from dissolution. Kirra could not see Senneth's face, buried against his black vest, but she could see Tayse's. She turned silently away and walked alone across the width of the room.

CHAPTER
26

DINNER conversation was interesting, to say the least. Kirra had been set among a handful of high-ranking nobles, including marlords Rafe Storian and Martin Helven and their wives. Rafe, as usual, felt no qualms about speaking his mind.

"Casserah! By the Lady's silver tears, what was that all about? Is that Halchon Gisseltess? I thought he was confined to his estates! Were you and that Brassenthwaite girl trying to arrest him in the name of the king?"

Before answering, Kirra spared a moment to savor his description of Senneth as *that Brassenthwaite girl*. "Well, no, but we did express surprise at seeing him here," she replied. "What is Mayva about, to invite such a man to her house? The king will be gravely displeased."

"It's not Mayva. It's her husband," Martin said. He was a heavy, balding man whom Kirra had always considered both smart and likable, if a little too cautious to suit her impetuous style. "He's Gisseltess kin. He probably extended the invitation."

"Does it matter? He's on Nocklyn land, and Nocklyn shall pay the price," Kirra replied.

Clera Storian leaned forward and her topaz pendant swung forward just far enough to reveal her housemark. "But who cares about boring old Halchon Gisseltess," she said. "Did you *see*? Senneth Brassenthwaite flung herself into the arms of a Rider! Is there a scandal brewing there?"

"Senneth Brassenthwaite," Martin repeated. "I haven't seen her since—she could only have been a child. Who could ever have predicted she would—well. She's led a strange life, has she not?"

"Missing for close to twenty years!" Clera exclaimed. "And she comes back and turns out to be some kind of strange mystic—and you just know her poor father must be cursing in his grave—and *now* she's consorting with soldiers? With common men? Kiernan will have to lock her up! Or she'll destroy the reputation of Brassenthwaite."

Kirra toyed with the stem of her glass and tried to decide how much Casserah would say. For herself, she wanted to throw the water in Clera's smug face and stalk to a different table. But she kept her voice cool, even uninterested. "It's difficult to lock Senneth up someplace she doesn't want to stay," she said. "And I don't think Kiernan feels like trying. Go ahead and ostracize Senneth if you like—she won't mind. She's only here to protect Amalie. She doesn't care for approval from—from anyone, really. Certainly not from the Twelve Houses."

"But Casserah," Clera said urgently. "A *King's Rider*? And a *serramarra*? Even if she is the most disreputable serramarra in the history of the realm?"

Kirra's fingers tightened on the glass, and then she took her hand and folded it in her lap. "The most amazing serramarra in the history of the realm," she said. "My father and the king honor her highly. You might choose to remember that."

Rafe Storian shook his head. "And yet these are perilous times for the king himself," he said, lowering his voice and looking around. "I am happy to see his daughter here with us tonight, but I have to wonder: Is that enough to quiet the doubters? What happens next?"

Fortunately, the uneasy state of politics interested everyone—except Clera Storian—as much as Senneth's breach of propriety, so talk turned to other topics. Kirra listened, but when she heard nothing new in their prattle and gossip, she let her attention wander to the other diners. Yes, a good number of them appeared to be whispering together and then cutting their eyes in Senneth's direction, their faces showing shock and dismay. A few of them looked between Senneth and Amalie, then whispered some more. It didn't take much imagination to guess those conversations: *Can a woman with so little judgment be trusted to guard the princess?*

A few—only a few—seemed more amazed by the appearance of Halchon Gisseltess in their midst than in the inappropriate behavior of a serramarra. Most of the people present were from the southern Houses, of course, and all of them had a long history of flouting the king, at least on minor matters. They were probably amused that Halchon had disobeyed an injunction. Many of them would probably head to his side tonight and ask after his health and perhaps make a deal or two. . . .

Possibly an hour of the dinner had elapsed before Kirra allowed herself to look for Romar Brendyn and try to assess his reaction. She always put some effort into *not* looking for Romar, but inevitably, before any meal or ball was ended, she had located him in the assembly. Tonight, he was seated between Amalie and Mayva, with Valri and a handful of other notables at his table. His face was thunderous. Kirra could see Mayva's mouth moving very fast as she attempted to either distract him or convince him that she had meant no treason. Lowell, sitting at the opposite end of the table, watched his wife with a closed expression and did not appear to be making any attempt at conversation with the women seated beside him.

Kirra wondered if Romar could order the king's guards now accompanying Amalie to escort Halchon back to Gisseltess. But even if he could, she thought he probably would not. Amalie's safety was more important than Halchon's disobedience. And they had ample reasons to worry about Amalie's safety. . . .

She looked a little longer before she found Senneth, sitting so quietly at her own table that she had almost managed to disappear. The lords and ladies who'd been seated next to the erring serramarra all wore the careful expressions of people attempting not to appear outraged. While she watched, though, Kirra saw no one turn to speak to Senneth, even to offer her a plate of bread.

For a serramarra who cared for the goodwill of her fellows, it appeared to be the gravest offense in the world to show public affection for someone outside the nobility. Kirra had never thought she would be able to do it. To love a soldier or a smithy or a serf—to be cast out of society forever—would she have the courage? She chafed at the responsibilities of noblesse oblige, and her magic put her on the very edge of respectability for virtually everyone in this room, but so far they had all continued to accept her, to allow her to step into their houses and sit at their tables. But if she were to marry a poor man, a tenant farmer, a tavernkeeper's son, she might never be permitted to cross these thresholds again. Could she throw so much away for love? Did her place in society matter to her so little that she would never rue her bargain?

Was any love so great that it was worth ruining a life for? Was she capable of a love that grand?

Her eyes went back to Romar. Not a serf, of course, but just as ineligible in his own way. But, oh, so attractive in every other! For so many reasons, she would be a fool to fall in love with him—more foolish than Senneth had been to fall in love with Tayse. But she did not know, in this case, if she would be able to govern her heart. The consequences would not include banishment from her social circle, but she suspected they would be even more devastating in their own way.

She was better off avoiding love completely. She did not seem capable of making intelligent choices.

"What would your father say, Casserah?" Rafe Storian was asking her. She had absolutely no idea what conversation had gone on around her while she had sat there thinking of impossible lovers.

But she smiled anyway and picked up her fork. "No one ever knows what my father would say," she replied. "You'll have to ask him yourself."

AFTER the meal, they were all shuffled into yet another adjoining room to indulge in the arts. Mayva had imported a trio of very fine musicians who played complex and accomplished pieces on a variety of instruments while the guests circulated around the room admiring a collection of paintings and statues. Between musical numbers, a plainly dressed young woman stood on a small stage and recited rather grim poetry. Kirra thought Mayva got points for creativity at her little soiree, but she still didn't enjoy the evening. From the expressions on the faces of the people near her, no one else did, either.

She was making desultory conversation with the people who showed any interest in speaking with her, and wishing she had Senneth's knack of vanishing, when Romar Brendyn caught her attention again. Or maybe she was looking for him, even though she was pretending she wasn't. But she saw him turn politely away from one discussion, place a wineglass on a servant's tray, and step to one side as if to engage someone else in conversation. And then he stepped beyond that group and beyond the next likely group and so made his way by gradual stages to the wall and then the servants' entrance. With one quick backward glance, he slipped out the door and disappeared.

On the instant, Kirra decided to follow him.

She made her way with equal circumspection to the exit and glided through. The hallway was dark, as no one wasted much illumination on servants, but it was pretty easy to tell where he had gone. Ahead and to her left was a door that led to the kitchens and the sound of women arguing; the door across from it appeared to open onto the gardens. Romar had no doubt gone outside, making his nightly escape from the close and disagreeable company of the gathered nobles.

Kirra stepped through the side door and found herself in a vegetable garden, surrounded by the pungent smell of ripening tomatoes and tall, ghostly stalks of corn. Romar was nowhere in sight. She hurried through the neatly kept rows and pushed past a tall wooden gate, still swinging as if someone had just walked through. She was far enough from the house now that no light from the windows lit her way, and the fragment of moon overhead was not much help. Was that a man's shape twenty yards in front of her, moving purposefully away from the house? Or was that just the shadow of a shadow, some odd condensation of darkness, and nothing she cared about?

But she was only a few minutes behind him. He could not have gotten far. She was taken by the notion that he had come out here for some sort of rendezvous, and not just for his usual evening constitutional. With whom could he be meeting? Mayva's husband, Lowell, to deliver in private a furious condemnation of his lapse of judgment? Rafe Storian, to discuss how one of the middle Houses intended to show its fealty to the throne?

One of the lovely young women with soft black hair and creamy white skin who didn't mind Romar's brusque manners because she was enchanted with his blond hair and quick smile?

He didn't seem like the sort of man for idle dalliance. But, of course, Kirra knew better.

She could not help herself. She had to know. She stood for a moment, hands down at her sides, concentrating, feeling her muscles soften and shift, feeling her bones grow hollow and light. Her clothes melted away. Her skin was coated with feathers. When she opened her eyes, she was a snowy owl, and she could see everything.

Lifting off silently, she cruised low to the ground, following the direction of that mysterious shadow. It didn't take very long to catch up and discover that it was indeed Romar, moving steadily toward what was undoubtedly an appointment of some sort. Soon enough, he left the manicured grounds most closely surrounding the manor and veered off toward a wooded area on the back end of the property. Kirra grew more cheerful as she decided no gently bred serramarra would follow him this far, on foot, at night, just to flirt by moonlight. If he was meeting someone, it was another man.

Indeed, once she followed him into the stand of woods, where it was even darker, she caught the first rumbling sound of male voices. She flew ahead, dodging outflung branches and trailing vines, to find a small convocation gathered around a tiny fire. Ten or eleven men, it looked like, none of them easy to see in the uncertain light. From what she could determine, three were wearing fine silks and a variety of small gems; they were lords of some degree and had probably been eating dinner two tables over from her earlier in the evening. The other six were more plainly dressed in darker colors with flatter textures. She wondered if they had entered the compound in stealth, without passing the checkpoint at the gate. Not too reassuring, if such a maneuver was easily accomplished. She listened to their low conversation and realized that all the accents were those of cultivated men.

Romar was coming to an impromptu meeting with members of the Thirteenth House.

Kirra settled soundlessly on a convenient tree limb a few moments before one of the lords spotted Romar. "I see someone. Do you think that's the regent?" And then, more sharply, "My lord? Is that you?"

"It is Romar Brendyn," he said, not hesitating to identify himself as he stepped out of the dark overhang of the woods into the firelit clearing. "I have come as you asked."

What a fool, Kirra thought, even as she admired him for his courage. This was a man who had been abducted while close to his own lands, attacked while the guest of a prominent noblewoman, and only spared by unforeseen circumstance from the fate of being burned alive in a wayside inn. And yet, solitary and unafraid, he attended a secret conference in an unguarded place attended by men he probably could not name. She was astonished he had lived so long. It seemed impossible he would survive his tenure as regent.

The very thought made her small heart cold. She shifted on her perch, trying to hear every word.

"We are all busy and expected elsewhere," said one man in a brisk voice. Kirra thought it came from one of the more well-dressed participants—no doubt one of Mayva's most favored vassals accorded the high privilege of being invited to the ball. "Let us get straight to the point."

"I am listening," said Romar.

"What can you offer the lesser nobility, as our patrons choose to call us?" said another voice, teasingly familiar. The speaker was a dark, large shape that did not come near enough to the fire to be identified. He wore the plainer clothes that indicated he had not been among the revelers. "We are tired of being judged inferior. We want equal voice, equal honors. We want rights and powers that are given to our brothers and cousins of the Twelve Houses."

"You would take lands away from their hereditary owners?" Romar asked.

"*I* would. They have held it long enough," said another man, but other voices spoke over his.

"We would take nothing from anybody," said the heavyset man. "But we want our own property, given to us outright and not to be disposed of at the whim of a marlord who might be small-minded or stupid or vindictive. Why should there not be twenty Houses instead of twelve? Some of us would be willing to consolidate. Others would intermarry. We ask for only an equal place with our brethren."

"You realize I cannot guarantee such a thing," Romar said. "I can promise to carry your request to the king. I can promise to advocate for you if Amalie ascends the throne while I am regent. But I have no power to decree such a change."

"You have the power to tell the king of our demands," growled one of the men. "You can tell him of the trouble we will cause if he does not listen to us."

Romar looked steadily into the darkness where the speaker stood. "I do not think you will get far with Baryn if you speak of 'demands' and 'trouble,'" he said. "He is a reasonable man, and he expects others to act with civility."

"We have been meek and civilized long enough," said the heavyset man. "We are almost out of patience."

"I cannot help you if you do not listen to reason," Romar said. "I believe your position is legitimate. I believe the king may be moved to deal with you. But I am less likely to take your side if you resort to threats and violence."

"And would you take our side if you were dead? Eh?" said another voice from the darkness. Even Kirra, with her predator's eyes, could not determine where the disembodied voice originated. "Would the king take our side if your life was at stake, and the deeds to our property doubled as your ransom?"

Romar's face, clearly visible by the soft firelight, grew stiff. "I came here in good faith. And now you would threaten me? How does that make me any more eager to espouse your cause?"

There was a muttering of dissent among the gathered men. It was clear some of them were not eager to engage in violence to make a point—but some of them were.

"Maybe, but the king would know we were serious if you were dead!" one of them called out.

The man Kirra took to be one of Mayva's vassals appeared to be staring past the circle of firelight. "Who said that? Dalwin? Ordway? Don't talk like that."

"Sometimes it takes a little blood for a king to know you're serious," another man said.

"I don't want to hear any more talk of bloodshed," the vassal said. "We agreed to present our petition to the regent and urge him to support us."

"Some of us did," a man replied, and again the vassal peered into the dark. Kirra was guessing that some of these men didn't know each other all that well—that there might be one or two here who were virtual strangers to all the others. In that case, there might be something she could do. . . .

She dropped from her tree limb to the ground while the men continued to argue. She caught Romar's voice more than once, sounding wholly unafraid, and the vassal's, and that of the heavyset man, who appeared to favor some kind of radical gesture this very night. She tried to ignore them so she could focus on the chore at hand, unfurling her white wings and stretching them to their full extent. Tipping her head back and craning it toward the heavens. Extending her curved claws into a flatter, fuller footprint.

Shifting her weight. Altering her outlook. Changing her shape.

When she opened her eyes again, she was human and male, dressed in nondescript dark clothing and heavy boots. She eased her way past tree trunks and shadows toward the bright point of the fire, circling around the back of the group so it would seem she was just moving from one place in the gathering to another. She hung back far enough to keep her face out of the light, but shouldered her way between the portly man and someone in court clothes who hadn't spoken much.

The big man was speaking again. "We have been biddable too long! We have done as we have been told! And we have been shunted aside and treated like common merchants. It is time our bloodlines were acknowledged and our status was established. The king must recognize us—or reckon with us. I say we take this man into our keeping and hold him until the king meets with us."

Kirra allowed herself to give a cynical little laugh. A few people turned to look in her direction, trying to puzzle out who she was. "You must not have been at Kianlever if you think that's a good idea," she said.

She heard someone next to her whisper to his neighbor. "Who is that, Salzton?" His friend replied, "I can't tell."

"What does Kianlever have to do with us?" the heavy man demanded.

"Maybe nothing, maybe something. *I* don't know who sent armed men into the court to attack the princess and your regent here." She waved a hand at Romar, who was staring fixedly at the spot where she was standing. Surely he couldn't see her. Surely no one could. "But the assault lasted fifteen minutes, and when it was over, there were twenty men dead, and none of them was the regent. That mystic woman they've got set up walls of fire—*fire*, inside the ballroom!—and the King's Riders cut down every last enemy. Out in the garden, so I heard, one of those other damn mystics turned into a wild animal and clawed the face off of one of the men sent to find the regent. You can take Romar Brendyn tonight, and you can put him anywhere you like, but I don't think he'll stay there long. And I don't think you'll live past the night."

There was another uneasy mumbling from the crowd. Clearly some of them had heard about—or witnessed—the massacre in Kianlever. She heard someone ask, "And how did he escape from the house in Tilt? No one has ever explained that," while another voice hissed, "Quiet."

"I don't want to draw the attention of Senneth Brassenthwaite," said the man Kirra thought was Mayva's vassal.

The big man, still standing in shadow, spoke in a sneering tone. "You won't. She's here to protect the princess. She won't go haring off after missing regents."

"She would if the princess asked her to," Kirra said, a shrug in her voice. "The man is Amalie's *uncle*. Of course she'll send her pet mystics after him! Don't you understand? We are *stuck* with this man. If we kill him, we lose everything. We have to negotiate."

"Would *you* want to negotiate with someone who had just threatened to take your life?" another voice asked. She thought she saw the glint of firelight off of metal. Someone had drawn a sword. "We have no leverage with the regent now."

"I understand desperation," Romar said. He still sounded as calm as if he was standing in the king's courtyard discussing crop rotation with farmers. "But your colleague speaks the truth. My death would not go unavenged. I have more friends than you realize."

No one else seemed to recognize that as a threat, but Kirra did. She tried to listen to the noises around her, a little distance out from the campfire. If she had been in animal shape, she would have been able to hear better, would have been able to tell by scent if other bodies were approaching, closing in by stealth on this assembly of malcontents. Was that the sound of a booted heel against a buried root? Was that the whine of a blade against its scabbard?

"Will you be our advocate?" the well-dressed lord asked. "Will you take our words to the princess—and the king?"

"I will do what I can," Romar promised.

"That is not good enough," someone said, and lunged forward with a blade.

"Colton!" Romar cried, and suddenly the whole scene was a melee. Kirra was not the only one to leap forward to try to knock the sword from the assailant's hand; the camp was almost perfectly divided between those who threw themselves around Romar to defend him, and those who battled forward to attack. Kirra found herself in the center of the small group surrounding him, her back against his chest as if to make her body a living shield.

"I appreciate the gesture, my friend, but don't you think you'd be a little more effective if you carried a sword?" came Romar's voice in her ear. Incredibly, he sounded amused.

"I—I forgot to bring one," she gasped. Even shape-changing wouldn't turn her into a warrior. She scarcely even understood the proper grip on the hilt.

"That's all right. You have other ways to defend me—and yourself," he said.

Impossibly, he knew who she was.

She did not have to answer, as the darkness was suddenly roiling with a furious motion, and what seemed like fifty men poured into the small clearing. Yes, she'd been right—Romar's captain and a cohort of his soldiers had followed the regent to this dangerous assignation. They dispatched the dissidents in short order, hampered a little by the darkness and Romar's insistent shouts of "No killing!" He clamped his left hand around Kirra's wrist and dragged her with him as he pushed through his line of defenders and over to Colton's side. In his right hand, he held a sword. He had come to this party a bit more well-prepared than Kirra had expected.

"Who have you caught? What have you found?" Romar demanded as soon as he reached his captain.

"A few of them ran into the woods and we didn't go chasing

after them," Colton said. "Too dark and too much chance of ambush. There's four we caught, and another three that didn't run. What do you want to do with them?"

The three who hadn't run were the men in fine clothes and high favor, all of whom looked both subdued and aghast. "My lord, I did not realize that some of my friends felt so—would offer you—my lord, please believe me, not all of the lesser lords are so free with talk of violence," said Mayva's vassal. He sounded absolutely appalled. "I realize, if they do not, that we have no hope of winning your favor by such ill-judged antics. I can understand your rage. But I swear to you, many of us would have no part in such bloody dealings."

"I believe you," Romar said. "But you must understand that I cannot put myself in the position of begging the king for favors for men who would like to kill me. I must know who among your friends is peaceful, and who is murderous."

The vassal looked perplexed. "I don't know. These men I recognize, but of these four only Horace spoke out against you. The big man who talked so wildly, and the other one, the one with the blade—I didn't know them. I thought they must have come with others who were invited. They were strangers to me."

Romar towed Kirra into the firelight. *Bright Mother blind me*, she thought, and kept her face tilted down. "Do you recognize this man?" he asked. "I think he arrived late to the gathering."

The vassal shook his head. "No. I thought that—no. Do we have spies in our midst? Someone who has gone to some trouble to infiltrate the highest ranks of the Thirteenth House?"

Romar nodded. "It would appear so. You have honest men looking for reform, and opportunists looking to turn your discontent into rebellion. It is hard to tell them all apart."

Colton had pressed close enough to audit this conversation. "We'll take these four back to the barracks with us and see what we can find out," he said casually. Kirra shuddered a little to wonder what methods he might use to discover information.

"Carefully," Romar told him. "These men have ties to gentry. You might have the head of the Nocklyn guard called in before you start asking questions."

Colton nodded toward Kirra. "What about that young man? We could find out who he is."

Again, Romar's hand tightened around Kirra's wrist. "Oh, this is someone I recognize," he said. "He thought to come here to lend me support. He is not one of the dissenters. But I am not pleased that he put himself at risk this way."

She gave him one quick, incredulous look. "If we are to speak of *risk,* my lord—"

He laughed. "I knew my men were in place. I was not afraid."

"Yes, that would appear to be your trouble," she said rather sharply. "You never are afraid."

"What would you like me to do, regent?" the vassal asked in a humble voice.

"You—I would like you to come see me in Ghosenhall in a few weeks' time," Romar said. The look on the lord's face was sheer amazement. Romar continued, "Bring with you some of the men you absolutely know and trust. None of these strange, shadowy figures who might be enemies. We will talk over your proposition. I can guarantee nothing except that I will listen."

"Yes, my lord. Thank you, my lord," the vassal said, bowing very deeply. His well-dressed compatriots followed suit.

"Now, I believe you have a social engagement to get back to," Romar said to the would-be malcontents, the smile back in his voice. "As do I. You and your friends return to the Towers. I will speak a few words with Colton and follow you in a moment or two."

Another series of bows and the three men hurried off. Kirra had to think they were cursing the whole night's work and debating whether it was really safe to go to Ghosenhall in a few weeks and meet with Romar there. But maybe. Men desperate enough to chance midnight meetings in the company of unreliable allies must be passionate about achieving their goals. Property. Prestige. Parity. She wondered if her aunt and uncle felt their lack of status as keenly as this group appeared to, and thought they probably did. Certainly they nursed a great enough bitterness against Malcolm Danalustrous. She had always thought that they disliked him for marrying and then forgetting their sister, but perhaps they would have resented him anyway. The thought made her feel strange, as if the colors of the world had suddenly shifted, as if her perspective had narrowed down or widened and she could no longer trust the evidence of her eyes.

She was careless with her Danalustrous heritage, but it was

integral to her sense of self. She was serramarra; everyone knew instantly what that meant and offered her the respect of her position. Who would she be if she was nobody? How much would she care?

"We'll escort you back to the house, my lord," Colton was saying. "And then we'll take these fellows off."

"Oh, I think we can find our way back in safety," Romar said. "My friend and I can both defend ourselves."

"Better not," Colton replied. "Some of those men ran, but they might not have run far. We'll come with you at least as far as the house."

Romar sighed and acquiesced. "Very well," he said, and they all began moving forward. He still had not released Kirra's wrist, and now she tugged on it.

"Give me my arm back," she said, exasperated.

"I think not," he replied, and continued strolling along, dragging her with him. Colton set a rapid pace, and his men and their prisoners were forced to keep up. There was almost no conversation until they were within sight of the mansion and it was time for Colton to turn his party toward the barracks.

"I'll come see you in the morning," Romar said.

"Very good, my lord. Be careful."

"I always am."

Colton did not bother to reply to that remark, clearly untrue, just shepherded his men off into the darkness. In a very short amount of time, Kirra and Romar were left alone.

CHAPTER
27

T HEY were standing in the middle of the back lawn that sloped away from the mansion. It was almost too dark to see anything, and Kirra had her head turned away from Romar's insistent gaze, but she could tell he was studying her as if all the lines and contours of her face were entirely visible.

"You were the last person I expected to see at tonight's little escapade," he said finally. "But I suppose I should know better by now. You appear every time danger threatens me. Soon I will come to rely on your intervention and I will prove so careless with my life that you will need to stand beside me at all times, just to keep me safe."

She was tempted to pretend she had no idea what he was talking about, that she was not the person he thought she was, but it seemed pointless. He had recognized her the minute she raised her voice, disguised as it was. "How did you know me?" she asked instead.

"I think I will always know you. No matter what form you assume or what company you keep. The essential nature of your soul is imprinted on my heart. You will never be a stranger to me."

At that she smiled and lifted her head. "Very pretty. Next time I will come to you as a spider or a snake, and we will see how quickly you recognize me."

"Come to me in any guise," he said, "as long as you come to me."

He leaned forward as if to kiss her. She put her free hand up to push back hard against his chest. Her heart was pounding so heavily she had to struggle to take a breath. "Now that would be a scandal greater than even Senneth has stirred up," she said, trying to laugh. "The regent of Ghosenhall is caught kissing a strange young man on the back lawn of Nocklyn Towers."

"Then change for me," he begged. "Be Kirra. Just for now. Just for this minute."

"That's foolish."

"Be foolish for me."

She shouldn't. It was stupid. He would kiss her if she was Kirra. Even now she felt the pressure of his body as he strained forward, as he clearly showed his desire and his intention. It didn't seem to matter to him that she was in this body, unfamiliar and not suited to his notions of romance. He knew her in whatever body she crafted.

Slowly, watching the expression in his eyes as she did it, she re-shaped her face, re-colored her hair, took on the curves and height and shell that defined Kirra. It made her feel strangely vulnerable, ridiculously feminine, to have her own gold curls tumbling down her back, feel her very own smile lifting the corners of her mouth. Even the dress she manufactured was one of her own, a red so dark it looked black in this poor light.

"So," she said. "What do you think of me now?"

He kissed her so hard there was no air to breathe; his arms crushed her body, rearranged her ribs. She wanted to shove him away, she wanted to hold him tighter, she wanted that kiss to end the world. Suddenly he released her from his suffocating hold, but he did not let her go. Now his hands were on either side of her head, buried in her hair. Now he was kissing her all over her face, her cheeks, her eyes, her lips again. Between kisses he whispered her name.

She couldn't think. She couldn't tell him to stop. She felt her body turn liquid and her blood rejoice. It was as if she was changing into someone new, a wholly unfamiliar shape, a woman who had never existed until he kissed her. It was a transformation more complete than any she had ever wrought on herself, and she was not sure she would ever know how to turn back into the person she had been.

When he finally let her go, she gulped and fought for air. She turned away from him, not wanting him to see her face. She staggered and he caught her arm again, but she jerked her hand away and he allowed her to go free.

"You can't blame me for falling in love with you," he said. "If not for you, I wouldn't even be alive."

"I think maybe I'll let you go next time," she said, still turned away, still trying to recover her breathing.

He laughed softly. "There will be no more next time," he said. "Nothing will make me risk myself again. I could not bear the thought of dying and thereby losing you."

Now she did look at him, making herself stand straight, acting like a reasonable woman. She tried, she tried to remember his wife, the kind and devoted paragon. She could not bring the image into focus. She said, "You don't have me. So you can't lose me."

"I want to have you," he said.

"We are nothing but trouble for each other."

"I don't care," he said. "I look at you and I see heartache, and I don't care. I think of you, and I know loving you will hurt everyone else I love, and I don't care. You may end up hating me, and I may end up mourning you the rest of my life, and I don't care. I want you too much. I want this moment, this night, anything you can give me. I love you. And all your shifting and all your laughing and all your protesting will not change that."

She shook her head, not to contradict him, but to signify that she did not understand. "I am so restless," she said. "I cannot stay in any one place for more than a few weeks, a few days. My friends are people like Senneth, who is as fidgety as I am, and Cammon, who is as strange. You have asked me why I have not married and that is one reason—there is no one I can bear to be with, settled cozily in one house, for all my days. So I have been used to thinking of myself as an inconstant and uncommitted woman." She straightened a little, turned herself to face him full on. "But I know that I would only be able to have you in bits and pieces, during snatched moments in dark corners, a day here, a day there. And it is not enough for me. I would want to be with you during all those other days, too, for months at a time, for years. Don't you think that's ironic? That I would finally fall in love with a man I would always have to be leaving, and he is the one who makes me want to stay?"

"I will settle for the stolen hours, if they are all I can have," he said. "I will settle for your smile across the room, your hand on my shoulder when I ask you to dance. I will take whatever you are able to spare me. There is nothing I can promise you, I know that—nothing I can give you, no offer I can make—except my love. Whenever you want it, for as long as you will have it. Even if I never see you again, I will love you the rest of my life."

"I cannot bear that thought," she said. "Not ever seeing you again. But there is so much about this I cannot endure."

He had released her earlier, but now he lifted his hands again, rested them on her shoulders. "Can you bear for me to kiss you again?" he asked. "For I feel I must."

She lifted her face. "I could not bear it if you did not."

More gently this time, he took her in his arms, more gently laid his mouth against hers. She was aware of every inch of her skin, alive with sensation, aware of every place that his body met hers. *I have to have him,* she thought, but it was not so clear as that; there were no words in her head. Merely, she pressed against him more closely, lifted her arms to wrap them around his shoulders. Something bubbled through her, and she thought it might be happiness. Or recklessness or mischief or desire. Or all of them, wrapped in a swirl of magic.

For she was a shiftling, and she could make any ordinary object of the world change shape. Her dress she turned into a scrap of cotton and lace, letting it fall to the ground. Romar actually gasped as he felt her turn nude in his arms. His hands roved down her back, came up to cup the curve of her shoulders, but he still held her against him, more tightly now, as if to shield her from view.

"Can you do that for me?" he whispered in her ear.

She was laughing now. So it had been happiness after all. And a little mischief. And certainly desire. "I can," she said. And then his clothes were gone, even his boots, just a few ribbons of silk and leather lost in the tall grass.

They were both naked, clinging together, kissing each other with a mad fervor under the thin, chilly moon and the startled constellations. They were close enough to the great house to hear occasional bursts of music, too far—or so Kirra hoped—for anyone out for an evening stroll to see them. Not that she cared. She cared about nothing but the feel of this man's hands on her body, his skin against her skin. She kissed him with a sort of desperation, trying to get closer.

"Can you conjure up a blanket?" Romar whispered against her mouth, and again she laughed. She pulled him down with her to the grass, where her spread fingers manufactured a soft quilt from so many leaves of clover, and they lay together, body to body, heart against heart. The music from the house swelled and receded; the summer night lay against them like an exhalation of breath. They made love by starlight and swore promises by moonlight. Kirra thought she might never be so happy again.

THE soiree was long over by the time they returned to the house, moving separately and in stealth. In fact, most of the lower story of the mansion was in darkness, light trickling out only from the kitchen windows and the servants' quarters.

"Do you think anyone missed us?" Romar asked.

"My friends might have noticed my absence, but they wouldn't have been alarmed," Kirra said.

"Why? Do you often slip away?"

She grinned. "It's hard to keep track of any mystic," she admitted. "All of us like to be alone from time to time. But they wouldn't be alarmed because they know I can take care of myself." *And because Cammon would know if I was in trouble,* she thought, but she didn't add that. Best not to really dwell on what other emotions Cammon was able to pick up on when he tried. "What if someone was looking for you? Amalie, for instance? Or anyone else?"

"They will have to wait till morning to be reassured, I suppose. But Amalie would check with Colton before she became truly worried, and he could let her know I was safe."

"Still, I think it is best that no one sees us returning together at this hour after a long unexplained absence," she said. "You go in by the way we left. I'll find another route."

"No," he said at once. "You go in the back door. I don't want you circling the house at night, trying for other entrances. I'll do that."

She laughed and kissed him quickly on the mouth. She

wondered how long such unnecessary protectiveness would
seem charming. Not long, she thought. "I'll use the same
door," she said, "but I'll take a different shape. No one will notice me."

He took a breath and she thought he was going to say something like *I hate to think we must spend our lives lying and
pretending.* He might have thought it, but he didn't say it aloud.
"Then I will see you in the morning?"

"Perhaps not till the evening. Perhaps not until the ball."

"You will dance with me, I hope."

She couldn't help laughing. Dancing would seem very
tame after tonight. "My lord, I will be happy to."

"Serra, I shall live for the moment."

She kissed him again, then allowed herself to melt into a
small familiar shape. Kitchen cat, calico-colored. Without a
glance back at him, she trotted across the last margin of the
lawn, wound her way through the garden, and nudged open the
back door. She could hear voices down the hall as women
worked in the kitchen, scrubbing the last pans and complain-
ing about someone who hadn't done her fair share of chores.
Kirra was quickly through the ballroom and down the corridors leading to the main stair. Bounding up the steps, she listened for sounds of activity down the halls. Not many people
seemed to be astir; it must be later than she had thought.

On the landing between the second and third stories, she
paused and listened again. No footfalls; no voices; no one
nearby. Smoothly and soundlessly she made her transformation back into Casserah, having to think about it a moment before she remembered exactly what she'd been wearing and
how her hair had been styled. Great gods, but she was tired.
She leaned against the cool stone wall for a moment, thinking
about all the events this day had held, from the meeting with
Halchon Gisseltess to the abandoned lovemaking on the back
lawns. In between, more transformations than she could immediately remember. No wonder she was tired. No wonder she
suddenly felt lost and exhausted and utterly alone.

She climbed the last flight of steps and turned into her own
hallway. The Rider named Coeval was stationed outside
Amalie's door and gave her a curt nod when she put her hand
on the doorknob. Her room was partially lit by a branch of

candles near the bed. The alcove where Melly lay was entirely in shadow, but Kirra heard the maid stir as she shut the door.

"Don't get up," Kirra called in a low voice. "I'll put myself to bed."

Melly must have been even more tired than Kirra, for she muttered something indistinguishable and subsided onto her pillow. Kirra quickly undressed, cleaned herself thoroughly with water from the pitcher and basin, and donned one of the prim cotton nightdresses that Casserah favored.

Now the exhaustion was compounded by a sense of loneliness and unutterable loss. *Wild Mother watch me, will I always feel this sad every time I love him and have to walk away?* she wondered. *I will not be able to withstand this many times.*

She stood by the bed and stared down at the cool white sheets, thinking that if she lay down, she would not be able to close her eyes. Her mind would give her back all the pictures of the day, her body would curl up with desolation and want. She considered crossing to the alcove and shaking Melly awake, forcing the maid to talk to her till she herself was too tired to summon another syllable.

Instead, she put on a robe, took a single taper from the candelabra, and headed for the door. "If you're awake, go back to sleep. I don't know when I'll return."

She stepped into the hallway, nodded at Coeval again, and walked the ten paces to the next door down. Not even bothering to knock, she pushed the door open and went in.

Cammon, Hammond and two soldiers wearing the black and gold of Ghosenhall were sitting around a table, playing a card game. Like her own room, this one was half in shadow. She could see that someone was sleeping in the big canopy bed, but she couldn't tell who. All the men had looked up when she entered, then returned their attention to the game. All except Cammon, who laid his cards aside and came over to her.

"Are you all right?" he asked in a low voice. His speckled hazel eyes were fixed on her face, but she noticed that he did not look unduly worried.

"I'm not sure," she answered just as quietly. "I wanted to talk to Tayse or Senneth, but I guess neither one is here."

"Senneth's with Amalie. If it's urgent—"

"No. Where's Tayse?"

Cammon's sweet smile appeared. "Out walking around. Checking to make sure everything is secure. He'll be back in an hour or so."

Of course. How perfect. Kirra had thought she'd had a secret tryst with her forbidden lover, and Tayse had probably spotted them the moment they first shed their clothes. She wouldn't think about that. "There was an incident," she said. "The regent met with some of the lesser lords, and a couple of them wanted to harm him. But Colton was there, and everything ended well, but it was—unsettling. I just wanted Tayse to know."

"Do you think it had anything to do with Halchon Gisseltess being here?"

She shrugged and laughed. "I don't know anything anymore!" she replied. "It's all so crazy! Every time we turn around someone else is trying to kill somebody. It's worse than the trip we took a few months ago."

Cammon grinned. "Halchon Gisseltess didn't try to kill anyone tonight," he said. "Unless I missed something."

"And how did Tayse know to come running into the ballroom this evening?" she demanded. "Did you tell him something was wrong?" Cammon nodded. "But how did you know? Could you hear us in your head—shouting or something? Me or Senneth?"

"Both of you," Cammon replied. "From Senneth all I got was one quick shriek. Then nothing. That would have been enough—I was already running for Tayse. But from you I got this continual sort of low growl. Like Donnal when he's a dog and he's mad about something. I knew you were afraid, but I knew you weren't in any immediate danger."

"Tayse told Halchon Gisseltess he would kill him if Halchon ever touched Senneth again."

"I think he will." Kirra just looked at him, and Cammon continued, "Don't you think so? Eventually? Tayse will kill him."

Kirra felt a little shiver go down her back. "No one, not even a King's Rider, can just murder a man because he wants to. And he certainly can't murder a marlord."

Cammon shrugged. "Well, I can't see the future. But that's what I think."

Kirra leaned against the door and closed her eyes. For a moment, talking to Cammon, she had forgotten her weariness, but now it all came rushing back. "I wish this was all over already," she whispered. "This war, this rebellion, whatever it's going to be. It's so tense. I'm so tired. And there's no end to it."

"You need to go to sleep," Cammon said, pulling her to him in a brotherly hug. "Go back to your room and lie down."

She shook her head. "I don't want to. I'm—Donnal's guarding the princess and I'm not used to—I just didn't feel like being alone. I'd rather stay here awhile and talk to you. Maybe I'll play cards. Are you gambling for money?"

Now his grip changed and he was urging her forward, toward the shadowed bed and its unidentified occupant. "Then lie down in here for a while. I bet you'll fall asleep."

She resisted a little, but eventually allowed him to push her across the room. "Who's already sleeping—oh, no, that's Justin. He won't want me in the bed with him. Maybe I can just curl up on the floor."

"He won't mind. He's already asleep. He won't even notice."

"Of course he will."

"No, really, he's a dullard. Come on, lie down."

She was too tired to turn around and walk out the door. Carefully, she settled onto the bed, hoping to disturb Justin as little as possible, and smiled up at Cammon as he arranged the covers over her. "Goodnight then. Thank you."

"Go to sleep," he said, and put his hand over her eyes.

When she opened her eyes again, it was morning.

CHAPTER
28

IT was a moment before Kirra realized where she was, even who she was, and she drowsed on the bed a few minutes, lazily assessing her situation. Sunlight coming in through an unfamiliar window, so it was daylight at some house she was visiting. Her pillow spread with dark hair, so she was not here as herself. That's right, she was Casserah. A warm body curled against her back, so Donnal must be—

No, Donnal was guarding the princess and she was in love with Romar Brendyn and last night she had sought refuge with the Riders and Cammon had urged her to lie down and share a bed with—

She jerked awake so violently that the body behind her startled instantly upright, and she knew before she even turned over that Justin's first action would be to grab a dagger. She was close enough to feel his muscles relax from their corded readiness as soon as he realized there was no danger. She shifted a little so her back was still to him but she could see him over her shoulder.

He was sitting up, he was shirtless, and he indeed had a knife in one hand. The expression on his face was quizzical as he gazed down at her. "Good morning," she said, her voice a touch malicious. "I hope this isn't an unpleasant surprise."

He laughed. "I knew you were here."

"You did not. You were asleep when I lay down beside you."

He gave her a look that said she was unutterably stupid if she thought he would ever sleep through an event like that. "So what happened?" he asked. "Last night?"

So many ways to answer that question! "Another incident involving some lords of the Thirteenth House. I came to tell Tayse, but he wasn't here."

She thought he would say, "So why did you stay?" but he didn't. She realized he really wasn't surprised to find her beside him in the bed. Not just because he probably *had* woken up when she joined him, but because it didn't seem strange to him that Kirra would have sought out the other Rider in the middle of the night. Whether her news was great or small, Justin himself turned to Tayse at every juncture; he expected everyone else to do the same.

Actually, it might be more than that, Kirra thought, sitting up and pulling her robe more tightly around her body. Justin expected the six of them to always turn to each other, no matter what the crisis. He might not have any idea why Kirra needed comfort, but he would have expected her to get it from someone in their small, strangely bound group. He wouldn't even have thought it through; Justin was not a great one for self-analysis. He would have woken up, seen Kirra beside him, realized she was not bleeding, noticed that Cammon was not alarmed, and decided that he was playing whatever part had been assigned to him for the hour. And gone back to sleep without worrying about it.

For a moment, Kirra wished she could be as simple as Justin.

Someone across the room stood up, and she realized there were other people in the room. She looked around quickly and counted three: Cammon and Coeval, yawning on sofas pushed against the wall, and Tayse, who appeared to have just risen from a mat on the floor. Hammond must be taking his shift outside the princess's door.

Tayse was headed in her direction, and he pulled up a straight-backed chair beside the bed. "What happened last night?" he asked. "I talked to Colton around three in the morning."

"Then you know most of it," she said, and launched into the tale. She was just finishing up when there was a knock on the door and Senneth stepped inside.

"Does anyone know—oh," she said, and stuck her head back out. "Never mind. She's in here."

Senneth entered, followed by Donnal, shaped like himself. *Donnal* had been looking for her? Hadn't he given all his attention to Amalie, with none to spare for his own serramarra? But then Senneth plopped down next to her on the bed and gave Kirra that faint smile.

"Melly was worried," Senneth said. "Apparently you didn't sleep in your own bed last night."

Donnal and Cammon came to join them, Cammon sitting cross-legged on the mattress at Justin's feet, Donnal leaning against one of the bedposts. Kirra heard the door to the room open and shut as Coeval left.

Just for a moment, just the six of them.

"I had a wakeful night," Kirra said, lightly enough considering the true circumstances. "I thought companionship might settle my mind. And who better to seek for kindness and compassion than my old friend Justin?"

"It's who I always look for," Senneth said.

"She snores," Justin commented.

Donnal's response was instant. "No, she doesn't."

Justin gave him a malicious look. "Little trick she's picked up while you've been hovering over the princess."

"Well, you kick," Kirra said, trying to distract Donnal. He looked genuinely furious. "I probably have bruises."

"Good thing you didn't kick back," Tayse observed. "He's likely to pull a blade and stab you before he's even fully awake."

Justin and Kirra both laughed. Cammon stirred on the bed. "So what are we going to do about everything?" he asked.

Tayse glanced at Senneth. "And there's more 'everything' than you know."

Again, Kirra recounted the tale of Romar's midnight adventure. "It's hard to tell," she said. "But I had this feeling. Some of the lesser lords were there to genuinely negotiate. Some were there to stir up trouble. Are there two factions in the Thirteenth House?"

Senneth looked tired. "Why not?" she said. "There are multiple factions everywhere else. It's impossible to keep straight where any of the alliances lie."

"Or one sincere group among the lesser lords, and someone like Halchon Gisseltess exploiting them with well-placed agents," Tayse said. "Since he is here, we have to assume he is exerting some influence."

Now Senneth looked a little sick. "I was not expecting him," she said. "I wish that I—with him—I can't—" She shook her head. "All my magic leaves me."

"You don't need magic," Tayse said, his voice a little rough. "You have my sword."

"Yes, well, leaving out the possibility of slaying him on Mayva's dance floor, what are we going to do about him?" Kirra asked.

She watched as Senneth and Tayse exchanged glances. "I don't think there's anything we *can* do," Senneth said. "We don't have the authority or the force of arms to return him to Gisseltess."

"I've sent a message to the king," Tayse said. "If he orders it, we can assemble the Riders and the guard sent to accompany Amalie, and escort the marlord back to his property."

"He brought fifty men with him," Justin spoke up. "We have twenty. The odds aren't good."

"The regent may lend us his troops," Tayse said.

"Then who protects Amalie?" Kirra asked.

"She stays in Nocklyn with us till the guards return," Senneth said. "How could Mayva protest? Surely we mystics can keep her safe inside these walls."

Donnal shifted his weight. "I could get to Ghosenhall in a day," he said. "The king could send more troops to escort Amalie home."

Amalie? Not "the princess"? Kirra thought. "I don't think the king will see Halchon as the priority," she said. "I think he'll want the Riders to stay with Amalie. But he may want her to come home."

"In the past we've all agreed that cutting short her journey would send the wrong signal," Senneth said. "Do we still agree on that point? Or is now the time to cut our losses?"

Cammon spoke up. "What's changed?" They all looked his way, Senneth and Kirra craning their heads to see him sitting behind them on the bed. He shrugged. "What's changed?

Halchon Gisseltess is here. Has he threatened her? No. Is she in danger from him? It seems like he's only flouting the king, not trying to assassinate the princess. Why is she in any more danger now than she was before?"

Kirra and Senneth exchanged glances. "As always, Cammon's right," Kirra said.

"It just *feels* more dangerous," Senneth grumbled.

Tayse said, "The next question is: Is Halchon Gisseltess continuing on to Rappengrass? Which is where we head next."

"He wouldn't have the nerve!" Kirra exclaimed. "Ariane Rappengrass would block him at the border."

Tayse shrugged. "So then, we do not need to change our plans for him. We stay for the ball tonight. In the morning we leave for Rappengrass and the marlord goes back to his House. Unless the king gives us orders to act as the marlord's escort, which we all doubt. He will want us beside Amalie no matter who else roams free."

"Valri will want us to go back to Ghosenhall," Cammon said. They all looked at him again. "She will! She's afraid."

Justin nudged him with his foot, still under the sheets and blankets. "She doesn't think four mystics and four Riders and twenty of the king's best soldiers can keep one princess safe?"

Cammon knit his eyebrows as he thought that over. "I don't think she's afraid for Amalie's physical safety," he said at last. "I think she's afraid of something else."

Now they all sent glances bouncing between each other. What in the silver hell did he mean by *that*? Tayse said gently, "Afraid of what?"

Cammon shook his head. "I don't know. I find Valri impossible to read." He sounded a little aggrieved. "Which is very strange. I can't pick up any of her emotions, any of her thoughts, except fear."

Now Senneth and Tayse were watching each other as if communicating without words. Senneth said, "Not so good, when the queen of the realm is afraid of—something."

Kirra sighed and pushed herself to her feet. She needed a real bath now, a sink-to-her-neck immersion in a tub of soapy water. "Well, I don't know what we can do about Valri," she said. "I don't know what we can do about Halchon. I don't know that we can do anything, except dress for a ball tonight and go dancing."

Tayse nodded and they all shuffled to their feet. The Rider said, "Everyone stay alert and everyone be careful. We don't need complications of any kind from here on out."

Kirra, already heading for the door, turned to look back at him. He was watching her. *He knows,* she thought.

DONNAL caught up with her as she was heading back to her own room. "Do you have to spend the entire day getting ready?" he asked, his voice wistful. "It doesn't seem like a naturally beautiful woman would need more than a few minutes."

She smiled at him, conscious of a complex surge of emotions. Delight, guilt, constraint, anger. Unexpected and unwelcome, all of them, since Donnal had always been her easiest companion. Why was it now suddenly so hard to settle back into the old familiar relationship? "Did you have a distraction in mind?" she asked.

He nodded, grinning. "Mayva Nocklyn's husband has organized a hunt to bring in game for the dinner table. Any of the lords who've brought their own hounds along are welcome to add them to the pack."

She felt illicit excitement skitter down her back, a smile of mischief light her face. "You mean to join the pack?"

He shrugged, an answering smile on his own dark face. "I thought it would be fun."

"They say Nocklyn is good hunting country. Better than Danalustrous."

"Nothing's better than Danalustrous."

"Let me just warn Melly that I'll be gone all day."

Half an hour later, they had joined the frenetic pack of dogs boiling in the courtyard of Nocklyn Towers, barely contained by the twenty or so noblemen on horseback. Kirra noticed that a few women were mounted as well—those who showed to advantage on horseback, or those who thought a little equestrian skill might make them appear more desirable to a marriage-minded lord. Mayva was not among them, though Lowell was leading the hunt.

Romar was not among the group, either, which Kirra thought was just as well. She would be mortified if he recognized her, depressed if he didn't. And there was Donnal. No, better that the regent indulged in other pursuits this afternoon.

They set off, a maelstrom of paws and hooves, Kirra and Donnal racing with the other hounds toward the wilder lands that crept up on the eastern edge of Nocklyn Towers. The day was warm, the air was rich with the spices of summer, and Kirra felt fine. She was in motion, Donnal beside her, and everyone else who knew her would be horrified by her behavior. This, for her, was almost the definition of a perfect day.

They were gone four hours, chasing down birds and rabbits, fetching the bloody carcasses back to the baggers and bounding off after newly spotted game. "That's a damn good bitch," she heard one of the baggers say to another. "She's brought in more than any of the others."

"That black mixed-breed—he's a fine one, too," his companion replied.

"Who do they belong to? They're not Nocklyn dogs."

"Don't know. Haven't seen anyone call them."

"Someone who doesn't deserve dogs this good," the first man groused. "I'd run them every day if they were mine."

The other bagger snorted. "You couldn't afford dogs like those."

Kirra thought that was definitely true.

They were back at the Towers by mid-afternoon. The exercise and the excitement had combined to leave Kirra completely worn out, but in a relaxed and agreeable way. Surreptitiously changing shapes in the stairwell, she returned to her room yawning but pleased with herself. All her muscles felt like they had been stretched and readjusted; her mind was swept clean, her heart was at ease. She didn't look as good as she felt, she realized, as she entered the room and saw Melly's scandalized expression.

"I don't think I even want to know what you've been doing," the maid said finally.

Kirra caught a glimpse of herself in the mirror and laughed unrepentantly. Her dark hair was a tangle of knots, her plain dress was rumpled and grass-stained, and there was a drop of blood on one corner of her mouth. She wiped the red away with a finger.

"You probably don't," she replied. "I want to sleep for a while. Then I want a bath. How much time do I have before dinner?"

"Three hours, more or less. I need two hours to dress you."

"Then let me sleep for an hour."

Kirra had settled on the bed and covered herself with a light sheet when she realized Melly was still watching her, trouble on her plain face. "What?"

Melly shook her head. "You've been behaving oddly the past day or so. I don't know what to make of you."

Kirra closed her eyes. "I've been so circumspect up till now," she said drowsily. "Anyone will tell you. This is the way I naturally am."

THREE hours later—rested, bathed, and styled—Kirra slipped out her door and crossed the hall to join the others in Amalie's room. "Aren't we an elegant group," she commented as she entered. As Casserah, of course, she was in deep red, her dark hair loose around her shoulders and twined with crimson ribbons. Amalie was all in gold; she actually sparkled in the candlelight. Valri wore her usual severe green, this time lightened with knots of gold embroidery worked into a pattern in the wide, smooth skirt. Senneth's brilliant blue turned her eyes cobalt and her fine hair almost a milky white.

"You're glowing," Senneth remarked. "You must have spent the day doing something you shouldn't have."

Kirra laughed. The day. Last night. Possibly tonight. Her blood was sparkling in her veins. "It would be so dull to always be good," she said demurely. "Are we all ready to go down to dinner?"

This meal was a little less dramatic than the one the night before. Halchon and Sabina Gisseltess were present again, but both Senneth and Kirra avoided them, so there was no need for tense conversations and forceful interventions by hulking Riders. Kirra had drawn as tablemates two of the lords who had joined the hunt that afternoon and were describing to their rather less enthusiastic dinner partners the various shots that had brought down particularly wily game. Kirra concentrated on eating the grouse that she may have actually fetched for a bagger and on not laughing out loud.

No one was inclined to linger at the meal. Everyone was eager to move on to the ballroom, and soon enough the entire company had disbanded and reassembled in the great, domed room. Mayva had tastefully decorated with the Nocklyn standard so

that in the four corners stood huge ochre-colored vases filled
with tall stands of wheat; curtains of the same two colors swathed
all the windows. But she had added a pretty touch. Strands of
shimmering artificial gems featuring all the colors of the
Twelve Houses wound around window frames and pillars, then
looped along the crown molding. Kirra paused a moment to
count the jewels and found a disturbing addition. Along with
the Fortunalt pearls, the Helven emeralds and the Brassenthwaite sapphires, Mayva had strung moonstones to honor the
Pale Mother. The Twelve Houses were represented, but so was
Lumanen Convent.

It was getting harder and harder to convince herself that
Nocklyn Towers might be loyal to the king should it ever come
down to war.

"Serra Casserah," came a voice behind her, and Kirra felt
herself turn to glitter and pulse. Romar Brendyn. "It is so early
in the evening. Surely you have not given away all your dances
already?"

She turned to smile at him, trying to hold on to some of
Casserah's coolness. The orchestra was still warming up, dis-
cordant but full of promise. "Why, no, my lord. I have just been
standing here bemoaning my lack of partners," she replied.
"Do you have time to spare a dance or two for me?"

He bowed very deeply. "Merrenstow always has time for
Danalustrous," he replied.

She gave him her hand. "Then by all means let us express
our politics with the polonaise."

They laughed through the whole dance, though they said
very little and their conversation was essentially meaningless.
But they were so happy. They could not look at each other
without grinning like fools, so they would turn their eyes away
and make some inane comment on someone else's dress or
partner. Kirra thought that anyone watching them must think
they were the Pale Mother's own idiots, struck dumb by divinity or mischance and allowed to attend aristocratic balls out of
someone's misguided pity.

Just before the music ended, Romar's hand tightened on
Kirra's, and his smiling face looked suddenly eager. "Can I see
you tonight?" he asked. "Somewhere—anywhere?"

She felt herself flush from her toes to her hairline, but it
was the heat of excitement, not embarrassment. "Maybe—I'm

not sure how," she murmured. "Every door in my hallway opens to the room of someone I know."

"Mine, too," he replied. "Rafe and Clera Storian on one side of me, Seth Stowfer on the other. But I am not opposed to moonlight and grass stains if you are not."

She laughed and instantly had to fight to put a vivid memory out of her mind. "Leave your window open tonight," she said. "I will come to you in another guise."

Again his grip tightened; his eyes were momentarily intense. "As long as you take your true shape for a little while."

"I would not deny myself that privilege," she said softly.

The music ended. They exchanged elaborate bows and curtseys. "I don't think I have any more dances to spare for you tonight, my lord," Kirra said in a shaky voice. "I find you a curiously unsettling partner."

"Then we will not dance," he said. "We will look for other ways to communicate."

She could only be glad Seth Stowfer appeared at that moment to ask for the favor of a dance. She absolutely had no reply.

The evening progressed in a tolerably enjoyable fashion. More than one of her partners commented on Casserah's unnaturally buoyant mood, but Kirra found it hard to repress her high spirits. She felt giddy, actually, silly as a girl, and all at the thought of what might come after the ball. How could Senneth contrive to look so staid? How could she contain a love that was anywhere near this monumental? Perhaps she had just settled in to her happiness, that was all. Perhaps, during that leisurely return to Brassenthwaite, Tayse by her side, she had been just as joyous, just as dizzy, as Kirra felt now. Kirra would have to ask her.

Although. Better not. The fewer people who knew about this affair, the better. Senneth's discretion could be trusted unconditionally, but talking became a habit. Next Kirra would be discussing her love life with Cammon, with Justin, with Donnal.

No. Never that.

Some of her exhilaration left her, and she was more subdued as she whirled around the room with Darryn Rappengrass. Yes, she told him, she and all her friends would be at his mother's party next week. No, she did not believe she had ever attended such an event in Rappengrass. Yes, she was quite looking forward to it. No, she had not heard from Kirra lately.

"Well, I have sent her an invitation, express to Danalustrous," he said, smiling. "Perhaps she will change her mind and come join us."

"You never know," Kirra replied.

Once that dance had ended, she searched the ballroom till she found Senneth, doing her best to disappear. In fact, Kirra had to locate Valri first and then stare at the surrounding stonework until she was able to pick Senneth out from the walls.

"How does Amalie ever find you?" she demanded when she finally tracked down her quarry. "Wouldn't that be a terrible thing, if Amalie was looking for you and you'd melted away?"

Senneth laughed. "Amalie never seems to lose sight of me. I think she just remembers where she left me and always comes back to that spot."

"Maybe she's like Cammon, and she's impervious to magic."

Senneth snorted. "No one's like Cammon."

Amalie herself waltzed up a few minutes later, golden and glowing. Toland Storian, still trying to make up to her for past transgressions, was the partner depositing her back beside her chaperones. He bowed very low, kissed her hand, and turned with some reluctance back to the throng.

"Has our Amalie made a conquest?" Kirra marveled. "And of such a sulky boy?"

"He seems very devoted," Senneth said.

"I can't stand him," Amalie said. "But I try not to show that. He'll be marlord some day."

"More and worse marlords in the other eleven Houses," Kirra said cheerfully. "You probably won't be able to stand any of them."

They talked in much the same vein for the next few minutes. Kirra had her back to the dance floor, so she couldn't see if anyone approached them, but suddenly Senneth's face went cold and her whole body stiffened. Kirra spun around to find Halchon Gisseltess right behind her, bowing low to the floor.

"Serras," he said in his beautiful voice. "Majesties."

Valri quickly moved up a step to stand on one side of Amalie; Senneth was on the other. Kirra positioned herself be-

tween Senneth and the marlord. "Ah, you decided to stay another day," she drawled in Casserah's bored voice. "I thought
you might have gone home by now."

"Home, when I feel so welcome here?" he asked.

"What do you want?" Senneth asked flatly.

He bowed again in Amalie's direction. "What every man
wants this night," he said. "A dance with the beautiful princess."

"No," Valri, Senneth, and Kirra said in unison.

"I'll be happy to take a turn with you," Amalie said.

They all stared at her. "Amalie, he cannot be trusted to even
touch your palm," Senneth said in a low voice. "He is not one of
the marlords you need to flatter and placate. He is dangerous."

"I'm not afraid," Amalie said, and held out her hand.

Halchon closed his fingers over hers and led her onto the
floor. The three of them were left gaping as Halchon and
Amalie dipped gracefully into the cotillion. The marlord appeared to hold her in an avuncular grip, though his smile was
a little sinister. Amalie seemed perfectly relaxed and her own
smile was unforced and genuine.

"The day I get that girl safely back to Ghosenhall is the day
I allow myself to lie down and die," Valri said.

The day you *get her back safely?* Kirra wanted to ask, but
she had to admit to general sympathy with the sentiment. Senneth asked, "Is this why the king has kept her locked up so
long? Because she is so fearless as to seem almost foolhardy?"

Valri shook her head. "She's not foolhardy. She is—I don't
know what she is. She's dancing with Halchon Gisseltess."

"I say you set him on fire," Kirra suggested. "Just on general
principle."

"I don't think he'll succumb to my flames," Senneth said
regretfully. "Or I would."

"I need a drink," Valri said. "Anyone else want some wine?"

Even Casserah bent her usual rules under these circumstances and accepted a glass of rich red liquid. Valri was on
her second goblet by the time the music ended and Halchon returned his charge.

"I enjoyed that immensely," he told Amalie, bowing once
more. "Perhaps we can dance again at some other event."

"I doubt it," Amalie said in a sunny voice. "I don't like you.
Oh, Valri, could I have some of your wine?" As she spoke to
the queen, she turned her shoulder on Halchon, ignoring him

as effectively as if he had learned Senneth's spells of invisibility. After a moment of stunned silence, he stalked away.

Kirra and Senneth were left staring at each other, Kirra summoning all her strength to keep from giggling. "It just gets more entertaining by the moment," she managed to say.

"I think I need a second glass of wine myself," Senneth said.

But Kirra didn't think Casserah would fall so far, so she made her excuses and wandered away. Another dance with Darryn, a light and shallow conversation with Mayva, and the evening slowly progressed toward midnight.

She had taken an empty seat in a shadowy alcove between two back pillars when another woman joined her in a puff of silken skirts. "Oh, my feet are already sore," the woman exclaimed. "And you know the dancing will go on another two hours at least. I just have to sit awhile and rest my toes."

Kirra was trying not to stare, but she could not think of any reason Sabina Gisseltess would have for seeking out Casserah Danalustrous.

CHAPTER
29

It took her a moment, but Kirra finally found her voice. "Yes, I find that both the dancing and the conversation get wearisome after the first hour has passed," she said.

A look of distress came to Sabina's face. Her cheeks paled and her tremulous lips turned down. "I'm sorry—did you want to sit by yourself for a while? I'll go somewhere else."

"No. Of course not. Your conversation has to be more entertaining than Toland Storian's."

Sabina looked uncertain. "I suppose it depends on what you would wish to talk about. Many people think I have very little to say."

Kirra laughed. "You have teenage sons, do you not? Most parents are happy to talk about their children."

"Yes, but not so many people are interested in *hearing* those stories," Sabina retorted.

"Well, you can pick the topic, if you like," Kirra replied, actually amused. "Land improvements. Ballgowns. Trade routes. Taxes. What courses you preferred at dinner. I will strive to appear fascinated by anything you say."

"I wanted to ask you a favor," Sabina blurted out.

Kirra kept her face impassive. "Certainly, if it is in my power."

"I want a chance to talk to your friend Senneth."

It was harder to appear nonchalant at that. "I can take her a message."

Sabina shook her head. She looked both purposeful and desperate, a bad combination. "Now. Tonight. I need to talk to her. I need to tell her—it's important."

Kirra glanced out at the dance floor. Halchon was partnered with Mayva, and both of them looked bored. "I assume your husband mustn't know you're speaking with her."

Sabina's face registered fleeting terror. "No. He—no."

Kirra nodded. "All right. Let me think." The ballroom was connected to the dining room by a short hallway lined with four other doors. Kirra knew, because she was curious and had investigated, that one of them was a small pantry where the servants stored extra linens and wineglasses should these items be instantly needed on the dance floor. "There's a little room right off the ballroom where you can talk in private. I'll make sure Senneth is there—in an hour. That will be enough time from now so that even if your husband is witnessing our conversation he won't think your actions have anything to do with what we've discussed."

"Where is this room? How do I find it?"

Kirra grinned. "I shall send someone to your side to guide you there. A handsome young man in Danalustrous colors. No one will be surprised if you slip away with him for a little flirtation."

Sabina laughed softly but somewhat wildly. "*Everyone* would be surprised. It would not be the sort of thing I do."

Kirra turned to give the woman a good hard look of appraisal. None of this seemed like the sort of thing Sabina would do. She looked like the tiniest, most helpless thing, and Kirra couldn't imagine that she wasn't completely dominated by her husband. Was this a trap of some sort? Had Halchon sent her to lure Senneth from Amalie's side? With that possibility in her head, would Senneth even agree to the meeting?

Sabina met her eyes. "What? You don't trust me."

"I am always open to the possibility of betrayal."

Sabina nodded. "Yes. I can see that—yes. What can I do? What can I say to make you believe that I come to you on my own, without my husband's knowledge?"

Kirra wished Cammon were here so that he could tell her if

the marlady lied or told the truth. But adding even one more player to the mix seemed dicey in the extreme. If Sabina really were bent on deceiving her husband, the last thing she needed was a parade of mystics calling attention to her behavior.

"Whether you are lying or telling the truth, I think Senneth will want to hear you out," she said slowly. "I will take the measures I deem necessary to keep everyone safe. Remember. One hour. A young man in Danalustrous colors will come for you."

"I'll be ready," Sabina said.

Seth Stowfer appeared just then, bowing to the marlady and asking for a dance. Belying any evidence of sore feet, Sabina jumped up and allowed him to lead her away. She didn't even glance back at Kirra.

Kirra started making the rounds.

First to the great door that led to the main hall, where Tayse was stationed just outside. "Something odd just happened," she said. "I think we might want the rest of the Riders here."

She told her story, and he nodded. Motioning to one of the servants, he sent the man to collect reinforcements.

"Try not to look conspicuous," she said. "We don't want Halchon to wonder if something's going on. But while Senneth is not standing there overseeing Amalie, I think the Riders had better be."

"I'll watch from the door," he said. "And the others will stay out of sight. But I think you're right."

Next back to the ballroom to find Romar and tell *him* the tale. "While Senneth is gone, I think you should be dancing with your niece," she said. "You should be able to defend her from any assault for as long as it takes the Riders to cross the dance floor."

"You have a poor opinion of my fighting skills," he commented. "I could defend her for longer than that."

"It might not be necessary," she said. "But—I can't tell. I don't want to take stupid risks."

He arched his eyebrows, and she felt her whole face kindle in a blush. "Stupid risks with *Amalie's* life," she amended.

"Ah. As long as there isn't a moratorium on risks in general."

She shook her head. "You deserve to live and die alone."

"Maybe," he said. "But not tonight."

Once everyone else was in place, she sidled through the

crowd to Senneth's side. Valri was actually sitting down, no doubt dizzied by her intake of alcohol, but her eyes were fixed unwaveringly on a spot on the dance floor. Kirra didn't even have to look to know the queen was watching Amalie. Senneth, only slightly more relaxed, was spreading her attention more generally through the entire crowd.

"I've made an assignation for you," Kirra told her in a teasing voice.

Senneth gave her an inquiring look. "Is he young, handsome, and noble? More suited to my station in life than a King's Rider?"

"Yes, I was mortified to hear you gossiped about last night at the dinner table, so I have stepped in to matchmake for you," Kirra replied. "I know your brothers will appreciate it."

"Thus are the bonds between Brassenthwaite and Danalustrous strengthened even more."

"Though I can't imagine you'll find yourself romantically drawn to this particular individual," Kirra said.

"Do you suppose you might give me a name? Or shall I go to this meeting wholly unprepared? Where and when am I having this tryst, by the way?"

"Tonight. About half an hour from now. In the little storage pantry off the hall to the dining room."

Senneth nodded. Like Kirra, she was inclined to familiarize herself with her surroundings and had obviously noticed this room already. "And the name?"

Kirra leaned so close she barely had to breathe the syllables. "Sabina Gisseltess."

Senneth's eyes widened, but she showed no other change of expression. Kirra almost thought she wasn't surprised, which was highly irritating. "Ah," was all she said.

"I've alerted Tayse and he's assembling the Riders. I've told Romar to guard the princess while you're gone. Even if it's a trick, I think Amalie will be safe."

"I don't think it's a trick," Senneth said.

"What do you know?" Kirra demanded.

Senneth shook her head. "Nothing. I'd never met her till last night. But she just struck me as—" She shook her head again.

"Someone afraid for her life."

Senneth nodded. "Yes. And wouldn't you be if you were her?"

"Yes," Kirra said. "But I don't know that I'd run for help to the woman my husband would murder me to marry."

Senneth gave her a wide, brilliant smile. "Who else could possibly help her?"

Kirra drifted away from Senneth, drifted through the ballroom, drifted out the door to the servants' hall. As always in every great house, this hall was shadowy and cool, with faint sounds of laughter and bustling coming from the direction of the kitchen. It might not be safe to change here, so close to other people; at any point, a footman could round the corner and stumble across her. So Kirra did it in stages, first shortening her hair, then roughening her features, then turning her red ballgown into red breeches topped by a red waistcoat. Eventually she was a more soberly dressed man—keeping only the red waistcoat—with short dark curls and an earnest expression. The ruby on her hand as well as the color across her chest proclaimed her a man of Danalustrous.

Now she strode confidently into the ballroom and glanced around. Senneth was gone. Amalie was dancing with her uncle. Kirra could see Tayse's dark shape hovering just outside the great doorway. Halchon Gisseltess was deep in conversation with Rafe Storian and Seth Stowfer. Sabina stood chatting with a few insipid-looking women in Nocklyn colors. No doubt wives and daughters of some of the more favored Nocklyn vassals.

Kirra crossed the dance floor, trying to look casual about her direction, pausing now and then to smile at a pretty girl or exchange greetings with a young man about her own age. Sabina seemed completely unaware of her approach and turned with a start when Kirra touched her on the arm.

"Marlady," she said, bowing with all the flourish of a good-looking young lord. "I see you are not dancing."

The vassals' wives and daughters turned away, sighing with envy. The young Danalustrous lordling was very handsome indeed.

"No, I—but I would be happy to take a turn with you," Sabina said rather breathlessly.

Kirra took the marlady's hand and led her into a sedate quadrille. She would have to concentrate; it was easy to forget she was dancing the man's part. Sabina showed no inclination to make conversation, so Kirra asked, "Have you been enjoying yourself?"

"Oh—yes—it's been—yes, I have," Sabina replied. At this rate, Kirra couldn't imagine her conversation with Senneth was going to turn up any interesting news at all. "And you?"

Kirra could not help a wicked smile. "Very much so."

"Are you from Danalustrous?" Sabina gathered her courage to ask.

Kirra nodded. "Serra Casserah told me I should come ask you to be my partner."

Sabina grew calmer at that. So she had not been sure this young man was the promised courtier. "I have not noticed you before," she remarked. "Have you been here this whole time?"

Impossible not to laugh when asked such questions! "Indeed, I have. But I have not mingled much till tonight."

"Will you be going on to Rappengrass?" Sabina asked somewhat wistfully. "My husband and I will be returning home."

"The serramarra is going on to Rappengrass, I suppose, and she will not travel without me," Kirra said. "So, yes, I will be heading there next."

They made similar halting conversation for the duration of the dance—and it seemed very long—while Kirra slowly edged them closer to the necessary doorway. She turned them so Sabina's back was to the dance floor while Kirra could scan the room. Halchon was still engrossed in his conversation and no one else appeared to be paying them much attention. Kirra tightened her grip on Sabina's hand and pulled her from the room.

Into the hallway, a few steps down, three knocks on the closed door. Senneth opened it instantly, gave Kirra one quick look of amusement, and nodded gravely to Sabina.

"My lady," Senneth said. "I am eager to hear what you have to say. We must talk quickly, though, for I don't know who might come to use this room."

"I'll guard the door and turn away curious servants," Kirra said.

Sabina looked doubtful. Senneth said, "He can look quite ferocious. Come inside."

The door closed between them, but this was one conversation Kirra was determined to overhear. Keeping a watchful gaze on the hallway, she pressed her ear to the wood and listened.

Sabina didn't waste any time. "You know my husband is planning a war," she said, sounding as if it was taking all her resolve to keep her voice from quavering.

"We all have had some suspicions of that," Senneth replied. "Do you have proof?"

"I have names of lords who have agreed to band together with him in an uprising. And how much they have agreed to commit to the cause."

Senneth sounded surprised. "Written down?"

"No. I have played hostess to a succession of visitors for the past year and a half. When I could, I listened to conversations. Now and then, my husband has let some information slip. And his mood was always easy to read. When someone agreed to join with him, he was remarkably pleasant. When they did not—" A small silence. "I am fairly certain of the list."

"Can you tell me?"

"Rayson Fortunalt and Gregory Tilton. Rafe Storian is toying with the idea, but he has not yet committed."

"What about Nocklyn? Siding with your husband, I am guessing."

"No—that is, I am not certain. I think Lowell is afraid to do anything too drastic while Els is still alive. At any rate, I know Halchon is not sure of Nocklyn."

"That's interesting," Senneth commented. "I would have put Nocklyn down as a traitor even before Rayson Fortunalt. Who else?"

"Heffel Coravann turned him down, but several of his vassals came by stealth to make deals of their own. The same is true of Eloise Kianlever and her lords—she said no, but some of her vassals said yes. There could be bloody uprisings within the Houses that would instantly alter where the king might look for allies. Baryn will not be able to quell those mutinies because he will be faced with an assault on his own territory."

"Do you know when this is slated to occur?"

"No. I believe Rayson and some of the others are raising funds and do not want to move until they have enough money to pay troops. Rayson at least is engaged in some shipping venture and he absolutely refuses to join any rebellion until his cargo is safely home."

"So we have some time. Weeks, maybe. Months?"

"Months, I would say. Not much longer."

"Where do they plan to attack first?"

"I'm not sure. But my husband keeps talking about the day he is installed in Ghosenhall. He might envision one great battle in the royal city, with all the other Houses tamely throwing down their arms once he is on the throne."

"I cannot see Merrenstow or Brassenthwaite reacting so mildly."

"You must warn the king," Sabina said.

"I will. He is aware that—but we have not had such specific information before. It is terrible news you bear, my lady, but I am glad you have brought it to me."

"I'm so afraid," Sabina whispered.

There was the sound of rustling cloth; Kirra imagined Senneth had put her arm around a weeping marlady. "If your husband suspects you have told me these things, I fear you will be in very grave danger," Senneth said.

"I am in danger already. My husband wants me dead."

That was true, and Kirra and Senneth both knew it, but it was even more shocking to realize that Sabina knew it as well. "Then leave him," Senneth said.

"How can I? No matter where I might go, he would track me down. If I tried to leave him, he would kill me for certain."

Kirra could only imagine the expression on Senneth's face, the expression she wore whenever something helpless fell under her protection. "Come with me. My friends and I will keep you safe."

That elicited a small, hopeless laugh from Sabina. "Oh, I don't think even you would be able to protect me, serra. He is impervious to your fire, is he not? And he would be happy for an excuse to hurt you. I do not want to provide that excuse."

"Then go somewhere else. To Rappengrass. Ride out with Darryn in the morning."

"And bring my husband's wrath to Ariane? I could not. I could not bring such destruction to the House of a friend."

"I hate to think of you going back with him, frightened and wholly alone."

"You have just described the entire sixteen years of my married existence."

"Are you worried about your sons? I will undertake to bring them to safety as well."

"My sons! Oh, they adore their father. They have had no interest in me since they were old enough to hold a toy sword. I wish I could tell you that I stayed on their account, but—no. It is fear that holds me in Gisseltess. No one there loves me enough to make me want to stay."

There was another short silence and then Senneth said abruptly, "Take off your pendant."

"What? My pendant? Why?"

"Give it to me."

More rustling and the sound of Sabina's bemused voice. "All right, but—I don't know what you could—here."

Kirra had to think to remember what sort of jewel the women of Gisseltess usually wore to cover their housemarks. The emblem of Gisseltess, of course, was a black hawk holding a small red flower. Kirra believed that the traditional stone was onyx, often set with a small garnet. Though Sabina could have been wearing something more colorful, just for the sake of fashion.

"What are you doing?" Sabina asked fearfully.

"I am—you know I have some mystical ability," Senneth replied. "Sometimes I can bestow some of that power onto an inanimate object—store it there, so to speak. I am putting some of my magic into your pendant. When you need strength, when you need courage, take hold of this stone. You will feel some of my power seep into you. It will help you through."

This was the second time Kirra had witnessed Senneth taking a common object and infusing it with magic—or pretending to. She had never tried such a thing herself, and she found it hard to believe it actually worked. Then again, this was Senneth, and she had abilities no other mystic had ever displayed. And even if she did nothing but create a faint fiery glow around her chosen object and solemnly promise the owner that it was now imbued with magical power, and the owner believed her and thus was heartened—well, where was the harm in that?

But Kirra rather thought there was a transfer of magic.

"I must go back to the ballroom now," Sabina said nervously. Her voice was a little muffled, as if she had tilted her head down to refasten her pendant. "If my husband has missed me—"

"He will see you returning to the dance floor on the arm of a handsome Danalustrous man," Senneth replied. "Will that be so bad?"

A despairing laugh from Sabina. "Almost as bad as the truth!"

"Then go now. And think about leaving Gisseltess. I believe I could find you sanctuary somewhere."

"You are very kind," Sabina whispered. "I knew you must be, for my husband to hate you so much."

Senneth laughed. Kirra heard her footsteps cross the small space and hurriedly straightened up. The door opened and Senneth peered out. She gave Kirra one brief, expressive look and then glanced up and down the hall. "Any visitors?"

"Not even a servant has crept by."

"Good." She motioned Sabina out, and Kirra took the marlady's arm. "You two go back to the ballroom. I will go out through the dining room and circle around to another entrance."

"If Halchon has noticed that we were both gone—" Sabina began. The hand she had laid on Kirra's arm was trembling.

Kirra had to fight to keep from dissolving into laughter. "I know," she said to Senneth. "Come in by the main entrance. Make sure someone glimpses you in a passionate embrace with Tayse. Not even Halchon will suspect that you were off hearing confidences from his wife if you're seen pursuing illicit romance instead."

Senneth frowned at her. "I cannot think why serra Casserah wanted to bring you in her train," she said. "You have a debauched mind."

"Serra Casserah would make the same suggestion if she was standing here," Kirra replied. "It is a good one and you know it."

Sabina—who clearly should have more pressing matters on her mind—looked shocked. "Serra Senneth! No! Not even for my sake should you consider consorting with someone unsuitable!"

Kirra laughed. "The very thing you should not have said if you didn't want her to do it."

Senneth gave her another repressive look. "You two go back to the ballroom. I'll give some thought to what I should do next."

Sabina gripped the mystic's hand. "Thank you."

Senneth smiled. "You're the one who risked herself to bring me news. Why are *you* thanking *me*?"

"For—just for existing, I think," Sabina said. "For being someone I feel I can trust."

Senneth nodded. "And you can. Always. Now go."

Still Sabina hesitated. "Tell your brother—your *brothers*—that I asked about them. And tell them I am well."

"I will certainly do that," Senneth said gently. She would not look at Kirra. "Now you must return."

Kirra stepped down the hallway and Sabina perforce followed, her hand still upon the young man's arm. In a few moments, they were through the doorway, through the crowd clustered along the walls, and back on the dance floor. Kirra didn't think they'd been gone more than fifteen minutes. No one seemed to have missed them. Romar was standing on the perimeter of the dance floor, smiling down at his niece and wholly ignoring the hovering Valri. Halchon was still engaged in what now appeared to be an argument with a group that had swelled by three men. Opinions seemed to be passionate, but no one appeared to be angry. If he had been looking for his wife, he gave no sign.

"I believe you are safely through this exercise, my lady," Kirra said, smiling down at Sabina's small, worried face. "Would you like a glass of wine? Shall I find you another partner? Or would you like to sit awhile and recover from your adventures?"

Sabina managed a shaky laugh. "I think I would like to sit quietly by myself," she said. "*With* a glass of wine."

Kirra guided her to an arrangement of stiff-backed chairs striped in the Nocklyn colors. "I'll be back in a moment," she promised.

In a few minutes, she had secured a drink for Sabina, bowed one last time, and crossed the dance floor with the aimless circumlocution of a man who wasn't quite sure what to do with himself next. She finally made it to the servants' hallway, but had to pass a few moments pretending there was a problem with her shoe as a small parade of footmen traipsed between the kitchen and the dance floor. Finally—a period of solitude—and she changed herself back to Casserah by increments. If anyone had noticed her disappearance down this hallway half an hour ago, and now saw her reemerging, they would think she had been stealing sweets from the cooks or creeping out to the gardens by the kitchen door. She reentered the ballroom, smiled at a young lord, and dipped back onto the dance floor as if nothing had transpired at all.

CHAPTER
30

It hardly seemed fair to expect the evening to hold any more drama. The clock had just struck two, and a few guests had already begun to trickle out, when a crash at the main entrance caught everyone's attention. Kirra whirled around to first look for Senneth, and found her across the wide room with a hand on Amalie's shoulder. Next she tried to determine the source of the commotion. She expected to see Tayse and Justin engaged in some kind of confrontation at the main entrance, but it wasn't Riders who poured into the ballroom in a dark phalanx. It was a regiment of royal soldiers in black and gold, at least fifty of them, all sober, heavily armed, and primed to fight. At the head of the troop was Romar Brendyn.

He strode heedlessly through the couples on the dance floor, who cried out and tumbled back from him, and a wedge of soldiers followed. More soldiers streamed in and split to either side of the doorway till there was a line of them completely enclosing the room. They made a heavy dark circle of containment around the gaudy colors of ball dresses and fashionable waistcoats.

Romar came to a halt in front of Halchon and Sabina Gisseltess. "Marlord," Romar said in a ringing voice. "Your escort has arrived to take you back to Gissel Plain."

Kirra put a hand to her mouth to push back her delighted

laugh. Across the room, she saw Senneth manage to maintain her stony expression, but Valri looked maliciously pleased. Halchon's body clenched in fury, but he kept his face smooth and his voice relaxed.

"I am not yet ready to return to my home."

"Servants are even now packing your bags. Your carriage is at the door. I cannot imagine what holds you here."

"I come and go as I please," Halchon snarled, losing some of his restraint. "If you think your impudence has carried the day—"

"I think a hundred of the king's men carry the day," Romar replied, his voice contemptuous. "You are in violation of his majesty's direct orders to confine yourself to your property. You will be returned to that property. Now. You will not set foot off of your own land again until the king has lifted his interdiction."

"I. Am. Not. Ready. To leave," Halchon spat out. He lifted a hand as if to signal men of his own. Romar caught him around the wrist and twisted his arm sharply.

"Do you really want bloodshed? Now? Tonight? Do you really have the manpower on hand to win a skirmish like this?" Romar demanded, scorn still dripping from his voice. He flung Halchon's hand away. "Do you want to see swords rip through ballgowns? Do you want to humiliate your Nocklyn friends? Then call for your men. But most of them are already under guard and could not respond to you if they would. You are well and truly taken, marlord. Accept it with grace or accept it with violence. But you are going back to Gisseltess."

A smoldering moment while the two men stared each other down, then Halchon jerked himself to one side. "Sabina," he said to his wife in a tightly controlled voice, "you might want to fetch a cloak. We're returning home tonight."

"Someone else will fetch her anything she needs," Romar said. "I myself will take both of you directly to your coach."

Halchon's eyes brightened with hatred but he did not lose composure again. He merely gave Romar one swift nod, then took Sabina's arm in a hard and painful grip. "My dear," he grated out. "We must be going."

Sabina herself looked as small and frightened as a child dreading a terrible punishment. Her face was so pale her lips looked bloodless, and even across the width of the ballroom, she appeared to be shaking. Kirra could imagine how cold her small hand was, locked inside Halchon's. The marlady did not say a word, merely hurried alongside Halchon as he stalked out of the ballroom behind Romar, taking two steps for every one long stride of her husband's. Soldiers folded around them until even Sabina's blond hair was lost in their insistent darkness.

Everyone in the room stayed exactly where they had been standing when the soldiers swept in, and they stared toward the door until all the soldiers were gone. And still they stood there, and still they stared, and still no one said a word. They could hear, rumbling down the hallway from the main door, the muffled sounds of organization and departure—the shouts of men, the creak of leather, the strike of hooves against the ground. It seemed to take very little time for Halchon and Sabina Gisseltess to be on the road, though it took forever for the sound of the soldiers' horses to finally die away.

Not until then did anyone on the dance floor move. Not until then, it seemed, did anyone breathe. Then suddenly there was a collective sigh of breath and a shocked, excited babble of voices. Kirra looked again for the faces she knew. Senneth and Valri had closed ranks around Amalie, and now Senneth was leading their small group toward the door, through the knots of people gathered together in intense conversation. Mayva had collapsed onto one of the striped chairs and was sobbing into a handkerchief while five well-dressed women hovered around her, offering what sympathy they could scrape up over their shock and glee. Lowell was nowhere to be found. Romar had not returned to the dance floor. If there were still Riders at the main entrance, they were not visible from Kirra's vantage point, though she imagined they had followed Senneth up the stairs to Amalie's room.

Start to finish, this was a night Kirra could not imagine living through twice.

There wasn't much Kirra could do for Mayva; other hands would urge her to bed and try to calm her down. So she slipped out the door, up the stairs, and into Amalie's room, where her friends had already gathered. Tayse and Justin were leaning against the walls, Cammon and Donnal were sitting on the floor, and Senneth, Valri, and Amalie had disposed themselves in the formal chairs.

"What happened?" Kirra demanded, sinking down onto

Amalie's bed. "How did—I thought we didn't have time to call soldiers in from Ghosenhall!"

"These were from Gisseltess," Tayse said. "The regent sent for them as soon as we discovered Halchon was here—last night. The soldiers were already on their way. They had left as soon as they realized he was missing. Romar Brendyn's messenger found them on the road, a half day out from Nocklyn."

"Did they explain how he had evaded them to begin with?" Valri asked coldly. "The king will want an accounting of that."

Tayse gave her an unreadable look. "I'm sure some trickery was involved. Halchon Gisseltess is a man who does not mind using subterfuge. And I doubt the soldiers had been given orders to kill, which would restrict their ability to hamper him. I'm guessing their assignment there was largely ceremonial. I expect that will change."

"Wasn't Romar wonderful?" Amalie exclaimed. "So fierce and unafraid. I was never so proud of him."

Kirra agreed silently; Senneth did so aloud. "Indeed, yes, he played his part perfectly," Senneth said. "The king's champion. That one act will go a long way toward convincing the marlords he will be an excellent regent."

"If we need a regent," Valri said swiftly.

"Yes," Senneth acknowledged. "If we need one."

"What now?" Kirra asked. "Are the Gisseltess men really under guard? Do they go back to Gissel Plain or on to Ghosenhall for punishment?"

"Under guard and on to Ghosenhall," Tayse said. "Some of the king's men, and some of the Merrenstow guard, will accompany them."

"And we go on to Rappengrass?" Justin asked.

"Of course," Amalie said.

Donnal spoke up. "Is the princess safer or more in danger now that Halchon Gisseltess is under guard again?"

Tayse's eyes were on Amalie. "I think we must always assume she is in some kind of danger, and prepare ourselves accordingly."

"I don't think she's the only one," Cammon said. All eyes turned in his direction, and everyone wore a questioning look. "The only one in danger," Cammon clarified. "I think Romar should be guarded, too."

Justin laughed. "He seems well able to handle himself."

Cammon shook his head. "He takes risks. And he's a target. And there is—there's a sort of hatred directed toward him. I can feel it all the time, all around him. Senneth might be right—what he did tonight might make people believe he will be a very strong regent. But that will just put him in more danger. I think there are plenty of people who don't want to see a strong regent behind the throne. And he doesn't strike me as the kind of man who is willing to guard his back."

Valri threw her hands in the air. "So we must spend our energy protecting *him* as well? We hardly have the resources to keep Amalie safe! If she won't go back to Ghosenhall, then send *Romar* back. We can't afford any distractions!"

The rest of them laughed at that, though Kirra could tell Valri was not entirely jesting. Truth to tell, Kirra was in sympathy with the young queen, and she believed Cammon was right. There had been ample evidence that *someone* would be happy to see the regent dead, and equal proof that Romar disdained to take extraordinary precautions. A bad combination. She could already feel herself starting to worry.

"The regent seems like a reasonable man," Senneth said. "I think if we explain to him our concerns, he will be willing to show some circumspection. And perhaps we just include him in our watchful circle. Donnal, you and Cammon are always aware of dangers that threaten the rest of us—expand your awareness to include the regent as well. Tayse, Justin, you and the Riders keep tabs on him. Amalie—"

"I will tell him to be careful," the princess said sunnily. "He will do it for me. He knows how much I value him."

I will ask him, too, Kirra thought. *For I do not think he would want to make me live without him.*

THEY did not talk much longer. The hour was so late by this time that they had no hope of getting on the road tomorrow before noon if they were to get any amount of sleep before they left. One contingent stayed behind in Amalie's room. The rest of them stepped into the hall and exchanged a few more words before seeking their own places.

"You will sleep at the princess's window again tonight?" Kirra asked Donnal. She watched idly as Tayse gave instructions to Hammond, the Rider now stationed outside Amalie's door. Justin and Cammon disappeared into their own room, both of them yawning.

Donnal nodded. "Tonight and every night. I think she likes to know I'm there."

Kirra smiled and put a hand to his cheek. "Such knowledge cannot help but make her sleep more soundly," she said. "I always dreamed more easily knowing you were nearby."

He smiled back at her, but his dark eyes were sad. "I am still near you, serra," he replied. "Never doubt that. Not even for a princess, not even for a queen, would I abandon you."

For a moment she thought she might cry. "You must be so tired," was all she could bring herself to say. "You can sleep tomorrow in the coach."

"We both can," he said. And without another word, he changed himself into an owl and went skimming through the narrow corridors. Kirra did not watch long enough to see what aperture he found that let him out into the night air and back to the sill at Amalie's window.

She stopped in her own room just long enough to change out of her ballgown and freshen her face. Melly stirred but did not wake up, and Kirra left her a note:

I have business to take care of. I will be gone much of the night. Do not worry if I am not here in the morning.

Ridiculous that she should have to reassure a maid. She was not used to being answerable to anyone. She was not used to being so closely watched.

She was not used to assignations in the dead of night, either, but she thought she might find herself getting accustomed to the stealth and the lying.

Still in human form, she glided from her room, nodded at Hammond, and tiptoed down the stairs. The ballroom was almost entirely empty by now, though Kirra caught sight of a few revelers still clustered together in the middle of the floor as maids cleaned around them. She crept down the servants' hallway and outside, pausing a moment to enjoy the fresh night air against her skin. Then she made her way farther out, past the kitchen gardens to the decorative flower gardens some distance from the house. It was too dark to admire roses and hollyhocks, but she sat on a stone bench and watched the upper-level windows of the house. She was guessing Romar was still out settling Halchon's men or conferring with Colton, and indeed the window to his room was dark. She would wait there and dream by starlight until he was ready for her to come to him.

She had been in place about twenty minutes when she caught a glimpse of a shadow moving across the lawn. Her first reaction was fear—another assassin, sent for Romar or Amalie—because the shape moved with the muscular certainty of a born soldier. But then the shadow drew closer and assumed familiar proportions, and she realized it was Tayse, out doing his nightly patrol.

A smile of undiluted mischief shaped her mouth.

Silently, swiftly, she rearranged her features, stretched her spine, colored her hair, until she was the exact image of Senneth. Rising, she crossed the lawn to intersect Tayse while he was still a few steps away from the garden. She made no effort at concealment, and he spotted her instantly, coming to a halt and waiting for her. She stepped close enough to put a hand on his shoulder, close enough to kiss him if she would.

"Tayse," she said, in Senneth's voice. "The night is so cool and beautiful. Come into the garden with me for just an hour or two. Everyone in our care will be safe that long."

His unreadable face was even harder to decipher by thin moonlight. "I wish I could," he said, sounding suitably regretful. "But I'm afraid your father would have me dismembered and Senneth would set her brothers on me if I transgressed so far."

She laughed and let her hand fall. "How did you know?" she demanded. "I am perfect in every detail! And you can hardly even see my face in this light."

"Your hand is cool," he said. Despite his unmoved expression, she had the feeling he was deeply amused. "Senneth's skin is always warm."

"Damn," she said. "I can't manufacture heat."

"You are dangerous enough without that particular weapon."

She laughed again. Despite the fact that Tayse had not fallen for her deception, she was happy and excited, pleased with the whole world. "Still," she invited. "You could come back to the gardens with me. You could pretend you didn't know. Senneth could hardly blame you for loving someone who looked so much like her."

He studied her a moment from his dark eyes. "I think you have already embarked on enough forbidden romances to waste any effort trying to seduce me," he said.

It was like a slap across the cheek; it was like a father's reprimand. It caused her to step back a pace and lose much of her happy mood as she returned to her true form. "I wasn't serious," she said.

"I was," he replied. "You're setting up camp in dangerous territory, Kirra, if you think to keep Romar Brendyn as your lover."

She couldn't believe it. *Tayse*, who could scarcely be forced to offer a personal opinion, giving her a lecture on the most private relationship of her life. But she was not the type to meekly endure a scold. "That's richly ironic," she said hotly, "coming from you. The man who took as his lover a woman forbidden to him by any consideration of class or standing. I would think you would be most understanding of someone who loved where it was most likely she would find despair."

"The difference is, Senneth was free to love me back if she so chose," Tayse said solemnly. "The difference is, I could hurt no one but myself by loving Senneth. Your infatuation with Romar Brendyn could ensnarl two Houses in conflict and break three hearts. Don't think I value your own heart any less when I say it is not worth that price."

"You wouldn't have given her up," she said very low. "If Senneth was married. If she was married to Halchon Gisseltess, as she could have been, and you had met her and fallen in love with her. You would not have closed your own heart and walked on by."

He was silent a moment. "No," he said at last. "If I had found Senneth as the marlord's wife, desperate to escape, I would have done what I could to aid her. I would have helped her, and loved her, and I wouldn't have cared what punishment might have come to me because of it. But I would have been silent about my love, if I thought it would hurt her in any way."

"That's not fair," she said, truly angry now. "Love is about more than *hurting* someone or *not hurting* someone. Love is about joy. And sometimes about sorrow. Love is about great emotion, and it is stronger than any simple rules about right and wrong."

"That's the most selfish thing I've ever heard you say."

She wanted to hit him. She wanted to change from human to lion shape and claw him across the chest. He didn't give her an opportunity to reply; he just kept on speaking. "Love is about caring for another human being so much that anything you do, anything you say, is calculated to keep that person safe. You want Romar Brendyn, and I understand that, but you can't expect me to be sympathetic. I would never do what you are doing. I would never put someone I loved in harm's way. I would die silent and alone before I ever did that."

"You haven't loved often enough to know what you would do," she whispered. An unforgivable thing to say.

But he didn't even wince. "I wouldn't waste love on anything less."

She turned away from him, furious and close to tears. "No one—not my father, not my sister, not my friends—has ever told me how to live my life," she said over her shoulder. "Why would you think I would listen to you?"

"I didn't," he said.

It was too much; she could not continue the conversation. She shook her head, put her hands up and waved them in front of her, closed her eyes and felt the blood fluttering under her skin. Good; she would take all that agitation, all that motion, and she would turn herself into a creature of swift nervous energy. She concentrated, she narrowed down, she was small and quivering and restless in the grass. A hummingbird, a creature that could not for a moment stay still. No natural bird of this type would be awake at this hour, but Kirra's tension was enough to overcome the hummingbird's sleepy impulses. She trembled into the air, a jewel made for the fitful wind, and hovered over him.

The stern disapproval on his face did not matter to her at all. She watched him for a moment, waited for him to speak again, but he said nothing. With a flirt of her feathers, she pirouetted in the sky.

There was a light in Romar's window. She flew toward it without a moment's hesitation.

ROMAR was standing in the middle of the room, watching the window. His boots lay on the floor, his vest and shirt across the back of a chair. He wore only his trousers, and the skin of his chest gleamed in the wavering light cast by a branch of candles. His face was creased, the muscles of his arms bunched as he watched the window, waiting for her. As soon as she darted through the casement, his entire body relaxed into a laugh.

"Kirra," he said, holding his hand out.

She settled on his palm as delicately as a petal falling, her feet dancing against his skin, her wings still madly beating. Not as madly as her heart. The smaller the creature, the more rapid the heartbeat, Kirra knew, but she was not sure, even in this shape, she could long endure the desperate pounding of her pulse.

"Kirra," he said again, lifting his other hand to stroke against her throat, down her back. She was not even human and his touch made her blood thicken with desire. "Very pretty—I admire this form very much—but do you think, for an hour or so, you could take your own shape? It has been a whole day since I have seen you as Kirra, and I miss you so very much."

She fluttered out of his hand and dropped to the floor, hoping something solid under her feet would make her a little more steady when she changed. But no. Human now—herself now, all golden curls and familiar body—she was just as dizzy. Her heart raced on at an even more rapid rate. It had been easier to breathe when she was a bird.

"Romar," she whispered, unable to fully find her voice.

But there was no time for talking. He snatched her to him, kissing her with a fervor that approached desperation. Magically, his clothes were gone, her clothes. Without seeming to move, they found themselves lying on his bed. Kirra thought she would die if they did not make love, now, instantly; and then they did, and she thought she would die of happiness. Impossible that anyone in the world had ever felt this way before. Nothing had ever been as wonderful, as devastating, as this.

OF course, Kirra being Kirra, it was not long before laughter came back to her. She lay face-to-face beside Romar in the rumpled bed, running her hand idly up the hard ridges of his arm.

"You have a most beautiful body," she told him. "Powerful. I like to feel your muscles."

He shrugged and she felt the ripples under the skin. "Any soldier, any man who wields a sword, has muscles like these. Or better."

"So if I were to undress—Justin, for instance—"

He kissed her swiftly. "You had better not. I am very jealous."

"One of the other Riders. Or Colton, even. I would find their bodies to be as impressive as yours?"

He grinned. "As strong, certainly. As impressive? Well—"

She made a fist and laid it, oh so gently, against his chin. "I see you are an arrogant man, like any lord from the Twelve Houses."

"Indeed, no. Humbled and grateful that any woman as beautiful as you would condescend to spend any time at all with me."

"Yes, it is a sacrifice," she admitted, now tugging at his hair, his beautiful dark blond hair. She loved the way it curled around her fingers. "Oh, horrors, Romar Brendyn is expecting me, I must go to his bed tonight or he will be very disappointed."

He laughed. "Well, I would have been. But if it is such an onerous chore for you—"

"If he were handsome, if he were noble, if he were brave, *then* I would not mind so much consorting with him under cover of darkness. But as it is—"

He kissed her again, forcing her head back against the pillows and pulling her tightly against him. "There would be many reasons for you not to come here tonight," he whispered when he lifted his head. "You don't need to list them."

"I can't think of any," she replied, and kissed him back. "Though I *do* think you're brave and noble," she said at last, when she had had enough kisses to satisfy her long enough to try conversation again. "The way you outmaneuvered Halchon Gisseltess tonight! I was quite impressed. Senneth thinks the nobles will take notice as well—that you have earned your reputation tonight."

"I was glad the soldiers were able to mobilize so quickly— glad they were able to breach the Towers as they did. It was more a matter of luck than bravery, on my part anyway."

"Oh, well, a lucky man—I don't know if I'm so impressed by that," Kirra said, pretending to turn away. "Maybe I should look elsewhere for my lover."

He pulled her back and they wrestled a little, laughing, until he had pinned Kirra's hands above her head and thrown a leg over her knees to hold her in place. "I am lucky that you love me tonight," he said, smiling down at her. "How lucky will I have to be to hold you forever?"

Her own smile was full of both merriment and warning. "You know you cannot hold me by brute strength," she said. "You know that at any moment, even now, I could turn into some other shape and slip out of your hands."

"I know that," he said. "How do I keep you? For I want to."

"Just love me," she said.

He bent down to kiss her again. It was the answer she wanted, and the rest came after. She thought that he did not need to worry; there would be nothing he could do to drive her away.

CHAPTER
31

T HEY were on the road a little after noon, everyone a little ill-tempered. Amalie was quiet, Senneth and Valri looked tense, and Tayse was downright grim. Even Kirra, who had never been happier in her life, was made irritable by lack of sleep and the necessity of undergoing yet another few days of travel.

Unable to face the effort needed to stay on horseback, she climbed into her coach and thought she might try to sleep away the early hours of the journey. Donnal and Melly were already inside, dozing in opposite corners. Kirra settled herself into a third corner and bunched a cloak behind her head for a pillow. She was asleep only a few minutes after the whole caravan had gone in motion.

When she woke, her head was against Donnal's shoulder, his arm was around her waist, and Melly was gone. The carriage still rocked forward at a steady pace, so they were still in transit.

"What time is it? How long have I slept?" she asked through a yawn, rubbing her eyes.

"About three hours."

"How did Melly get out?"

A laugh. "We stopped about an hour ago for a rest."

"Have I been leaning on you this whole time?"

"I don't know. I was asleep myself till the break."

"Has anything exciting happened?"

"Not exciting enough for them to wake us up."

"Good. Then I want to go back to sleep. But wake me up again if we stop. I'm hungry."

For a moment, his hand lifted to rest on her hair. She thought he was going to say something, and with a great effort kept her eyes open so she could pay attention. But all he said was, "All right. Go back to sleep."

It was always easier to sleep with Donnal beside her. Either the warmth of his body or the comfort of his presence or the sheer knowledge that nothing, *nothing*, could harm her while he was nearby made it a simple thing to close her eyes and slip into dreaming. Kirra did not wake again until the motion of the carriage stopped, and Donnal stirred against her.

"Supper break," he said, shaking her shoulder. "Do you want to get up?"

They joined the others for a quick meal, and Kirra took the chance to freshen up as well. She was feeling much better, both rested and cheerful, and she laughed so much over the meal that Justin walked away in annoyance and Cammon watched her with surprise. Tayse gave her one comprehensive glance and then turned most of his attention to Senneth.

It hardly mattered. She felt splendid. She was ready to go riding for the rest of the journey. They were moving through the unaligned territory between Nocklyn and Rappengrass, mostly flatlands spiky with skinny pine trees and brushy undergrowth. Pretty enough country with the occasional spectacular view. Kirra commandeered a horse and saddled up just as Tayse gave the order to move out. It was no surprise that Romar pulled his horse alongside hers as the caravan slowly got under way again.

"You've been sleeping, haven't you?" he accused. "Resting in the carriage. While I have been drooping in the saddle, scarcely able to keep the reins in my hand."

"Yes, I'm feeling quite refreshed," she replied. "The coach is empty now. You could nap for the rest of the journey."

"I doubt we've got more than another hour of travel ahead of us," Romar replied. "I don't think Tayse wants to keep Amalie on the road once it's dark. I assume he's aiming for an inn somewhere along the road."

"It hasn't occurred to me to ask before," she said, trying to make her question and her face innocent. "When we stop for the night on the road, do you bivouac with your men or take a room?"

He grinned at her, clearly not deceived by her nonchalant manner. "It depends on the weather, usually," he said. "On cold nights or wet ones, I sleep indoors. On fine nights, out with the men."

She turned her face up as if to test the wind on her cheeks. It had been hot and stuffy in the carriage, and the air was still close with the accumulated heat of summer. Not a single cloud cluttered the fading blue of the evening sky. "I feel certain it will rain tonight," she said. "I feel certain you must stay indoors."

"I'm not so sure," he said, keeping his voice serious. "Colton told me that the Merrenstow men are restless. He thought I should take my next few meals with them, be available to listen to grievances. I thought I'd take my place beside him at a campfire tonight."

She was sure the expression on her face was ludicrously crestfallen. "*Really?* Well—of course—I mean, I understand how important it is to keep the faith of your men—"

He burst out laughing. "No, I was joking. No Merrenstow soldier would ever whine about such things! If he did, we'd boot him out of our guard. I'm taking a room."

Now she felt giddy again, as if she had been spinning in circles. But she kept her face solemn. Two could play this game. "I am sure you must share your quarters with Colton," she said. "He deserves a soft bed after a hard day of riding."

He eyed her with a grin. "No, indeed. Colton is required at the campfire. I don't believe he's ever slept inside an inn his whole life. Possibly he's never slept under a roof. I'll have to ask him sometime. A very hardy man, my captain. No soft living for him."

"Then—you'll be—quite alone?" she asked with exaggerated delicacy. "All night?"

"Unless there's a willing barmaid or girl from the taproom—"

She hit him, hard, on the arm, then was instantly appalled. Not that she'd struck him, but that someone might have seen. But there was no outcry, no one turned in the saddle to stare at them, and Romar himself was grinning.

"That hurt," he said, rubbing his arm. "I suppose I should be glad there weren't claws on your fingertips at that particular moment. I was joking again, you know."

"I know. I would have made the same kind of joke if positions were reversed. It just—caught me by surprise."

He was silent a moment. "It is you I want in my bedroom tonight, Kirra," he said. "If you ever had any doubt. If you needed me to say it. Tonight, and for as many nights as we can manage. That's not much to offer you but I—"

"I will be there," she interrupted. "I will come to you. Anytime you want me—anytime we can be alone together."

He was watching her, his head turned sideways so he could see her, his expression rueful and a little sad. "Think of all the times, from now on. Years and years from now," he said. "We'll be at Ghosenhall together. Or Rappengrass or Brassenthwaite or wherever we might meet. And some of those times you might have a husband in tow. Sometimes I'll be accompanied by my wife. But sometimes one or both of us will be alone. And we'll be in a room, with twenty or fifty or a hundred other people, and we'll look at each other, and we'll know. We'll *know* that we want to be together that night, but we won't be able to say the words out loud, because the king will be listening, or your father, or Kiernan Brassenthwaite. How will I be able to tell you, yes, it is safe for you to come to my room? Shall I wear a ruby ring on the days I can welcome you? Tie my hair a certain way, wear a particular hat? Maybe I shall just drop a specific word into conversation. 'Hummingbird,' I'll say, no matter what the season, and everyone else will look at me strangely, but you'll know. You'll know I'm talking to you. You'll know I want you, and you'll come to my room, and you won't leave till morning."

"There is an old tale in Danalustrous about a marlord who was in love with one of his vassal's daughters," Kirra told him. "He was married, of course, and had three sons, and a cold and suspicious wife. And there would be many occasions when the vassal and his family would come to stay for a few days at Danan Hall. The marlord and the young lady devised this system of signals to communicate with each other during dinner, or during a ball, or anytime there was a roomful of people and they could not speak."

Romar appeared fascinated. "What? What did they do?"

"The marlord would cross his arms upon his chest with his fingers tucked to his ribs. But then, while she watched, he would free one finger of his right hand, or two, or three, and lay them casually along his arm. This meant, 'Come to me at one—or two—or three.' And she would go to him. If he pulled his signet ring from the finger of his left hand and put it on his right hand, that meant, 'It is not safe for you to come to me tonight. Unlock your door and I will come to you instead.' If he wanted her to meet him in the gardens, he would pick a rose from one of the flower arrangements and carelessly pull its petals off while engaged in conversation with someone else. If she thought her father was watching her too closely for her to get away, she would lift her pendant and absently kiss it, then lay it back across her throat again."

"Very subtle," Romar said. "What if one of them made the gesture, but the other one was not watching and missed it?"

She laughed. "Wouldn't you be watching?"

"Yes," he admitted. "Any more codes?"

Kirra flattened the palm of her left hand against her cheek, then curled it into a fist and laid it against her heart. "Sometimes, no matter how much they wanted to, they could not find a way to get free for the night. So they would send each other this signal, which meant, 'I love you, I will love you always.' I'm sure there were many nights that was the message they had to send."

"How is it you know this?" he demanded. "How long ago did these people live?"

"It depends on who tells the tale. Sometimes they lived two hundred years ago, sometimes three or four hundred years. They might not even be real. But I think they are."

"And the story's been handed down over that much time?"

"Oh, yes. I think I learned it when I was a child. It's part of Danalustrous lore. There's a set of portraits—my father's grandparents—hanging in one of the back galleries. She's leaning her cheek against her hand; he's got his fist against his heart. Very subtle, but everyone who knows the story knows what their postures mean. 'I love you, I will love you always.'"

"That's sweet," he commented. "How does the original tale end? The one with the marlord and his mistress?"

She recoiled a little from the word *mistress*, but not so much that he noticed. "Unhappily, I'm afraid. Apparently the marlady learned to interpret their signals, and one day she met the young lady in the gardens before the marlord could arrive. Again, the tales vary on how the girl met her end, but suffice it to say that it was the last assignation she ever kept."

Romar was staring at her. "She *died*? The marlady had her killed?"

Kirra felt her laughter bubble up. "Strangled or stabbed through the heart, yes. Everyone dies badly in the old folk tales, you know. No such thing as a happy ending."

"Yes, but they don't all end with *murder*," he exclaimed. "What happened to the marlady?"

Kirra laughed again. "Bore the old lord two daughters and another son. Happily ever after for *her*, I suppose."

"Perhaps it's time to invent some hand gestures of our own—ones not freighted with such a legacy," he said.

"I think, whatever our own story holds, it is not murder in a garden at midnight," Kirra said. "We are safe from that at least."

Romar didn't answer, but there was no time for more private conversation anyway. Cammon dropped back to ask if she knew where they planned to spend the night, and Romar spurred over to confer with his captain. Dusk was beginning to fall, so Kirra was not surprised when, about thirty minutes later, their course took them through a bustling market town and Tayse waved them all over to an inn on the outskirts.

It was always a long, laborious chore to determine where the armed escort would camp—since some of them, at least, needed to be close enough to the princess to defend her in case trouble arose, but no inn yard could accommodate all the soldiers in their party. Kirra, Senneth, and the royal women never bothered with these details. Followed by their own servants, they entered the inn, found accommodations reserved for them, and were ensconced in their rooms before any of the soldiers had been settled.

Kirra managed a quick bath and a change of clothes before there was a knock on her door. Senneth stood outside. "Hungry? Some of us are going down to the taproom for a late meal."

She'd had dinner on the road, but riding always built an appetite. "Good. Let me tell Melly I'm leaving."

The party that gathered downstairs in a few moments was weary but convivial. Romar, the four Riders, the princess, the queen, and the serramarra were joined by Donnal, Cammon, and Colton. Kirra liked the ratio of men to women. She always enjoyed masculine company and could not keep from flirting with anyone who responded, despite the fact that Casserah would not have. She sat between Justin and Cammon, arguing with them over stupid details, drawing Hammond and Colton into the discussion whenever they seemed to be paying attention. Senneth, Romar, Tayse, and Coeval were having a much weightier discussion at the other end of the table, while Donnal appeared to be telling stories to Valri and Amalie that were so humorous neither woman could stop laughing. That was unusual, Kirra thought. Donnal was only talkative around people he liked very much, and sometimes not even then.

"So, what do we expect in Rappengrass?" Cammon was asking, drawing her attention back to the conversation at hand. "We've had assailants in Kianlever, Coralinda Gisseltess in Coravann, and Halchon Gisseltess in Nocklyn. What comes next?"

"The ocean floods the whole territory," Hammond guessed.

"War opens," Justin said pessimistically.

"We have a lovely time. Everyone is charming. *That* would make this stop unique," Kirra said.

They all responded in the negative and began inventing more disasters. Plague. Earthquake. An uprising of vassals. "I know," Cammon said. "We're invaded by Arberharst."

"Do they have much of a navy?" Hammond asked with interest.

Justin shook his head. Kirra thought, *Great gods, now they're going to discuss military strategy!*

"Not that I ever heard," Justin said. "An army, though—a good one. Did you ever come across any of their soldiers when you were there?" he asked Cammon.

Cammon nodded. "Oh, yeah. Troops of them going through the port cities all the time. Even my father was afraid of them, and he generally thought he could outwit anyone."

"So, say they hire ships to transport cavalry to Gillengaria," Hammond said.

"Infantry," Justin corrected. "Too much trouble to ferry over horses. All that way? A nightmare."

"There were horses on the ship I arrived on," Cammon said.

"Sure, but hundreds of them? Like you'd need for an army?"

Kirra stopped listening to the words, though she let the rhythms of argument and counterargument make a pleasant staccato accompaniment to her thoughts. She was watching Romar, engaged in his own debate, which seemed to require arranging beer glasses like some kind of diagram on the table before him. Tayse disagreed with him, pushing the glasses aside and drawing a picture by pulling his fingertips through spilled wine. Senneth sat watching them, a half smile on her face. Unless Kirra greatly missed her guess, Senneth was experiencing much the same emotion Kirra was feeling right now. *Men and their wars and their quarrels. But how I love some of these particular men.*

Romar was watching Tayse intently; Kirra did not think he even realized that she was covertly surveying him. He sat back in his chair, crossed his arms on his chest, and shook his head emphatically. She could see his lips shape the word "no" and then the syllables of a vehement denial, though she could not actually hear what he said. Tayse and Coeval didn't give him a chance to finish before they launched into their own counterattack.

Still arguing with Tayse, Romar lifted one finger and laid it across his arm.

Come to me tonight at one o'clock.

Kirra felt her skin heat as her blood careered through her veins. Not that the invitation was unexpected, not that she was planning on sleeping in her own room, but she was left breathless by the excitement of planning a secret meeting in such a public place. No wonder that vassal's daughter had not been able to resist her doomed romance. What a thrill, what an exultation, to know the man you loved—so handsome, powerful, and forbidden—wanted you so badly he would tell you so before all of his friends.

But she could not pass up the chance to tease him. Keeping her eyes on Justin, though she had no idea what he was talking about, she lifted her pendant idly to her lips. *I am too closely watched. I cannot get free tonight.* She chanced a quick look at Romar to find his face creased with indignation. She tried not to laugh, but she couldn't help herself. She dropped her pendant and shook her head. *Only joking.*

"What? What did I say that was funny?" Justin demanded.

She honestly had no idea. "You're not funny, you're boring," she said. "Talk about something else."

He rolled his eyes. "Ballgowns and hairstyles. Right, that's not boring."

"Anything's better than war stories."

"How long before we arrive in Rappengrass?" Hammond asked, so they turned to travel talk instead. The meal progressed and finally ended, and the lot of them dispersed to find their beds.

Where some of them would sleep that night, and some would not.

KIRRA returned to her room for about an hour to brush and rebraid her hair and wash her face for a second time. Melly was busy mending a tear in one of the red dresses and muttering over the lack of some cleaning supply not in stock at the inn.

"I'll be gone much of the night," Kirra told her. "Don't wait up for me, and don't worry."

Melly gave her a straight look—almost reproving, as if she knew very well where Kirra had been these last few nights. It would be just like Casserah to have a servant who felt free to scold her, not that Casserah would care what a maid said. Casserah didn't care what anybody said. "I won't wait up, but I *will* worry," Melly said. "The Pale Mother knows there's no telling *what* mischief you might get yourself into. Changing shapes whenever you please and going out courting trouble."

Kirra laughed. "I never get myself into trouble that I can't handle."

Melly's gaze dropped to the fabric again. "That's what many a young woman before you has thought."

So she did know. Red and silver hell. This was why Kirra had never wanted to burden herself with servants. Kirra crossed to the door and waited a moment, listening to the quiet in the hall. No one seemed to be stirring. "Don't wait up," she repeated, and stepped outside.

Amalie's room across the hall, Coeval at the door. She nodded at him gravely, as if she pondered matters too serious for him to comprehend, and strode along the hall. Down the steps, out into the deserted courtyard. As soon as she was sure she was deep enough in shadows that no one would be able to see her, she changed. Romar had liked her hummingbird well enough to want to employ it as a code word; therefore, she would assume that shape again.

She launched her tiny body into the air, paused to sip nectar from a night-blooming flower, and made a fluttering, indirect circuit around the exterior of the inn. Plenty of windows were open as guests sought to cool their rooms with the fresh night air. Some were shut; one was guarded by a white owl, drowsing on the sill. Kirra darted above him, winging away as fast as she could. He hadn't seen her, or if he had, he had not realized who she was. He didn't even open his eyes as she hurried past.

The Wild Mother was kind. She had made sure Romar's room was not adjacent to Amalie's. No mistaking the regent's room, for the shutters were open wide, the room was aglow with candlelight, and Romar himself stood at the window, scanning the night sky.

She flew over and hovered right before him, her wings beating the air so mightily they could not be seen. He stared at her a moment, not smiling, then he held out his hand. She dropped into his palm and let her wings fall still. It was not possible that her small heart could beat any faster. He drew her inside and latched the shutters behind her.

CHAPTER
32

NOT until Kirra was on her way back to her room did she
encounter any trouble, and even then it came from an unexpected source. No cats in the shadowed courtyard to pounce on
her as she shifted shapes. No late-arriving guests to ogle her as
she stepped back inside the inn. Even the clerk was asleep behind his desk and did not see her enter. She had just hurried
down the hallway and had her right foot on the stairwell when
Justin entered from the back door, obviously heading in her direction.

"What are you doing up?" she asked without thinking.

"My shift at the princess's door," he said. His sandy eyebrows
gathered into a scowl. "Why are *you* out roaming around?"

She shrugged. "Restless. Sometimes I wander."

Now his frown was even blacker. "Where did you wander to
tonight? Romar Brendyn's bedroom?"

She was so stunned she could only gape at him.

But Justin wasn't done. "What do you think you're doing,
Kirra? How could you be so stupid? Chasing after a married
man—"

It took her that many sentences to recover. "I don't think
this is any of your business," she snapped, and put her hand on
the rail.

He knocked it off and moved to block her before she could run past him up the steps. She had never seen Justin so furious. Astonishment, more than the physical barricade of his body, kept her in place.

"This is wrong—this is stupid—you can't go after Romar Brendyn, you can't," he railed. "Half the young lords in Gillengaria are in love with you, and you'd throw yourself away on a man you can't have? Where's your pride? Where's your honor? You shame yourself and him and his family and *your* family. If you—"

"I don't want to hear this from you! Let me pass!" she exclaimed, making as if to push past him, but he would not budge.

"I don't have a family! I have no one to hurt by my actions, but I wouldn't behave this way," Justin continued. "But you! You're a daughter of Danalustrous. And you're styled like your sister! Have you thought how you might damage her reputation by your behavior? You owe it to her—"

"Justin. I will not have this conversation with you. I *will* not."

"You owe it to yourself," he persisted. "Don't you know you will only end up breaking your heart? How can this man make you happy? How can he do anything except hurt you?"

"My heart, my hurt, are *not* your concern!"

"You owe it to Donnal," he said.

She stopped trying to brush past him and stood staring at him. Her own face, she knew, was stricken. His was still dark with fury and concern. "Donnal doesn't know anything about this," she whispered.

"Of course he does! Donnal knows where you are every minute of every day, even if you aren't shaped like Kirra, even if you cannot see him watching you. What do you think he's thinking? What do you think he's feeling?"

She shook her head. "I cannot—my life is—I cannot live my life for Donnal's sake. We are further apart than Tayse and Senneth. There is—you don't know—"

"He loves you."

"I'm not free to love him in return!"

"That's not it!" Justin struck back. If he hadn't been almost whispering, he would have been shouting in her face. But both of them were keeping their voices lowered in the hopes of not waking the clerk or drawing the attention of customers still in the taproom. "You take him for granted. You think he will always be there, when you think about him at all. Don't you know how precious every friend is? Don't you know how quickly you can lose people—lose anybody at all?"

Justin himself had lost everybody, mother and sisters and some of his friends; he never talked about any of those losses. Kirra put her hands across her eyes and realized she was trembling. With anger, with weariness, with sheer emotion, she didn't know.

"I do not want to lose Donnal. I do not want to lose anyone," she said, speaking very distinctly. "But I cannot live my life for him. For my family. For anyone but myself. I am sorry if that shocks you. I am sorry if that disappoints you. I cannot live my life to please you, either."

"You owe me more than this," he said in a low voice, and her eyes flew open. She dropped her hands.

"*What*? I owe *you*?"

He was shaking his head. "You are the first noblewoman I ever believed in. The first serramarra that I didn't hate."

"There's Senneth," she said dryly. "And you do so hate me."

"Senneth doesn't count. She's—she's Senneth," he said, and he didn't have to explain any better than that. Kirra knew what he meant. "But you—I had spent my life despising the aristocracy. For their wealth, their arrogance, their ease. For having so much while everyone else had so little. But you—" He shook his head again. "You're different. You live a life that matters. I respect you." His voice changed. "Or I did."

Now she was the one shaking her head. "You can't—I'm not—damn it, Justin, how I live my life has nothing to do with you! How you live your life has nothing to do with me! Do I chide you every time you take up with a barmaid? Do I care if you've slept with every serving girl from here to Ghosenhall? Do I—"

He was staring at her. "I haven't," he interrupted. "I don't. I want to be like Tayse. It's not good enough unless it's love."

By the laughing silver goddess, the unreliable Silver Lady. Fierce, abrasive, impossible Justin was a romantic at heart.

She closed her eyes again. She was suddenly so tired that she almost dropped her head forward to rest it against his chest. "I love him, Justin," she said in a low voice. "And I cannot have him. But I will have what part of him I can steal. And nothing you say, nothing anybody says, can change that. And if you think I've betrayed you and every single one of the Twelve Houses, well, then, so be it. This is the path I choose."

His hands were on her shoulders; he pushed her back and shook her, just a little. "You're so lost on this path."

She pulled herself free and he released her, standing aside so she could finally climb past him. "Every path is tangled and overgrown," she said over her shoulder, not looking back at him. "All of us are lost."

So that was not a restful night, but she found herself too edgy the next day to want to sleep the hours away in the coach. Possibly because whenever she closed her eyes, as she had the night before, her mind replayed for her Justin's words, Justin's face. Even when she clenched her hands and willed herself to remember Romar's face instead, Romar's hands, Romar's body. What she saw was Justin's anger. What she heard were Justin's reproaches.

Easier to find a horse and ride the whole day, contending only with the discomforts of the body.

They had been on the road for about three hours when Senneth shook herself loose of a conversation with Valri and brought her horse alongside Kirra's. "You look tired," Senneth commented.

Kirra gave her a sideways glance. Justin, Tayse, Donnal (if you believed Justin), and possibly Cammon all knew where she had spent her recent nights. Impossible to believe that one of them had not informed Senneth, who might have figured it out on her own. "Nocturnal activities," Kirra said briefly. "I'm already braced for your disapproval."

Senneth smiled faintly but without much amusement. "I'm in no position to tell anyone else how to walk away from love."

"Exactly what I told Tayse," Kirra said, nodding darkly. "But that didn't stop him."

"But I know from experience that hearts can withstand more punishment than you'd like to think," Senneth added. "You can hurt a lot more and for a lot longer than you'd ever believe. I hate to see a happy girl like you fall into pain and despair."

"I am perfectly capable of deciding how much unhappiness I can bear," Kirra said. "I will take care of my own life, as I told Justin."

Now Senneth did look amused. "Justin?"

Kirra nodded. "Yes! Last night. He caught me on the stairs, returning from—returning to my room. He stood there and yelled at me for ten minutes. I was never so astonished. *Justin.*"

Senneth was trying to smother a smile. "I overheard him lecturing Donnal the other day, too."

"For what?" Kirra said waspishly. "Spending too much time flirting with the princess?"

Senneth lifted her eyebrows at that. "Not exactly, but perhaps indirectly. He said Donnal had left you too much to your own devices. Or words to that effect. He implied that Donnal was overlooking his primary responsibility. You can imagine how well Donnal took such an accusation."

Kirra laughed shortly. She could. "This is almost impossible to believe. Why would he care? Justin has no use for Donnal and he can't stand me."

"Actually, I think you're wrong there," Senneth said thoughtfully. "More than any of us, I think, Justin considers the rest of us to be his family. You'd expect Cammon to be the one who turned us into kin, and to some extent he has, but I don't think Cammon would be quite as lost as Justin would if the rest of us were suddenly to disappear. You know, Cam finds people to love him everywhere he goes. People are drawn to him, they want to protect him or be his friend. Justin—it's harder for him. Basically, we're all he's got."

"There's the Riders," Kirra pointed out. "All fifty of them."

Senneth nodded. "Yes. Those are his peers, the people he wants to think well of him. The people he's comfortable around. But we're the people he loves. We're the people he would fight for till the death." She turned her head and smiled at Kirra. "Even you. He would defend you with his life."

"No," Kirra said in a very disgruntled voice, "he's more likely to strangle me and leave my body for the dogs."

"You know that isn't true," Senneth said. "And you'd fight for Justin. You would. If he was in trouble and it was in your power to save him, you'd do it."

Kirra opened her mouth to refute this and found herself unable to reply. *Bright Mother blind me,* she thought, her mood blighted even more by this revelation. *I actually care about Justin.* "Well," she said, scowling now, "since I can't imagine any situation that Justin couldn't fight his way out of, I don't suppose I'll ever be called on to prove my loyalty."

Senneth loosed a peal of laughter and wouldn't stop laughing even though Kirra shushed her and various members of their party sent inquiring looks her way. Cammon kneed his horse over and rode on the other side of Senneth.

"I don't suppose you'd be willing to share the tale?" he asked hopefully.

"If you're as good as everyone says you are, you'll already know what we're talking about," Kirra snapped, and Senneth laughed even harder. She was clinging to the saddle horn, doubled over; Kirra thought it was possible she might fall to the ground. "Stop it," Kirra hissed. "People are going to think you're having a fit."

Cammon was watching Senneth in some bemusement. "Do you think I should offer her a drink of water or something?"

"Just ignore her," Kirra said. "That's what I'm going to do."

Senneth managed to regain some control, though her mouth was still wide with laughter. "So *do* you?" she asked Cammon. "Know what we were talking about?"

Cammon shrugged. "Something about Justin. He's mad at Kirra, too. But he didn't seem to think it was funny."

That set Senneth off again. Kirra rolled her eyes. "I think I'm going to ride in the coach for a while, after all," she said to Cammon. "You can watch over the madwoman. If her frenzy gets any worse, call for Tayse."

Cammon looked doubtful. "You're the healer. Maybe you should stick around. What if she—I don't know—stops breathing or something?"

"Right now, I would find that a blessing," Kirra said and reined her horse back. Senneth was still laughing.

Once she had turned the horse over to one of the men and climbed back in the carriage, she finally did fall into a fitful sleep. Even when she woke, even when the caravan came to a halt for an afternoon rest, she did not emerge again. She couldn't think of anyone in the whole party that she actually could endure. Only one that she even wanted to talk to—and from him she wanted more than conversation.

Let the night fall soon.

. . .

ANOTHER small town, another picturesque inn, another convivial dinner in the taproom.

Another illicit trip to her lover's room, traveling in disguise.

This night, no one intercepted her, no one reprimanded her, no one watched her but the moon. Kirra crept back into her own room an hour or two before dawn, and stood there a moment, listening to the sound of Melly's even breathing. Remembering Romar, his skin warm against hers, his mouth against her own. Her body was flushed with something more primitive than happiness, more triumphant than love. Satiated desire, perhaps, laced with a greed for more.

She did not know how she would ever be able to give him up.

THEY were making good time the next day until the second carriage lost a wheel. The efficient Colton rounded up the men who had fixed the axle during their last mishap, while Tayse and Justin grumbled about the inconveniences of traveling by cart.

"Won't take but an hour to fix," Colton assured them. "We ought to be at Rappen Manor before nightfall."

"And if we're not, we're not," said Senneth practically. "We can't do much about it."

Kirra was considering joining Amalie and Valri for a mid-morning snack when Donnal came bounding up and licked her hand. He was shaped like his familiar black dog today, and he had spent the morning sleeping at Amalie's feet in her coach. Or so Kirra surmised. He had climbed into that coach right behind Senneth when they embarked, and he had been a hound then. Kirra had noticed.

But now he was frisking around her, restless and obviously wanting her attention. "What?" she demanded, and he responded with a deep bark. He dashed off a few paces, came back, barked again. "You want me to follow you? Is that it?" Another bark signified that she'd understood.

She glanced up to see Cammon watching them, an unreadable expression on his usually open face. "We're going off for a walk, in case anyone misses us," she called, and he nodded.

They were passing through an area thickly wooded with

those tall, thin pines, and it didn't take long before the curves
of the land and the tangles of the trees hid them from view of
their own party. Time for a change. "Hold up a minute," Kirra
said, and pretty soon she was on four feet right beside him, a
purebred retriever with gleaming golden fur. Donnal came
over to nuzzle her ear, then tore off through the undergrowth.

She instantly followed, and for about thirty glorious minutes they played chase and capture. Donnal happened upon a
pool, deep in shadow and tasting of leaves, and they both
thirstily lapped up water. Just for a lark, Kirra dove in and
splashed from one side of the narrow pond to the other, before
leaping out and shaking herself to dry off.

When she looked for Donnal again, he was standing there,
shaped like himself.

Not until she followed suit, assuming Kirra's body and
Kirra's hair, did she read the trouble on his face.

"Donnal," she said, coming close enough to put her hand
on his arm. She could feel the water from her damp hair turning the back of her gown wet. "You look—is something
wrong?"

"I'm leaving," he said.

It was as if he barked like a dog again or spoke in some
other language that she could not comprehend. For a moment,
she didn't know what he meant. On some level she had understood him, for her body strung with tension and her heart
stopped beating, but her mind could not sort out his words.
Could not process them. Could not believe he had said them.

"Leaving?" she repeated finally, her lips stiff. "For where?"

"I don't know."

"Danalustrous?"

"Probably not."

"For how long?"

He merely looked at her.

Now her heart started up again, knocking against her ribs
in slow, painful strokes. It was her lungs that stopped function-
ing this time; she could not take in any air. "You're leaving
me," she whispered.

He nodded.

She could not ask him why. She knew why. Justin had been
right; Donnal knew about Romar. She could not tell him he
was wrong; she could not beg him not to go. *Stay, I will give*

him up for your sake. Stay, it will be different tomorrow. She had nothing to offer him.

She could not live if he left her.

There was nothing to say.

She wanted to ask him if she would ever see him again, if he would come find her in six months or a year or ten years, once this infatuation with Romar was past, once her father had bullied her into marrying some eligible Twelfth House lord and she had settled into something like an ordinary life. It would never be the same, of course. She could not expect him to be her companion, her shadow, her pet, her vassal, ever again. But perhaps he would visit her from time to time. Let her know that he was still alive and well. That he had forgiven her. That she still owned at least a tiny portion of his heart.

But she had held on to him for too long without giving him enough in return. She could not now try to make a noose with words to hold him, even part of him.

"I can't say good-bye," was all she could manage.

"I love you," he said, and bent in to kiss her.

He had never kissed her before, and she closed her eyes to imprint the feeling on her lips forever. His mouth was gentle, undemanding. It was clear he was taking away a memory. His hands rose to cup her face; his fingers felt so familiar against her skin. She leaned in, putting more pressure into the kiss, thinking if she could just absorb enough of him, it would not be so bad once he had left.

When he lifted his head, he kept his hands on her face. He was smiling; he looked entirely at peace. "Wild Mother watch you," he said, then folded both his hands into fists and laid them against his heart.

While she stared at him, abandonment striking her to the soul, he changed into a hawk and launched himself into the air. A moment she could see him, weaving his way out of the dense branches overhead, and then he was out of sight.

His hand to her cheek, his fist to his heart. *I love you, I will love you always.*

He was gone.

SHE changed herself back into the retriever because she didn't think she could find the camp if she had to rely on her

human senses. Didn't think she could see the path in front of
her for the tears, and the dog, at least, didn't cry. She didn't know
what she would do when she came upon the caravan, how she
would resume human shape and wave cheerily to everyone
and climb back into her carriage and survive the day.

She didn't have to.

Cammon was waiting for her, sitting in a scrap of grass on
the side of the road, holding his horse's reins while the animal
took the opportunity to graze. He didn't scramble to his feet
when she trotted up, weary as if she had run from Ghosenhall
to Rappengrass in one day. He merely held out a hand, and she
ducked her golden head under his fingers, grateful for the
smallest gesture of kindness.

"I told Tayse to move on out," he told her. "Said I'd wait for
you. He didn't want to, but Senneth told him to go ahead. We
have to catch up with them before Rappen Manor, though."

She turned her head and licked the inside of his wrist. He
laughed, but his face still showed concern.

"Will you be all right by then?" he asked. "I mean—all
right enough to pretend?"

For an answer, she stretched out beside him on the grass
and laid her head in his lap, closing her eyes.

"Yeah. That's what I thought," he said, slowly pulling one
of her silky ears through his fingers. "Well, they're moving slow.
It'll be easy to catch up. Let's just sit here for a little while."

So, perhaps, after all, nothing momentous would occur in
Rappengrass. All the excitement had transpired on the road.

CHAPTER
33

THE caravan made it to Rappen Manor about an hour before sunset. Kirra had taken human shape and slipped inside her own carriage during a late-afternoon break, managing not to speak to anyone except Melly. "Wake me when we arrive," she said, and closed her eyes. Of course she did not sleep. She felt as if she had been battered by some illness, wracked by fever for days. Her body actually hurt as she shifted position on the cushioned seats.

It was both a relief and a horror to arrive at Rappen Manor, a gray fortress on high ground closely guarded by soldiers wearing the maroon sash of Rappengrass. A relief because finally she would have some distraction from her own distressed, inchoate thoughts. A horror because now she would actually have to function. Speak. Laugh. Listen. She was not sure she could do it.

Ariane was not awaiting them, but Darryn was, handsome and youthful and smiling. "Majesties! Welcome to my mother's house. We are so pleased to have you here, both of you. Serra Senneth, serra Casserah—welcome to you as well. Serra Senneth, I know you have visited my mother often, but I do not believe serra Casserah has been to Rappengrass before this."

Kirra gave him her hand and attempted a smile. "No, it is

my first visit to the southern Houses. I am most impressed with your fortifications."

He laughed. "The story goes that my great-great-great-and-some-odd-greats-grandmother did not feel her near neighbors respected her ability to hold property. So she had the Manor built to withstand attack and siege. There's been so little war in Gillengaria in recent centuries that I can hardly tell you how well it would hold up today."

Kirra cast a glance up at the narrow turrets, let her eyes linger on the grilled gate, just now hoisted to allow them to pass. "You might have your chance to find out," she said softly.

"I hope not," he replied.

"So do I."

Darryn turned a little to address them all. "There is a dinner tonight, of course, and afterward there will be music. The ball is the day after tomorrow—we think it will be very grand, and we hope you all enjoy it. I will have you shown to your rooms now. Let me know if there is anything you require."

Kirra could think of many things she required, none of which Darryn would be able to provide. No one else spoke up with any particular wants, and so they all filed in behind a parade of servants to partake of the hospitality of Rappen Manor.

THE dinner would have been delightful if one had been in the mood to be delighted. Kirra sat between one of Darryn's brothers and a lesser lord from Fortunalt, both very attractive, and was able to admire the bounty of Ariane's table even though she could hardly bring herself to choke down a bite. She hoped that Casserah's legendary coolness would be blamed for her lack of animation, though she worked hard to keep a civil expression on her face.

"You've made practically the whole circuit this summer, haven't you?" the Rappengrass serramar observed at one point. "A little wearing, isn't it? That's what Darryn says."

"I admit I have found myself thinking about home these last few days," she said. "But I am very much looking forward to your mother's ball."

The Fortunalt man looked up. "Traveling with a whole party, aren't you? The princess, the queen, the regent, and dozens of guards, is that right? Must be hard to find lodging for the night."

She smiled briefly. "We pay well. That makes it easier."

"Would drive me mad," the Fortunalt man said with conviction. "Traveling with all those people. Hard enough to make a trip with just a few companions, because everyone wants to start at a different time, or stop at a different time, and someone's always wandering off. Can't imagine how you can get fifty people going the same direction at the same time."

"We're led by a King's Rider, and he's very ruthless."

"And it wouldn't be so bad if you liked them all, or most of them," Darryn's brother said. "Are you friends with everyone in the group?"

"Some of them," she said. "Even the ones I don't know well I have found to be fairly agreeable. The others I've managed to tolerate. And we've left one or two behind on the road."

One, anyway. The most important one.

I will never see Donnal again, she thought.

BY the end of the meal, not only was her stomach one burning knot, but her head was pounding. She thought of asking Senneth if she could borrow Tayse, who knew some secret trick for curing Senneth's recurrent headaches. She would have, if she'd thought the same methods would work on her. But Senneth's headaches tended to be by-products of magic or anger. Kirra thought her own was concocted of despair. She didn't think even Tayse's strong hands could throttle that emotion away.

She knew she would not be able to sit through an evening of music no matter how exquisitely played. She must escape to her room and sleep, or sob, or do something to alleviate her profound depression. It was almost a relief when Romar approached her obliquely, almost accidentally, as the diners rose and milled about before moving to the salon.

"Serra," he said, his voice formal but his eyes warm. "Perhaps we might sit together as the harps are played? You know so much more about the gentler arts than I do. I thought you could explain to me which players are gifted and which are merely competent."

She managed a smile, but barely. "I think I will go up to my room right now and not leave again for any reason," she said, trying to convey with innocent words the information he most wanted to know. "I find I am reacting in an unfortunate way to something I ate earlier in the day. Most unpleasant. I cannot stay for the music." *I cannot come see you. But I cannot tell you why. I am sad because another man I say I do not love has left me because I say I do love you. How could I speak those words? How could you possibly understand? I do not understand myself.* It was unlikely Romar knew that Donnal had left the caravan. It was unlikely, even if he knew, he had figured out why. She was safe to plead illness. It would not be hard to believe.

Romar looked instantly concerned. "Shall I send for someone? Senneth? Or I'm sure the marlady employs a healer of some kind."

"No, no, this is a passing thing. I just need sleep and solitude."

He still watched her. "You have not had much rest these past few days, I know," he said.

She couldn't help a smile at that. "And there have been many nights I have lain awake, not yet ready to fall asleep," she said demurely. "I think such evenings are starting to take their toll."

"I hope you will feel much improved in the morning."

She smiled again. "I'm sure I will."

She turned away and excused herself repeatedly as she cut through the crowd, back toward the formal doorway. Naturally, the one person she encountered was the person she least wanted to see—Justin, on his way to guard the salon while Amalie sat inside it. His face wore its usual expression of scorn and fierceness, carefully cultivated to show he was dangerous and unimpressed by nobility. When he caught sight of her, his face momentarily darkened—more scornful, more ferocious—and she read anger and condemnation in his eyes. *He* knew, if Romar Brendyn did not, that Donnal had left. And why.

But something on her own face snagged his attention, and his expression changed, became suddenly alert and inquiring. He caught her arm as she would have stalked right by him.

"Are you all right?" he demanded.

She shook herself free. "Fine."

"Should I get Senneth?"

"I'm fine. I'm going to my room. I'm tired."

He said nothing else for a moment, merely watched her. She thought she could see him considering and then rejecting any number of other comments, everything from abuse for her stupidity to sympathy for her pain. Finally, he said, "Cammon's in our room. Just down the hall from yours. If you need someone."

This was meant to be kindness, she knew, and she was almost undone by it. "Thank you," she whispered, because the tears had made her throat close up and she could not speak normally. "I just want to be by myself."

He nodded and stood aside to let her pass. She practically ran up the stairs and down the hall to her room, flinging herself on her bed. She had wept hysterically for maybe ten minutes before she felt Melly's soft hand on her shoulder. It had not occurred to her that someone else would be in the room, and she struggled to sit up, to compose herself. But she could not do it. Melly wiped her face with a damp cloth and murmured something inarticulate and soothing, and Kirra just gave up. She turned her face back into the pillow and sobbed herself to sleep.

KIRRA woke late and reluctantly, and then only because someone was calling her. "Serra. Serra. There is a message from the marlady. Serra, you cannot sleep all day."

She rolled over on the mattress to try to locate the voice, reorient herself to her surroundings. Dark hair on her pillow, a worried young woman bending over her, bright light streaming in through unfamiliar windows. She was Casserah, this was Rappengrass, and it had to be past noon. *Bright Mother blind me,* she thought, and sat up.

"What time is it? Is something wrong?"

"Everyone else has just gone down to lunch. Nothing's wrong. You've gotten a note from the marlady, who would like to see you. I didn't know—I didn't want to wake you but— Are you sick? Serra Senneth said I should let you sleep as long as I could."

Kirra dangled her legs over the side of the bed, then sat there a moment, assessing. How did she feel? Rested; that was a nice change. A little foggy from too much sleep, but that would surely pass. There was a lurking sadness in her heart, hiding in a dark vaulted chamber and unwilling to be examined too closely, but she could breathe. That was another nice change.

"So, Senneth has come by this morning?"

Melly nodded. "And Cammon. And two of the Riders."

Kirra could not help smiling at that. The very act of smiling eased some of her pain, which made her realize just how much pain she still was feeling. Hell and damnation. "What does Ariane want?"

"She didn't say. Just that she would like a private audience with you. Today."

"I suppose I'd better get dressed then."

"Are you hungry? I had some food brought up."

Kirra checked again, but couldn't find hunger among her range of wants. Still, she supposed she should eat something before she met with Ariane. "Yes, thank you," she said, summoning a smile. "You are very good to me."

"That's not hard," Melly said, turning away to fetch the tray. "You're very easy to care for."

IT was not quite an hour before Kirra was dressed, fed, reasonably focused, and on her way to see Ariane. As a servant led her through the ornate halls of Rappen Manor, Kirra could not help but notice Rappengrass soldiers everywhere. They were visible out every window that overlooked the lawns, training or lounging; the room where she was finally taken was guarded by six men, all grim-faced and heavily armed. So it had been several months ago when Kirra had come here last, shaped as herself, Senneth at her side. Ariane Rappengrass clearly was taking no chances with her own safety—or that of her guests.

The heavy door was opened by Ariane's steward, a cadaverous, humorless man who had always had a fondness for Kirra. "Serra Casserah," he said and waved her inside.

Ariane was standing across the room, just beside a wide desk. The whole chamber was furnished in deep colors, maroon and bronze and purple, the somber effect somewhat mitigated by the glorious sunshine pouring in from three high windows. Ariane herself looked just as serious as her furnishings, with her severe hairstyle, the grave expression on her broad features, and the black color of her dress.

"Thank you, Ralf. You may go," she said, dismissing her steward as she came around the desk toward Kirra. A smile lightened her face somewhat; she took Kirra's hands and studied her a moment. "Casserah. It has been a long time since I've seen you. I cannot believe you are twenty-one already. I think of you still as a thin and somewhat clumsy sixteen. You have become so poised."

Not everyone in the nobility liked Ariane Rappengrass, but everyone in House Danalustrous did, so Kirra allowed herself to smile warmly in return. "I resent being told you ever thought I appeared clumsy," she replied. "I assure you, even when I was at my most awkward, I considered myself *quite* adroit. I suppose, when I am thirty, I will look back with dismay at the gaucherie I display now."

"I doubt it," Ariane said. "From everything I hear, you are very polished."

Kirra laughed. "Has Darryn been telling tales of me?"

Ariane drew her over to an embroidered crimson sofa and they sat. "Oh, Darryn is filled with admiration for both you and your sister. He said that Kirra has better hair but you have better insults."

Kirra choked and then laughed aloud. "And I thought I was always so kind to him! I'll have to treat him to real disdain during this visit so he can see me at my best."

"Yes, do that. It will please him so much."

There was a polite knock on the door and a servant entered with a tray of refreshments. Neither of them spoke until the food had been arranged on a small table and the servant had withdrawn again.

"So, I am wondering what you've learned on this jaunt across Gillengaria," Ariane said, pouring tea and handing a cup to Kirra. When Kirra was silent, Ariane looked up with a smile. "Is that too blunt? Surely I cannot be wrong in thinking your father sent you on the circuit to gather information about the state of the realm."

Kirra sipped at the tea, which was really too hot to drink. She wasn't sure how to answer. "My sister came back from her travels earlier this year, full of dire warnings about rebellions being plotted in the south. My father is not sure how much turmoil is real, how much is just—posturing—by the southern Houses."

"My own guess is that there is a very real chance for war," Ariane said flatly. "And that I sit in the middle of a combat zone."

Kirra nodded. "So my sister said. And she was anxious to hear my father say aloud that he would support the crown if the Houses divided."

Ariane looked at her sharply. "And he would not say so? Surely Malcolm would never side with rebels! Particularly rebels led by Halchon Gisseltess."

Kirra drank a little more tea. "My father would—no. He would never rise against the king. But he might do everything in his power to hold back from a war. I believe he would stay neutral if he could."

"He can't," Ariane said.

"He thinks he can."

Ariane replaced her cup on the table as if she was afraid she might spill it if she held it much longer. "So Malcolm would desert us," she said, clearly angry. "I thought we could count on Danalustrous."

"War is not here yet," Kirra said gently. "He may have a different answer if it arrives."

The marlady gave her another keen look. "And you? Now that you have been named heir to Danalustrous? What if war came while you were installed in Danan Hall?"

Harder and harder to answer this as Casserah would. "You know that I seldom stir beyond my own borders. Danalustrous is first and foremost in my heart, and I would do anything in my power to keep it safe. But I have to admit, I do not think Danalustrous would be safe if the rest of the world was rent by war. I think sides would have to be chosen. And I would never, under any scenario you could devise, choose to cast my lot with Halchon Gisseltess." Kirra drained the teacup and set it down. "And neither would my father," she added. "If he takes sides, he will fight for Baryn. With you. With Brassenthwaite."

"Yes, and with who else?" Ariane said with a certain grimness. "Did you happen to pick up any clues about Nocklyn and Coravann and Kianlever while you were journeying across the continent? For I am sure Fortunalt is against us. I wonder just how alone we will stand."

"I have no specific knowledge," Kirra said, since she didn't think she was authorized to repeat Sabina Gisseltess's whispered words to Senneth. If they were even true. If the woman even knew who was allied with her husband and who was not. "I can tell you my impressions. Heffel Coravann feels much like my father does—he wants to stay neutral, and he seems to think he can. Eloise Kianlever would declare herself for the king—but some of her vassals could be convinced to put their loyalty elsewhere, and she may well have an uprising on her hands. Nocklyn would appear to be wholly given over to the Gisseltess connection—and yet Els is still alive, and Mayva was not happy at the chaos that churned in her house when Halchon Gisseltess came to call."

"Yes, Darryn told me the whole tale," Ariane replied. She sounded astonished still. "That Halchon had the nerve to travel when Baryn had confined him to his estates! Well, that alone should tell us the caliber of the man. I believe there is nothing he would stop at."

"I believe you're right. He spoke quite nakedly of his ambition when he confronted Senneth earlier this year. Have you heard that tale as well?" When Ariane shook her head, Kirra told the story. "Senneth and Kirra met him in Lochau recently. He all but came out and said he was ready to wrest the throne from Baryn's hands, for Baryn is old and weak and has only one rather questionable heir. He also told Senneth he would be willing to forgo a war if Baryn would name him heir instead—"

"He would never repudiate Amalie that way!"

Kirra nodded. "*And* he thought the other eleven Houses would agree to this plan if he, Halchon, discarded his current wife and took a more politically powerful woman as his bride." She waited expectantly.

Ariane was staring. "No. Did he—did he mean *Senneth*? She despises him! Oh, terrible as it is, I almost wish I'd been in the room to hear him make that proposal to her! What did she say?"

"I forget the exact words—or maybe Kirra never told me," she added hastily. "Something along the lines of she'd rather see him dead. In any case, I don't think that should be a contingency you consider as a real possibility. She'll never marry him. But that isn't going to keep him from pursuing the throne."

Ariane sighed and passed a hand over her strong features. For a moment, she slumped on the sofa and appeared much more like a tired old woman than a formidable marlady. "And so we come back to war," she said, and dropped her hand. "As does every conversation I have these days."

"We could talk of something else," Kirra said, because she

thought Casserah would have. "Family and friends, for instance. I have met two of your sons during my most recent travels and I liked them both a great deal. How are your other children? And grandchildren? We could spend the next hour discussing them."

Ariane sighed again and looked even more tired. "Unfortunately, we could," she said. She glanced at Kirra, then stared blindly out the window at the bright sunlight. "I am most happy that you have come to Rappengrass, for I don't believe I've ever had the chance to entertain you at Rappen Manor before, but I have to say, I was wishing Kirra would come as well. I would ask her—" She spread her hands and said nothing more.

Kirra waited till the silence had stretched out a few moments. "She was here a few months ago and you asked for nothing."

"A few months ago my granddaughter had not fallen ill with red-horse fever. Now—now she is so sick they think she will die within the month. I am talking to you of uprisings and loyalties, but half my heart does not care at all if war comes to Gillengaria. Half my heart is up in that sickroom with Lyrie. I would sacrifice Baryn, I would sacrifice Rappengrass itself, to keep her alive."

Kirra felt a bolt of melancholy strike dead center into her heart, already tender with losses of its own. "Red-horse fever," she said. "I've heard of that. It's—they say it cannot be cured."

Ariane nodded. She was looking down at her hands. "That's what they say. I've had all kinds of healers in— mystics and physicians—those trained in magic and those trained in science. No one has been able to do anything for her except ease her pain for a day or two. I thought that Kirra— well, she's the best healer I've ever seen. I thought maybe she could do something that the others could not."

Now Kirra was the one to sit for a minute in silence. She already knew she had no antidote for this particular illness; she already knew she could not rout this poison with her hands. It was pointless to speculate, to wonder how she might insert herself into the sickroom, to hope that this time, with this child, her magic might be more powerful than death. It was stupid to think she could defeat someone else's despair even though she could not defeat her own.

"Casserah?" Ariane asked. "What did I say? I'm sorry—I

did not mean to offend you. Of course I am happy that you are here. I was not saying that I preferred your sister. I was just—"

Impulsively, Kirra took hold of the marlady's hands. "Ariane—I believe I can trust you. And the secret is not so terrible, really. It is just that I have been keeping it for many weeks now and had had no thought of revealing it, even to you."

Ariane looked wholly bewildered. "But—what secret? Casserah, you do not have to tell me anything that you—"

Kirra squeezed her hands more tightly. "Kirra. I'm Kirra. I have traveled the circuit pretending to be my sister because my father thought Casserah should meet all the nobles. But she refused to leave Danalustrous, so I agreed to a masquerade of sorts—"

"You're *Kirra*?" Ariane repeated, holding on to the one piece of information in that tumbling speech that made any sense to her. "But you—oh, this is just like you, it really is."

Kirra laughed, and dropped the other woman's hands. "Yes. But I don't see any reason—I mean, by now I've met everyone Casserah was supposed to impress—why can't I be Kirra from today on? We'll say Casserah was called back home. A message from my father. I have come to take her place during the final ball of the summer season. *You* will not be offended. And I can throw off a disguise that, truthfully, has become a bit difficult to maintain."

Ariane still looked slightly dazed. "But you—why would you do this? I mean, I'm happy to have whichever sister from Danalustrous chooses to grace my court, but—"

"Because I do not dare pretend Casserah has any magic," Kirra said, entirely sober now. "The fact that I am a mystic has done my father much harm—or would have, if he cared for anyone's opinion but his own. I cannot let there be even the slightest suspicion that Casserah also carries such a taint. I cannot go to that sickroom as my sister and touch that child and bring even a small measure of relief to her body. I can't do it. If I want to go to her, I have to go as myself. And Ariane, I don't know if there is anything at all I can do for her, but I want to try."

Ariane was trying not to cry. It was shocking to see tears on that strong, imperturbable face. "If you could do anything—anything at all—I would be so grateful—"

Kirra rose to her feet. "Give me an hour or two. It will take me that long to leave the Manor as Casserah and return as Kirra."

Ariane stood beside her, looking just a little shaky. "No one would even have to see you leave," she said. "None of the guards is watching for stray nobility on the way *out* of the gates. But you will have to come through the checkpoints like any other visitor or someone will grow suspicious."

Kirra smiled, then leaned in quickly and kissed the older woman on the cheek. "I can manage this," she said. "Be ready to receive me again in a couple of hours."

So it was that, solitary and on horseback, Casserah Danalustrous slipped out of the gates of Rappen Manor, and Kirra Danalustrous rode in. No one had stopped or questioned Casserah, who had been plainly dressed and not particularly notable; but Kirra had to explain to five different guards who she was and why she had chosen to visit. A half dozen nobles, coming and going on their own pursuits, witnessed her arrival. Those who knew her waved and called out greetings. Those who didn't looked curious and pleased when they learned that Malcolm Danalustrous's wildest daughter had chosen to come to Rappengrass for the summer ball.

The one gauntlet she had not expected to run unfolded just as she dismounted at the front doorway to introduce herself to yet another guard. "Can you send for Ralf?" she finally demanded with some of Casserah's haughtiness. "He knows me and will verify that I am allowed inside your doors."

"Indeed, serra," said the guard, respectful but unyielding. "The steward has been sent for."

"I appreciate that," she replied.

Their slight altercation had caught the interest of a lively party that had just stepped outside to tour the gardens. Kirra paid the group no attention until four people detached themselves from the larger mass and approached her.

"Kirra?" came Senneth's voice. "I thought I recognized you! What are you doing in Rappengrass?"

Cursing inwardly, Kirra turned to greet Senneth, who was accompanied by Amalie, Valri and—something of a surprise—Cammon. She should have hunted up her friends before making her transformation; the explanations would have been much less awkward then. "Senneth! I had hoped you would still be here." She dropped a curtsey. "Majesties."

Senneth turned to Cammon, who was staring at Kirra uncertainly. "Cam, you remember Kirra, don't you?" she said, malice in her voice.

"That's—that's Kirra?" he said faintly. "Oh! Of course it is! You look so much like your sister. Hello."

Cammon always had trouble telling when someone was in disguise. She probably looked no different to him now than she had yesterday, when she was shaped like Casserah, or even when she was wearing the form of a mountain lion. Unless someone told him, he would have no idea how he should address her, what role she had assumed now.

"She looks nothing like Casserah!" Amalie exclaimed, coming forward to give Kirra her hand. "But how good to see you again! I don't think we've met since I was a little girl. Everyone says such marvelous things about you. I have been hoping you would come back to Ghosenhall soon. I'm Amalie, if you don't remember me."

Kirra curtseyed again. "Your majesty is too gracious."

"Have you come to join your sister for the ball?" Amalie asked.

"Yes, why are you here?" Senneth asked, obviously still enjoying herself. "I didn't think your father would be able to spare both of you at the same time."

"In fact, he can't spare us both. Casserah has already left. I was a few hours behind the rider who came with a message from my father, asking her to return."

"Oh, no! I hope nothing dreadful has happened?" Amalie cried.

"No, no. Actually, if you want the truth of it, I think Casserah wrote *him* earlier, begging him to allow her to come home," Kirra said easily. She should have thought of a better story; she was improvising as she went. "In fact, I think she *threatened* to leave even if he didn't give permission, so he told her she could come home but not till I could be sent on my way to replace her. And here I am."

"I'll miss your sister. We all will," Valri said in her dark way. Kirra wondered if she could possibly be sincere. "I thought she was a very intelligent girl. Hard to sway. Not very impressionable."

"Well, *that's* all true," Kirra said. "I hope she behaved with reasonable friendliness to all the important parties."

"Indeed, she could hardly have been more charming," Senneth said. "I thought she might make a match of it with Darryn Rappengrass, but she told me later she thought he was more your type. I never did really get a feel for the kind of man she might like."

Kirra thought she might have to kill Senneth, right there in front of the guard. Fortunately, Ralf appeared in the doorway, bowing very low. "Serra Kirra," he said. "Your sister told us that we should be expecting you. You will be staying in the room that had been reserved for her. The marlady asks that you come see her as soon as you've had a moment to freshen up."

Now Senneth's gray eyes were sharp as she realized there was more to this visit than a whim of Kirra's. "Would you like me to show you to your room?" she asked. "It's right down the hall from mine."

"Not necessary," Kirra replied. She tried to send a message of reassurance. *This is a private matter between Ariane and me. Do not be concerned.* "I'll be by to see you as soon as I can. We'll have a lot to catch up on."

Ralf stooped to take Kirra's bag. Senneth hesitated, still unsure as to whether or not she should really leave. Cammon touched her on the sleeve.

"Everything's all right," he said in a voice too low for the guard to overhear. "Let's take Amalie to the gardens."

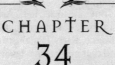

CHAPTER
34

TWENTY minutes later, Ariane led Kirra to the upper level of the fortress, where the family members had their suites. All of Rappen Manor was impressively and tastefully furnished, but this top story was particularly beautiful, Kirra thought. The stone floors were covered with wool rugs in rich hues; stained glass was set in all the windows, throwing wild jewels of color across the stern gray walls as the sun glittered through. The scents were homier, of candle wax and wood polish and fresh linen just now washed and folded and put away.

Ariane laid her hand on the knob of a door down the end of the wide main hallway. "She is probably sleeping," she said in a low voice, and stepped inside.

The room was darkened, curtains drawn against the afternoon sun, and smelled faintly of pungent herbs. Homemade medicines, Kirra guessed, mixed to ease the patient's pain. She made out a few vague objects in the semidarkness—a bed, a dresser, a couple of pieces of furniture. A small shape lay under thin covers on the bed. Two chairs were drawn so close to the bedside that the people sitting in them could touch the sleeping girl without even stretching.

As Kirra and Ariane stepped inside, a man stood up from

one of the chairs. The woman sitting beside him glanced over, but did not rise. Her face was pale against the dark fabric of the chair; her face was indifferent with exhaustion.

The man approached them and spoke in a whisper. "No change. She's sleeping now."

"I have brought someone to see her," Ariane whispered back. "Kirra, this is my son-in-law, Marco. That's my daughter, Bella, sitting by the bed. Marco, Kirra Danalustrous. She's a healer."

He made a sound that might have been a sigh or might have been the faint laugh of hopelessness. He did not bother with social niceties or even address her by her title. "Healers have not done us any good to date."

"No, and I have not had any luck curing this particular disease," Kirra admitted. "But I might be able to ease her pain a little, if she is indeed feeling pain now."

"Yes. Now, always," Marco replied. "That would be a blessing, though a short-lived one."

"I have your permission to touch her? Lyrie, is that her name?"

Marco stood aside and gestured toward the bed. "As long as you do not hurt Lyrie any more, you may try what you like."

Kirra approached the bed, nodding at Bella, who watched her without making any response. Gingerly, Kirra perched on the mattress, careful not to displace the frail body. Keeping her fingers as gentle as she could, she gripped the thin wrist and felt for the child's slow pulse.

Lyrie opened her eyes and looked straight up at her. Not sleeping after all. Kirra guessed the child was about eleven, though she was so wasted and fragile that it was hard to be certain. Her eyes, huge in her gaunt face, were liquid with pain and the wisdom that came from enduring unendurable things. Her face was as square as Ariane's. Kirra wondered if she also had Ariane's strength of character and indomitable spirit.

"Hello, Lyrie," she said softly. "My name is Kirra. I'm a healer. I understand you've been sick a long time."

Lyrie did not answer, but her head moved slightly on the pillow. *Yes.* Kirra continued, "I don't think that I can do anything to make the illness go away, but I might be able to stop the pain for a while. Should I try? Or would you rather I did not?"

"Try," Lyrie whispered. "Please."

"All right. I will."

She tightened her grip on the girl's wrist and put her other hand on the hot, dry skin at the base of Lyrie's throat. The covers were down far enough for Kirra to see the diamond-shaped housemark burned into her chest. She could feel the pain coiled along every joint, clustered at every nerve; she could feel the acid heating the blood as it coasted through every vein.

Her hand pressed harder on Lyrie's wrist, turning itself into a sieve, skimming the poisons from the blood. She moved her other hand to press down hard on Lyrie's heart, as if using her own weight to displace the knots of pain that clogged the girl's body. Lyrie's eyes widened, with discomfort or the tingle of magic, Kirra could not tell. She kept up the pressure on the veins, on the chest; she pictured the blood clean, the body exorcised. Lyrie's hot skin cooled beneath her fingers. Lyrie's tight mouth loosened in wonder.

"It doesn't hurt anymore," the girl whispered. "To breathe. It doesn't hurt anymore."

Kirra smiled at her, easing off a little. "Good. Can you make a fist? Do your muscles ache when you try to lift your arm?"

Lyrie balled her hand and punched at invisible enemies in the air. "No," she said, her voice growing stronger. "No, even my shoulder feels fine, and for the past few weeks—"

Kirra lifted her hands as Lyrie wriggled and sat up. Behind her, she could hear Bella stirring. Marco had already circled the bed and was standing on the other side, staring at his daughter with cautious delight. Kirra said, "Be careful. You might feel a little dizzy. Magic can have powerful effects."

Lyrie's face was wreathed with smiles as she settled her back against the pillow. "I don't care. I'd rather be dizzy. Oh, thank you so much, you—I can't remember your name—thank you, thank you—"

"Kirra," she supplied, smiling broadly in return. "I don't know how long the magic will hold. A few days, at least, before the pain comes back, maybe longer—"

Someone pushed past her. Bella, flinging herself on the bed. "Baby? You're feeling better? Baby, look at you! You're sitting up! Has the pain gone away? Would you like to eat something? Can I hug you? I don't want to hurt you—"

For an answer, Lyrie threw her arms around her mother's

neck. Kirra wasn't sure which of them started sobbing. She stood up and moved to stand beside Ariane, who was staring at the figures on the bed as if she could not trust her good fortune.

"It won't last," Kirra told her very quietly. "A few days."

"A day would be good enough," Ariane replied just as quietly. "I cannot express my gratitude. I have no words."

Marco had come around the bed to join them, leaving his wife to her joyful reunion with his daughter. "You cannot know what this means to us," he said earnestly to Kirra. "She has not spoken or eaten or allowed us to touch her for two weeks now—"

"I have only bought you a day or two—"

He put a hand to her shoulder. He was not much taller than she was and he looked her straight in the eye. "I would give up all of Rappengrass for an hour."

"I wish I could do more," Kirra said.

He dropped his hand, turned so he could watch his daughter smiling up at his wife. "No one can. There is no cure. And do you know the stupidest thing, the hardest thing? There *is* a cure. There is an herbal mix that you can feed to dogs and horses, and it will heal them in a week. No matter how sick they are, how far along the disease has progressed. But feed those herbs to people and they die. I know three families who have tried it. Every child has passed within a day."

Kirra stood in the dark sickroom and felt as if she had been seared by lightning.

A disease that affected animals and had migrated to humans. A disease that could be treated in animals. Not in humans.

But if humans could be transmogrified just long enough for the medicine to take hold—

Forbidden. A shape-shifter could not work the magic that would turn a living man or woman into any other creature. The Wild Mother would not allow it. The spells did not exist. Kirra did not know how to do such a thing, even if the act was not the severest transgression she could imagine. It was impossible.

But if she could save a life—

Forbidden.

Folk were already afraid of mystics and their uncontainable powers. If anyone suspected a shiftling had the power to transform *others* into random creatures against their will, no shape-changer would be safe. They would all be stoned in the streets, victims of a not unreasonable fear. *If mystics can change little girls into animals to heal them, they can change all sorts of people into animals to harm them.* Once acquired, such knowledge could not be unlearned—and it was such a tempting piece of knowledge. It would be so easy to turn it from a virtuous cause to a wicked one.

But if she could save this girl's life—

Her hand closed on the lion-shaped charm she always carried in her pocket. It felt smooth and warm under her fingers. She thought she could detect a small, buried heartbeat flickering through the striated stone, almost as if it was alive.

"Kirra? Kirra? Is something wrong?" Ariane's voice in her ear, Ariane's hand on her wrist. "Did you—did it drain too much energy from you to work your magic on Lyrie? Should you sit down? I can get you something to drink."

Kirra shook her head, forced herself to smile. "No. I'm fine. I was just thinking about what Marco said."

Marco, who was also staring at her, looked surprised. "What did I say?"

"I was thinking how sad it was that animals could be saved and children could not."

He nodded, his face darkening. "Tragic," he said. "I am so bitter that I almost cannot speak."

Kirra caught the sound of Lyrie's laugh, breathless but unmistakable. Bella called to Marco and gestured him over. He excused himself and hurried to the bed.

Kirra glanced over at Ariane to find the marlady staring at her. "What are you thinking?" Ariane demanded in a slow voice.

Kirra shook her head. "Things I cannot say aloud."

But Ariane was clever—as clever as Malcolm Danalustrous, who understood everything. She had already reviewed Marco's comment, thought over Kirra's abilities, and analyzed what might have made Kirra stand there gaping like a half-wit. She knew exactly what Kirra was thinking—and she did not look shocked at all. Instead, she said in a very quiet voice, "Can you do it?"

Kirra shook her head. "I don't know. I never have."

"If you can—"

"It is prohibited."

"If you can—then I want you to try."

"Ariane—"

"I will beg you, if you want. I will give you anything. You can marry my son and inherit my property. If you can save this girl."

"If I could save her, I would do it without inducements. I don't know if I can work the spell."

Ariane stared at her another moment. "*Try,*" she breathed.

Kirra stood for a moment, utterly motionless. Then she nodded. "Let me see what I can figure out."

BY an amazing stroke of good fortune, Senneth was back from her outing with the princess and the princess was taking an afternoon nap. Therefore, Senneth was not in Amalie's room, Coeval informed her kindly, but across the hall with the Riders and "that strange boy."

Better and better and better.

Kirra entered the room without knocking and found her luck still holding. No other outsiders present, not even Hammond, just Cammon and Justin and Senneth playing cards and looking bored, Tayse stretched out on the room's double bed, taking a chance to sleep.

"Sen," Kirra said, locking the door behind her. "I need to talk to you."

Justin glanced at her, glanced back at his cards, and then jerked his head up. "What are you doing here?" he demanded. "Why are you Kirra?"

"Is she still Kirra?" Cammon asked in some relief. "Just make sure someone tells me if she's ever Casserah again."

"I'll be Kirra for the rest of the trip," she said impatiently. "Senneth—"

Senneth had come to her feet. Her face was concerned but the posture of her body indicated strength and purpose and determination. It was impossible to feel afraid or defeated when Senneth was in the room. "What's wrong?"

Tayse, who had looked to be comatose a moment ago, rolled to a sitting position and swung his legs over the side of the bed. "Don't tell me Halchon Gisseltess is back," he said.

"Nothing so simple," Kirra said. "I need—an opinion. I need advice. I don't know what to do."

There was a moment's studied silence, and she realized they all thought she was speaking of her illicit romance. For a moment she wanted to laugh out loud; she actually had not thought of Romar for the entire day. Donnal, yes. Donnal she wished was here at this conference, for he could help her more than any of them. He was the only other one who understood shape-shifting; he was the one who could help her work through the spells or tell her flat out she would be a fool to try them. But Donnal was gone. She would never see Donnal again.

"Advice about what?" Justin finally asked.

She ignored him; pretty much she ignored all of them but Senneth. She kept her gaze on Senneth's gray eyes as she slowly told her story. "Ariane's granddaughter is dying of redhorse fever. It's a disease for which not even mystics have a cure. Her son-in-law just told me that when horses and dogs get this same disease, they can be treated with an herbal potion and they survive. But the same potion will kill a human."

Senneth's face sharpened; she thought it through as quickly as Ariane had, as Kirra had. "I thought you didn't know those spells."

"I don't."

"What spells?" Justin demanded.

Tayse had crossed the room so silently that he was standing beside the card table before Kirra had even realized he was moving. "You want to change this child into an animal?" he asked.

"I thought that was forbidden!" Justin exclaimed.

Kirra glanced at each of them in turn. "It is. And I don't know if I can do it. And I don't know if I *should* do it. I don't know if that suddenly means—" She waved her hands, unable to explain.

"Means that mystics are even more fearsome than people believed they were," Senneth supplied. "Means that you put yourself and every other mystic in danger by proving how very powerful we are."

"Yes," Kirra said.

"But a little girl is dying?" Cammon asked. "Well, you have to do what you can to save her. Don't you?"

Kirra gave him a brief, tight smile. "I don't know if I can do this. I've never done it. What if I try to change her—and I kill her?"

"She's going to die anyway," Senneth said.

Kirra nodded. "But I don't want it to be at my hands."

"Practice on someone else first," Cammon suggested. "Practice on me." They all looked at him in silence. "What?" he said. "I'm not afraid."

"Thank you," Kirra said. "But I don't think you'd be a good choice. You're too open to magic. Even if I *could* change you, it wouldn't prove anything. I would need to practice on someone ordinary."

"I wonder if Melly would do it," Senneth said.

Kirra considered. "She might. She seems to trust me. But what a thing to ask someone! Especially a servant! Would she only agree because she cannot afford to offend House Danalustrous? I would not want to take advantage of her that way."

"Then perhaps Ariane could supply someone who would be willing to undergo your experiment. One of her vassals. An older man who does not have much left to live for," Senneth said.

Tayse snorted. "Even old men tend to want to die with some dignity," he said. "And being turned into a dog—or unsuccessfully turned into a dog—sounds like an ignominious end."

"Yes, and even if I can manage the transformation *into* another creature, I don't know if I can reverse it!" Kirra exclaimed. "I mean, I might have to leave him as a dog forever! Not a bad existence, speaking as one who's lived it from time to time, but certainly not one that most people would choose!"

"You would have to explain the risks very carefully," Senneth said. "You would have to find someone willing to volunteer."

Kirra gave a short laugh. "Ariane would, I know it. She would be willing to do almost anything at this point to save her granddaughter."

"Ariane Rappengrass cannot be spared," Tayse said.

"I know. But her son-in-law, maybe—he seems to love his daughter enough to risk his life."

"I'll do it," Justin said.

They stared at him.

He shrugged. "I will. I'm no more afraid than Cammon is."

Kirra shook her head, tried to speak. It was hard to find her voice. "Justin," she said. "I don't know that you can be spared, either."

He smiled at her, jaunty and cool. The Rider who feared nothing. The street urchin who gambled with his life every day. He had not even looked at Tayse to get the other Rider's permission, something he always did almost as a matter of course. "I trust you," he said.

"I'm not sure I trust myself."

"You can do it," Cammon said. "I'll help you."

Kirra looked at him helplessly. "How?"

He held out his hand. "Give me that charm you always carry."

She flicked a look at Senneth, who was trying hard not to smile. This was Cammon at his most eerie. How did he know about the little lioness? And why could he possibly want it now? Kirra fished it out of her pocket and handed it to him. "Why?"

Cammon's fingers closed over the figurine and Kirra felt a jolt of power lick through her veins. She stiffened and bunched her fingers into fists. Senneth was watching them both curiously. "What just happened?" Senneth asked.

"Cammon. He did something."

Cammon seemed wholly nonchalant. "Kirra picked up this little piece from the Wild Mother's shrine. It's some kind of amplifier. Like the moonstone is a damper. It's rich with the wild god's power."

"Then—shouldn't Kirra be the one to hold on to it?" Tayse asked. "If she's going to be playing with the wild god's magic?"

But Senneth got it first. "Cammon's an amplifier, too," she said quietly. "He has power of his own, and he can channel it through this charm, feed it to Kirra. Or at least he thinks he can."

Cammon grinned. "Pretty sure I can."

Kirra's voice was strangled. "Oh, he can. I can feel it. It's like a fever, only better than that. My veins feel like they're full of sparks. Am I glowing? I feel like I should be."

"You look the same," Tayse said.

"Let's get started," Justin said. "What do I do?"

Kirra looked around, nervous and distracted. "Um—I suppose—get on the floor, on your hands and knees."

"Do I need to take my clothes off?"

She shook her head. "No. They'll be the easiest part of you to change. Just get comfortable."

Justin settled himself on the floor, resting on his heels, hands braced before him. "Will it hurt?"

"Well, it never hurts *me*, but I don't know. It shouldn't. If it does—if it does—cry out or raise a hand or—or do something, and I'll try to stop. But Justin, I don't know if I can—"

He cut her short. "All right. I'm ready."

She knelt before him, put her hands on his shoulders. She had never done this spell before, but she knew she had to touch him to make it work. His muscles were relaxed under her hands. He stared straight into her eyes, but she could not read fear anywhere on his face.

Cammon stood behind her and she could feel him like a blacksmith's forge, radiating magic as if it were heat. Her own skin was flushed with it; her hands felt hot enough to burn through Justin's shirt. If someone cut her open now, she was sure her blood would run opal.

She closed her eyes and imagined Justin as a dog. Some scruffy butterscotch mutt, the kind likely to be found in any back alley snarling over a scrap of food, face crossed with old scars, rangy and fit and mean. Even the bigger dogs were afraid of him, and the small ones whimpered at his approach. But his plumed tail showed a ragged elegance; his eyes were dark with intelligence. This was a dog that could be cleaned up and put to good use if someone had the patience to train him. . . .

She heard Senneth's gasp and her eyes flew open. That very dog sat before her, a little lighter in color than she had visualized, with a brighter, more inquiring expression. Her hands—too hot to even feel the transformation as it occurred—fell limply to her sides. He sat there very still, watching her, as if he didn't realize he was no longer human, as if he didn't know what he should be expecting.

"Justin," she said in a quiet voice. "You've successfully made the transition. Can you tell? You can stand up—you can move around—"

The dark eyes dropped, and he lifted first one paw, then another. Somewhat hesitantly, he came to all four feet and took a few tentative steps—and then a few more, as he got used to his unfamiliar body. Suddenly he bounded across the room, leaping across a low table just for the pleasure of feeling his muscles stretch, jumping to the bed and down to the floor again. The open window caught his eye. He scrambled over to it, put his forelegs up on the sill, and peered out. Whatever he saw pleased him, and he released three short barks.

That pleased him even more, and he dropped to his feet again, barking joyously. He had a deep, throaty voice, musical and appealing, and it was clear he loved the sound. Barking still, he bounded back over to Kirra where she knelt on the floor, and knocked her over with exuberance. She flung up a hand to protect herself, but too late; he had already licked her across the face.

"That's Justin," Tayse said dryly.

Kirra elbowed him away and he dashed over to Senneth, licking her fingers and frolicking around her feet. She laughed and leaned down to scratch the top of his head. Kirra pushed herself back to a sitting position and looked at Cammon over her shoulder.

"You can tell he's a dog, can't you?" she said. "I mean, I know you're never blinded by magic, you always see the essence of things, but you can tell he's changed, can't you?"

"Sort of," Cammon said. "I can tell he's a dog but—he still looks like Justin. I would never mistake him for an ordinary animal."

The sound of Cammon's voice caught the mongrel's attention. He left Senneth's side and flung himself at Cammon, bringing both of them to the floor. Cammon yelped with laughter and the two of them wrestled for a few minutes.

"A boy and his dog," Senneth said. "It's so touching."

Tayse looked at Kirra. "Was that hard?"

She shook her head. "It's frightening how easy it was."

"Will you be able to change him back?"

She nodded.

"I don't think he wants to be changed back," Senneth said.

"Even if that were his preference," Tayse said, "she has to prove she can do it, or the whole experiment is worthless."

Justin pulled himself off of Cammon and trotted back to

plant himself in front of Tayse. Now he barked out a long, earnest sentence, as if he was trying to communicate, as if he really thought they might understand him.

Kirra looked at Cammon. "So? What's he saying?"

Cammon was tucking his shirt back in his trousers. "No idea. Sounds like he thinks it's important."

"Time to end this," Tayse said.

Kirra couldn't help herself. She whistled as she would have to any of her father's hounds. "Here, boy," she called. Justin's head pulled around as if he would respond, and then it was clear the insult registered. He planted himself more firmly, lowering his head in an attitude of defiance.

"Oh, yes," said Kirra. "I'd be able to pick him out of a pack any day."

He didn't move off when she scooted over to sit next to him, though. He did lick her wrist when she put one hand on the top of his head. "Settle down," she commanded. "I have to concentrate. You don't want *this* to be the part I get wrong, do you?"

He gave a big doggie yawn, his pink tongue curling in disdain. She looked at Tayse. "Can't I just leave him like this?"

Tayse barely smiled. "No."

Justin's tongue brushed her hand again. She put both palms on either side of his narrow face and said, "Sit still." Cammon came over, so close she could feel his knee against her back. That sparkling heat filled her again, made her veins sizzle.

This time she didn't close her eyes. She stared down at the dog and thought of Justin, with his sandy hair and scoffing expression and warrior's reflexes. She hated him and she loved him and he was her friend, and she conjured him up from memory and will.

His metamorphosis was as rapid as Donnal's always were. One moment, a mutt. The next, a man, crouched on the floor with his face between her hands. There was a frozen minute when no one spoke or moved, and then Justin pulled himself free and stood up. He was laughing. Kirra had never seen him look so absolutely given over to delight.

"*That's* something I want to do again!" he exclaimed. "I never had so much fun! And think of the possibilities! Tayse, can you imagine? She could send a whole battalion of soldiers across enemy lines, disguised as cats or squirrels or birds, and once they were in position, they would be turned back into men—"

"Precisely the reason people fear shiftlings," Senneth murmured.

"How were your senses? Did you lose your regular thought processes?" Tayse wanted to know.

"No! It was—it was strange, my body felt strange, but I—and my eyes were different, what I could see—but I could hear things and smell things—it would take a little practice, I think, but I could run a race in that shape, or catch a rabbit or—just be a dog."

Cammon reached down to pull Kirra off the floor. She said, "You don't lose your sense of self. It's filtered a little, but it's still there. It's hard to explain."

Tayse looked at her. "*Could* you really change a whole battalion of soldiers and send them across enemy lines?"

She laughed nervously. "I don't know. I didn't even know I could do this."

"Something to think about," Tayse said.

"Later," Senneth said. "Today she has a little girl to heal."

CAMMON accompanied her to the dark room in the upper story. Ariane, Bella, and Marco were all still there. Lyrie was sitting up in bed, eating what looked like toast. She smiled and waved from across the room when Kirra stepped through the door.

Ariane met them before they had gone three paces. "Well? What have you decided?"

"I think I can do this. I think I can try," Kirra amended. "I am afraid to make promises. But someone must explain to Lyrie—"

"She wants to do it," Ariane interrupted. "I asked her—when you were gone—I told them all what you were thinking."

"And they agreed? All of them? Because if I make a mistake, it will be a terrible one."

"Marco has already been to the stables and gotten a bundle of herbs from the head groom. He told the man that one of the house dogs had fallen sick, and the groom told him how to mix the potion. Everyone wants to do this, Kirra."

"I just want you to be sure."

"I'm sure."

But she asked Lyrie, too, when she seated herself once more on the side of the bed. "You understand what I want to do?" she asked, studying the wide, eager face.

"Yes. You're going to turn me into a dog. And I'll take medicine for a week and then I'll be better."

"If everything works. If the magic holds, if the potion is just right, if I am able to do the spells. Lyrie, I have never done this before, and I—"

"I want to," the girl interrupted. "Please. I don't care if it hurts."

"It won't hurt," Cammon said.

Lyrie and her relatives all looked at him. "This is Cammon," Kirra said hastily. "He's also a mystic. Not a shape-shifter, a—Well, a man with strange gifts. He's going to help me."

He smiled down at Lyrie. Impossible, but he seemed entirely at ease. "I'll be able to tell if something's going wrong," he said. "If something's hurting you. I'm good at reading people's emotions."

Lyrie looked interested. "Will you be able to talk to me when I'm a dog?"

"Probably not," Cammon said.

Bella leaned forward and touched Lyrie's hand to get her attention. "Baby, you understand you'll have to be a dog for a few days. A week. You understand it takes a long time for the medicine to take effect."

"I know," Lyrie said.

"She'll be able to understand you," Kirra said. "She'll hear everything you say. She'll *think* like a little girl. She just won't—look like one. Her body will be shaped differently. Her spirit will not change."

Bella looked terrified, but she nodded. "All right," she whispered. "Then let's get started."

It went just as it had with Justin. Lyrie sat in the bed, trustfully looking up at Kirra; Cammon stood behind her, waves of magic rolling off his body. Kirra put her hands on Lyrie's face and pictured a beloved, shaggy spaniel—small, dark-haired, sunny-tempered. This time, she felt the flat skin turn to curly fur beneath her fingers. She saw the skull melt down, the body reshape. She saw Lyrie transformed before her eyes.

Bella took a short, sharp breath and pressed her hand against her mouth. Marco did not waste time with astonishment. The instant the alteration was complete, he was kneeling on the bed beside his daughter, a bowl of shredded meat in his hand. Kirra could see how the ground green leaves of the herbs were mixed in with the main dish.

"Here," he said, holding it to his daughter's short, pointed nose. "Eat this. We want you to start getting well."

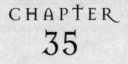

CHAPTER
35

AFTER that, Kirra knew, it was going to be hard to consider any other event of the Rappengrass stopover to be anything but anticlimactic. She danced back down to her room, Cammon at her heels, evanescent with magic and success.

"You're going to need to sleep for a while," he warned her, and she didn't believe him.

"I feel wonderful. I feel—really, I feel like I'm flying, and I *know* what it feels like to fly."

He pushed her toward her own room. "Trust me. Lie down for a little bit."

"Am I going to get a headache like one of Senneth's?"

"I don't know. But I think once the euphoria's gone, you're going to feel like red hell."

He held his hand out and she took the lion charm. The instant it left his palm, she felt her own body sag; hundredweights lined every bone. She staggered back, fetching up hard against her own door. "Oh," she said. "It was you."

"Well, some of it was me. Some of it was your own magic. But you'd better sleep now."

"I think you're right," she said. She fumbled with the door latch and he had to help her inside. Melly was there to lead her to the bed, asking questions, exhibiting real concern. Kirra let

Cammon offer explanations or reassurance, she didn't care. She tumbled to bed and was almost instantly asleep.

Twilight had fallen by the time she awoke—at least two hours later, she judged. She was famished. She sat up in bed, wondering if there was anything in her room that would pass for food. She couldn't wait till dinner. Perhaps she had already *missed* dinner. She'd have to take hawk shape, she'd have to hunt, she had to eat now, she was so hungry—

"Are you awake? Cammon said you'd be starving," came Melly's voice and, bless that girl, she approached the bed with a tray of fruits and pastries. "This was all I could get from the kitchen, but dinner's in an hour. You've got time to dress and go down."

Kirra was cramming food in her mouth in a most unlady-like fashion. "Yes. Yes, I certainly do want dinner. Let me wear—I don't care—anything that fits."

"Did you change your wardrobe when you changed yourself?" Melly asked, sounding curious rather than accusatory. "Because if you didn't—"

Kirra laughed. "Oh, a dress is a simple thing to convert," she said merrily. "Just pull something out and throw it on my back. I'll make it fit."

Fifty minutes later, her hunger only partly appeased, she headed downstairs, dressed in angelic blue and feeling a resurgence of well-being. Ariane had mentioned that tonight's dinner would be an informal buffet. Guests would mingle and talk and pause to eat and mingle some more. It sounded most charming. Especially the eating part.

Kirra had forgotten, while she was practicing miracles, that she had changed into a shape that most people here were not expecting. So when she stepped into the dining room, set up with buffet counters and a random arrangement of tables, she was almost instantly taken by surprise.

"Kirra! What are you doing here?" someone squealed, and she found herself enduring Mayva Nocklyn's breathless embrace. "You look wonderful! Casserah didn't say you were coming."

Oh—yes—Casserah. Time to make explanations. Edging over to the food trays, Kirra lightly tossed off her version of the truth. *Casserah got homesick and said she wanted to return to Danan Hall. My father sent me to take her place. Oh, yes, Casserah's already gone. We passed each other on the road. . . .* Mayva, it turned out, was not the only one who wanted to hear the story. Darryn and Seth Stowfer and Eloise Kianlever and all the nobles she'd had a single conversation with over the past few weeks each approached her with the same astonishment and set of questions. Everyone seemed happy to see her, though, and that was gratifying.

"A very elegant girl, Casserah, but not really warm," Eloise pronounced. "She frightens me a little, to tell you the truth. No one that young should be so self-possessed."

And the real Casserah would intimidate you even more than I did, Kirra thought. "She was born that way," Kirra said. "But tell me, how are *you* doing? It's been ages since we've talked."

Romar was not in the room when she first walked in—she had searched for him as soon as she had filled her plate—but after the guests had been gathered for an hour or so, she saw him stride through the doorway. He scanned the crowd, seeming to look for someone he didn't see, then made his way to Amalie's side. Kirra watched for a moment, trying to curb her smile, then ambled over, a plate of cake in her hand.

"Maybe you should ask Senneth," Amalie was saying. "I don't like to think that you—oh, there's Kirra. I haven't seen you all evening."

Romar turned so fast that he actually spilled a little of his wine. The expression on his face was comical—surprise, delight, worry, and just a hint of desire—but he wiped it off before Amalie could glance back over at him.

"You know Kirra Danalustrous, don't you? Her sister was called home, and Kirra has come to take her place."

"Yes, indeed, Kirra and I shared a very adventurous journey back from Tilt this spring," Romar said, putting his glass down. He dried his fingers on a tablecloth, laughed, and held out his hand. "Good to see you again, serra. I hope you've been well."

"I am doing splendidly," she replied, giving him a deep curtsey. "I am delighted to be at Rappen Manor! I felt very glum to be left behind while Casserah was having all the fun. I'm glad she went home."

"Oh, but I'll miss her," Amalie said.

"Nonsense," Kirra said. "I'm sure you'll like me much better."

Her high spirits amused Romar, she could tell, particularly after her edginess the night before. "I assume you'll be staying for the ball tomorrow night?" he asked.

"Absolutely! I've missed all the other balls. I'll certainly be here for this one."

"Come back with us to Ghosenhall afterward," Amalie invited. "My father is holding a dinner party for some foreign ambassadors. I know he'd like to have you there."

Kirra hadn't given much thought to where she would go after Rappengrass, unofficially the last stop on the summer circuit. "Perhaps I will," she said. "It sounds most intriguing. Ambassadors from where?"

"Arberharst and Karyndein, which is even farther west than Sovenfeld. I think the people will be quite exotic."

"I'll be there," Romar said. "If that's any inducement."

Kirra laughed. She had to put some effort into it not to sound giddy. "It most certainly is."

"Good," Amalie said. "I'll write my father to expect you."

Eloise Kianlever claimed Amalie's attention then. Kirra and Romar allowed themselves to step a few paces away to have what passed for a private conversation under such circumstances.

"Why are you really here?" Romar asked in a low voice. "I'm elated to see you, of course, but I can't think of a reason for the change."

"Ariane's granddaughter is very sick and she was hoping I could heal her. It seemed best to attempt such a maneuver when I could appear as myself. Anyone who knows Casserah would believe she is entirely capable of leaving someone's house simply because she's bored with the whole social round. Time for Kirra to make an appearance."

"And could you? Heal the little girl?"

She laughed again. By the Wild Mother's woolly head, she felt so *good*. "Yes. I believe I did. We won't know for a few days."

"And will you really come to Ghosenhall for the dinner?"

"Of course. Any reason I shouldn't?"

He shook his head. "I was afraid to hope you would come. Another few days to spend with you—what a gift from the gods that would be."

"Well, of course, I would be coming to see the *ambassadors*, not you, precisely."

He shook his head again, smiling now. "Then we shall have to make do with what time we have left while we are together here. My room is on the second floor, overlooking the front drive. Will you come to me tonight?"

"Any reason I shouldn't?" she repeated, whispering now.

"No," he replied, his voice very low. "And every reason you should."

BUT it was strange that night, different. She was happy when she first arrived, wandering in through his open window like a painted moth, all dusty colors and love of light. As soon as she was shaped like a woman again, he kissed her hungrily, embracing her so tightly that her ribs protested. She had a sudden, sharp memory of Donnal's gentle kiss good-bye, and it made her turn vague and heavy in Romar's arms, despite his passion.

He did not seem to notice. "It has been so long since I have held you," he said with a groan when she pulled free and took a deep breath.

"Only one night."

He kissed her again, even harder. "One night, and I could hardly bear that. How will I stand all the nights in between? When you're gone and I'm back in Merrenstow?"

Back in Merrenstow with your wife. She didn't say it, but the thought cast another cloud over her joy. The world seemed suddenly full of inconstant people. "You must find other women to love instead," she said, her voice light, making a joke of it.

He wasn't amused. "That's not funny."

She pulled back even farther, though his arms remained loosely linked around her waist. She feigned a smile. "You could lie with a redhead one night," she said, casting her hair back, curly and flame-colored. "Bed a blonde the next." Now her hair was a silken river of yellow, running down her back and spilling across his arms. "Then a dark-haired girl—"

He grabbed her by the shoulders and shook her. "Stop it. Stop that. I don't want other women. I want Kirra."

She twisted free and moved away. "Kirra will do for now," she said. "But when you can't have Kirra—"

He followed, caught her arm. "I will wait till I can have Kirra again."

"I won't hold it against you," she said. "If you take another lover while I am away. Just tell me what she looks like, so I will know what shape to assume when I creep to your bed one night in her place—"

Now he jerked her into his arms again, covering her face with kisses. His own face was riven with remorse; she thought she caught a glitter of tears in his eyes. "No one will take your place, no one," he whispered in her ear. "Why would you talk that way? Why would you say such things?"

She could have pulled herself free or changed into some smaller shape and melted out of his arms, but she didn't want to. She wanted him to hold her, reassure her, pledge his love. She wanted him to love her so much he was worth giving up everyone else. "Because I am so afraid," she whispered back. "Because I love you so much and I cannot have you. Because sometimes it is easier to believe I mean very little to you, so that I can pretend you mean very little to me."

His hands were buried in her hair, his thumbs tangling in the thick curls. His own hair was unbound and she could see its darker gold mingling with hers, falling forward to form a sort of curtain over their faces. "Then I cannot make it easier for you," he said. "For you mean everything in the world to me, and I cannot pretend otherwise."

He kissed her then, not allowing her to respond. She had no reply to make, anyway, nothing that expressed her feelings any better than a kiss. They fell to the bed, still embraced, still desperate, and made love as if they might never see each other again.

THE day of the ball passed, as all such days did, with a coiled laziness that would unfold to a near frenzy as the hour of the event drew near. Kirra slept late, dressed casually, and made a quick trip up to the third story of the Manor. Lyrie was curled in a tight black ball in the middle of the bed, Bella sleeping beside her with one hand tucked into the fur on the back of the spaniel's neck.

Marco greeted her with a smile. "The medicine seems to be working already," he said. "She passed a very restful night, and this morning she—well, she was playing like a puppy. It's very strange. She's an animal, a *dog*, and yet I can tell it's Lyrie. The way she watches me, the way she comes over to sit beside me— this whole experience should be so odd, and yet it doesn't feel odd, because I can tell it's her."

"But she's better, you said? I'm so pleased!"

"I can't even put into words how I feel," he replied. "Or even guess how to thank you."

"Thank me later," she said. "When she's well."

Leaving the sickroom, Kirra spent a good half hour tracking down her friends, who were nowhere inside the house. She eventually found most of them—Senneth, Amalie, Valri, and Cammon—down in the gardens. They were sitting on a blanket under a huge tree, sipping lemonade, and watching other guests stroll past. Justin stood, very straight and very fierce-looking, a few paces behind them.

Kirra plopped down and said, "Doesn't anyone ever ask who this young man is who follows the princess around everywhere? He's certainly not a noble, and he's *certainly* not a guard. Don't they wonder what his function is? Can I have some lemonade?"

Senneth passed her a glass. "He's her gigolo," she said.

Cammon scrambled to his knees, managed a shaky head-stand, and tumbled back onto the blanket. "I'm the royal fool," he said.

"He's my friend," Amalie said.

Valri gave her a stern look. "Princesses don't have chance friends drawn from the lower classes."

Cammon looked hurt but resolute. "Should I go, then? I will."

Now the young queen turned her impossible green eyes on him. "No. Of course not. We rely on you to help keep Amalie safe. We just must be prepared to answer questions about you. Though none have come up so far."

Amalie looked mutinous. "He's my friend," she repeated. "Just as Senneth is. And Kirra. And Justin. What's the point of being a princess if you can't pick your friends?"

A shadow moved over them and resolved into a man as Romar dropped to the blanket beside his niece. "As far as I can tell, there are no other advantages to being royalty," he agreed. "So don't let them make you give up the ones you love. Hello, sweet." And he leaned over and kissed her on the cheek.

"Well, I won't," Amalie said.

Kirra carefully rearranged her skirts and didn't look at him. Romar wasn't royalty, but perhaps the comment had been aimed at her as well. *I won't give up the ones I love, either.* "So is everyone feeling rested and beautiful for the ball tonight?" she asked.

"Not rested, not beautiful, but *relieved*," Valri answered in her dark voice. "Finally. The last event, and then we can go home."

"My opinion exactly," Senneth said. "I don't care if I never attend another dinner or another dance as long as I live."

"But you're coming to the dinner party back in Ghosenhall, aren't you?" Amalie asked a shade anxiously. "You said you would."

Senneth smiled at her. "Yes, of course. But after that, I'm disappearing for a few weeks. No matter what favor your father asks of me. You won't need me once you're safe at the palace."

Kirra thought it was highly unlikely Baryn would allow Senneth to slip away like that now that she had proved so useful, but she didn't say so. Her attention was caught by a dark figure pacing deliberately up the flagged walkway of the garden. Tayse, dressed all in black, looking even more dangerous than Justin. Must be time for the Riders to change shifts. "'Disappearing for a few weeks,'" she repeated thoughtfully. "Where will you be going? Will you be traveling alone? Perhaps you should bring someone with you for company."

Senneth smiled. "Perhaps I will."

"So, when do we leave?" Valri asked. "Tomorrow morning? I can be packed tonight by midnight."

Kirra studied her feet. "I won't be able to leave for a few more days," she said, elaborately casual. "But you don't have to wait for me."

"And why is that?" Romar asked.

"I told you. Ariane's granddaughter is sick. I think I need to stay until I'm sure she's well. In case there's—something more I can do for her." *So I can change her back from a dog.*

Cammon's strange eyes were on her face. "I'll wait with you," he said. "So you don't have to travel back alone."

She smiled at him. He had to wait with her; she wasn't sure she could do this by herself. "That's kind of you."

"The rest of us then," Valri said. "Tomorrow?"

"I can't," Romar said, and Kirra's heart skipped a beat. He would manufacture some excuse to linger at Rappen Manor a few more days, and they could travel back to Ghosenhall together. She hadn't allowed herself to hope for that possibility; she knew he was eager to stay with his niece's entourage. "I could go the following day, though, if you all want to wait."

Kirra's little flare of excitement died and she kept her eyes down so he wouldn't see her disappointment. Senneth asked, "What keeps you here another night?"

"I've been invited to attend a dinner. Apparently there's no Shadow Ball in Rappengrass, but something not too dissimilar. The marlady's vassals and a few friends gather at a dinner party the night *after* the ball, so they can discuss everything the nobles said and did and what effect all this saying and doing might have on their own lives. I've been to a couple of the Shadow Balls, and it seems to please the Thirteenth House. So I said I would go to this as well."

"I don't think you should," Cammon said.

There was a short pause, full of enough portentous silence that even the Riders, conferring a few feet away, turned their heads to stare. Romar looked annoyed, but Kirra could see that Senneth's face wore an expression very like her own, full of tension and dread.

"Cam," Senneth said in a quiet voice, "why shouldn't the regent attend this dinner?"

"I think somebody wants to kill him."

Amalie gasped; Valri straightened up and looked severe. Senneth motioned the Riders over and they dropped to their knees on the edges of the blanket.

"What's wrong?" Tayse asked.

"Lord Romar says he's been invited to a dinner party tomorrow, hosted by some of Ariane's vassals," Senneth said concisely. "Cammon says he shouldn't go because someone wants to kill him."

"How can he possibly know something like that?" Romar demanded, vexed.

"If Cammon says it, it's true," Justin said.

"Uncle, you can't go," Amalie said, putting her hand on his sleeve. "Leave with us tomorrow morning."

Tayse kept his dark eyes on Cammon's face. "Do you know who wants to kill him?"

Cammon shook his head. "No. It's just this feeling." He glanced around the circle of alarmed or doubting faces. "You know I said something the other day. That I didn't think he was safe. But not until he mentioned this dinner did it seem—did I know—I can just tell. There's something wrong. Something's been planned. For the dinner."

"Uncle Romar, you *can't go*," Amalie said more urgently.

"She's right. He can't," Tayse said.

Romar shifted impatiently on the blanket. "I appreciate your concern. I find it hard to believe Cammon could—but I'll take him at his word. I'll be cautious. I'll bring Colton and—"

"Not good enough," Tayse said.

"Still," Senneth said thoughtfully. "If he went, forewarned, and someone tried to murder him, and we could stop it—we'd learn who among the Thirteenth House is plotting against the king."

"*If* you could stop it," Valri said. "But could you?"

"Tayse and I go dressed in Merrenstow colors as his personal guard," Justin said. "Senneth, too."

"Me," Cammon said. "I could tell when someone was approaching him with a weapon in hand. Well, probably I could."

Tayse shook his head. "Still not good enough. We'd be in the courtyard or out in the hallway. Too far to help."

"I'll go," Kirra said quietly. "Shaped as Lord Romar. Whoever is plotting against him will try to kill me instead."

Now they were all staring at her.

"No," Romar said before anyone else could speak.

But Tayse was nodding. "That's a good plan."

"How is that a good plan?" Romar exclaimed. "The woman can't even hold a weapon! She can't defend herself! Someone approaches her with a sword—or throws a dagger at her—"

"She changes," Senneth said. "She's a hawk. The blade never touches her."

"What if she's not fast enough?"

"Put chain mail on under her clothes," Tayse said. "It will turn a knife aside long enough for her to alter."

"If the knife is aimed at her heart! What if it is aimed at her throat? Or her head?"

"I think I can outmaneuver it long enough to escape," Kirra said.

Romar was shaking his head. "No. No. You think it's too dangerous for me to go, fine, I won't go. But don't send Kirra, either. Let the whole Thirteenth House rise up in rebellion, but don't send someone else toward assassination in my place."

Kirra laughed. "I won't be assassinated."

He looked at her, and the naked terror in his eyes struck her to the heart. "I could not bear it if you died," he said quietly.

Tayse rested his big hands on his knees. "It's up to Kirra," he said. "I think Senneth's right. This is an ideal opportunity for us to discover who among the Thirteenth House is allied against the king. But it *is* risky, even with the rest of us in place."

"I'll go," Kirra said. "I want to."

"No," Romar said. "If anyone goes, it's me."

Tayse gave him a stern, heavy look. "Regent, you cannot be risked. You are too valuable."

"So is Kirra!"

"I would hate to lose her, but it would be a personal loss for me, for her friends, for her family," said Tayse. "If you were killed, it would be a blow to the kingdom. This is what it means to be one step away from the throne, lord. That you cannot always fight your own battles. That your life matters more than another's."

"It doesn't," Romar said. "Not more than Kirra's."

"I want to do this," Kirra said, smiling at the whole lot of them. Amalie looked terrified, Valri uncertain, and Romar was stiff with protest, but the other four were watching her with trust and approval. They were not afraid for her, just as none of them feared for themselves. "I think it will be fun."

"'Fun,'" Romar repeated, and shook his head again. "No, no, no, as often as I have to say it, no."

Justin was watching him steadily. "Is it because she's a woman?" the Rider asked.

"What? No! Well—maybe," Romar said, risking a quick glance at Kirra. She could read that look. *It is because she's the woman I love.* "Partly."

"Because, no offense, lord, but if I had to choose one of you to be on my side in a fight, I would pick Kirra," Justin said. Astonishment made Kirra's mouth fall open, but he wasn't done yet. "You're not a bad swordsman. I'd trust you at my back, but Kirra is clever. And she's got a range of skills you simply don't possess. And nothing frightens her. If we're going to send someone to this dinner in your place, Kirra's the one to send."

"And I think we send someone," Senneth added.

"I'm not sure," Amalie said.

Senneth gave the princess one long, unsmiling look. "Majesty, you know we could be headed toward war. What we learn tomorrow night may help avert it. Isn't it better to risk one life than to see thousands cut down in fighting?"

"I'm going to go," Kirra said. "It's up to the rest of you to keep the regent from following me and spoiling the adventure."

"We'll assign Coeval and Hammond to hold on to him," Tayse said with a glimmering of a smile. "The rest of us will be with you."

THAT wasn't the end of it, of course. There was more than a full day, and night, to get through before the vassals' dinner party, and Romar used almost every minute of those intervening hours to try to change Kirra's mind. He followed her from the gardens, arguing. At the ball, he danced with her half the night, still arguing. When she came to his room late that night, he spent more time trying to convince her to abandon this plan than he did making love to her.

"I should hold you here by force," he said finally as he lay beside her in bed, gazing at her by candlelight. "Tie you to the bedpost. Keep you here until that damned dinner is over. I should never have mentioned it."

She sat up, holding the blanket to her chest, and laughed at him. "Do you really think it is possible to keep me against my will?" she demanded. "Don't you realize that I can turn into any shape I desire and free myself? My stepmother despaired of me when I was a child because it was impossible to punish me. I couldn't be locked in my room. I would not sit still for a beating. No one has ever been able to control me. And you will not be able to do it now."

He leaned forward, buried his head against her shoulder. "I am so afraid for you," he whispered. "You are so reckless. And even if I could prevent you from risking yourself tomorrow night, there will be nights after that, and after *that*, that you do foolish things and I will be helpless to stop you. I love you. I want to keep you safe. I am used to being able to command men and shelter women. I cannot accustom myself to the fact that you will not accept my protection."

She slipped a hand under his chin and tilted his face up. "I never will," she said. "I do not want to be protected. I do not want to be sheltered. I am not helpless, and I will not be held."

"Then what can I do?" he whispered.

She leaned down and kissed him. "Just love me for what I am."

CHAPTER
36

THE day after the ball passed languidly and with a great deal of boredom. Most of the other nobles were involved in elaborate leave-takings of their own, loading up coaches and saying their farewells, so the front courtyard was a constant jumble of activity. Kirra passed a quiet couple of hours on the third floor of the manor, watching Lyrie alternately sleep and play. Her fur was developing a healthy shine; her pointed black nose was cool when she nuzzled Kirra's hand.

"Still improving?" she asked Marco.

He nodded. "Visibly. Every day. Every hour."

Kirra was idly scratching Lyrie's stomach, since the little spaniel was on her back before the mystic and they were all disposed on the floor. "I don't know how I can conceal this magic," Kirra said slowly. "I don't know how I can save this one life, and know how to save hundreds of others, and not do it."

Marco watched her. "Are you afraid of what people will think of Lyrie if they find out she was cured by magic? I don't care. Tell anyone."

"There will be a taint on her," Kirra warned. "Enough people distrust magic that they will distrust people who have been touched by it."

"I don't care," he said again.

"But it is not even her I am thinking about so much," Kirra

said. "I am thinking about how much people already fear mystics, and how this will exacerbate the fear. And I am weighing that against the other lives I know I could save. And I am trying to decide what to do."

"Save the lives," Marco said without hesitation.

Kirra ruffled Lyrie's soft fur. "I have not saved her yet."

"No," Marco said. "But you will."

I N the evening, they all gathered in the Riders' room, just down the hall from Kirra's. Romar had lent them Merrenstow livery, one set even big enough for Tayse to wear, and Tayse, Justin, Senneth, and Cammon had arrayed themselves suitably. Romar had been consigned to the care of Coeval, and Hammond had been left to guard Amalie.

"Not ideal," Tayse admitted. "But I told Romar that he could help protect Amalie by spending the evening with her while we were out, adding his own sword and Coeval's to her protection. That seemed to comfort him, and he said he would do it."

Both Tayse and Justin looked indefinably different to Kirra when, instead of the black and gold of Ghosenhall, they wore the checkered black and white of Merrenstow. They looked less ferocious, a little more tame.

A misperception, Kirra knew.

By contrast, Cammon looked no more like a soldier than he ever did, even in a set of clothing that fit him much better than his usual ragged trousers and shirt. Senneth had trimmed his hair, so it actually fell with some neatness around his face, and he wore the requisite weaponry, but he just didn't hold himself like a soldier.

"You're the one they're going to go for first if anyone starts picking off Romar's men," she told him.

He grinned. "Good. I think I can surprise them."

Senneth, oddly, looked just the same. It didn't matter what Senneth wore, Kirra reflected—a ballgown, traveling clothes, a guard's uniform—she looked purposeful and strange. Not precisely dangerous, not the way the Riders were, but unusual enough to make a man think twice before accosting her.

"All of *us* are ready," Senneth said pointedly. "What about you?"

Kirra laughed. She was still herself, still wearing a summer gown and allowing her hair to fall unbound down her back. "I came to get that chain mail Tayse promised me. Then I'll go to my room and change. Then we can leave."

Cammon was watching out the window. "The carriage just pulled up."

"All right. Give me a few minutes." Tayse handed her a man-sized vest of interlocking metal circles, so heavy she almost dropped it to the floor. "Oh, *this* will be fun to wear all night."

"I think you'd better," he said seriously. "Magic is well and good when you have a moment to prepare, but chain mail will keep you alive when you're taken by surprise."

"Five minutes," she said, and hurried down the hall to her room.

Melly wasn't there since Kirra had expressly sent her away for this particular hour. She had a feeling Melly would be about as enthusiastic about this enterprise as Romar had been, and she didn't feel like another argument. Anyway, she didn't need help changing in and out of these clothes. She stripped off her dress, stepped into simple leggings and a cotton shirt, and settled the chain mail over her chest. *Damn*, but its weight made it hard to breathe. She resisted the temptation to convert it into something lighter, less restrictive; she respected its abilities as much as she respected her own.

And then she stood in front of her mirror and changed herself into her lover.

The intelligent, restless face; the brown eyes; the dark gold hair, tied back with a black ribbon. All these were as familiar to her as her own features, her own skin. The well-muscled body that was such a pleasure to touch—that she could manufacture, too, without a moment's difficulty. She dressed him in formal black, with touches of the Merrenstow checkerboard at his throat and pocket.

By the Red Lady's burning hand, he was her idea of the perfect man. She could stand here and stare all night, in love with her own reflection.

A last lingering look, then she spun on her heel and strode out into the hall, automatically adopting Romar's stance and gait. At the door to the Riders' room, she paused a moment, hand upon the knob. Then she smiled, and knocked instead.

Justin opened the door, but she brushed past him before he

could speak. She addressed the whole room in Romar's voice. "Is there anything else you need from me before you set off on this ill-judged adventure?" she asked. They all stared at her, uncertain. Well, Cammon was trying very hard not to laugh. Obviously he had not been fooled. "Or have you changed your minds? Where's Kirra?"

"She's down the hall, lord," Senneth said. "Preparing for her part."

She pivoted for the door. "Then perhaps I'll check with her."

Justin moved without much subtlety to block her exit. "No. Lord. I think it's best you return to Amalie's room and let us finish our preparations on our own."

"I just wanted to wish her luck," she told him impatiently.

"She's got us. She doesn't need luck," Justin said with a little smile.

She swung back to face the others, carefully avoiding looking at Cammon. "I could come with you," she said, as if struck by fresh inspiration. "I'll stay in the coach. That way, if no danger threatens, Kirra and I can exchange places sometime in the middle of the evening."

"Which is exactly when danger would strike," Tayse said. "Why don't I take you back across the hall? Where I will be sure to ask Coeval and Hammond why they let you leave your niece's room."

She opened her mouth, but before she could reply, Cammon started laughing. That was enough for the rest of them; they knew instantly they'd been tricked. Justin shoved her on the arm so hard she staggered back a few steps.

"We ought to just let you go by yourself," he said in disgust.

"I'm sorry," Cammon said, still laughing. "But that was too good."

Senneth and even Tayse were smiling. "I don't think we need to worry about you *not* fooling the vassals," Senneth said.

"Very good," Tayse said. "Time to go."

IT was about an hour by coach to the estate of Domenic Ayr, Ariane's primary vassal. A boring hour for Kirra, since she rode alone inside while the other four accompanied her on horseback. On the trip back, someone was definitely going to be persuaded to sit in the coach with her and keep her company.

She let petty considerations drop away as she disembarked before Domenic's house, an attractive but not particularly large manor graced by a profusion of roses along the front walk. She was late; the lord was not at the door to greet her. A footman showed her instantly to the dining area, and she took a quick look around before her name was announced.

About twenty men and a handful of women were gathered in the room, already seated around a highly polished table and consumed with debate. Kirra recognized many of them from her earlier visits at Shadow Balls. There was Kell Sersees from Kianlever, Bat Templeson of Coravann, both accompanied by their wives. There was even Coren Bauler, with whom Senneth had had a memorable one-sided flirtation in Fortunalt last winter. Kirra recognized faces from Storian, Merrenstow, and Tilt. None from Danalustrous, thank the great gods. There were a few other individuals who looked familiar, though she could not assign names to them. And that man, portly and self-satisfied, standing by the sideboard conversing with Domenic Ayr—he looked familiar.

He looked like the man who had led the attack against Romar at the bonfire in Nocklyn.

"Lord Romar Brendyn of Merrenstow, regent to the king," the footman intoned, and all conversation in the room ceased. Chairs scraped on the stone floor as the diners pushed their seats back and rose, some of them bowing or curtseying, some merely giving her cool nods of acknowledgment. Kirra kept her expression grave, as Romar would have, and responded with a slight bow of her own.

Domenic hurried across the floor to greet her. "Regent! I am so pleased you were able to join us after all. Do you know everyone?"

"Some. Not all."

"Let me introduce you around the table and then we will be seated. Dinner is ready even as we speak."

She paid close attention as introductions were made. Yes, every House but Danalustrous was represented. The heavyset man was from Storian, though Domenic mangled the introduction and she couldn't catch his name. Storian. That seemed wrong. Unlike Cammon, she couldn't automatically tell when someone was lying, but something about this man rang false to her. His name or his affiliation or his face or—

His face. His body. That was it. Like her, he was in disguise. Like her, he had changed himself from his proper form. There was a mystic among the Thirteenth House lords, and he was allied with the rebellion.

He would be the man to watch during dinner.

The meal itself was excellent, a variety of well-cooked dishes chased down with copious amounts of wine. Kirra drank sparingly and did more listening than talking, as Romar would have. Conversation veered from earnest to envious to hilarious as it covered everything from new taxes to the privileges of the wealthy to recent personal disasters that became much funnier in the retelling. Those sitting closest to Kirra made a point of including her in their conversations, bombarding Romar with questions both political and social. From them she got the impression she had picked up on other nights at the Shadow Balls—even at that ill-fated bonfire in Nocklyn. These were people who were eager to better themselves, hopeful that a regime change might improve their fortunes. Most of them, or so she gathered, wanted peaceful change; they were willing to work for recognition and honor.

Then who were the rebels? Was this really a meeting of conspirators? Did anyone here truly want to kill Romar Brendyn?

When conversation became general, as it did every twenty minutes or so, it tended to revolve around universal preoccupations—land, the succession, and power.

"Els Nocklyn promised us," one of the vassals's wives was saying in a stubborn voice. "Before he got sick. He promised us another hundred acres. I know serra Mayva would honor the promise, but I can't get in to see her, and her husband—" She made a fatalistic motion with her hand.

"Gisseltess lords keep their promises," said a guest who was wearing a vest embroidered with the hawk and the rose. A Gisseltess man. "But sometimes you have to wait till it's convenient for them to be fulfilled."

"I'm tired of waiting on promises," said the Storian man in disguise. He looked straight at Kirra. "Lord Romar, what can the king promise us that our own lords can't? What can he grant us?"

That was blunt. But she had seen Romar field this same question before, and he hadn't flinched. "I can promise nothing on behalf of the king except that I will tell him you want a conversation with him," she said, her voice firm and ringing. "Make up a delegation. Come to Ghosenhall. I will guarantee you an audience. But more than that I cannot guarantee."

The Storian man leaned forward, his bulk displacing some of the plates before him on the table. "But will he listen? Will his daughter listen if her father is dead? Will *you* listen, once the king is gone?"

"The king is still very much alive," she said in a pleasant voice. "I would not consider negotiating elsewhere, if I were you."

"The king will not live much longer," said the Gisseltess man. "We all wish him well, of course. But he is old. What happens when he is gone? We have the patience to wait—but not if waiting brings us nothing."

"Send a delegation to Ghosenhall," she repeated. "Ask to meet with his majesty and his daughter. I will join the negotiations."

"Yes, but will you argue for us?" a pale woman demanded.

"I will if the proposals you put forth are reasonable."

"Thirteenth House yourself, or very near to it," purred the false Storian man. "You own fine properties and your blood is pure, but you'll never inherit Merren Manor. How does that feel? Don't you hate your marlord cousin—just a little bit?"

She was shocked at her own reaction, which was one of arrogance and outrage. *I am Twelfth House, you ratty upstart pretender,* she wanted to say, on Romar's behalf as well as her own. Well. That was telling. She had always believed herself an egalitarian, open to every man's virtues, and here she was poised to defend bloodlines at the slightest hint of insult.

Romar, she thought, would not have felt the same uncharitable emotions. Romar would have shrugged and said, "I honor my cousin. I respect him. I manage my own affairs and let him manage his." Therefore she said the words anyway, in his voice, and thought it was a much better response than her own.

The heavy man still sneered, but Domenic Ayr toasted her with his wineglass. "A diplomat," he said. "Just the kind of man we need sitting next to the king—or next to the princess."

Conversation turned to less dangerous topics then, though Kirra caught other people at the table eyeing her speculatively for the next few minutes. She waited until no one was paying much attention to her, then signaled a servant.

"I need to speak with one of my guards. Can you fetch him? I will wait at the doorway."

"Certainly, regent. One in particular?"

"Yes, the younger one. Cammon."

She excused herself from the table and left the room, standing just outside the doorway in the outer hall. She could still watch the diners eating and arguing. None of them seemed alarmed by her brief absence.

Cammon came bounding up seconds later. He didn't look alarmed, either; he knew she wasn't in danger. "What?"

"There's a man in there. I think he's clad in magic. Can you tell me what he really looks like?"

Cammon peered inside the room. "Well—where is he?"

"Between the man in the maroon jacket and the man with the white beard. Right now he's tearing apart a piece of bread with his hands."

"He's overweight but not huge. Almost bald, but not quite. What hair he has is blond, going a little gray. His cheeks are very red, as if he's been drinking a lot, or shouting at someone."

"That could describe a lot of people. Not wearing any House colors? Doesn't have a huge scar across his face? Anything that would help identify him?"

"No."

"I wish I could see him. I wonder if I'd recognize him."

"Do you have your little lion with you? Give it to me."

She fished it out. "You're always surprising," she commented, and dropped it in his hand. Instantly, she felt her veins quiver with fire; the muscles along her back strung with tension. "Now what?"

"Look at him," Cammon directed. "I think, when I touch you, you'll pick up some of my magic. Maybe enough to help you see him truly. I don't know. I'm only guessing."

She focused on the portly man, just now gesticulating with some energy at the lord across the table from him. Cammon moved behind her and laid his palm along her spine; she could feel the pressure of his hand even through the links of chain mail. For a moment, she was dizzy. The room before her danced as if she viewed it through waves of heat. Then her vision sharpened and her eyes felt hot and she was staring across the room at a man she knew.

Heavyset, ruddy, fair—that was how he had always appeared. Angry, purposeful, calculating—that was a side of him she had rarely seen. Berric Fann, her uncle. A man who hated her father and who was, or so it appeared, plotting against the king.

She said nothing for so long that Cammon prodded her with his free hand. "Kirra? I mean, my lord? Is something wrong? Do you know him?"

She nodded. "I do."

"Is that good?"

How could he have changed shapes, altering himself just enough so that she did not recognize his face? He used to have only the slightest magic in him, barely enough to erase the freckles on his skin, and even that he had lost with age. Or so he had told her, just a few weeks ago. Clearly, that had been a lie—clearly, he had lived a lie all these years. It turned out he *was* a mystic, with a significant amount of power, and he had always concealed his true strength. Kirra remembered all the summers she had spent at his house, chattering away about everything she had been taught, the spells she had learned from Senneth and her other tutors, the discipline, all the tricks she had developed to channel and heighten her ability. He had learned right along with her. He might have had very little magic, a scrap, a sparkle, but he had made the most of it, thanks to her tutelage.

"Kirra?"

He had *lied* to her, lied to everybody, sat out on that lovely, peaceful farm and devised strategies for bringing down the king. No doubt he was plotting against Danalustrous as well, trying to foment rebellion among the lesser lords, pretending it was for his dead sister's sake but really because he was power-hungry himself. He was not the man she had thought he was, the one who showered her with gifts and called her his favorite niece and taught her the dance steps she was too stubborn to learn from Jannis but that she had to know, every serra did. He was not the man who had saved a kitten from the barn litter so that she could name it, who had taken her riding through his own estates and explained crop rotation and good husbandry. He was not the man she had thought loved her. Not the man she had thought she loved.

Now Cammon pinched her so hard on the forearm that she almost yelped. "Kirra? What's wrong? You know him?"

"He's my uncle."

"And he shouldn't be here?"

"He shouldn't be here in disguise. He's the same one who wanted to kill Romar around the bonfire back in Nocklyn."

"I thought a lot of people wanted to kill Romar that night."

"Yes, but he's the one who really tried. And he was—I'm not sure—I think it's possible he was in Tilt. One of the men who was responsible for kidnapping the regent. He didn't look exactly like this, but he—I don't think he has a lot of power. Just enough to shift his features and alter his shape a little. There was a fair, heavyset man in Tilt. I think it might have been him."

"I suppose it's good that we know this," Cammon said cautiously.

"I suppose it is."

"Do you want me to get Tayse?"

"No. But if something happens—if there's trouble—look for this man. I think he'll be in the middle of it."

A small silence from Cammon. "I will, but—what does he look like? To everybody else?"

She closed her eyes briefly. Really, sometimes it was almost more trouble than it was worth to get Cam's help on anything. "Sort of like you see him now, but his hair is darker and he's wearing a black jacket with gold braid. He's pretending he's from Storian."

"Maybe we don't have to wait for trouble," Cammon said. "Now that you know. Maybe you can leave."

"I don't want to leave. I want to see if he talks to me."

"I'm getting Tayse," Cammon said. "We'll stand right outside the door. Right here."

He dropped his hand and her vision blurred. She had to put her palm out to the wall to keep her balance. When she looked inside the room again, her uncle was gone, and in his place was a stout, sneering, swaggering stranger. "Give me back my lioness," she said, and Cam restored it. It made a very small but infinitely comforting weight in her pocket. "This trip just keeps getting stranger by the day," she said.

Cammon grinned at her. "That describes every trip I've ever taken."

She strolled back into the dining hall and reseated herself

just in time to accept a plate of cobbler from a servant. "More wine, my lord?"

"No, thank you. I'd appreciate some water."

"Very good."

She ate the cobbler without tasting it, audited the conversation without hearing it, answered questions without having any idea if her replies made sense. Her father had always hated Berric, never bothering to explain why. She had supposed it was because Berric so obviously despised Malcolm, and Malcolm never felt the need to accept criticism graciously. But now she guessed that her father had some inkling of the depths of Berric's animosity—that her father distrusted her uncle, probably purely on instinct. But Malcolm's instincts were generally good.

Kirra felt like such a fool.

It was worse than that. She felt like a child suddenly abandoned. For so many years, the Fanns had been her refuge, her place of safety. They had been the people who loved her no matter what she did. Was Beatrice aware of Berric and his deceptions? Did she, too, possess hidden magic and aspirations to higher status? Had all their protestations of affection been false? Had they welcomed her and made a fuss over her and treated her like a favored daughter not because they loved her, but because they thought they could use her in a bid for more land and power?

First Donnal had left her. Now the very memories of her aunt and uncle had been blackened and destroyed. Everything she had believed defined her, everything that had ever secured her, had frayed apart and left her drifting in a hostile wind. It was very hard to sit at this table, feel the chair against her back, the glass in her hand, and keep herself from disintegrating. She felt her own magic flicker through her fingers. Without much effort, without even conscious volition, she could undergo a disastrous change right here, dissolving into component parts of muscle, hair, and bone.

Someone looked at her oddly, and she wondered if she had made a noise or, more probably, failed to answer a pointed question. *Concentrate.* She was not Kirra Danalustrous, lost and left behind. She was Romar Brendyn, regent of Gillengaria, proud man and property owner, and some of the people in this room were not her friends.

"Sorry," she said. "I've received startling news."

"Nothing too bad, I hope," one of her dinner companions said.

"I don't have all the details yet. But please forgive my rudeness! What were we talking about?"

Gradually she eased herself back into the conversation, even managed to laugh once or twice. She offered her opinion on the merits of the wine, agreed that last winter had been a bad one, and hoped that the harvest was good. Like the rest of her companions, she rose to her feet when her host did and followed the whole group into a sparsely furnished room down the hall.

This part of the evening, she quickly surmised, was designed to allow informal conversation between clusters of visitors who might not have had a chance to talk over dinner. More wine was available, and a half dozen lords pulled out pipes and tobacco. The women unfurled their fans to blow the smoke away. A fire burned in a great hearth even though the windows were open to admit the warm night air. The walls were lined with hunting trophies—bear heads and deer antlers—as well as crossed swords and a display of daggers. This was the sort of room where deals were made and plans were formulated and individuals hammered out the details of governing the kingdom.

For this particular interlude, no doubt, Romar had truly been invited to the dinner.

Indeed, over the next hour, Kirra was approached by vassals in ones and twos, airing quiet grievances or expressing hope for future projects. Most of them seemed prosperous and content, willing to work within the existing system as long as their own needs could be attended to. Indeed, Kirra found most of their requests quite reasonable and hoped she sounded passably intelligent as she discussed road construction and possible dam sites. These were the lesser lords and ladies as she had always believed them to be—honest, outspoken, ambitious, and sensible. The sorts of people any marlord would be pleased to have as vassals.

It was a little past midnight when Berric Fann approached her.

She had just said warm farewells to a couple from Rappengrass who were interested in expanding their fishing ventures, so she was standing alone for the first time all evening. She was wondering if she should ingratiate herself into an existing conversation or wait till someone else approached her with a question when she made a half-turn to find Berric almost upon her. He was smiling. He held a glass of wine in each hand.

"Thirsty work, talking all night," he said in the most amiable voice he'd used so far. "Red wine or white? I brought you some of each."

"Red, thank you," she said, accepting the glass from his hand. All her senses had grown miraculously sharp. She felt as if someone had poured vinegar into her veins. "I'm sorry, I didn't catch your name. Storian was all I picked up out of Domenic's introduction."

"Mobry. Francis Mobry," he said, saluting her with the other glass.

"You have strong views, Lord Francis," she said.

He sipped his wine and watched her. "Do you object to them?"

"I believe a man is entitled to any opinion he chooses as long as he doesn't force that opinion on others through violence."

"Sometimes violence is the only way to get other men to respect your opinion."

"And are you intending to engage in violence anytime soon?"

His smile was decidedly unpleasant. "I am hoping your support will make drastic measures unnecessary."

He didn't appear to have a sword or even a knife anywhere on his body. It was hard to believe he intended to cut her down here in Domenic Ayr's house, in front of all these people. "And if I find myself unable to offer the support you crave?"

He shrugged his broad shoulders. "Then I—and likeminded men—will have to find ways to work around you."

"I think it would be a mistake to count me out of the game," she said, and took a mouthful of her own wine.

He watched her. "You don't even know what the game is."

Only when she swallowed did she register the bitter aftertaste. Only then did she realize Berric Fann really wanted to murder Romar Brendyn, but not even a full suit of armor would have shielded her from his malice. Berric employed more subtle weapons than swords and daggers. The wine had been poisoned.

CHAPTER
37

ONE swallow. Would that be enough to kill her? Probably not, for Berric still watched her with a predatory attention. She held the goblet in her hand and altered the composition of the liquid inside it. From wine to grape juice; from toxin to harmless herbs. She drank again, more deeply this time. Surely she had to down the whole measure of poison before she would fall dead.

"Then explain the game to me, Lord Francis," she said.

He had already finished most of his own wine. How had he known which color she would choose? Had both glasses been doctored? Had he already ingested an antidote? That was the most likely, she decided. She did not think he had enough shiftling power to modify the poison as she had done.

He relaxed a little, now that her glass was almost empty. He even smiled again. "Some of us are willing to see a weak princess on the throne. We are less eager to see a strong regent beside her," he said. "A young girl can be more easily controlled by a determined coalition than can a man with some battle experience and years of political maneuvering behind him."

"You don't know Amalie if you think she is easily manipulated," Kirra said, amused.

"Nonetheless. There is a faction who believes the regent

must go. Another faction believes he is our only hope for peaceful realignment of property, and they would like to see him standing one step behind the throne when Amalie comes to power."

"You keep assuming that Baryn will not rule much longer."

Berric made a dismissive motion. "His time is over. He will not be king another year."

She drained her glass and set it down. If he thought she was about to die, perhaps he would give her more details. Her stomach was starting to roil with protest and her hands were a little shaky. She might have less leeway than she'd thought. "You and your friends are contemplating assassination?"

"It is one option of many," he conceded. "But he's an old man. We might not need to hasten his death."

"Where does Halchon Gisseltess fit into all your plans?"

"He has made certain pledges. He is happy to see the Twelve Houses expand—to eighteen or twenty-four—if we support him when the time is right."

"And you plan to support him?"

Berric shrugged. "I am not so certain he is the man to back. I would be just as willing to see Amalie on the throne, frightened and conciliatory."

"So Baryn is your obstacle in either case," Kirra said. "But in the second scenario, you have only one additional impediment. And that is me."

"You," Berric said, drawing the syllable out with pleasure. "Yes, up till now, you have been the primary hindrance. But I don't think you will trouble us anymore."

It was not so hard to affect a look of fear, to let her eyes move from his face to the glass and back to his face. "The wine," she said, her voice strangled. "Was there something in the wine?"

He nodded, cool and pleased. "Don't worry. They say it causes very little pain. In any case, it quickly passes. You should be dead inside of fifteen minutes."

She put her hand to her throat, as if she was choking. Indeed, she was finding it hard to breathe, and not just because of the weight of the chain mail. Mystic, traitor, *and* murderer— her uncle was more despicable than she ever would have guessed. "What have you done?" she whispered. "You have killed me—

you have betrayed your country—you have brought shame to House Storian—"

He leaned closer, laughing a little. "I care nothing for Storian," he said with some contempt. "It is House Danalustrous I will see fall. Malcolm may have named that bastard girl his heir, but she will never live to take control of her property. I shall be ready to take advantage of any mistake she makes—"

Now terror spiked through her, running through her blood like silver. Her hands were shaking; she was sure her face was devoid of color. Red hot hell, the poison was taking effect too soon. Not only was it hard to breathe, it was hard to think. "Not Casserah Danalustrous," she said as fiercely as she could, clawing through the folds of Romar's white shirt, trying to loosen its collar. "*You will not harm Casserah Danalustrous.*"

He laughed again, a little more loudly. "Then the gossip is true, is it? Rumor has it that you and Malcolm's daughter have been very friendly as you traveled Gillengaria this summer. What a blow this will be to her to lose you so suddenly. Followed by the next blow of losing her land—and possibly her life—"

She swung up her free hand to strike at him, but she was so weak. She had waited too long; she could not call for help. Her body was breaking down; her vision was splotched with dancing spots. She really was going to die here at Domenic Ayr's little party, just as Romar had feared, just as he himself would have died—

Berric caught her arm and held her close as if to brace her. "Lord Romar," he said, his voice loud enough to be heard by someone standing nearby. "Have you had too much wine?"

Footsteps running nearer; a shape pushing between them; someone's hands pulling her from Berric's arms. Farther away, too far away to matter, sounds of dismay and outrage and the clatter of dropped china. Kirra wrenched her gaze upward, wondering how she could explain the situation to Domenic Ayr or Kell Sersees or whoever had rushed to her aid.

But she found herself staring up into Senneth's gray eyes. And she realized that the shadows clustering around Berric were the bodies of Cammon and the Riders. She saw the glint of metal—a sword at Berric's throat.

"What did you administer to the regent?" Tayse asked in an ominous voice.

Kirra just stared up at Senneth. "Poison," she mouthed, unable to vocalize the word. "I didn't take all of it. Help me."

Senneth nodded and lowered her to the floor. Around them, the sounds of conflict and argument grew louder; there were shouts and threats and the ring of blades. But no one broke through the band of defenders to disturb Senneth. The other mystic crouched over Kirra, keeping her cool eyes on Kirra's face and running her hot hands over Romar's infected body. Kirra could feel their warmth even through the chain mail.

"I can sense it," Senneth said. "I don't think there's enough here to kill you, but I'll burn it out anyway. Are you ready? It's going to hurt."

"Yes," Kirra tried to say.

Then fire arced through her, boiling in her gut and fanning out in all directions. She nearly screamed from the pain. Her heart roasted in her chest. Her bones liquefied, and her blood evaporated. She struggled for breath, but her lungs were seared beyond the ability to function. Ashes made a powdery trail down her throat.

The fire banked down and for a moment she felt like a great felled log, hollowed out by fire, only the outer form intact. Coolness seeped slowly along her skin, restoring some of her ordinary sensation. She had not incinerated after all. Cautiously, she sat up, coughing, all her muscles lax and rubbery. But the poison was gone, consumed in a blaze of magic. She felt weak but whole. Scarred but safe. "Red and silver hell, I am never asking you to heal me again," she gasped.

"You're welcome," Senneth said. "Glad I could help."

There was a scuffle a few feet away and Kirra turned her head enough to see Tayse shoving Berric hard against the back wall, knocking his skull against the stone of the manor. Even in disguise, Berric was big, but Tayse was bigger; he completely overpowered the other man. Blood was running in trickles down Francis Mobry's puffy face and it looked as though one of his arms had been broken.

"My lord regent! Your man! Stop him! He's going to—*stop him*!" This from Domenic Ayr, who sounded genuinely agitated. Similar cries were coming from many of the other lords. Kirra peered around Senneth to see why none of them was rushing to Mobry's defense and saw Justin and Cammon with swords upraised, making a threatening barrier against the crowd.

"You might be interested to know that you've changed back to your true self," Senneth murmured. "Sometime during the whole—cauterizing—process."

"My lord!" Domenic shouted. Other unfamiliar voices called out orders.

"Summon the servants! Fetch the house guards!"

"Put up your sword! Let me through! He will murder that man—"

"Help me stand," Kirra muttered, and staggered to her feet with Senneth's aid. Then, loudly as she could through her singed throat, she announced, "My guards are protecting me, as they should. Lord Francis tried to kill me."

There was a sudden wash of silence as the gathered crowd all gaped at the golden-haired daughter of Danalustrous where the regent of Gillengaria should have been standing. She could see shock, disbelief, and anger working across the staring faces as the others realized how they had been duped.

"I came in Lord Romar's stead because I was expecting an attempt on the regent's life," she continued, and now some of the expressions were horrified and some were calculating. "Lord Francis poisoned my wine. I very nearly succumbed. Did any of you join him in wishing the regent dead?"

A number of them did not know her; she caught whispers from the crowd as some asked and others answered questions about her identity.

"Serra," Domenic Ayr said blankly. "None of us—all of us—These nobles are all faithful to the crown and to you. Yes, there are grievances but—no one—even Lord Francis—"

"This is not Francis Mobry," Kirra said, making a quarter turn to see that Tayse had finally stopped battering Berric against the wall and was now lashing the man's hands behind his back with a leather cord. Unlike Kirra, Berric hadn't allowed his violent ordeals to undermine his magic. He was still shaped like the lord from Storian.

But he was staring at her with an expression that was sheer Berric. Just this minute, it was clear, he had seen her for the first time, realized that he was not the only individual who had traveled here tonight in disguise. Only now did he see how close he had come to killing his sister's daughter.

"*Kirra?*" he exclaimed, his voice rich with all varieties of anguish.

She nodded ironically. "Uncle."

So that was as bad as it could possibly have been, Kirra thought later as they made their way home. After all, she did not ride back in the carriage alone. Senneth sat beside her to make sure she didn't fall into a faint, while the bound Berric rode on Senneth's horse. "He must go to Danalustrous," Kirra had said, but Tayse had shaken his head.

"He must go to the king. We will take him with us when we depart in the morning."

In the morning, when everyone in the world would leave her behind.

She did not know how she would have the strength to go to Romar's room, even to tell him what had happened. She was so tired. She had been betrayed by love, churned by poison, and rent by magic in one short hour. She was not even positive she would find the strength to climb the stairs to her own room, let alone go sneaking through the manor on unauthorized business.

But she need not have worried on any count. Justin carried her in from the carriage, and Romar was waiting for them outside Amalie's room. So she had the supreme pleasure of greeting her lover from the arms of another man, unable to summon the energy either to protest or explain. Romar stared at all of them, and Kirra merely closed her eyes and rested her forehead against Justin's checkerboard sash.

"A bad night, but not as bad as it could have been," Senneth said, pausing at Kirra's doorway before following Justin in. "Let me settle her and then I'll come tell you the tale."

"But she's—is she—"

"She'll be fine."

Melly was already at the bed when Justin laid Kirra down with unwonted care. "Serra! Are you—what happened? Did she—"

"All she needs is sleep," Senneth said. She gazed down for a moment, her face stern. "Sleep," she repeated, this time speaking to Kirra. "Don't go creeping off in the middle of the night."

"I won't," Kirra whispered. "If you won't leave tomorrow before I wake up."

Senneth smiled. "Deal." She turned to go, then turned back. "I'm sorry," she said. "About your uncle."

Kirra nodded and closed her eyes. "My father won't even be surprised."

"If you're the only one to mourn him, that only makes it hurt more," Senneth said quietly.

Kirra nodded again, her eyes still shut. "I can't imagine any way the pain could be worse."

"Try to sleep. We'll see you in the morning."

A few footsteps and Senneth was gone, the door closing behind her. Melly quickly and competently pulled Romar's clothes off of Kirra's body and wiped her face with a wet cloth. Or maybe Kirra only dreamed she did. She was already asleep.

THERE was no time to say good-bye, really, in the morning. The carriages were drawn up in the front courtyard and most of the luggage was loaded when first Amalie and then Valri had to hurry back to their rooms to see if they had left any items behind. Gathered to make the journey was virtually everyone who had traveled together this summer—all of the princess's men, all of Romar's, the regent, the Riders, and one mystic.

Kirra was a little surprised at who had opted to stay behind, not giving her much chance to argue about it, either. Cammon, whose presence she required. Melly, who adamantly refused to return in the carriage that Kirra sent on with the others. And Justin.

"I'm not really going to need your protection on the road to Ghosenhall," she told him. "I think Cammon and I will be able to detect and fend off anyone who means us harm."

Justin shrugged. "I'm coming with you, anyway."

"Four for cards," Cammon said, grinning. "I'm glad he'll be with us."

Amalie hugged her good-bye, Valri said a cool farewell, and Senneth gave her that faint smile. "See you in Ghosenhall in a week or so."

There was no private moment to take her leave of Romar. He stood a little apart from his men, holding his horse's reins, watching all the commotion with a mix of impatience and humor. It was entirely natural that she would approach him, hold her hand out, make a laughing little speech that recalled their exploits on the road. They were far enough away so that no one could overhear their conversation, but she did not want anyone to read sadness on her face. Not even Romar.

"I'm sure Senneth told you of my misadventures last night," she said. "Traitors uncovered and murders averted. I'm very glad I was there in your place."

"She told me all of it," he said, his voice more intense than hers, though he too was working to maintain a pleasant expression in case anyone was watching them. Since everyone was watching them. "I am so sorry you had to learn of your uncle's treachery this way. I understand he spent the whole ride back begging Tayse to allow him an audience with you this morning."

"I do not wish to speak with him," she said. She was glad he had already been bundled into the empty coach so she didn't even have to see him one last time. "Maybe some of my hurt and anger will have dissipated by the time I arrive in Ghosenhall, and I can beg the king for clemency on his behalf. But I don't think so."

"He doesn't deserve clemency. He tried to kill you."

"He tried to kill *you*," she corrected. "A greater crime in my eyes."

"How long before you will be in the royal city?" he asked.

"We will leave here when Ariane's granddaughter is healed. Another three or four days, I think. Four of us traveling by horseback should make better time than your big group. We will be there only a day or two after you, I would expect."

"Travel safely," he said, taking her hand again. "You carry precious cargo."

She laughed. "A few changes of clothing and a pair of shoes?"

"My heart." With his free hand, he trailed his fingers across her cheek, then made a fist and touched his chest. "Until Ghosenhall," he said and released her. Swinging to the back of his horse, he nodded at her and trotted over to join the others.

She was left trying not to stare and trying not to cry. It was a relief when the caravan finally got under way and she was left in the relative quiet—and loneliness—of Rappen Manor.

• • •

THE next four days were strange, but blessedly peaceful. Kirra spent much of her time sleeping, making up for all the hours of lost rest on the road. Even when she was awake, she sometimes spent hours lounging in her room, reading old romances Ariane lent her. Naturally, she visited the sickroom every day, to find Lyrie frisking about the room, playful as a puppy.

"She looks well, but there's still a trace of blood in her stool, and that has to be all gone before she's considered healed," Marco told her that second day. "If you don't mind staying a little longer—"

Kirra shook her head. "I knew when I began this I would need to linger through the whole recovery. I'm content."

One afternoon, she and Darryn took a pack of dogs and went out hunting. They rode past what Kirra thought had to be the limits of Ariane's property and spent so much time talking that they bagged very little game. But the exercise and the undemanding companionship did her good. When they returned, she was relaxed, windblown, sunburned, and exhausted.

"You don't look much like a serramarra," Darryn commented as he handed her down from the saddle. "You look more like an urchin."

"Even when I look like a serramarra, I have a tendency to behave like an urchin," she told him. "This is closer to my true appearance."

That night after dinner, Ariane commented in a grossly unsubtle fashion on the friendship between Kirra and Darryn. "Thank you for entertaining my son," she said. "He is so delightful in your company."

"Darryn is always delightful."

"I wish you would marry him."

Kirra laughed out loud, not at the suggestion but at its boldness. "If I ever feel like marrying, I will keep that in mind."

Ariane waved a hand. "You could live here. Or at Danalustrous. Or split your time between Houses. Whatever made you happy."

"It tends to make me happiest to be free to roam wherever I want."

"Surely you'll get tired of that life sometime. And it's time Darryn was married."

Kirra stopped laughing. "You're serious."

"Yes."

Kirra thought of all the reasons she didn't want to marry. Not now, not Darryn, maybe not ever, not anyone. There was a man she loved, and she could not have him, and she was not willing to compromise.

Two men, her heart said, *and you cannot have either of them.* She shook her head as if to silence some small, whispering voice.

"I am not, at the moment, feeling particularly marriageable," she said finally. "And that is no reflection on you, your son, or your House. I think you'd best look elsewhere for Darryn's bride."

It was easier, much easier, to spend her evenings with Justin and Cammon, who expected nothing from her, not charm, not a blood alliance, not even rational conversation. The two men had continued bunking in the bedroom down the hall, though it had really been an acceptable billet for soldiers only when they had been required to guard the princess. But most of the manor was empty, since all of the summer guests were gone, and Ariane didn't care, and so they stayed.

During their days, she learned, Justin and Cammon spent most of their time working out in the training yard with Rappengrass men. In the evenings, they either diced in the barracks or came back to their rooms to play cards with Kirra. Melly resisted being drawn into their circle, repeating that it wasn't right for serramarra to be socializing with servants, but Justin and Cammon wore her down. So she joined them if the hour wasn't too late, and learned from Justin the card games she didn't know, and soon she was beating them all pretty handily.

"I think Melly likes our Cammon quite a bit," Kirra murmured to Justin one night when the other two were engaged in an animated argument about the best way to play a particular hand. "Maybe they'll make a match of it. What do you think?"

He gave her a sardonic look. "I think Cammon's like the rest of us," he said.

"The rest of who? The Riders? The general population?"

"Us. The six of us," he clarified. "He'll fall in love where it's most extreme, and where his chances of success are least assured."

The words made her go blank with shock—because Justin

had said them, and because they were true. The four of them who had admitted to love so far had not chosen the objects of their affection with an eye toward happy endings. "Tayse and Senneth," she objected faintly.

He nodded. "Who could have predicted they'd be able to pull it off? If you heard the tale in the barracks one night, you'd be thinking it would turn out another way."

She glanced over at Cammon again, who had spread all the cards on the floor and seemed to be giving Melly some kind of lesson in mathematics. "He's only nineteen. He's too young to fall in love anyway, with someone suitable or unsuitable."

"When he does, I'm telling you, it will make the rest of us look like we weren't even trying."

RESTFUL as the interlude at Rappen Manor was, pleasant as the days were, Kirra almost fell on her knees to thank the Wild Mother the day that Marco proclaimed his daughter cured.

"We even had the groom come in to look her over—he's the one who cares for the dogs, you know, as well as the horses. He said he wouldn't have thought she'd ever been sick if I hadn't told him," Marco reported. "And she seems so strong, and she looks so healthy. I think it's time."

"I think it's time, too," Kirra said.

For the day the magic was to be reversed, the same people gathered in Lyrie's room who had gathered when the magic was introduced—Ariane, Bella, Marco, Kirra, Cammon, and Lyrie herself. Today all the curtains were drawn back and the windows were opened. The heavy scents of late summer curled over the sill and settled on the floor like rose petals. Kirra had knelt on the rug, Cammon standing fast behind her. Lyrie was bounding around the room with such energy that it was actually hard to catch her attention. When Marco chased her, she took off across the floor, glancing back to see if he was following.

"She thinks it's a game," Kirra said.

Marco was exasperated. "She won't even sit still long enough for me to explain!"

Cammon bent down, snapping his fingers. "Lyrie. Lyrie. Over here. Kirra and I need to work with you."

Something in his voice snagged her interest—or, who could tell? He seemed to have a gift of communicating with animals, so perhaps he was using some wordless mental speech. In any case, she responded instantly, trotting over to sniff his outstretched hand.

"Sit down for a minute," he said, still in that hypnotic voice. "We're going to transform you back to your human shape. Right now. We need you to concentrate. It's going to feel strange. But everything will be fine."

Lyrie promptly sat back on her haunches and watched them both with bright, eager eyes.

Kirra tossed him a look from over her shoulder. "You're spooky sometimes."

"What? What did I do?"

She ignored him, focusing on Lyrie instead, placing her hands on the spaniel's head. She knew the instant Cammon wrapped his fingers around the lioness charm, because she could feel magic thrum through her joints and muscles. Even her hair felt alive with it; she felt her golden curls tighten with energy.

"Lyrie," she said and the dog's dark eyes met hers. But it wasn't a dog Kirra was remembering, it was a little girl, with a broad, thoughtful face and her grandmother's strength of purpose. Kirra had seen her wan and weak, but she was pretty sure this was a girl who knew how to laugh, who could fling herself through the house with noise and excitement. A girl who could face death, who could endure magic, and not give in to fear.

This time, Kirra saw the transformation, as deliberate as most of her own. The pointed face softened and grew rounder between Kirra's hands; the dark fur lightened and smoothed out. The shoulders bulked up, the knees developed a bend. Lyrie stretched, and folded in, and pulled herself out of her own shadow—and there she was, a girl sitting on the floor, pink-cheeked and clear-eyed, bursting with health and vigor.

Bella breathed a prayer and broke down sobbing, stumbling into her mother's arms. But Marco gave a shout and dove for the floor, enveloping Lyrie in a ferocious hug. "Papa! Papa! I'm me again!" Lyrie squealed as they rolled together in an exuberant ball across the floor. "Did you see? It's me!"

Bella broke from Ariane's embrace and dropped to the

floor, her arms outstretched and her face wet with tears, and Lyrie scrambled over on her hands and knees. "Mama! Look at me! And I'm *well*! I can tell, I feel so good! Look at me!"

Kirra could feel herself smiling so brightly that her face hurt, and this despite the fact that she was crying a little, too. Ariane just looked at her and shook her head, tears pouring down her own cheeks. *I cannot express my emotions,* that's what that headshake meant. Kirra felt much the same way.

She thought it was time to give the family some privacy to revel in their joy, but there was one coda to perform before this episode was over. "Lyrie," she called. "Let me just check you one more time. I'll be able to tell if the fever is completely gone from your body."

Instantly, Lyrie came to stand before her, her parents on either side of her, unwilling to let go. Bella's face was pinched with a renewed fear—could the gift be revoked?—but Marco emanated happiness. He had witnessed magic, and he would forever after be a true believer.

Lyrie herself looked happy but calm, at ease with miracles. *This one will be hard to overawe in the future,* Kirra thought. *This one will keep her head no matter what turmoil goes on around her.* Lyrie smiled trustingly up at Kirra. "Thank you, serra," she said very politely. "For saving my life."

Kirra had to laugh. "And did you enjoy being a puppy for the past ten days?"

"Oh, yes! It was so much fun. But I'm glad to be a girl again."

"That's how I always feel," Kirra replied. She laid her palms against Lyrie's cheeks, innocent of fever. She touched the girl's arms, chest, hips, knees, back, looking for lurking infections. Nothing. All the organs clear, no bones under siege. The blood ran through the unspoiled veins like laughing rapids.

Kirra dropped her hands and gave the whole family an encouraging smile. "Cured," she said. "She has defeated the fever."

Now Bella and Marco threw their arms around Lyrie again and Ariane rushed over to join the communal embrace. Kirra jerked her head toward the door and Cammon followed her out, closing the door behind them. When she extended her hand, he dropped the little lion charm into her palm. It was as if she had been in giddy motion that abruptly stopped. She waited till she adjusted to the heavy sensation of ordinary existence, then hid the charm in her pocket.

"What now?" Cammon asked.

"We pack. We leave tomorrow at dawn."

CHAPTER
38

As expected, the four of them made excellent time on the road to Ghosenhall. Theirs was a compact, efficient group that easily navigated all kinds of terrain, from the forest of northern Rappengrass to the plains of central Helven. It was so much simpler when they didn't have to worry about coaches, axles, or lodging to accommodate more than fifty people every night.

Indeed, after the first night, they didn't bother with commercial lodging at all. At the end of that first day's ride out from Rappen Manor, they had all been pleased to find two rooms to rent over a small tavern perched by itself at a crossroads. The food had been passable and the beds comfortable enough, and none of them had any reason to complain.

But Kirra found herself lying wakeful, staring at the dark shape of the shuttered window, thinking even darker thoughts. The last time she had slept in a roadside inn, she had crept from her bed and changed herself into a bird and gone seeking the room of Romar Brendyn. She had lain with her heart against his heart, his cheek against her cheek, hearing him whisper her name so often that it came to sound as natural as his breathing. She wanted him to be here, this night, so she could search him out. She knew that she would never again be able to stay at any kind of inn without wondering where Romar's room was and how quickly she could get to it. He was inextricably mixed up with her expectations of travel; he would accompany her on any journey she took for the rest of her life.

The next night, she insisted they camp out.

And every night after that.

Only Melly really complained, and even her sighs were halfhearted. Justin, of course, was always happy to prove he didn't require material comforts, and Cammon never cared where he was as long as he was with people he liked. So they made sure they found reasonable campsites each night before sunset, and they gathered fuel because Senneth wasn't there to provide sorcerous heat and light, and they cooked the game Justin usually managed to catch at some point during the day. If they weren't too tired, they played cards for a while or fell into idle conversation. Justin cleaned his weapons every night while Melly mended various items of Casserah's clothing. Cammon and Kirra were left with most of the cleanup. Everyone seemed content with the arrangement.

On their fourth day out of Rappengrass, Justin returned empty-handed from a noontime foray out to find food. "No luck," he said in a grouchy voice. "We'll have to eat dried rations tonight."

"We're only a day from Ghosenhall. I don't think we'll starve," Kirra said.

"I saw some wild berries back a little ways," Melly said. "If you want to wait awhile, I'll go pick some."

"I'll help," Cammon offered.

Justin was watching Kirra. "I want to hunt," he said.

She shrugged. "Fine. I'll sit here with the horses while you all go traipsing off."

"No," he said. "I want to hunt in animal shape."

Cammon's head swung around sharply; Melly's eyes widened in disbelief. "Oh," Kirra said. She thought about it. "Any preference?"

Justin was grinning. "Whatever's comfortable for you."

Kirra was grinning, too—no, she was laughing. Melly was horrified, but Cammon looked intrigued, and Kirra knew, she *knew*, that if Senneth or Tayse were here, this little game would not proceed for another second. Magic should not be played with. Kirra had gambled with Lyrie's life because the stakes were so high. But there were so many reasons it was a bad idea to practice her shape-shifting skills on Justin, here off the main road somewhere in the sparsely wooded northern stretch of Helven, for no reason except that each of them thought it would be fun. Cammon wouldn't stop them—it wouldn't occur to him to try. Melly might offer a protest, but she would never dream of gainsaying a serramarra.

And Kirra had never been one to walk away from deviltry.

"Let's make it easy on both of us," she said. "You've already been shaped like a dog, so we both know that works. Let's try that."

"*Serra*," Melly breathed.

"It's all right, Melly. Don't worry," Kirra said. "We've done this before."

"Do you want my help?" Cammon asked.

"I think—let's see if I can do it by myself. Here, I'll put the lioness on the ground, right by you, but don't touch it unless it looks like I'm having trouble."

"Say, if I'm half-dog and half-man," Justin said.

"Though I might like you better that way," Kirra said.

Melly turned around, a hand over her eyes. "I can't watch."

"You really don't see much," Cammon said in a comforting voice. "It's not disgusting or anything." Melly strangled a sound that could have been a snort.

"Get down," Kirra said, kneeling. Justin dropped to a crouch beside her, balancing himself with one set of fingers against the ground. She placed her hands on either side of his face. "Watch me."

His eyes fixed unwaveringly on her face; he was serious now. She took a deep breath and held it, searching for reserves of magic in her body. This was hard, harder than she'd expected without the boost of Cammon's power. She felt the silent spell gouge a heavy track through her chest. Her ribs contracted from effort. But there was Justin, now a sandy-haired dog, floppy-eared and disreputable, springing to his feet and barking in a mad frenzy of excitement.

"By the Pale Lady's silver tears," Melly breathed. She'd whirled back around and was staring at the apparition. Who, truth to tell, was behaving more like a street mongrel than a dire act of sorcery, growling low in his throat and then throwing himself at Cammon's chest. Cammon laughed, and the two of them fell to the ground, wrestling. "That's—that's *Justin*?"

"And wasn't I right? Isn't he better like this?"

"I can't believe the goddess doesn't strike us all with light-ning."

"Well, this is the third time I've done this, and so far she doesn't seem too interested," said Kirra cheerfully. "We're go-ing to go hunting for a while. Tie up the horses and go get those berries. We'll be back in an hour or so."

A minute later, Kirra had slipped into the shape of her fa-vorite retriever, more elegant than Justin but just as playful. She nipped him on the shoulder and darted into the woods that lined the side of the road. He tore after her, plumed tail stretched behind him, mouth stretched in a canine grin.

She wasn't sure they'd actually catch any game, but the af-ternoon promised to be enjoyable.

They chased each other through the undergrowth for the next half hour, rousting out plenty of grouse and rabbits but not reacting quickly enough to overtake any of them. Every once in a while Justin gave up on hunting altogether and just stood in some tangle of weed and bramble, barking because he liked the sound of it. At one point he wandered off, following some scent that didn't interest Kirra, and she settled back on her hind legs, yawning hugely. If he was gone for any length of time, she just might flop to the ground, right in a pile of dead leaves, and take a short nap. The sunshine and the exercise were wearing her out.

Without warning, Justin jumped her from behind, pounc-ing on her with all four feet and taking her neck between his jaws in a mock grip. She yelped and rolled to her back, dis-lodging him, then sprang for his throat. He was too quick for her, though—Rider reflexes, even in dog shape. He darted aside and circled her, waiting for an opening, his mouth wide in a panting grin, wholly unmoved by her low growl of warn-ing. She leapt at him, biting his flank, then kept running. Within five paces, he'd caught up and knocked her to the ground.

If she'd been human, she would have been laughing so hard she wouldn't have been able to keep to her feet. She felt light and joyous, irresponsible and carefree, as she always had when playing with Donnal. They would chase each other across the woods, into the water, through the air, changing shapes, changing sizes. Now *that* would serve Justin right—she could transform herself to a lioness, or a bear, and he would not be able to counter. Unlike Donnal, he would have to stay as she made him, respond only to her call, rely entirely upon her magic—

She was human again so abruptly that Justin yapped and backed off. She hadn't even meant to change. She hadn't realized her body planned to take another shape. That of a woman, sitting on the ground, sobbing into her hands.

She would never play through the woods with Donnal again, never see his dark face, recognize it no matter what form he took. Never hear his voice. He was gone.

Justin had crawled forward again, belly low to the ground, tail down, whining. His cold nose nudged her hand, and, when she pulled away, lifted to burrow against her neck. She turned her face aside, but his pink tongue lapped across her cheek; he lifted one wiry paw and scraped at her shoulder. Unmistakable dog language for *what's wrong with my person?* She kept her face averted and he grew more insistent, back legs on the ground, both his paws on her shoulders. He barked once, right in her ear, and it startled her so much she almost started laughing. He licked her face again, this time catching the corner of her mouth. She knew he could taste the tears on her cheeks. He barked again.

"All *right*," she said, turning to look at him and grabbing his scruffy face between her hands. "I'm all *right*. Don't worry. I'll turn you back into Justin. In a minute. Just—give me a minute."

He settled back but kept his gaze intent on her face. She dropped one hand to her lap, kept the other on his head, scratching between his ears. She was almost moved to pour her heart out, to talk to him as she had always talked to Donnal when he followed her in animal shape—but this was Justin; this was neither Donnal nor one of her father's hounds, not nearly as safe to confide in. So she said nothing. She just looked away and waited for the tears to stop.

Apparently Justin decided that might take a while. He folded himself down to the ground right beside her and rested his head on her thigh. Giving a mighty sigh, he yawned and closed his eyes. She kept her fingers in his fur, absently stroking his head. They stayed that way until she heard Cammon's voice, lifted to call their names.

. . .

A<small>T</small> the end of that journey, Ghosenhall seemed like some mythical city of grace and refinement, so beautiful and so long-sought that it could not possibly be real.

"We've found paradise," Kirra said as, tired, hungry and a little dirty, they finally rode through the great gates of the royal city.

"Maybe not paradise," Justin said, "but it's home."

"Not for me," Melly said with a sigh. "Home's another long journey away."

The Rider glanced at Kirra. "How soon will you be leaving for Danalustrous?"

"Not sure. The dinner's tomorrow night, if I've reckoned correctly, which means there's probably a semi-formal function tonight. You know, for all the people who've arrived a day early. I imagine I'll stay a day or two after the main event." *As long as Romar is here.* "But Melly's right. It's time to be getting back to Danan Hall."

"Make sure you say good-bye," Cammon said.

"Where are you going tonight?" Justin asked him. "Off to your mystic friends? You could stay a night or two at the barracks. Hear all the gossip."

Cammon nodded. "Sure. That'll be fun."

"I wonder when Senneth and the others got here," Kirra said. "I bet we're only a day or two behind them."

Justin grinned. "Maybe we beat them."

But at the gates to the palace itself, they were informed that the royal caravan had arrived two days ago, everyone safe but weary. Kirra had been expecting the usual inquisition she had endured every other time she had tried to enter the palace grounds, but the presence of a Rider at her side made for a whole different experience. The guards had merely called Justin by name and waved the rest of them through. Kirra had had to rein back on her horse to ask for information about the princess's party.

"And I'm right? Tomorrow is the formal dinner?" Kirra added.

"Yes, serra."

"Good. I was afraid it might be tonight," she said, and caught up with the others.

"We'll ride up to the door with you," Justin said so nonchalantly that she had to stop and realize that he didn't really have to. Inside the royal compound, she was about as safe as a person could be, and the pathway to the barracks lay in a completely different direction. But she had finally started to figure Justin out a little. *The six of us . . . We'll ride with you. . . .* When he said "we" or "us," he meant this small core of friends that he hadn't even known existed a year ago, and hadn't really liked when they were first thrust upon him. Except for Tayse, of course. He had always worshipped Tayse. But the rest of them had surprised him by coming to mean so much to him. She thought he must still be astonished by his depth of feeling.

"You can take my horse for me," she said casually.

He nodded. "Will do."

Milo, the royal steward, was waiting at the door when their ragged little group rode up. "Serra Kirra," he said in that voice that never showed dismay or disapproval. "The king will be glad you're here. Your usual room has been reserved for you."

Kirra slid from the saddle and unhooked her bags. Melly was also on the ground and retrieving luggage. Kirra handed her reins to Justin and gave him a friendlier smile than she usually bothered to show him. "Thanks," she said. For returning the horse to the stables. For feeling the need to guard her on the way back from Rappengrass. For comforting her while she cried and never mentioning the incident again. "I'll swing by the barracks before I leave."

He nodded carelessly, as if it didn't matter, and turned away, already talking to Cammon. Kirra smiled and followed Melly up the stairs to the grand entrance of the palace.

SENNETH wasn't in her room. It seemed inappropriate to seek out Amalie or Valri, who would take on much different personas, Kirra thought, now that they were back in the royal compound. She didn't dare go looking for Romar in broad daylight in the king's palace. So she had to impatiently get through the intervening hours until dinner, unable to catch up on any good tales of the road.

Melly convinced her to nap, and then she luxuriated in a real bath, all scented soap and hot water. Melly seemed so eager to style her hair and help her with her clothes that Kirra submitted, just sitting and standing as Melly directed.

"This is the last time, though," she warned. "Tonight and to-morrow night. I'm getting tired of being fussed over."

"I know," Melly said with a smile. "That's why I want to do it."

When Melly was done, Kirra was wearing a gown of deep violet silk edged with borders of velvet; against it, her hair looked bright as a pile of new coins. Melly had woven purple ribbons through the loose curls and set garnets and amethysts in Kirra's ears and around her fingers. The ruby pendant of Danalustrous hung perfectly in the narrow V of the neckline. Kirra's blue eyes looked smoky, tinged by the color of the dress.

"I hope I look this good tomorrow," Kirra said, admiring herself in the mirror. "Thank you, Melly." *Thank you for your patience and care and good humor these last few weeks.*

"I was happy to do it," Melly said. *I would do anything for House Danalustrous.*

Kirra smiled and turned away. "Time to go charm the multi-tudes. I don't know when I'll be back."

"I won't wait up." *Because I know Romar Brendyn is here.*

Kirra was surprised into a laugh. "Good. Time you finally got a long night's sleep on a real bed."

She flitted downstairs toward the sound of voices and found twenty or thirty people gathered just outside the smaller of the palace's two formal dining rooms. She didn't get five steps into the room before someone called her name and she was drawn into light conversation. Senneth was across the room, looking bored but unable to break free from a confer-ence with some ancient-looking lord. Kirra waved and Sen-neth nodded, not breaking into the smile Kirra expected. Kirra raised her brows. Was something wrong? She tried to ease out of her unwelcome tête-à-tête and edge toward Senneth, but three more people caught up with her before she had even made it halfway across the room.

And then there was Amalie, descending on her in a swirl of gold skirts. "Kirra!" the princess cried, giving her a hug. So maybe it would have been permissible for Kirra to seek her out earlier in the day, just two old friends chattering the hours away. Amalie seemed to think friendship still held off the road. "When did you arrive? You must have traveled so fast!"

"I've only been here a few hours. But I was worried! I was afraid the grand dinner was tonight and I didn't want to miss it."

"No, it's tomorrow," Amalie said, and if she added something, Kirra missed it. Wild Mother still her wild heart, there was Romar a few feet away, standing with a small group. He looked almost as serious as Senneth, or maybe that was irritation on his face. The large woman talking to him at just this moment looked pompous and overbearing.

"Have you seen Senneth? Have you said hello to everyone?" Amalie was asking now.

"No—I've really just walked through the door."

Amalie took her arm and—*heart, please behave*—tugged her in Romar's direction. Kirra shaped her face with her most serene expression. "Uncle Romar, look who's arrived, a whole day before we expected her," Amalie said, as Romar's circle of friends parted to admit them.

Romar turned to them so smoothly, with so little surprise, that Kirra was sure he must have seen her when she stepped through the door. He was smiling, but something about his expression was shuttered. Perhaps, like her, he was striving not to let his emotions show in such a public place. Great gods, they'd been apart less than two weeks and it was already like some kind of breathless holiday when they were reunited. "Serra," he said very formally. "I trust you had no troubles on the road?"

"No, we were a small party, and we traveled without incident," she said, spreading her smile impartially over the other four people in the group. She didn't recognize any of them, though she thought the overbearing woman might be from Tilt. Or possibly Merrenstow, which explained why Romar was trying to be civil to her.

"You're Kirra Danalustrous, aren't you?" the large woman said, grabbing for Kirra's hand without waiting for introductions. "Pretty as everyone says. I'm Macey Carrostan from Merrenstow."

"Ah—forgive my rudeness," Romar said. "Serramarra Kirra Danalustrous. That's Lady Macey and her husband, George. Lord Gilbert Porrin. And my wife, Belinda."

She was holding Lord Gilbert's hand at the moment or Kirra would have fallen over. As it was, she felt the foundations of the palace shake and the walls pounce forward in one dark swoop. She could not falter; she could not scream. She could not crumple to the ground in a small, bleeding heap.

"Lady Belinda," she said, making a quarter turn and keeping her smile perfectly in place. "I didn't realize we would have the pleasure of your company for this event."

Belinda placed her little hand in Kirra's and offered a shy smile. She was small but not overly delicate. The bones of her face were prominent; her grip was strong. She had dark hair and a determined chin and the look of someone who was, quite simply, kind. But she was obviously a little dazzled at the exalted company she was keeping.

"I don't often come to court, but my husband says it's something I'll have to get used to," she said, giving Romar a swift sideways glance. "I must say, everyone has been most gracious."

I want to strike you. I want to hurt you. I want to see you run whimpering from the room. Kirra forced a smile. "Oh, people are pretty much the same everywhere," she said breezily. "Title or no. Some are pleasant and some aren't. But I'm glad you've enjoyed yourself so far."

She felt a touch on her arm and turned blindly to see who might have accosted her. Senneth. "Kirra, can I drag you away for a minute?" Senneth asked, giving everyone else an apologetic glance. "I need a favor."

Kirra shook her head in mock dismay. "She always does this," she informed the Merrenstow contingent. "It was very nice to meet all of you. I'm sure we'll get a chance to talk later."

And she allowed Senneth to pull her away. No, she leaned on Senneth with all her weight as Senneth helped her escape.

"I'm sorry, I'm sorry, I thought I would intercept you before you got down here," Senneth was murmuring in her ear. "She arrived this morning. I'm not sure Romar had any clue she was coming. Baryn must have invited her. There was no way to warn you—"

"Do I look all right? Do I look pale? Do I look like I'm going to throw up? Because I think I'm going to throw up. I don't want to embarrass Romar. I don't want anyone to notice anything—"

"You look fine. Do you want to sit down? I made Amalie put me at your table for tonight."

"I'm not going to be able to eat anything. Senneth, really, I'm going to start retching."

"Here. Sit down. Here."

Senneth pushed her to a striped divan situated at the edge of the room. Her hand was still on Kirra's arm, unbelievably warm, unbelievably reassuring. Kirra closed her eyes and concentrated on breathing, concentrated on not emptying the contents of her stomach here outside the king's dining room.

"If someone comes over and wants to talk to me, say that I'm faint," Kirra said. She was leaning back against the stuffed cushions, trying to keep her back straight, but she really wanted to bend over so her head touched her knees. Or lie on the cold floor, curled in a ball.

"No one will see us," Senneth said.

Kirra was able to summon a small flare of amusement. "What? You're using your invisibility spell on both of us?"

"Something like that."

Kirra took two deep breaths and slowly let them out. "I'm a fool," she said at last. "I should have expected—I should *always* expect—of course she would be here. It's surprising she didn't make the whole circuit with him this summer. Everywhere he goes, I should expect to see her."

Senneth made no reply, though Kirra could imagine a few choice words the other woman could have spoken. *If you had not allowed yourself to love a married man, you would not care if his wife was present or not.* True. True. She was a fool for so many reasons.

"I think I'm feeling a little better now," Kirra said. "I think I'll be able to stand up when dinner is announced."

"He made sure I met her," Senneth said. "I know he wanted me to tell you she was here. I thought I would—but then the king called me in and—I should have left a note. I should have given it to Milo. I thought I would see you before you walked in the room."

Kirra turned her head to stare at Senneth and found that the motion did not make her dizzy. She *would* be able to stand up. She wouldn't be able to eat a bite of dinner, of course—she'd change every forkful to water as soon as she slipped it into her mouth—but she would be able to survive the meal. She thought. "Of all the people in the room, you are the last one who needs to be apologizing," she said.

"It's just that you're breaking my heart," Senneth said.

At that moment, the meal was announced. Kirra relied on Senneth to help her to her feet, but after that she moved under her own power. A few more diners stopped them to greet the serramarra, and Kirra was astonished to find that she could smile and talk as if nothing had happened. As if nothing was wrong.

She sat at a table with Senneth and six others, and she continued to laugh and chatter so charmingly that she saw Senneth smile at her more than once. The food was served, and it didn't make her gag, though she put her plan into practice and altered every single mouthful. The man sitting next to her, a lord from Tilt, leaned over as dessert was passed around and touched her arm. "I'm following you home to Danalustrous and asking for your hand in marriage," he said. "No one ever told me you were so delightful."

The whole time, a voice in her head was screaming, was sobbing, was whispering that the world had ended.

CHAPTER
39

RAIN came as dawn's escort, moving in a little after sunrise and hanging around glumly no matter how many hours passed. While the gray skies perfectly suited Kirra's mood, she found it in her heart to pity the late arrivals journeying to Ghosenhall for tonight's event. Nothing worse than traveling in bad weather.

Half of her expected Romar to send a message to her room, begging her to meet him somewhere so they could talk in private. But such a summons would be risky, she knew, so half of her was convinced he would find no way to communicate. She was equally conflicted about whether she should stay in her room, hoping to hear from him—or leave, so that he had no way to reach her.

When the knock fell on the door, her heart clambered to her throat. But it was only Milo with a note from Baryn.

Can you see me at your earliest convenience? I am available at this very moment, if you are.

A strange day when you were disappointed to learn that your king wanted your company, she thought as she followed the steward down the stately halls.

Baryn was waiting for her in a relatively small study, a cluttered but friendly room where he clearly did much of the real work of governing the kingdom. He greeted her with a smile and a kiss on the cheek.

"Kirra! Such a marvelous thing. I send one sister off on a tour with my daughter, and a second sister comes back in her place." He grinned at her over his spectacles. A tuft of his white hair had come uncombed and was sticking up on the back of his head. He looked like a mad librarian.

"You know Casserah," Kirra said with a laugh. "Not a very sociable girl."

"Well, I hope you will tell her, and your father, how very highly my wife and daughter think of her," he said a little more seriously. She was not certain if he had figured out the deception and was really complimenting her, or if he actually wanted to convey his appreciation to Casserah. "They said she was intelligent, self-possessed, and always interesting, even when she did not appear to be enjoying herself."

Kirra laughed again. "Sounds like Casserah."

His smile quickly faded. "A bad business about your uncle, Kirra. I'm so very sorry."

Her own face turned grave. "What will happen to him?"

"For now he has been imprisoned. He is being questioned. We are hoping he can tell us if links exist between him and Halchon Gisseltess, and what other lesser lords might be involved in plans for small uprisings. So far he has chosen not to be very communicative."

"He has some shape-shifting skill," she forced herself to say. "So be careful. It is possible he will try to make himself look like someone else so he can flee the prison."

Baryn watched her with his faded blue eyes. "Do you want to see him?"

Kirra felt a chill settle around her heart. She should see him. She should ask him if he had ever loved her or if he had spent the last twenty-five years pretending. And if he had loved her, if he was able to convince her that he had—well, then, she should offer him something—forgiveness, some understanding, a willingness to listen to the bitter litany of how hatred had slowly driven him to treason. She owed that to him, if he had loved her. Because she had loved him.

But she didn't think she could bear it. Not on top of all the other betrayals.

"Maybe in a few months," she said. "When I'm not so angry with him. He will still be here, I presume." There had not been an execution in Gillengaria for the past hundred years. Surely Baryn was not going to revive the tradition.

"I fear he will be here most of the rest of his life."

"I will tell my father."

Baryn nodded briskly and turned the subject. "Did you meet either of the ambassadors last night?"

"No, I am hoping to manage that at tonight's dinner. What do you think of them?"

He moved his head back and forth in an equivocating motion. "I think they have some potential to be friends and allies. Trading partners, certainly. But I think the people of Karyndein are looking to start a war with some of their near neighbors, and as much as anything they're interested in friends who can supply armies. I am not much of an imperialist, as you know. And I think I will have plenty of use for my armies here at home in upcoming months. So I do not think I will be signing any except commercial treaties."

"I don't understand why people go to war," Kirra said.

"Don't you?" he said, a little rueful and a little amused. "Because they want something they don't have. Most trouble in this world is caused by people wanting something not currently in their possession."

She instantly wondered if anyone had been gossiping to the king about Casserah's possible affair with the regent. Valri was the most likely culprit—though the young queen had not seemed to think about or care about anyone except Amalie. *Red and silver hell,* Kirra thought. "Well, then," she said, as lightly as she could. "I suppose I have caused a few wars myself from time to time."

He looked at her sadly. "All of us have, my dear." He sighed and, for a moment, looked his full sixty-five years. "And Coralinda Gisseltess seems determined to start the next one."

Thank the gods. A change of subject. "What's she done now?"

"It's still only rumor. Apparently one of Els Nocklyn's vassals was overheard disparaging the Daughters of the Pale Mother and accusing some of his fellow lords of being fools for so eagerly accepting Coralinda's doctrine. A few days later, his house and grounds were burned. There's no sign of the man, his wife, his children—not even their bodies."

"Coralinda did that?" Kirra breathed.

Baryn shrugged. "Some say they saw a troop of men riding by that very day, dressed all in black and silver—the colors of the Lumanen Convent. Others say, no, they were wearing black and red. Gisseltess livery. I have sent a delegation to question the Lestra and do some further investigation, but I do not think I will discover anything conclusive."

"What has Els said?"

"He is too sick to send a message. His son-in-law wrote me a very cold letter saying that Nocklyn would take care of its own and that I need not launch any investigation. I think I shall have to find a way to establish a presence in Nocklyn—in stealth."

"If Coralinda really did such a thing—"

"Yes. I know. Inexcusable."

"Terrifying."

"Yes," he said again. "I know."

"I will tell my father that as well."

"When do you return to Danalustrous?"

This very minute, if I didn't have your damned dinner to attend. "Tomorrow morning, I think. I find myself feeling as Casserah must have felt for the first few stops along the circuit. Homesick."

"Then if you leave before I have a chance to speak to you again, travel safely. And thank you for all you have done for Ghosenhall."

I T was too wet to go outside, and Kirra found herself uninterested in participating in whatever indoor activities Valri had put together for the guests, so she went back to her room. Senneth had left a note, but only to mention that she'd be gone for a few hours on a trip into the city with Cammon. Melly was also gone, presumably running errands of her own.

There was literally nothing to do but sleep. Kirra lay herself rather gingerly on the bed, scowling because she wasn't tired in the least, and surprised herself by almost instantly dropping into dreaming.

A knock on the door woke her about an hour later. She sat up quickly, her hands going to her hair, and tried to convince herself that it could not possibly be Romar. The room was dim with the half-light of a rainy afternoon, but Kirra could see herself in the mirror well enough when she scrambled from the bed. A bit rumpled but flushed from her nap. Pretty. Sweet.

The knock came again, a little more hesitant. Kirra hurried across the floor to throw open the door.

Belinda Brendyn was standing there.

For a moment they just stared at each other, Kirra stupid from sleep and a sudden wild dread. *Why is she here, what does she know?* For her part, dark little Belinda Brendyn looked uncertain herself. The expression on her face could have been embarrassment, could have been worry. Could have been desperate determination.

"My lady," Kirra said at last, her voice utterly neutral.

"I'm sorry, serra. I hope I didn't come at an inconvenient time," the other woman replied. "I thought—I wanted to—I had something I wanted to ask you."

Are you in love with my husband? "I suppose it's something quite confidential," Kirra said, stepping back. "Come in, then." She shut the door behind her most unexpected visitor, and the two of them stood there a moment, looking at each other. Kirra decided she would not be the first to speak, no matter how uncomfortable the silence grew.

Belinda took a deep breath and Kirra braced herself. "They told me you were a healer," Belinda said.

The dead last thing Kirra had expected. "Yes. I am." Then, since that sounded so bald, "Are you sick?"

Belinda opened her mouth as if to speak, and then turned away to begin an aimless pacing of the room. Kirra stayed where she was, just inside the door. "I don't know. Perhaps not. It's just that I—it seems that I should have—and I've never dealt with mystics before. I have nothing against them, truly I don't, it's just that—they haven't come my way. I don't know if you can help me even if you would."

Bright Mother burn me in ashes to the ground. "I don't know, either," Kirra said as gently as she could. "Some hurts and illnesses I can cure. Some I cannot. What exactly do you suffer from?"

"I'm barren," Belinda whispered, and stopped her pacing.

What? "Barren?" Kirra repeated stupidly.

Belinda turned to face her. "I've been married more than a year now and I haven't conceived. I know that one of the reasons my husband wed me was so that I could bear him children, sons and daughters to inherit the property. And I've always wanted children. I was eager to have them, so I—but I haven't gotten pregnant. I'm so afraid there's something wrong with me. I don't want to disappoint Romar."

Oh gods, great gods, dreadful gods, how was it possible she would have to have this conversation? "Sometimes, my lady, it does take a little time before—"

"I know. That's what my mother says. And Romar has been gone a great deal, so we have not had as many opportunities as we—but still. I should have had a baby by now. I'm afraid something in my body is broken." She lifted her dark eyes and Kirra could see that she was crying silently. The expression on the pointed face sharpened to one of determined bravery, and Belinda said, "It is so important that I have Romar's baby. And I don't know how many more chances I will have."

"Why wouldn't you have many more chances?" Kirra forced herself to ask.

"Because I think—I'm afraid—I think it's possible he's fallen in love with someone else."

It seemed like a full minute before Kirra could bring herself to speak. "Is your husband a dishonorable man, my lady?" she asked finally in a very soft voice. "Would he abandon you for some other woman?"

Belinda shook her head so fiercely a few of her tears came flying off her cheeks like wet diamonds. "No. No. He would never do anything to shame me. He is—he is such a good man, serra. He is not—he is not the warm and gentle sort of person I always imagined I would marry. He is intense, and impatient, and full of this restless energy. Nothing slows him down, nothing holds him in place very long. But he is so passionate. He cares for so many people. You should see him with his mother, the lengths he will go to in order to make her happy. All his tenants would lay down their plows and die for him—he is such a good master. His estates are the best-run in all of Merrenstow. He would not desert the people who depend on him. He certainly would not cast me aside. But I think—I'm afraid—if he loves someone else . . . Serra, I don't think he's the kind of man who will be able to bring himself to love me, too."

Gods, gods, gods, gods. Kirra felt her heart shrink to a hard ball and then shatter inside her chest. The shards nicked the bowed ribs as they went careening out. She could feel the tiny welts, leaking blood and growing larger. "Do you know—do you have any idea—"

Belinda nodded. She put her hands up to wipe away the tears and stood there, trying to look very composed. "I got letters from some malicious *friends* while he was on the road," she said. "People couldn't wait to write and tell me how Romar danced with this woman in Kianlever, with that one in Coravann. But one name came up over and over again. Casserah Danalustrous."

Worse and worse and worse. "You think your husband is in love with my sister?"

Belinda nodded, and then broke down, speaking all her words in a rush. "Oh, serra, do you think it's true? Is she— would she—is she the kind of person who would take another woman's husband?"

Kirra almost could not speak. She had to try twice before she could get the words past her constricted throat. "No," she said truthfully. "Casserah would never do such a thing."

For a moment, Belinda looked hopeful, then her face crumpled again. "If not her, then someone," she said, despondent. "He was not at all happy to see me when I arrived. He was not cruel—you should never think that, but he—he was not there with me. He did not really kiss me when he kissed me. His heart is with someone else. I'm sure of it."

Kirra was sure of it, too. She absolutely could not think of a thing to say.

Belinda straightened her shoulders, gave her head a brisk little shake. "And if he loves her, he loves her," she said. "I cannot change that. But I am still his wife, and if he wants a legal heir, he must have a child with me. So, if he—when he—I want to be able to give him a baby. I want to be able to do that much for him. Can you fix me? If I am broken?"

This was her punishment for loving where she had no right to love. Now she had to feel compassion where she only wanted to feel hatred. "I will do what I can," Kirra said, finally coming deeper into the room. "Take off your gown. Lie on my bed. I will see what I can read in your body."

Belinda dutifully undressed, modestly leaving on her undergarments, and stretched out face up on the mattress. She was so small she looked like a child herself, her expression a mix of hope and fear. She looked like Lyrie. She looked like someone it should be impossible to heal.

But Kirra had healed Lyrie Rappengrass.

"Will it be painful?" Belinda asked as Kirra leaned over her, running her hands along the smooth skin of the other woman's arms and shoulders.

Kirra shook her head. "I don't think so. You might feel— something like a tingle. Something a little sharper than that eventually. Not real pain."

"Because I can stand pain. Don't be afraid to hurt me."

Sweet gods. "I won't hurt you."

The blood seemed clean. The heart was strong. Kirra could find no ruptures in the bones. She ran her hands impersonally over Belinda's ribs, brushed the hips, let her palms rest on the soft little mound of Belinda's stomach. All sorts of organs in this general area, some of them cantankerous and quick to malfunction. All sorts of places for trouble to burrow.

There. Kirra pressed a little harder. There. In the red cavern of the womb. A sticky darkness, a hungry blackness, a thin, twisting rope of malice. That was the problem. That was the troll, the ogre, that chased away any small life when it tried to pass. Not an infection, precisely. Not some poison administered from the outside. This was an indigenous malady, cultivated from within, a cozy, clever and catastrophic disease. Kirra could read its potential even in its nascent form. This was an illness so virulent that it would, if unchecked, destroy its host within a year.

If Kirra did nothing, Belinda would die.

Her hands trembled, her whole body trembled, as Kirra stood there with her palms against Belinda Brendyn's body. It would be easy, so easy, to step back, fold her arms, shake her head. *I'm sorry, there's nothing I can detect. I see no reason you and your husband can't have a whole houseful of babies.* So easy to do nothing. She had crossed enough boundaries already on this latest trip, contravened both personal and mystical standards of behavior, it should not be hard to do it one more time. Step back. Lace her fingers together. Shake her head.

"Hold still," Kirra said, her voice sounding rough to her own ears. "You might feel this."

Her hands arched against Belinda's white lacy underthings; perhaps her fingernails bit through the thin silk. She could feel the magic lance through her, playing like domesticated lightning from her shoulders to her wrists. She heard Belinda gasp, then catch her breath. If the room had been a little darker, it would have seemed that phosphorescence puddled around Kirra's hands, making a faint luminous cloud over Belinda's small stomach.

The tarry black evil in the other woman's body was gone.

Kirra lifted her hands and folded her arms. *Too late, too late,* she heard a voice in her head cry. *You should have broken contact before the magic flowed through your fingers.* "I did find something," she said, keeping her voice as cool as she could. "I believe I pushed it away. I would think your body would respond now as it should—I think you and your husband should be able to have a baby."

Belinda sat up, swinging her legs over the side of the bed. She was too short for her feet to reach the floor. "What can I do to thank you?" she asked. "Do you charge a fee?"

"No. This is how I pay off my debt to the Wild Mother, who lavishes me with her gifts."

"The Wild Mother," Belinda repeated. "One of the old gods."

Kirra let herself be impressed that Belinda recognized the name at all. "She's the one I honor."

Belinda nodded. "Then I will thank her tonight in my prayers." She reached for her gown. "But you are the one I am truly, truly grateful to."

Kirra forced a smile. "Thank me when you're pregnant." Belinda pulled her dress back on, and Kirra turned away and began rooting through personal items she'd scattered over the dresser. Here was a little vial of lavender scent; this would do. "I have something else to give you," she said, closing her fingers on the glass until the cologne inside had been transformed into harmless water with no taste, no odor.

"Something to keep me healthy?"

Kirra turned to face her. "Something to help you keep your husband's attention."

Belinda almost smiled, but this was not a subject she could joke about. "A love potion?"

Kirra also found herself unable to smile, though she tried. "Not exactly. It's a—a potion of forgetting."

Belinda took the sealed jar from Kirra, looking uncertainly between the lavender water and Kirra's face. "I don't understand."

"It's old magic. Folk magic," Kirra said. *Completely improvised-at-the-moment magic.* "Take the liquid in this jar and—and—one of your own tears. Put them into something your husband is about to drink. It will make him forget any woman but you. So the legends say, anyway. I've never had cause to try to use this particular potion before. I don't know if it will work."

Belinda looked again at the vial in her hand. "Will it make him forget other things? Important things?"

"No. Only—only any woman he has ever been interested in except you. It will take a day or two before it is totally efficacious. But soon he won't think of that other woman at all."

"I would like to believe that," Belinda said wistfully.

"I think you should try it, anyway," Kirra said. Her throat hurt when she spoke. The slivers of her heart had sliced her chest to ribbons; she was having trouble breathing. "But use it today. Tonight. Before tomorrow morning, anyway. The ingredients don't last long once they've been spelled."

Belinda watched Kirra with her dark eyes. "I don't know how I can thank you," she said.

Kirra shook her head. "I wish you wouldn't even try."

IMPOSSIBLE that there was still the dinner to get through. Impossible that there was one more task, even harder, she would have to do. Impossible that the gods had added this to her list of trials.

CHAPTER
40

SENNETH was at Kirra's door, dressed in the dull bronze that seemed to be her favorite color for formal wear. Melly had insisted that Kirra wear Danalustrous red. Its reflected fire was all that put any color in Kirra's cheeks. Even so, she was still too pale.

"Tell yourself, 'Six hours, and this is over,'" Senneth suggested, leading the way downstairs. "That's what I do. 'I can endure another five hours. Look, only four more hours to go.'"

"Six hours seems longer than I can manage."

Senneth glanced at her and shrugged. "Then don't go. I'll tell Baryn you were sick. He's got plenty of other highborn ladies to fill his tables."

"No. I have to go. It's—I have to—I'll be fine."

Anyone would wonder at the significance of that disjointed sentence, so surely Senneth did, but she did not comment. "I was out with Cam today," she said instead. "Buying him some decent clothes. And all of a sudden he turned to me and said, 'What's happening to Kirra? Right now?' Of course, I didn't know."

There was a question in her voice. Kirra shook her head. She couldn't possibly answer that without breaking down, and she could not break down as they were twenty yards shy of the dining hall. "How can he do that?" Kirra asked. "And what else is he capable of?"

"Very good questions," Senneth replied. "I don't know the answer to either."

They had scarcely stepped inside the salon when Valri approached to guide them to Baryn's side. He was standing with a contingent of strangers who were dressed in odd clothes and looking very fierce. By contrast, Baryn himself appeared tall and elegant. For a change, his gray hair was smoothed down under a thin gold circlet and his silken clothes were perfectly arranged. He almost looked kingly.

"Ah, there are two of my favorite serramarra!" he greeted them. "My dears, let me introduce you to some very distinguished guests."

He rattled off names and titles so quickly that Kirra could not keep track of which collection of syllables denoted which short, scowling man. Or perhaps she just was not paying attention. Senneth seemed to manage just fine, engaging the most ferocious of the strangers in a conversation about shipping and even winning a smile from him. Kirra, too, lived on land that bordered a coastline; she knew all about the value of ocean trade. But she couldn't think of a thing to say. She audited Baryn's conversation with two of the other men, smiled when anyone looked at her, and thought, *Five hours and forty-five minutes.*

Much too long.

Finally they all went in to dinner. She thought this would be better because she was sitting down, but it was worse. Senneth was not at her table, so she had to fight through the conversational thicket on her own. Toland Storian was seated on her right, so she had to pretend, for the whole interminable meal, that she could tolerate him. And from where she was sitting, Romar Brendyn was in her direct line of sight. She had to spend the entire meal watching him.

When she could not stand it, she watched his wife instead.

Belinda wore a deep pink gown, edged with the Merrenstow checkerboard at the neckline and the wide wrists. Very pretty; a flattering color for her, a flattering cut. She seemed fully engaged in the conversations around her, her dark eyes narrowed with intelligence, her comments brief but apparently informed. Now and then she glanced at her husband as if for reassurance or approval, and then her face was so hopeful and so full of love that Kirra felt her own face grow tense with the effort of holding back tears.

Romar did not often cast glances at his wife. He was in what Kirra sometimes thought of as his professional mode. He was here to do a job—represent the king—and he would do it well even if he found it unpleasant. So his own expression was guarded, though his eyes were alive with interest. When he spoke, the very set of his mouth was decisive; he illustrated points with quick, controlled gestures. Once he picked up his knife and fork and held them like weapons, demonstrating something that Kirra could not determine. His dark blond hair was tied behind his head, so the defined angles of his face were exposed. Not a courtier's face. Not a soft one. This face belonged to a man who would stand fast against any attack, who would fight to the death for his most cherished beliefs.

A man who would not give up something he wanted without a long and bruising battle.

While she watched him, he leaned closer to the man across the table from him, arguing some detail. He pulled a small red rose from one of Valri's centerpieces and plucked off one petal at a time, then arranged them on the white tablecloth before him as if amassing troops for a skirmish. The other men nearby bent forward to watch his armies of rose petals march into formation.

Kirra's face was hot with wonder and desire. The plucked rose, the scattered petals. The old Danalustrous signal. *Meet me in the garden tonight.* She picked up her wineglass and sipped from it, hoping to calm her fevered pulse.

Someone was talking to her. Someone close by. She blinked twice and tried to concentrate on her near surroundings. "Perhaps I could come visit you and your sister at Danan Hall," Toland was saying in her ear.

Kirra gave him a winsome smile, completely false. She was still breathless. "I'm sure Casserah would like that," she said. "But I can't promise I'll be there."

"Someone said you were leaving for Danalustrous in the morning."

"I am. But I never stay anywhere for long. It is never wise to count on me."

• • •

THE meal went on and on. More courses, more wine, a welter of after-dinner sweets. Then speeches. A few toasts. More wine. Finally, the slow, disorganized migration to one of the drawing rooms, where a pale young boy was already seated, playing at a harp, and servants were circulating with more trays of food.

Kirra was one of the last to enter the room. One swift glance around was enough to tell her Romar was already gone.

She stepped back across the threshold and practically ran down the brightly lit hallways. This was Ghosenhall. She knew every twist and turn. She could sneak in and out of the palace by any number of circuitous routes and not worry about running into curious servants or gossiping young serramarra. There were a dozen gardens at Ghosenhall, which could have been problematic, but only one was really near the palace itself and offered a formal maze of rosebushes, lilies, and fountains. She had no doubt that that was where she would find Romar.

It was cool outside, but the rain had temporarily stopped. Grumbling black masses of clouds overhead promised that the storms would return soon enough. Kirra ran lightly down the wet flagstones of the garden, her red skirts gathered in her hands, a shadow herself among the spindly shadows of bushes and ornamental trees. It was so dark she could make out almost nothing. If Romar was already here, would he be able to see her?

A figure stepped out of the darkness and snatched her against a warm body. She recognized his scent, his shape, great gods, the texture of his skin beneath her hands. She was crying; she knew she was crying, and laughing, too, as he kissed her and broke away to whisper her name and kissed her again.

"Kirra. Dear heart, I am so sorry—*Kirra*. Not this way, never this way, I swear to you I would not have let this happen—"

"I know—it's all right—I know, I know—"

"As soon as I said her name, I knew you did not realize she was here—but I could not—how could I—and then I had no way to tell you—"

"I know. I know. Shh, it's all right—"

He was crying, too. She could feel his cheek damp with tears when she brushed his face with her fingers. For the first time since she had met him, she had to hope she was stronger than he was. She had been drawn to him partly because of his strength, his restless energy, his quick male pride. But these were the very traits that would work against her now. She knew before he said it that he was not going to give her up.

"This changes nothing," he said. "I know it is dreadful, it is a shock to all of us, but I still love you. I will not leave her, but I love you, I have to have you. When can you meet me? Where? I am returning to Merrenstow for a few days, but I will be leaving again in a month or so. You can come to me wherever I am."

She kissed him, pulling his head down to hers, pushing her fingers through his hair till they encountered the ribbon tied at the back of his head. Like a mischievous child, she tugged on the bow, and his hair came loose, spilling over her shoulders, over his face. "I love you," she said against his mouth.

He kissed her urgently, then pulled back, trying to see her face in the darkness. "You will meet me? You will come to me?"

"Send me word of where you are."

"At Danalustrous? I should write you there?"

She kissed him again. "Yes. Danalustrous. That's where I always return."

That seemed to satisfy him; he didn't realize she had not promised. He kissed her again, holding her so tightly that she almost could not breathe. But that didn't matter. She didn't want to breathe. She almost did not want to live.

She kept her hands laced in his hair, as if all she cared about was feeling its subdued radiance beneath her palms. But her fingertips were tracing the contours of his head, and her fingertips were dense with magic. This was a form of healing, she had decided, a way of seeking out a disease and destroying it. But now she was searching for memories, hunting down emotions. Now she was planning to excise images, cauterize the sharp, bloody wounds of desire. She looked for a specific kind of poison that had lodged in his body, had slipped past the hard shield of his skull, webbing itself throughout his mind so that he could hardly have a thought that was not tainted.

She could drain that poison away. She could leave him healed of Kirra.

He kissed her again, harder, more desperately. "I wish I could come to you—tonight," he muttered between kisses. "Do you sleep alone? I could—come to you. I could tell her—the king sent for me. I cannot—see you ride away tomorrow—and know I did not have—another chance to be with you."

"Not tonight," she gasped back, her fingers tightening in his hair, because she did not want to do this; she did not want to work the magic. Just one more night with him. Was that too much to ask? *Wild Mother, watch over me,* she thought. "There is no time."

"Then when? When?" He kissed her again. "I must see you—"

"Send word to Danalustrous," she whispered, and flattened her palms against his head. She held her mouth to his in an intemperate kiss while magic streamed from her body into his.

It would not take effect immediately, she knew. He would recover over a period of time, as a man might recover from a fever, weak at first, stronger as the days unfolded. There would be moments when he was dizzy, not sure why, catching at a bedpost or doorframe to keep his balance. But he would grow stronger. He would forget he had ever been unwell. His life would resume its former rhythms, untroubled by memories of an old fever.

"I cannot live without you," he murmured against her mouth.

"I know," she said. "I know I will die without you."

THEY left the garden hand in hand till they got close enough to the palace to be seen. Fresh rain was just beginning to fall.

"Your skirts," Romar said. "They're all wet. And a little muddy."

Kirra laughed. "I can dry them with one pass of my hand. You go in first. You are more likely to have been missed."

He paused, one hand on the door, and looked back at her. "I will see you again soon," he promised, and disappeared inside.

Disappeared from her life.

She stood there as long as she dared, letting the rain patter on her head, make tear-sized stains on the red of her gown. She was close enough to the salon to hear the low rumble of conversation, and she wondered if anyone was looking for her. Senneth, no doubt, who would immediately realize that Romar was missing as well. Who else would notice? Who else would wonder and worry?

She stepped inside, brushed all traces of rain from her clothing, paused at a small mirror in the hallway to check any damage to her hair. Not as badly mussed as Romar's, though he had remembered to retie his ribbon before returning to the palace. She patted a few curls in place, pressed her fingers to her lips, which looked puffy and much-kissed. A little magic, so. A very demure and composed serramarra stared back at her.

She could do this.

She slipped back inside the salon and accepted a glass of water from a passing footman. Within minutes she had eased herself into a small group of laughing young women, all of whom were speculating about what it might be like to be married off to a Karyndein ambassador.

"That dark-haired one, he was very short, but—did you notice his hands? I thought I would faint when he touched me."

"I hear the women in Karyndein are treated like goddesses. The wealthy class is *very* wealthy."

"I wouldn't like to be so far from home, though."

She spotted Senneth across the room, talking to Seth Stowfer but watching Kirra. Kirra summoned a small smile and a little shrug. She glanced at the large, ornate clock hanging on the wall and surreptitiously held up a single finger. *One hour to go.* Senneth smiled and returned her attention to her own conversation.

So that final hour went, Kirra slipping from group to group, speaking to everyone she thought Baryn would want her to acknowledge. She was never unaware of Romar, standing near the center of the room beside Baryn and Valri, holding his own series of earnest conversations. Every time she glanced at him, he was watching her, even while he appeared to be discussing some complicated commercial agreement with the foreign ambassadors. Every time she moved to another part of the room she would find he had repositioned himself so that she was still within his line of sight.

I cannot stand this anymore, she thought suddenly, as the hour ticked past two and still few of the guests had left the room. She could hear the ominous clash and roll of thunder outside and knew that the promised storm had stampeded in.

The air wafting in from the half-open windows was cool and inviting; the scent of rain was very strong.

She had to get outside. She had to go somewhere she could breathe.

Senneth wasn't looking at her, so Kirra could drift across the room, aimless and unnoticed, smiling insincerely at anyone who caught her eye. At the doorway she paused, and took one last look at the handsome crowd, all bright dresses and sober jackets, excited laughter and soft, scheming whispers. Hard to guess when she would be back at Ghosenhall again.

Romar was watching her, of course, his body shifted slightly from his last stance so he could track her progress. She put a hand to her cheek as if to feel for heat, then pressed her palm to her heart as if to check that it was still beating.

I love you, I will love you always.

He nodded, and she slipped out the door.

Down the hallway, down another hallway, out the great front entrance watched by a host of guards.

"Raining out there, serra," one of them cautioned her, and she nodded.

"I know. I like the rain."

She fled down the massive steps, straight into a downpour, soaked to the skin within a few paces. She could not see for the raindrops, for the tears, so she moved blindly over the slick grass, into the sheets of falling water. Her first thought was to make for the gate, to flee the palace drenched and on foot, but the rain was falling so hard she could not even be sure she was headed in the right direction. Uncertain, despairing, she made a quarter turn, took a few steps—turned again and started off on another route. The palace was somewhere behind her, but now she was so disoriented she did not know which direction she was facing, if she was headed for the barracks or the stables or the back lawns.

It didn't matter. She didn't care. She stumbled forward as far as her feet could take her, but it wasn't far. Something tripped her and she fell to the muddy ground, collapsing in a red puff of soggy skirts. She was sobbing. She could not push herself back to her feet. Her body shook with the force of her weeping; her ribs had tightened so brutally over her heart that she could not draw breath. On her knees already, she bent double so her head was almost to the ground, and let the rain batter her with unrelenting misery.

She wanted to change herself to some small armored creature that would not feel the rain and would not hate the mud and would not remember what it meant to love or cry. She wanted to change herself to stone, or to dirt, or to rain itself. She wanted to obliterate herself, disintegrate here, leave behind nothing, not even pain.

She did not have the strength. She could not move, she could not alter. She merely lay in the remorseless storm and wept.

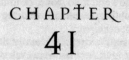
As soon as Kirra realized she was awake, she squeezed her eyes shut tight. She felt rested and serene, but a small anxious part of her knew she should be in the silver pit of hell. If she didn't open her eyes, if she didn't even think, she might not remember why.

It was daylight, that she could tell by the quality of light playing across her closed lids. Daylight, and she had slept for some hours, because her body felt restored and relaxed. Soft bed under her, Donnal's warm body beside her—what could be so terrible that she had to work to try to forget it?

She moved, and the shape next to her adjusted. Heat streamed in steady waves from Donnal's side of the bed. He must have taken the form of a bear or something equally large and full of energy. What Melly would think when she saw a bear in Kirra's bed—

But if Melly were likely to see them, Donnal would never be so careless as to—

But Donnal—

But Donnal was gone because Kirra had fallen in love with Romar Brendyn. And last night Kirra had disenchanted Romar, laying her own hands on his head to—

Her whole body spasmed with pain and she sat up, gulping for air, her hands at her throat as if to pry off someone's choking fingers. The shape next to her stirred and sat up. Not Donnal, of course. Senneth, her pale hair in disarray, her kind face creased with worry, her whole body radiating that generous and comforting heat.

How had either of them gotten to this room? All Kirra remembered was rain and mud and darkness. And tears so bitter they had probably permanently salted the ground where they had fallen.

"What happened?" Kirra said faintly. She moved her hands to investigate her face, her hair. Her eyes were sticky from last night's weeping. There were twigs in her matted curls.

Senneth watched her closely, gray eyes giving nothing away. "What part don't you remember?" she asked cautiously.

"I remember leaving the ballroom and wandering out in the storm," Kirra said. "But I don't know how I got from outside into this room. With you."

"Cammon knew something was wrong. He took Tayse out in the storm to find you. Tayse carried you inside and Cammon came to get me. You were crying."

Kirra made a small, helpless gesture at that. *Of course I was crying.* "I feel—I don't feel as terrible as I think I should. How could I even fall asleep after that? Senneth, I—oh, I can't even talk about it—"

"You broke it off with Romar."

"Worse than that. I—I made him forget me."

Senneth looked at her, eyebrows raised. "Forget *you*? Serramarra Kirra Danalustrous?"

"Forget his love for me," Kirra said, her voice very subdued. "Forget the emotions I inspired. He'll recognize my face, maybe even remember a conversation or two, but not how he felt about me. Not—some of the things we shared. I went into his head. I found his love for me and cured it like a disease."

Now Senneth's face showed deep compassion, but all she said was, "That would explain the despair."

Kirra shook her head. "So how could I—I can't believe I could even stop crying."

"Well," Senneth said. "You're not the only one who's a mystic."

She watched, waiting for Kirra to figure it out. Kirra stared back at her, trying to reconstruct the rest of the night. Vaguely she remembered hands and voices in the dark. Vaguely she recalled the ease with which Tayse had lifted her off the ground, remembered sobbing into his wet shirt. She had been so cold, so wet, so miserable, so certain that no comfort could exist in the entire world.

And then Senneth's hand on her arm, the heat from Senneth's body chasing away the chill and some of the sense of loneliness. But Senneth did not have the power to soothe the frantic mind, discipline uncontrollable emotions. There had been another hand clasping hers, another voice whispering hope and reassurance.

"Cammon," Kirra said flatly.

Senneth nodded.

Kirra felt a prickle of unease or wonder dance down her spine. "What did he *do*?"

"He said he—made it bearable. He said he gave you peace."

Kirra stared at Senneth a little fearfully. "He can do that?"

A small smile from Senneth. "Apparently so. I'm beginning to think there's not a lot our Cammon can't do."

Kirra passed a hand over her eyes. The longer she sat here in bed, the more she became aware of aches and stresses on her body. Not good for anyone to lie in the rain weeping, even if the period of duress was short. She must look as bad as she felt, hair wild and skin wan and bruised. "I have to leave," she said.

"Leave the room? I can go if you want to be alone."

"Leave Ghosenhall. I have to go home. I have to go now."

Senneth was silent for a moment. "I wish I knew what to say to make everything better. I can't come up with any words. I'm so sorry. I will do whatever you want. I'll come with you to Danalustrous if you like."

Kirra dropped her hand, moved to a tiny smile. "No. You should stay in Ghosenhall and spend time with your much more accessible lover, whom you scarcely got a chance to see the whole time we were on the road."

Senneth smiled back. "Tayse would come with us, of course. He does not permit us to be separated."

"Ah, now *that* is the sort of thing I need to hear to heal my heart," Kirra said. "That makes me believe love is possible. For some people. Some of the time."

"I think we should come with you."

Kirra shook her head. "No. I want—I can't tell you how

much I need to be by myself. I'll take hawk shape and fly home. I won't even bring Melly with me. It will make her angry to be left behind, but I cannot deal with her concern. I need to be—I need to remember the secrets and magics that make me familiar to myself."

"And what will you do in Danalustrous?"

Kirra rearranged a pillow behind her back and leaned against the headboard. "There's a place. A small island off the coast," she said slowly. "It's become a sort of isolated colony for people with red-horse fever. They go there to die and to make sure they infect no one else. My aunt and my—my uncle told me about it a couple of months ago. I think I'll go there. I think I'll take what I learned from Lyrie Rappengrass and heal as many of those people as I can."

"You realize that word will spread quickly that you have mastered the art of changing someone other than yourself."

"You think I shouldn't go?"

"No, I think you should. How can you not bestow the gift of life when you hold it in your hands? And maybe you will heal yourself as you heal those others."

"Maybe. It seems too much to hope for."

"We'll come with you, if you like," Senneth said again.

Kirra actually laughed. "No! This is a shiftling's journey. But I thank you for the offer."

"Will you at least stay another day so I can be sure you're all right?"

Kirra shook her head. "No. I'll eat something, and then I'll go." She gave Senneth a direct look. "So let me say good-bye now."

"You can't go without seeing the others."

Kirra sighed. "I know. I promised Cammon I'd find him before I left."

"And Justin."

Kirra sighed with more theatricality. "*And* Justin. But you can take my farewell to Tayse, can't you?"

"I can." Senneth leaned over and gave her a warm hug. "Good-bye. May the Bright Lady light your journey. May the Wild Mother guard your back. And may whatever god watches over Cammon heal your spirit."

Kirra laughed and held on tightly, just for a moment, just to soak up some of Senneth's incredible heat. It seemed to suffuse her whole body with light and gladness, snuggling with a little sigh around her battered heart. "You know I'll be back in Ghosenhall before the year is over," Kirra whispered.

Senneth pulled away. She was smiling. "Then I shall not be so sad to see you leave, for I will see you again very soon."

WITHIN an hour, Kirra was ready to go. She'd taken a quick bath, devoured a hasty meal, and explained to Melly that she was going on to Danalustrous alone.

"I'll have my father send guards to Ghosenhall to escort you home," Kirra said. "I would not make you travel by yourself."

Melly was concerned, but not for herself. "There are two Danalustrous men in Ghosenhall right now. Came in last night bringing a message for the king," Melly said. "I thought you and I might travel back with them. I think that's the better plan, serra. I don't think you should leave like this—no one knowing where you are or if something is wrong—"

"Melly." Kirra laughed. "That is how I always travel. I am always alone, and no one worries."

"Everyone worries," Melly shot back. "You just don't care."

Kirra laughed again and gave the maid a quick hug. "I'll tell my sister to double your salary and to make sure you never leave her service," Kirra said. "You're a treasure."

The last thing to do was keep her final promise and make her good-byes to Justin and Cammon. Neither of them were in the barracks, or the training yard, or anywhere she might reasonably expect to find them. She found herself scowling, wondering if Senneth had told them to hide in the city so that Kirra could not find them and, thus, could not depart. But then she had the inspired thought of looking for Cammon in the gated garden where the queen kept her raelynx. It took her another thirty minutes to quarter the back half of the king's property—which boasted any number of gardens and private woods—but she finally found the walled, overgrown acres that had become home to the red cat.

Luck was with her. Both Cammon and Justin were sitting on the ground outside the gate, half asleep in the warm noon sun. The raelynx rested on the other side of the grille, its pointed nose on its paws, its tufted tail twitching with remembered wildness.

All three of them woke when she was twenty yards away. The men came to their feet, but the raelynx merely yawned and returned to its nap.

"Finally. I found you. Now I'm saying good-bye," Kirra said when she was near enough. "See you again soon enough, I'm sure."

She made as if to spin and walk away, but Justin caught her arm and Cammon was calling, "Wait, wait, wait!"

She laughed and turned back. "Only joking," she said. "That wasn't a real farewell."

Justin dropped her arm, but Cammon came closer, peering at her with his strange, flecked eyes. "Are you better this morning?" he asked quietly. "Last night you—" He shook his head.

"Yes. Better. But not—" She searched for a word. "Well." It was insufficient but she couldn't think of how to phrase it. "I need to go. Thank you for—thank you both. For caring. That almost makes it possible to bear everything."

"You're going back to Danalustrous?" Cammon asked.

She nodded. "Now. This minute."

"We'll come with you," Justin said. "Give us an hour to pack."

Really, it was enough to make you think you were too frail to cross half a continent on your own. "No," she said. "But thank you. I'm used to traveling by myself."

Justin was stubborn. "You're used to having Donnal with you."

Well, that was an unnecessary stab to the heart. She talked around the sudden sharp pain. "This time I don't. I'll have to get used to traveling without him. I've managed just fine since we parted on the road to Rappengrass."

Cammon's eyes widened. "Donnal didn't leave you on the road to Rappengrass," he said.

Kirra and Justin both looked at him.

"He didn't! Well, he *did*, for a day, but he joined the caravan before we made Rappen Manor. He was there the whole time."

Kirra felt as if the muscles of her face had grown too slack to hold her jaw in place. "He was—Donnal's been with us—"

Cammon nodded vigorously. "Hawk shape, most of the time. Owl, eagle. Wolf once in a while, but mostly birds."

"In Rappengrass?" she said faintly.

He nodded again. "And on the whole trip back to Ghosenhall. I haven't seen him today, but I know he's still here. He wouldn't leave you. I don't think he can."

Justin was actually smiling. "Well, then. You can go back to Danalustrous by yourself. I'll agree to it."

Kirra could feel herself crying again, nothing like last night's wracking sobs, but stupid, mindless tears that seemed mixed of equal parts joy and hope and rue. *He has not left me. Donnal has not left me.* How could he love her still, how could he forgive her? What did she have to offer him when she was not sure she would ever be whole enough to love again? And nothing had changed between them—they were still serf and serramarra, titled lady and peasant's son. But he was her shadow and mirror; he defined her, he gave her back her image of herself. She could not be complete without him no matter what course her life took, whatever form she held.

She gripped Cammon's shoulders and shook him, still crying, starting to laugh. "Why didn't you tell me, you wretched boy?" she demanded. "Why didn't you tell me Donnal had not left?"

"I thought you knew! You never said!"

She groaned, clutched him tighter in a quick embrace, and released him. "I will never understand the way you think."

She turned for Justin, but Cammon grabbed her sleeve. "You're coming back, aren't you? Soon?"

"Sometime," she said. "I don't know when."

"Don't be gone too long."

She kissed his cheek. "I won't."

Justin caught her in a bear hug before she could think if she would shake his hand or kiss him on the cheek or merely speak a farewell. "We'll come after you if you don't return," he growled in her ear. "Don't be gone too long."

"I won't," she said. "Watch out for everyone while I'm away."

She pulled free and gave them both a blissful smile. She felt herself glowing. That was happiness, or perhaps euphoria, or at least an understandable reaction to the thought that *this* time what she'd learned wasn't bad news. She extended her arms, her fingers gathering into neat points, and tilted her head skyward, closing her eyes. Sunlight played along her cheekbones, her throat, laid a golden weight on her outstretched hands. She felt her whole body contract in response, grow smaller, lighter, elegant and deadly. She was a creature of wings and talons and swiftness and hunger. Eager to fly away.

She opened her eyes and made one sharp, gruff good-bye to the men standing there, earthbound and a little sad. But she was not sad at all. She beat her wings mightily against the heavy air and lifted herself aloft, weightless, windblown, a bauble of feathers and heat. It felt good to drift in one lazy circle above this cloistered compound of men, feel a surge of affection for everything, everyone she left behind, while feeling no compulsion whatsoever to stay. She flapped her wings to gain altitude, canted her body to change direction, and set her beak directly into the wind blowing gently from the west.

She had not traveled more than a minute when a shadow crossed her from above, then dropped to her level, settling in on her left just a wingspan away. She did not cry out a hoarse welcome, did not even glance over in his direction, but she knew he was there, silent and familiar, knew he would accompany her for every mile of her flight. The morning passed and the afternoon fell away from them and evening stretched up to meet them as they flew without stopping, straight on for Danalustrous.